Franco American Dreams

JULIE TAYLOR

Scribner Paperback Fiction
Published by Simon & Schuster

SCRIBNER PAPERBACK FICTION
Rockefeller Center
1230 Avenue of the Americas
New York, NY 10020

This book is a work of fiction. Names, characters, places, and incidents either are products of the author's imagination or are used fictitiously. Any resemblance to actual events or locales or persons, living or dead, is entirely coincidental.

Copyright © 1997 by Julie Taylor
All rights reserved, including the right of reproduction in whole or in part in any form.

SCRIBNER PAPERBACK FICTION and design are trademarks of Simon & Schuster Inc.

Designed by Brooke Zimmer
Set in Bauer Bodoni
Manufactured in the United States of America

10 9 8 7 6 5 4 3 2

Library of Congress Cataloging-in-Publication Data
Taylor, Julie, date.
Franco American dreams / Julie Taylor.
p. cm.
I. Title.
PS3570.A9416F73 1997
813'.54—dc21 96-29625
CIP

ISBN 978-0-684-83092-6

For my parents, Jim and Freda Taylor, with love

Acknowledgments

This book became a reality with the help and support of the following people, all of whom I owe a big, fat thanks: Chuck Adams, Kip Kotzen, Dr. Marie Saunders, Sandra Tabbernee, Cheryl Weinstein, my family (Orrs and Taylors), Zanni Boring, Mike Easterling, David Farney, Evan Fogelman, Ivy Garcia, Laura Hannebaum, Stuart Hazleton, Elizabeth Hurchalla, David Masello, Traci McKnight, Mudpie, Daniel Pinchbeck, Jenni Shrum, Dan Vossen, and, of course, Jay Brown.

Chapter 1

Here's the deal: I, Abbie McPhereson, am totally tired of boys who love me, adore me, can't live without me—until they have a six-pack coursing through their veins, then they're like "Abbie who?" My swan-necked self does not take kindly to being rated second-best to a Bud long-neck, you know? I simply do *not* need it. So that's why twelve seconds ago, at exactly 12:00 A.M. on January 1, instead of swapping saliva with the short Nicolas Cage look-alike who had been leeching onto me for the past twenty-five minutes, I stained my own well-manicured hand with deep purple lipstick and made a firm resolution to never go out with a boy who'd choose Rumple Minze over romance again. No more leaving the 7:45 flick early so we could make it to the liquor store before it closed. No more going to thirteen QuikTrips looking for a guy named Bubba who had some good weed. No more boys passing out in the middle of Christmas dinner at my parents' after nineteen cups of Aunt Ethel's eggnog. And, hallelujah, no more puke on my green patent leather stilettos. I am free of them: the drunken Dallas-dwelling dudes who, in my one and a half years at Dallas Design Institute, have clung to me like white cat hairs on a black cashmere sweater.

I am a free woman, and I feel good. So good that I flash a big smile to Shrunken Nick Cage as silver balloons fall from the ceiling, celebrating the arrival of the new year. As corks pop, I am sprayed with the bubbly two-dollars-per-bottle champagne that Club Unity is serving free of charge for the next half hour. The cheap pink liquid on my cheeks is a baptism, cleansing my soul of all the jerks who've invaded it during my nineteen years on the planet. Every effervescent drop that hits my face and dissolves into my tiny pores represents another loser from the past who is out of my mind forever. See ya, Jeffrey, the third-year college freshman with the Mad Dog addiction and the cute plaid shorts. Later, Frazier, the rehab veteran who couldn't face the day before washing down two Chocolate Zingers with four mimosas on the rocks. And goodbye-don't-let-the-door-hit-ya-in-the-ass-on-your-way-out, Parker, my majorest love, whose greatest accomplishment in life is his amazing ability to burp "The Star-Spangled Banner" without pausing for breath. Don't call me, boys, I'll call you.

The unbelievably loud rap music starts up again, jolting me from my thoughts and sending me into spasms of delight. I search the packed dance floor for my best pal and roommate, Georgette, who hates this club almost as much as she loathes boys now that Guy Number Three dumped her last week.

I finally see her standing next to the bar in a "Little House on the Prairie" dress, pale arms folded across flat chest, glass of the usual OJ, no ice, resting in a dainty, ringless left hand. I wave wildly, trying to catch her attention.

Shrunken Nick Cage observes my flailing limbs, assumes I'm doing a new dance step and instantly mimics my motions. I think he looks like an idiot until I realize I probably look just as stupid. Georgette spots my blonde locks, which are glowing under the black light, and runs over, leaving the boy who was hitting on her stone-cold.

"What is up, Georgie? Happy New Year, sweets! Does this guy not look exactly like Nicolas Cage?" I scream, pointing to Mr. Short who is now moving away from us, at last giving up his pursuit. I wonder if he thinks I'm bi? I'm sure I've just been dissed, but I don't care. I grab Georgette's arm and pull her to the edge of the dance floor.

"Abbie, to you everybody looks like somebody else. I look like Melissa Gilbert, you look like Cindy Brady in her grade-school days, Joe looks like . . ."

Her voice falters. Joe is ex-boyfriend *numero tres.* We hate Joe.

"Georgie, Joe looks like a single, dateless freak because that's exactly what he is. He's probably sitting home right now playing Yahtzee with his eight-year-old cousin, watching "Dick Clark's

Rockin' Eve" or something lame like that. And you, my dear, look like you could use a shot of vodka to go with that O.J."

I know it's kind of hypocritical to try to get my pal sloshed when I have just sworn off drunken boys forever, but Georgette is going postal. This girl *needs* a drink.

"Nope. Alcohol is not the answer, Abbie," she says, shaking her hand and pointing her index finger at me menacingly. Her finger looks like my grandma's speedometer, erratically moving back and forth, back and forth.

"God, you sound like an eighties Nancy Reagan ad. Just Say No, baby. But, speaking of saying no, I made an important New Year's resolution. Wanna hear it?"

Georgette nods solemnly, looking like she couldn't care less, but I pretend not to notice her vacant gaze.

"I am never, ever going to date a boy who drinks ever again. I mean it, Georgette. It's always been hard for me to figure out that just because someone needs you, that doesn't always mean he loves you. From now on, though, no more caretaking of drunken deadbeats—no way, José. I am my own person. In six short months, I will be done with the Design Institute. I'm cute, I have a fake I.D., I don't need support-top pantyhose and I deserve better than this, dammit!"

I'm on a roll. I look at Georgette, waiting for some sign of life.

"You know, Joe never took a drink. The whole eight months I was with him, he never took a drink."

This is too depressing. I pat her hand comfortingly, tell her I'll find her before last call and head toward the center of the dance floor. I check my watch—12:22. The club is wall-to-wall people—mostly alternative types: a typical Deep Ellum crowd. I see a guy from a textiles class I had three semesters back and jump between him and his date, shaking my booty, which looks pretty good in the little celery-colored flapper dress I designed a couple of weeks ago. Textiles Guy and his woman grin at me and continue to grind their bods to the beat.

I scan the crowd, scoping for sober babes. I see Short Nick Cage hanging on a big-banged bimbo in fluorescent spandex. God. I look around for anyone of interest. By the D.J. booth, I spot a familiar object: a daisy-covered hat I designed last year.

It brought in eighty bucks at a hip little boutique a few blocks away. I dance on my tiptoes, trying to catch a glimpse of the chick with the good taste and the charming chapeau.

I notice her bouncing Lucille Ball–red bob and admire the way her lean frame grooves to the beat. Yep, this girlie has style, no doubt about it.

It is kind of strange to see someone other than one of my friends wearing something I designed. I am, in a weird way, getting off on it. I can't take my eyes off the headpiece, which I can only see the back of. I want a closer look.

Waving goodbye to Textiles Guy and his chick, I gallivant to her area of the dance floor, contemplating an introduction. Perhaps she will ask me to autograph the *Over Our Heads by Abbie* tag. But I don't even have a pen on me. Biting my lip, I hope she won't be too disappointed.

After what seems like an eternity, I fight my way through the gaggle of dancers. I tap her go-going shoulder, admiring my handiwork. That hat rules.

She turns around with a perplexed look on her face. "Yeah?"

It's my turn to look confused. The gal with the awesome fashion sense is not a gal, she's a guy. I mean, he's a guy. A very hot, hot guy.

My mouth drops open, and I pray none of my drool drips on the black-and-white checkerboard floor. Out of nowhere, I remember my mom's honey-sweet voice: "Abbie Sue, you will meet many men in your life. But when you see the man who is destined to be yours forever, you will just know."

"Yeah? I'm sorry, do I know you?"

You will just know.

"Yes. I mean, no. Uh, I'm Abbie, as in *Over Our Heads by.*"

He smiles, looking at me like I'm loco. Say something, Abbie, say anything.

"Your hat—it's mine. I mean, it's yours, but it's my design. I designed it."

He continues to stare at me blankly. His gangly body has stopped gyrating and all of his attention is focused on me. He is so hot I want to cry. I smell alcohol on his breath.

You will just know.

"Oh, the hat. Yeah. I just got it this afternoon—four ninety-eight at the Salvation Army, the one on Elam and Buckner. Whoa, you really made it? As in, you know, made it? Coooool," says Hot Boy, stroking the hat's petals.

"Sal—Salvation Army?" Who would give away the coolest hat in Texas to the Salvation Army? And why would they sell it to the cutest guy in this zip code for less than the price of a Michael Bolton CD? Reality check. My inflated ego is going down quicker than a cheerleader on prom night.

"Yeah, that's my fave thrift store. Wanna dance?"

Mr. Perfecto's smile beckons. Since I am in love with this guy for real and he's my future husband, I nod and we start to boogie.

I vow to remember the retro song that blares—"Personal Jesus," by Depeche Mode. The first song we ever danced to. Maybe we'll play it at our massive tenth-anniversary blowout. I'll be smashingly famous and everyone will be dressed to the nines and we'll serve those little cucumber sandwiches like my cousin Traci did at her wedding last summer.

Mr. Perfect bumps into me—maybe he's dancing or maybe he's falling-down drunk, I can't tell. I stop daydreaming and bump back, doing that crazy dance move that was so popular in the seventies. Perfect grins at me and continues to get down, brushing a red strand of hair from his bloodshot eyes. Someone across the dance floor is blowing a whistle. A guy in front of the unisex bathroom's door is puking his guts out. Could this be love?

When the song is drawing to a close—that part where it keeps repeating "Reach out and touch faith" over and over again—I wonder if I should say something to the god-little-*g* of the dance floor. But what will I say? The choices are endless: "Want to father my kids?" "Do you like mayo or mustard?" "Who did you go to your junior prom with?" "Are you always drunk?" "Can I kiss your nose?"

I want to know everything about him, but I don't want to scare him off. So, as the tune ends and blends into an old Cure song, I nudge his ribs—wonder if he likes barbecue?—and say, "Hey!"

His eyes are closed. He's shifted into low gear and is moving seductively to the slow song. I want to jump him, but decide to nudge him again—harder this time. "Hey!"

His eyes open halfway and he grabs my waist and pulls me close. A gravelly voice growls into my left ear, "Heeeeey."

Goose Bump City. His hot breath on my lobe is turning me on way more than a Brad Pitt flick ever has.

Perfect lifts me up and whirls me around. The checkerboard floor spins, resembling a pinwheel gone berserk. My flapper fringe flies. Purple lips press against pale neck.

He sets me down but does not let me go. We dance hip to hip, à la Jennifer Grey and Patrick Swayze '87. His scratchy bowling shirt rubs against my bare chest. Feeling cute, I whisper, "What's your name?"

Perfect squeezes my shoulders tightly, then releases. He repeats this little motion five times, sending shivers down my spine and driving me into a frenzy.

"Sorry, I don't know Morse code, babe. Try English." I'm trying to sound cool, but my voice quivers. Great.

"It's Franco. Franco Richards." He slurs a bit on the last name, saying "Rishards," but I barely notice. My hormones are slam-dancing, my mind racing.

Abbie Richards. Abbie McPhereson-Richards. Mrs. Franco Richards. Franco and Abbie Richards.

"I like you, Franco Richards," I whisper, but I don't think he hears me since an earsplitting song cuts off the love ballad, silencing my sugar-sweet confession. A mosh pit quickly forms and Franco grabs my hand—aaaaaaaaah, we're holding hands—and pulls me in.

A huge dude with a goatee slams into my fragile form, almost knocking me down, but Franco pulls me up and puts his arms around my upper bod, shielding me from the slams and bams of the pit. We get hit and pushed by a bevy of boisterous moshers; we're bouncing around the circle like a pair of Mexican jumping beans. Somehow we stick together to the end. I feel like this is foreshadowing our future life together. Franco and I will be beaten up, knocked around, kicked and jostled, but we will stay together through it all, clinging together like argyle socks in a hot dryer. Okay, maybe I'm jumping the gun a little. I do not know this boy's interests, hobbies or background, but I know his soul. I want him I want him I want him.

The song segues into a slow number and the pit dissipates, everyone returning to their respective places on the floor. Franco and I stay where we are and dance, neither one of us saying a word. There is major eye contact as we groove for another forty-something minutes or so. Finally, Franco speaks.

"Hey, Hat Gal . . ."

Oh God, he just called me Hat Gal. I smile my most charming smile and wait. Will he ask me out? Beg for my phone number? Tell me I'm pretty?

"Wanna do a Kamikaashe shot with me?"

Not quite the words I long to hear. My New Year's resolution flashes in my mind as I nod and grab his callused hand. Just one shot won't hurt. Anyway, by the time we get married I'm sure he'll be a nondrinker.

As we approach, I see Georgette still hanging by the bar, looking crabby. Wonder if she'll agree to be my maid of honor? I can already tell there will be a fight over the dress, but I'm sure we'll work it out.

"Hey, sweetie, this is Franco. Franco, this is Georgette."

"Nice hat," Georgette says, her brows nearly scraping the ceiling as she blatantly checks Franco out. After careful scrutiny, she flashes me a thumbs-up signal inconspicuously with her right hand.

Franco, getting antsy, slurs, "Wanna do a Kamikaashe shot with ush?"

Georgette's grin fades and her thumb rotates downward. "So," she says in this really fake-nice voice, "what was your New Year's resolution, Ab?"

Pissed, I shoot her a dirty look and push past her to flag down the shirtless bartender.

"Two Kamikazes, puhleeeeease!" I holler, the bitterness in my voice directed at Georgette, who's looking at me like she's Wile E. Coyote and I'm Road Runner.

The bartender, so hot he's got to be gay, nods. He then quickly pours vodka, triple sec, Rose's lime and ice in a large silver container, shakes it vigorously and turns the metallic container upside down, straining the liquid, now almost exactly the color of Key lime pie, into tall, test tube–shaped glasses. I slap eight bucks on the bar—six bucks for the shots, two bucks for Mr. Washboard Abs—and grab the drinks. I hold one out to Franco, who's scanning the dance floor, and turn away from cranky Georgette, who whispers "Hypocrite" as I walk off. What is her deal?

"Hey, Franco, my treat."

He doesn't say thanks; just lifts the shot to his lips, points his chin toward the ceiling and empties the tube in one gulp. Then he looks over at me, wipes his mouth with his Bic pen–blue sleeve and says, "Gracias, Hat. What are you waiting for?"

I think, "I've been waiting for you, drunken you, all of my life," but instead say, "Nothing," and slam my shot, wincing. It's good, not much of an aftertaste, but I always wince after gulping a swig of alcohol, no matter how smooth the taste. A heavy drinker I'm not.

Franco slaps me on the back. "You okay?"

"Well, I don't need the Heimlich just yet. I'm okay. More than okay, actually."

"LAST CALL FOR ALCOHOL!"

Hot Bartender rings a pink cowbell, corralling the stampede that's heading toward the bar.

Franco squeezes my forearm, says, "My treat this time," and turns to join the rest of the thirsty clubgoers clamoring for the bartender's attention. I don't know if I want another, but Franco isn't asking, he's telling.

I walk over to Georgette, in her usual spot. She's still looking disgusted. Shocker.

"What is up with you, Georgette?"

"I am having a shitty time, Ab. All night I've wondered what Joe's doing, who he's doing it with and if she's skinnier than I am. And what is the one person who doesn't lie, doesn't fabricate, Miss Oh-Never-Ever-Again-Will-I-Go-For-A-Boy-Who-Drinks, doing? Drooling all over some tipsy, tanked-up alcoholic waste of hunky flesh who can barely stand up. Sure, he's very cute, but also very intoxicated. And does that deter Miss Abbie's hormones? No. But what can? Once you set your sights on someone, it'd take three professional wrestlers and a crowbar to get your polished claws out of him." Georgette hisses, her usually wide eyes now narrow, evil slits.

"I cannot believe you! Look, Georgette, I am not Joe. Joe screwed you over, not me. If I break a resolution to myself, I am not doing you, or anybody else, a disservice. And sure, Franco may be drunk right now, but my God, you don't even know the guy." Neither do I, really, but that's beside the point. "So please spare me the lameass judgmental bullshit, okay? The year's too damn old to hear a tired lecture, I swear to God it is."

Without a word, Georgette stomps off just as Franco returns, two shots of a fudge brownie–colored liquid in each hand. "Something I said?"

"Nope, something I said." I grab two of the shots, turn my back away from the bar, tilt my head until my ringlets brush my shoulder blades and pour the icy cold liquid down my throat. The licorice-tasting Jägermeister washes away my tension like Loving Care washes that gray right outta your hair—quickly, effortlessly, painlessly. Once the seventy-proof opium-based bev enters my bloodstream, I start to calm down. Georgette will be back—I'm her ride, after all. Even though I can't see her on the dance floor right now, I know I'll be seeing her soon. But will I be seeing Franco again anytime soon? He still hasn't asked for my phone number. I turn to the bar, trying to decide how I can ask for his seven digits without looking like I'm chasing him, which I guess I am. Two empty shot glasses rest on the black lacquer bar, a film of brown liquid still coating their insides. The spot where Franco had been standing just fifteen seconds before is empty.

I frantically look around the bar for the blue and red bowling shirt, the lean frame, the Bozo the Clown red hair. Desperate, I stand on the leather turquoise-and-orange-striped barstool to get a better view of the club. I feel mucho dizzy and sick. Is it getting hotter in here?

A fat chick in black Lycra—fat chicks always wear black Lycra, God knows why—bumps into my stool. That seventies commercial "Weebles wobble but they don't fall down" goes through my inebriated mind—unfortunately I'm not so lucky. The stool tumbles to the ground and I go with it; green fringe flying, blonde ringlets defying gravity. My body falls with a thud.

"Okay, it's one forty-five. TIME TO GO!" Hot Bartender screams.

Wait, I can't go yet—not until I find Franco. I get up and look around, my neck swiveling around like a garden sprinkler. I feel a tap on my bare shoulder. Franco, thank God. But when I turn around, I see a pissed-off Georgette. "So, I've decided to forgive you." She notices the stricken look on my face. "What is wrong, Abbie? Did you lose an earring or something?"

I look around the club desperately and mutter, "Something like that." Franco's nowhere in sight.

One of the many bartenders who's directing people out the front door nudges us. "The party's over, ladies. Move it or lose it." Instead of telling Mr. Hot that it doesn't matter, I've already lost it, I grab Georgette's arm and shuffle toward the exit of the almost empty club, one high-heeled foot in front of the other.

Chapter 2

"Only nine days until school starts!" Georgette screams, pulling my lime green comforter off my bed, replacing the lovely blackness I've been cocooned in for the past fourteen hours with harsh sunlight.

I squint and rub last night's black eyeliner from my eyes, covering my knuckle with a charcoal soot. "Soooo?" This is the first word I have uttered to her since New Year's Day, three days ago. She's been back from her dad's since yesterday, but I haven't been in a talking mood. When I'm depressed I play the solitaire version of the quiet game, make hats and eat foods that are bad for me. And believe you me, I am Depressed-with-a-capital-*D* at the moment.

"Soooo, cranky, get outta bed and enjoy your last two hundred–something hours of freedom!" Georgette is getting on my nerves. Even on a bad day, she's way cheerier than Katie Couric. That is, except when she is brooding over a boy. Judging from that smile on her face and the big red sorority-girl bow in her hot-rolled hair, I'd definitely say she's over whatshisname. And she's definitely pissing me off.

"Georgette, three short days ago I met the man of my dreams. My soulmate. I-am-peanut-butter-he-is-jelly. And I lost him. Wham, just like that, he's gone. One second he's kissing my chipmunk cheek and buying me shots, and the next he is vapor. Will I ever see him again? Was he an optical illusion? Will I die an old woman, living alone with twenty-six cats? Did I dream up—"

"God, Ab, I get the picture. I do, but enough already. You have been in this weird depression since I got back from Dad's and it is time to snap out of it. Chop, chop! Face the facts, Abbie. Franco was cute, way cute. Bowling shirts turn you on.

always have. He was wearing a hat you made with your very own hands. All these things, I understand, could cloud your vision. But he was also very fucked up—not just drunk, I think. I mean, he was drunk, no doubt about that, but I'd say there was also some drug use going on, and I'm not talking Tylenol here." Georgette dives onto the bed beside me. I sit up and cross my arms, ready for battle.

"George, you talked to the guy for two minutes. What did you do, follow him to the bathroom and ask him to pee in a Dixie Cup or something?"

"No, but my major is substance abuse . . ."

"As you love to remind me." As much as I love her, George will just not shut up about her damn major. It becomes quite annoying after awhile.

She shoots one of those nasty looks she's famous for my way. "My major is substance abuse. When someone is X-ing or tripping, I detect it. With my trained eye and observant—"

"You mean nosy."

"Uh, hm . . . my trained eye and observant nature—"

"George, your major is substance abuse, but have you ever done a substance? Nope. So how would you know anything about it?" My God, I've taken a karate class but it's not like I'm spouting kung-fuisms all over the darn place.

"I've read tons of books and I've—"

"You can't learn shit from books. How about enrolling in the school of life for a semester? Experience life. Live and learn, Georgette. Live and learn."

"Are you saying I have to be a druggie to counsel one? Puh-*leaze*."

"No, I'm saying that you don't know everything there is to know about drugs and drug users just because your major is substance abuse. And I know that maybe Franco was on something a little stronger than Flintstones Vitamins but I really don't care. We had a connection. I have thought about him for the past seventy hours nonstop. He is Mr. Right, I just know it. God, I know it! But right now he is also Mr. Lost, and I don't know what to do. George, I just don't know what to do," I say, tears of frustration and premenstruation welling up in my eyes.

"Abbie, I really didn't know you were so freaked over him. I mean, sure you've eaten five pints of Ben & Jerry's in the last three days, but you did the same thing when you heard 'My So-Called Life' got canceled. And you've been doing your usual depressed Charlie Chaplin impersonation, but I figured you were just getting your monthly visit from Aunt Flow. Man, this must be hardcore, huh?" I am really crying now—big, fat tears drop all over my Joe Boxer nightshirt. "God, I am really insensitive. Ab. Was it truly love at first sight?"

I wipe my wet cheeks with my plaid sleeve. "It is crazy. Insane. I've seen all the love-at-first-sight episodes of Oprah, Sally Jessy and Geraldo. I mean, I saw them but I didn't really believe them, you know? But this is just too weird. When I saw him, I really just knew. I just knew."

Georgette pats my arm as I draw my knees up to meet my Clearasil-covered chin. I tell her how when I was in eighth grade, I never had any boyfriends because I was so geeky and tall—way taller than most of the guys my age. But I was addicted to those paperback teen romance novels. I devoured them. I read like four or five a week. And there was this one series, Twosomes, that came out with a book about once a month. It was about the in-group at this high school in California or Florida or somewhere. And there was this guy named Woody in it. He was just so cool—funny, quirky sense of fashion, red hair, dug unusual girls. And I always thought if I ever got a boyfriend he'd be just like Woody. In my mind's eye, I created this image of Woody. I thought about him all the time that year, almost like he was real. I reread the three or four books that focused mainly around him at least ten times each. When my mom was fourteen, she worshiped Fabian; when I was fourteen, I worshiped Woody.

"And you know what? This is the crazy part: Franco looks just like Woody. Almost exactly. Except his hair is a little longer, and Woody had a mole to the right of that little crook under his nose that Franco doesn't. But other than that, they could be twins. Freaking identical twins." I say really fast, words spilling out of my mouth as rapidly as shiny coins from a lucky Las Vegas slot machine.

"Okay, you've lost me. Woody is a guy in a book series you liked. And Franco looks like Woody. I get that. But Woody doesn't exist, right? So how does Franco look like a guy who isn't real?" she says, like it's this big mystery.

"That's the thing. Woody was very real to me. I knew exactly what he looked like, what his interests were, what he thought about. Elvis lived in Graceland, we live in Dallas, Woody lives in here," I say, tapping my index finger against the side of my head. "And when I saw Franco, it just clicked. He was Woody. My Woody. I just knew it instantly. But then he was gone. I don't know, maybe it's some kind of poetic justice. Woody lives in my mind only, and now so does Salvation Army–lovin' Franco. But I keep thinking: Did I live it? Did I dream it? Who knows. I guess there's nothing I can do but sit here and suffer."

"Nothing you can do? Nothing you can do?" I see that look, and I know Georgette's flowery romantic side is kicking in. "Rent a billboard along Loop Twelve. Take out a personals ad. Wallpaper every Salvation Army in the town with flyers declaring your love and devotion. Stake out Club Unity for a million nights in a row. Do anything—but don't give up. You can't give up now!" Georgette hops up and puts her hands on my shoulders, shaking them slightly. "Ever heard that old song by Garth Brooks, 'The Dance'? It's about something like how life is better left to chance, and how he could've missed the pain but then he would've had to miss the dance. Screw the dance. Screw Garth Brooks. Screw that better-to-have-loved-and-lost crap. You, Abbie McPhereson, have to find your man. Go after him, hunt him down and go in for the kill! Take no prisoners!"

Georgette was a pom-pom girl in high school or some such shit—the squad all the chicks who didn't make cheerleader get shoved on—and she's never quite brushed that image off. During this monologue, she's a cross between a go-getter cheerleader captain and drill sergeant from hell. For the first time in days, my teeth come out of hiding as I flash Georgette a smile.

"You're right, Georgie baby. Like Greg Brady said: 'Winners never quit and quitters never win.' So, if I'm gonna stake out Club Unity tonight, there is one very important question we must consider," I say solemnly.

"What's that, Ab?"

"What the hell am I gonna wear?"

— — —

"HEY, KIDDOS. This is Georgette and Abbie and we're not feeling too gabby. *Beep.*"

"Hi, Abs, this is Mom. It's two o'clock Sunday. I'm just calling for the Franco report. Last night was night eight of Operation Club Unity, right? The whole family's dying to know how it turned out. Give me a call—collect, of course. I hope you wore your eyeliner last night—you know you have my eyes and we look dead without it. Okay, okay, call me. Now. Bye!"

I'm lying on my pink-and-orange-striped couch with half-dollar-sized cucumber slices covering my puffy eyes. After eight unsuccessful late nights in a row, I'm not up to talking to anybody—not even Mom.

If Franco had shown up, the stakeout would have been perfect. Well, this is a wee bit of an exaggeration—most of it was from hell. But I looked perfect, at least. I conducted eight pre-Unity beauty sessions, which included nightly pedicures and shaving above the knees. Then it was time for a good-luck dinner—Franco-American spaghetti. I have to admit, eight cans later, that I am a little sick of this entree. After the culinary cuisine, I pumped up my hair, sucked in my tummy and squeezed each evening into one of the sexiest little dresses my bod has ever been (almost) covered in. Hell, one night I even taped up my tits with silver duct tape so I could adequately fill out the bust of this awesome little Betsey Johnson number. But, alas, my primping was all in vain since Franco never showed. That fact hurts almost as much as pulling that tape off did.

I guess the endeavor wouldn't have been a total loss if a hot guy or two had hit on me during my Unity marathon. But apparently I had a neon sign on my forehead that said IF YOU'RE A GEEK, I'M YOUR GAL because I was a nerd magnet for every loser within a two-mile radius. Until this experience, I never would've believed so many boys still owned those eighties M.C. Hammer pants. I swear to God.

And to top off the eight days of eternal bliss, last night was a Unity special event—an Abbie grand finale, if you will: a *Tiger Beat* New Kids on the Block reunion concert. Girl, you know it's true: four hours with hundreds of screaming prepubescent chicks, four synchronized-dancing, screechy-singing, wannabe geeks and almost-crying, eyes-glued-to-the-door me. When they sang that "Step by Step" song, I had to leave. There is only so much a hip gal can take, you know?

Needless to say, they were not the most fun eight evenings of my life. But it was worth a shot, and now it's over. *Finito.* I promised myself that the eighth day would be my last, and it was. It only took God seven days to create the universe, after all. I spotted myself a day, just in case—but still no cigar. Oh, well. School starts tomorrow, and I'm too worried about graduating to spend one more millisecond harping on Mr. Wonderful.

I remove the cucumbers from my eyes and pick up the jade green compact from the coffee table. I open it and check myself out. Scary. God, I've got enough bags under these eyes to go on a two-week vacation. I bounce off the couch and jaunt to the bathroom—the only thing that can save me now is my trusty blue tube of white liquid concealer.

While I'm dotting under my eyes—four dots, evenly spaced apart, under each—the phone rings. Grand Central Station. Maybe it's Georgette, she's supposed to call from the mall. I sprint to the seventies Snoopy phone, my face looking like a page from a dot-to-dot coloring book.

"Hello?" I chirp, trying to give good phone in case it's someone of interest.

"Is this Vanna? Vanna White?" It's Pat, my best bud since ninth grade—God love him. The guy's the absolute most, calling me Vanna White and all. He does that shit constantly; we're talking total riot.

"No, Pat Sajak, but I do have white concealer dots under my eyes. What is up? Back from Daddy's in Cali?" Pat's originally from West Hollywood but isn't by a long shot the stereotypical Jeff Spicoli you picture when you think California Boy. I don't know why, but when I think of a West Coast fellow I always picture some bronzed god or something and they're usually never like that, not ever. But Pat lived in Tulsa through all of high school, so maybe that's what de-California-ized him.

"Back from Cali with the tan to prove it, baby. So how'd Saint Nick treat Abs this year?"

"Well, I got a Macintosh and two Cynthia Rowley dresses and then I met the boy of my dreams New Year's Eve but he escaped and is still missing in action," I say real quick, the syllables leaving my mouth faster than Franco left Unity.

"Whoa, Abbie. Haven't I told you? Handcuffs, sweetie, handcuffs. Then they'll never get away," he says, all cackling. A few years back, Pat told me he and his ex bought some handcuffs and I harped on it for-fucking-ever, like he will never live that shit down. The whole notion was kind of a turn-on, if you must know. I've never used them, though.

"Oh yes, you S&M master. Speaking of, how's Sal?" He's been dating this boy for a while who's cute and nice but totally insecure. We're talking male anorexia waiting to happen here.

"Still my guy," Pat said. "Our one-year anniversary was December fourteenth, and he got me a skateboard for Christmas."

"How'd he like the kitten?"

"Loved it, loved it. He named him Kiwi and keeps getting lip gloss all over his white fur from kissing him so much."

I sigh, wishing I had a boy to buy me a kitten that I could kiss and get glosser all over. I can't find a guy who'll buy me a damn pack of gum, much less a pet. "Y'all are too sweet. You really give me hope, Patrick. There are still normal cool boys out there! Even if they are all gay. So are you ready for school *mañana*?" Pat came to the Design Institute with me the summer after senior year, which seemed a natural move since he was constructing elaborate clubbing outfits before he was old enough to even be thinking of getting into a club. He rules, he really does.

"Hell no, I'm not ready for school. That's why I'm calling. Me, Sal, Ulysses and Dennis are going to the midnight showing of the original *Dracula* at Inwood. If you give a pint of blood, you get in free."

"Hello, have you forgotten who you're talking to? Your best friend? The one who hates needles more than she hates sewer rats?"

"What's a little suffering when there's a free movie involved? C'mon, I'll hold your hand, Ab. It'll be fun. I haven't seen your ass in a month. I'm having withdrawals."

"Uh—"

"Come on, Ab."

"Weeell, I don't know, I me—"

"For me, man. Pleeeeeeeease?" I can't take it when a boy begs. I just cannot take it.

"You buying the popcorn?"

"Light butter, extra salt—just the way you like it. And, what the hell, I'll even throw in a jumbo Dr Pepper."

"I guess it's a date," I groan, regretting the words before they're even out of my mouth. You put enough pressure on a girl like me, even one who hates needles and loathes Dracula, and she'll buckle every fucking time.

"We'll swing by around eleven. Oh, and wear black—as if you wouldn't anyway." Last year I was way into the black thing and wore only black for around two months. Pat will never let me live it down.

"Save the black fashion jokes, please. See ya at eleven."

I hang up quickly, happy once more. I love Pat—he is my best pal in the world, tied with Georgette. And Sal is the coolest, despite being a bit on the insecure side. Maybe life after Franco will go on after all. If so, I better make sure I've got something to wear. I head to my closet to prepare for my Franco-less future and my needleful night.

"GOD, LOOK at that line," Pat says as he pulls his little yellow Bug into the Inwood parking lot. I peek over Sal's shoulder and check out the crowd. Everyone looks pretty cool from this distance. All but two people are dressed in black—the oddballs are wearing matching red velvet overalls and big black satin capes. I put on another coat of stop-sign red lipstick and smear it majorly as Pat whips into a parking place between two station wagons.

"Thanks, Pat," I say sarcastically as I wipe the red wax off my cheek. Pat drives just like he talks—fast and furious. I should have known never to apply cosmetics when he was behind the wheel, but I am not thinking clearly. Frankly, I'm scared shitless. My needle phobia is in full effect.

"Abbie, you are freaking, aren't you?" Sal asks as we unfold ourselves from the Volkswagen. He's really pretty thoughtful and all, just annoyingly jealous of any male with a pulse.

I smile nervously and smooth out the wrinkles in my black fake-fur skirt. As I bend down to pull up my southbound tights, I notice my hands are shaking big-time now. Great.

"I think I should warn you. I haven't had a shot since second grade. And during that one, I cried for three hours and two nurses had to hold me down," I tell Pat and Sal as we walk briskly to the theater, anxious to get out of the forty-degree climate.

"Baby, don't worry. It's nothing, really. And Ulysses and Dennis are already in there—they survived and so will you," Pat replies as he grabs Sal's hand with his left and mine with his right, squeezing my fingers tightly.

"Yeah, Abbie, I'll be right by you, too," Sal says as we file in at the end of the line, giving me this weird sideways glance punctuated by a forced, thin-lipped smile. I wonder what's up with him until I realize I'm holding his man's hand. This is what I'm saying when I call him a jealous freak. I mean, I love Pat, but please, not like that. And besides, I'm not quite equipped to steal Pat away, even if that was my intention. Which it's totally not.

But frankly, as I count the people in front of us—sixteen—Sal's freak-out is the least of my worries. I cup my hands around my eyes and peek into the tinted windows of the theater. I make out two beds, a couple of nurses running around and a clear plastic thing full of a dark red substance that's got to be blood. From here, I can't see the needles, but I know they're in there. On the admission window there's a big sign that says: NO BLOOD DONATING=NO MOVIE WATCHING. NO CASH ACCEPTED. Oh God. I think I'm gonna be sick.

Pat and Sal are chatting about Kiwi and his cute habit of jumping into open refrigerators. I slap a smile on my face and pretend to listen, but all I can think about is the needle that will soon invade my arm and the excruciating pain that will accompany it.

As we get closer to the door, I remember the time I went to Six Flags Over Texas with my family. This roller coaster, Shock Wave, was the big draw and we wanted to ride it. We stood in line for over an hour, inching slowly closer and closer to the entrance. When we finally made it and it was our turn to ride, my little brother who was like seven at the time chickened out and refused to get on. He wouldn't budge. So we went on without him and it was awesome—two upside-down loops, a monster hill and a sideways turn. My mom, dad and I were all raving about it for the rest of the day, going on and on about how fun and scary it was. Well, this depressed my brother so much that he threw a tantrum and wouldn't stop crying that night at the hotel until we promised to go back the next day just so he could ride the stupid thing. That next afternoon he rode it nine times in a row. The kid's been a roller coaster junkie ever since.

I doubt the same thing will happen to me with needles, like I'll become an acupuncture addict or something, but I don't want to be a chicken like my brother was and then regret it like he did. I vow to be brave. Two minutes of hell will not kill me. When you consider how many minutes there are in a month or a week or a day even, two minutes is nothing.

When we finally get to the front of the line, Sal and Pat are still gabbing about Kiwi and I am still silently freaking. As a theater employee ushers us in, I feel like a death-row inmate on her way to the electric chair. The lobby looks more like an emergency room tonight. Pat and Sal lie down on the two beds, fill out a form and stick out their right arms. Two nurses stick needles into Pat and Sal's flesh, but neither of my pals flinch. I stare at the empty clear pouches, side by side, slowly filling up with blood.

"All done," the youngest nurse chirps loudly, removing the needles from their skin. "Next!"

Pat and Sal, still alive, hop off the beds. I lie down on the right bed, closing my eyes tightly. A feeling that can only be terror paralyzes every organ besides my heart, which sounds like a heavy-metal drum solo at the moment.

"You have to fill out the form first," the older nurse bellows, her Vienna sausage–shaped fingers shoving a clipboard under my nose.

I fill out the sheet of paper with a shaky hand. Tears hover at the brims of my eyes. God, I am a chicken. Pat grabs my left hand as I extend my right arm. When the sharp metal pierces my flesh, the tears escape and cascade over my cheeks. There is a needle in my arm there is a needle in my arm.

I start to sob. "Hold still, ma'am. Can you control your friend, sir? It's almost over, ma'am."

Pat: "Hang in there, Abbie baby."

Sal: "Abbie, popcorn awaits."

My sobs now have a life of their own. I haven't cried this hard since *Schindler's List* how-many-ever years ago. My makeup is history.

"It's over, it's over," Old Nurse says as she removes the needle from my arm. Pat bends over and kisses my forehead. Sal starts jumping up and down and cheering loudly. Oh my God, I need a bathroom *now*.

I get up shakily, feeling a little dizzy. No matter how good this movie is, that was so not worth it. "Where's the bathroom?" I ask, wiping my cheeks with my fingertips. Pat points westward and I stagger toward the pink door. The lavatory door starts to spin, like cherry icing swirling on hot vanilla cupcakes. My knees quiver violently. A boy exits the men's room, almost hitting me with the turquoise door.

"Franco?" I gasp. Then I hit the floor with a thud, fainting for the first time in my life in front of the last boy I ever expected to see again.

When I open my eyes, four blurry figures are closing in on me like carrion crows descending on a fresh animal carcass. "She's awake! She's awake!" Pat? A chubby paw sticks an Oreo in my mouth. "Eat this, missy, and your blood sugar will shoot right back up to normal." I close my lids and chew, trying to figure out what I'm doing on the floor. As I swallow the chocolate wafers and melt-in-your-mouth cream filling, my brain slowly kicks in. Dracula. Blood. Needles. Pain. Franco. Franco?

I open my eyes and wait for things to come into focus. Finally, I clearly see Old Nurse smirk at me and walk back to her makeshift torture chamber. Pat and Sal, arm in arm, look like worried parents. Pat extends his free hand to help me up and Sal cheers as I make it to my feet. "Hip hip hooray—you're okay!" But where the hell is Franco?

"Wasn't—wasn't there another guy crouching over me a second ago? I could swear I saw four people hovering over me," I say frantically as I try to revive my smashed curls with shaking fingers. Could I have dreamed the whole thing? It wouldn't be the first time I've created a situation in my mind that in no way exists.

Sal nods. "Yeah, some redheaded dude. But when he saw you were alive, he went into the theater."

Went into the theater? Went into the theater? Franco, boy of my dreams, saw me faint and went into the damn theater without even waiting to find out if I'm functioning?

"Yeah, Ab—listen, if you just want to blow this thing off, it's cool. You look like hell," Pat says, patting my shoulder.

"Flattery will get you everywhere, Pat. I'm okay. Just buy me that jumbo Dr Pepper and I'll live." I can barely form a sentence at this point. Who knows why he didn't hang around; whatever, the point is Franco's nearby, like in the same building as me. Soon we'll meet again, any second. If this isn't fate, I don't know what the hell is. My mom said I would just know, and after this encounter, believe me, I fucking know alrighty.

After Pat kisses my plucked brow and heads to the snack bar, Sal gets in my face. "Are you really okay, Ab? Because if you don't feel like staying, we can leave. I mean, five minutes ago you practically died and you were on the floor and—"

Have I mentioned Sal rambles? He does a bit. But he's very good-looking, so most people don't mind watching him talk even if they're not listening. "Listen, Sal, I'm fine. Really. But the deal is, you know that redhead? The guy who was just inches above my bod? Well, I want him. And we're not leaving this theater 'til I get him."

An I-can-relate smile comes to his lips. "Aaaaaaah, I get it. Lust. He is hot, what little I saw of him. But do you know him or what?"

"Sort of. It's kind of a screwed-up story, I'll tell you the details someday, but I'm serious—I feel like I love this guy." It's the first time I've said it out loud to anybody but George, but it sounds pretty coming from my lips. "I love this guy." I could bawl right now, just thinking about it.

"Love? Is this Abbie Never-Again-Will-I-Love-Another-After-Jerko-Parker McPhereson speaking? No way."

"I know, it's crazy. We met at Unity twelve days ago. I don't even know his middle name or his favorite Nintendo game, but I know I love him. With a capital *L*."

"God, that is so romantic. When I first met Pat at that fabric store, I loved him right away. I was with my boyfriend-of-the-week, who was a real asshole, and I saw Pat looking at the green lamé and I thought, 'Oh no, this is it.' It just hit me."

"Just like that?" Like I said, the guy can be a sweetie when he wants to be. I mean, he's awfully sincere.

His eyes dart to Pat, still at the snack bar. "Well, Pat looked so silly and serious checking out that god-awful puke green lamé, looking at it like it was some sort of precious spun gold or something. And I just wanted to ditch my guy right then and there and let Pat drape that ugly fabric all over my bod. But instead I scrawled my name and phone number on one of those free Threads + Less yardsticks and slipped it to him while my date was checking out the Speedo patterns. Ugh."

"Just like a teen romance or something! Or 'The Love Boat.' "

"Did I hear the *L* word?" Pat asks, handing me my big drink and tossing Sal a box of Milk Duds.

"Yep—and the boy of my affections is inside that theater, so let's haul ass," I say, already five steps ahead of them.

"What? Who?" Pat calls. But I don't answer—don't have time. Franco awaits.

I enter the theater, which is black as licorice. Pat and Sal are hot on my heels. I can't see my hand in front of my face, much less make out the guy of my dreams in the bevy of moviegoers.

"Franco! Franco!" I shrill, my voice barely louder than the movie's Dolby Stereo Surround sound. A chick with short black ringlets, think Betty Boop, twists around in her back row seat and shoots me a dirty look. Maybe I should just chill and wait 'til the end of the movie to find him if I want to keep all my body parts intact.

I turn around and grab Pat's earlobe, whispering, "Find us a seat."

He edges in front of me and heads to the front row, the only row with any vacant seats to be had. Welcome to Whiplash City.

I try to concentrate on the action on-screen, but my brain is full of Franco, Franco, Franco. God, we're in the same room, watching the same movie, breathing the same air! It blows my mind. I keep craning my neck, trying to spot him in the crowd. I wonder if he's looking for me too? The thought churns my stomach.

Finally, after what seems like an eternity, the credits roll. The flick is over. It's showtime. Should I wait until the lights go up, then try to spot him? Or stake out the lobby? I decide the lobby's the safest bet and dart toward it, not waiting for my pals. The aisle is kind of clogged, but I strong-arm my way through, calling "Franco! Franco! Franco!" at the top of my lungs. One jockboy I bulldoze into says, "Who the fuck is Franco?" but I ignore him. I don't have time for geeks or hecklers—I'm on a mission. And this time, for once, it doesn't look like "Mission: Impossible."

I make it to the lobby and check out the tops of heads. Blonde, brown, black, ballcap, shaved, gray, bald. But no red. Not a single red hair in the whole damn crowd! Okay, do not freak, Ab. Inhale. Exhale. Inhale. Exhale. Inha—oh God, there he is. By the door, it's him. Looking as hot as ever, breathtaking even.

I run to the door and grab Franco's leather-covered arm. "Franco!"

He whirls around. It's him, alrighty. "Yeah?"

"Hey!" Brilliant, Abbie, brilliant.

"Hey." He looks at me quizzically with empty eyes, waiting. Waiting for what?

"Remember me? Abbie? From New Year's Eve? We met at Club Unity. You were wearing a daisy hat that I designed. And we danced. Then did shots—Kamikazes and Jäger. Then I just saw you when I fainted and . . ."

"Okay, okay. Yeeeah, New Year's Eve. Uh-huh, that explains it."

"Explains what?" Maybe why he's so struck by my beauty right now?

"Why I don't recognize you. I was fucked on New Year's Eve. Fucked! God, I can't even remember coming home from the clubs. I was on so much shit that night. Man oh man. Crazy night, caaaarrrazy night. So what's your name? Tabitha?"

"No, it's Abbie. Abbie," I repeat, feeling like an idiot. For almost two weeks I've been stalking a boy who can't even get my name right. He's been my total existence yet he doesn't even know I exist.

"Oh yeah. Right. Abbie. Not-so-shabby Abbie."

Is that his way of telling me I'm cute? Who knows. All I do know is that this is going nowhere fast. I figure I better make my move pronto. Biting my lip, I take the plunge: "So, Franco, do you have a phone?"

"Yeah, doesn't everybody?" he asks, squinting at the parking lot through the smoky glass.

"Um, I guess. But, well, can I call you sometime on it?"

"Call me?" he asks, like he's never heard of the concept.

This is torture. I know I sound desperate, but the truth is I am desperate for this boy. "Yeah, call you. You know. I dial seven digits, your phone rings, you pick it up . . ."

"Oh, okay. Cool."

"Cool." He doesn't move a muscle. Nothing. "So, can I get your number?"

"Oh yeah, you might need that," he says, flashing that zillion-dollar grin. "I'm sorry I'm so completely out of it. I guess it might have been giving the blood, who knows. But here I am meeting a cool girl and I'm acting like an idiot."

He called me a cool girl. Cool. Cool. Cool. Cool. The word skips over and over my brain like a note from a scratched record. Looking into Franco's piercing blue eyes, I think how much I'd like to scratch his record.

"You're not," I titter, deciding to respond to the coolness comment by not really responding at all.

"Well, whatever, but my apologies anyway." He shakes his head from side to side. "I'm telling you, I feel really trippy. But the number, it's five-five-five, two-two-four-three."

"Wait, hold on," I say as I rummage through my purse for a pen. I usually have pens coming out of my ears, but the one time I really need one there's not one to be found. Of course. "Uh, I can't find a pen. But what is it again? I have a pretty good memory."

"Five-five-five, two-two-four-three. The easiest way to remember it is five-five-five, ACID."

"Five-five-five, ACID? As in LSD?" I croak.

"Yep. I was on that New Year's Eve, among other things," Franco says, chuckling. I emit a seventh-grade giggle although I'm not sure what's so funny.

"Well, okay, I'll call you then. Good to see you again."

"Ditto, doll. Call me, I'll be waiting." You take a guy like Franco, hot enough to fry an egg on, you doubt he's ever waiting for anything. But then you don't really care because you're getting heatstroke just being near him and all.

I smile my most charmingest smile and wave before turning around to find Pat and Sal. I wonder if he's checking out my backside. I wish I hadn't skipped all those step aerobics classes. I wiggle over to Pat and Sal, who are hanging by the bathroom doors, right about where I bit the dust a couple of hours before.

Sal grabs me as I approach. "Soooooo—that was him, right? How'd it go?"

I look into Sal's eyes, then into Pat's. "Oh God, I think I'm in love."

Chapter 3

"—Phereson?"

"I'm here, I'm here, I'm here!" I sing as I burst through the doors of room 106 at my home away from home—Dallas Design Institute—on the first day of my last semester, January 13. I am fashionably late, as usual, but unfortunately the boy at the front of the Runway Collection class—where is Mrs. Potter?—does not look amused. At all.

"Hmm, hmm. Well, darling, if you are going to be tardy don't bother coming," Stranger hisses, stroking his tiny black mustache with both of his manicured index fingers.

In response to this colicky outburst, I roll my eyes and plop into an electric-blue beanbag in the corner of the room.

"Okay, Parsons?"

"Here."

As Mr. Crabby drones on, I scan the room for Pat. I finally spy him sitting at an egg-shaped table with two chicks who are all decked out in club kid gear—such a tired look. Pat, in old-man cardigan and thermal, catches my eye and raises his eyebrows at me like, What is this guy's deal? I shrug and brush a stray strand of hair out of my eye, pissed. All I want to know is where the hell Potter is and why my school hired such a lame substitute teacher with an enormous attitude, somebody fill me in. Please. I have been looking forward to this Runway Collections class my whole college career—no attendance policy, ancient teacher and practically zero work. My kind of class, and the last one I need to get my Associate's. True, I wouldn't learn anything, but who cares? I just want the *A*. Unfortunately, little Mr. José freak has entered the scene. Curveball. Let's just hope he's not the proverbial rainstorm that drenches my parade, because this girlie doesn't groove on downpours.

"May I please have your attention," Cranky says, shaking—ohmigod—a pair of red and green maracas like they're plastic bags full of drumsticks and Shake 'n Bake. The guy's got an exaggerated accent straight out of a bad Cheech and Chong flick and has sort of a nervous tic with his eyebrow, like it's twitching or something. Not to be a bitch or anything, but it's really weird. The eyebrow's out of control.

A few people giggle but soon zip it once Freak gives them the evil eye. He turns to the board, trades the maracas in for a stubby piece of Mary Kay–pink chalk, scrawls *Señor Fredrique* and turns back toward us, glaring.

"Perhaps you have heard of me. I am"—dramatic pause—"Señor Fredrique."

Heard of him?

"I was the toast of Paris, in my day."

Yeah, right—watch out, Calvin. Who *is* this guy?

"The fashion world devoured me, savored me, then chewed me up into little pieces and spit my bloody remains on the New York pavement." He spits on the bologna-pink tile floor to illustrate this point. Gross. I am losing interest in this freak fast and I'm not alone. All around me, feet are shuffling, a few people are whispering, the girl next to me is smacking her Bubble Yum loud.

"So here I am now, teaching you children design techniques when you should be reading about me, Señor Fredrrrique, in your textbooks." He picks up the text—*Runway Collections and You*—from his little metal podium and starts ripping out the pages and tossing them on the floor. Major eighties *Dead Poets Society* flashback. I look at Pat and our eyebrows collectively scrape the ceiling.

"Yes, Señora Potter kicked the bucket. Heart attack, quite sudden. She's gone and I'm here. Your easy ride has just come to a screeching halt."

Community gasp.

Okay, let's get this straight. Mrs. Potter, blow-off teacher of the world, has joined the Choir Invisible. The woman who was going to salvage my grade point is six feet under. Can my life possibly get any worse?

"Here is the story. It's called Runway Collections. *Sí.* I take that to mean an entire fall collection designed and created by the end of the semester, at which time we will present our designs to the world at the First Annual Dallas Design Institute Style Gala. Everyone who's anyone will be there—Donna, Liz, Ralph—to witness your rise . . . or fall," he cries with a snicker as he drops to his spandex-covered knees. Potter's final project was to design a wedding outfit for Ken, Barbie or Skipper—a far cry from this assignment from hell.

"You, my friends, are responsible for providing the models, so you better give Cindy Crawford a call pronto. And the first person to book Cam, the CK One model, gets an *A* for the course. Period. And, on that note, if you are on yours, girls, I don't want to hear about it. No excuses. Either you do the job or you don't. The collection must have an underlying theme, include thirty pieces and be totally original. That means no club kid creations, *por favor*," Fredrique says as he glares at Pat's table.

Talk about drunk with power! It was one thing when he wanted us to design a fall collection—but to produce a full fall collection with thirty pieces? In one semester? I don't think there's any way it's humanly possible. I raise my hand, not believing this guy.

"Yes?"

"This isn't very fair," I whimper. Mature, I know, but I'm cranky. Mistake.

Fredrique glares at me, yanks off his fuchsia beret and hops up from the shredded-paper-and-spit-covered ground over to my corner. "Would you say it was very fair when *Vogue* said my last fall collection was perfect for work only if you work at a place with a drive-thru? No. But they did, and now I'm here. Life is not fair. It's one lesson F.I.T. didn't teach me that I will teach you if it kills me."

As he stomps off, I look around the room. Everyone—even the club kids—is looking at me sympathetically. Pat blows a kiss at my fire-engine red face. I feel tears welling up in my eyes. Abbie, you will not cry, baby. No way.

"Well, class, one more thing and you can go on your first field trip. For the next thirty *momentos*, walk around this little school. Experience everything on a fashion level. Then write about your experiences, type them up on your little computers and submit them for a grade *mañana. Adiós.*"

Fredrique hauls to the door, slips on some fifties rhinestone-studded cat's-eye shades even though it's not the least bit sunny outside and makes like a tree.

"Good riddance, asshole," I mutter when the door slams shut.

The whole class, myself included, is still sitting down, silent. It's like there's just been a big plane crash and we're all still in shock. Like we know something awful happened but the horrible reality of just how tragic it really is hasn't sunk in yet.

I jump up and run over to Pat. The room's silence is quickly being replaced with the sound of some major bitching and moaning. "Let's get the heck outta Dodge," I say as I pull Pat toward the door. "Field trip time's a-wastin'."

As soon as we hit the hall, Pat starts in. "God, is this guy on crack? Thirty pieces? Totally original concept? A theme, for Chrissakes? Hello, this isn't a senior prom, it's a freaking class. Someone needs to clue him in. I've got other classes besides his. Plus a job. Plus a life! I don't even have time to design thirty things, much less make every single piece from scratch."

I nod. "Sweetie, I know. He's a freak—insane. I mean, isn't this illegal or something? Last night, I almost die—I don't need this. And what is this Potter dead as a doornail thing? What is that all about? God, is there anything we can do?"

"Yep, our damn homework. We have twenty-one minutes before my next class. Experience, babe." I follow Pat down the hall, trying to look at the pink-and-white-tiled floor and light pink walls I've seen a trillion times before as if I am looking at them for the first time, but unfortunately it's not happening. Everything looks just as ugly as it did this morning. Concentrate, Abbie, concentrate.

"Hey, Pat?"

"Yeah?" he answers, distracted, looking up from the water fountain he's studying.

"If Franco was a dress, he would definitely be designed by Betsey Johnson."

"You, my dear, have lost it. Completely."

January 13, 11:15 P.M.

I finally saw him. Franco. At this Dracula movie I got stuck with a needle at. God, is this fate or what? He's defi-

nitely interested, it's obvious. 555-ACID, his number (!!!) in case I forget it. Yeah, right.

Will we name our first child "Count" after the first movie we sorta saw together? So romantic. Tomorrow is the second day of school. I couldn't call him on the first day of school—bad karma. To avoid looking desperate (who me?) I should definitely wait 'til Thursday to call. But what if he thinks I'm blowing him off—not calling for ninety-six hours? I mean, he's probably waiting for my call, why make my boy suffer needlessly? Wednesday around two, I'll call him. For sure. Forty hours away. God, forty hours really seems like a lifetime. Maybe tomorrow? In about fifteen hours? We live in apartment 15. That's a good omen, right? Okay, Tuesday it is. Franco, my sweet—Tuesday, you're mine.

"And that's why I think the office door looks like a patent leather platform shoe, size ten-B. Thank you."

A smattering of applause for the first oral report of the day. That was Frazier, a boy who thinks I'm a bitch. This is alright, because I think he's an idiot.

"Weak effort, Señor Johnson. Very weak." Fredrique drawls, scribbling something in his orange notebook. "Hmm, hmm. Next—Señorita McPhereson."

I smooth out my right sleeve and go to the front of the room. I am the worst at oral reports, the absolute worst. Like I won't even feel nervous at all and the minute I get up there in front of the crowd my hands start trembling and my voice starts shaking and my face gets all red and I'm like a sunburn girl with Parkinson's disease or something. I take a deep breath, look at Pat and begin.

"I walked down the hall nonchalantly, with no particular destination in mind. Then, suddenly, there it was: an open door leading to a place where few women have gone before, in more ways than one. I hesitated. Fear of the unknown gripped my pounding heart, filling my black Docs with lead. Was I brave enough to explore uncharted territory? A classmate of the Y-chromosome variety grabbed my arm and pulled me over the threshold. Cue the 'Twilight Zone' theme song: I had now officially entered The Men's Room." My voice is a bit shaky and I haven't looked up from my paper since word three, but otherwise things are okay. I grip the podium a little tighter and continue.

"A pungent cherry bubblegum aroma invaded my nostrils as I shuffled down the lavatory entry path. Anticipation filled my aerobicized bod as the tiled wall before me got closer and closer. Crossing my fingers that no boys would be draining the weasel as I played Nancy Drew, Girl Detective, I reached the end of the entry hall, veered to the left and saw them: three white urinals mounted to the wall, resembling Art Deco flowerpots. The two white sinks, soap dispenser, paper towel holder and pair of mirrors looked just like the ones in the chicks' room but I bet our mirrors get a lot more use." I look over at Señor Fredrique. "Uh, but maybe not. A dented steel trash can rested in between urinals number two and number three, its exterior quite like a second-grader's metal lunch box on the last day of school. Next to urinal number three, a deep mauve wall—the exact same color of this amazing Isaac Mizrahi dress I just bought—hid a white toilet that would feel quite at home in the girls' room. I concluded this is for doing number two or as a last resort when the trio of urinals are full. My final observation: no neato machines on the walls like we gals have. But, then again, we don't have those flowerpots either, so I'll just shut up. The End."

I look around, a bit freaked. It wasn't tip-top, nor was it a total disaster. I'm just happy the damn thing's over. A few people clap, Pat whistles and Ulysses shrieks. Fredrique says, "Yes, well . . ." and then calls on the next person. What does "Yes, well" mean?

I only half listen to the rest of the speeches, opting instead to doodle and think about my upcoming call to Franco—only nine and a half hours away. Near the end of class, Pat—who just gave his speech about the similarities of the doorknob and fellow classmate Susan Pritchet's earrings—grabs the notebook on which I've written *Abbie Hearts Franco* about a hundred and eight times in the last five minutes to examine it.

"God, Abbie, you are beyond obsessed."

Yes.

Chapter 4

"Hello, hello!" I holler as I walk in our apartment door and toss my black leather backpack in the corner next to the jumbo aquarium Georgette's dad bought her for Christmas.

"Hey, you Mrs. Paul's rejects," I say as I rest my hand on the aquarium glass, giggling at how the fourteen fishies—seven clown loaches, six hatchetfish and one tiger oscar—swim my way, expecting some flavorful fish flakes. I grab the yellow and brown plastic container from the fireplace mantel and pinch some yucky-smelling flakes between my thumb and index finger and drop them into the water. The fish go wild, acting like they haven't eaten in about a year. I feed them some more and call out to my roomie once again.

"George, are you home?"

Guess not. I flip on the TV—a "Dragnet" rerun is on in ten minutes—and head for the kitchen. The cabinets are depressingly bare. Two boxes of generic mac and cheese, four packages of ramen noodles, a bag of pretzels and a canister of Slimfast. The refrigerator unfortunately brings me no solace—a jar of mustard, carton of eggs, A.1, half a stick of butter and a carton of milk that expired four days ago. The freezer is my last hope. Fingers crossed, I open the door. Pay dirt. Hiding behind a bottle of ninety-proof peach schnapps and three trays of ice is a frozen pepperoni pizza. Whee!

I crank the oven to 425, pour a glass of water and settle down on the couch to watch Friday strut his stuff. "Dragnet" rules.

About the time the pizza's nearly history and Gannon and Friday have almost got the case solved, Georgette strolls in, looking like an R-rated version of her G-rated self. Even though I try not to, I crack up.

"Well, what do you think?" Georgette squeals while twirling around, her egg-white skin turning as red as my Lancôme lipstick.

"Why are you dressed like one of those 1-900 infomercial girls who purr 'Call me—I love to talk'? Ohmigod, this has got to be a dream." I'm not exaggerating. Miss Prude of America is wearing black dominatrix heels, a rhinestone-studded bustier, black spandex miniskirt and—nooooooo way—fishnet hose. "Are you trying out for a Metallica video or something?" Sometimes I crack myself up and now is one of those times. I'm rolling. Unfortunately, Georgette does not find me quite so hysterical.

"God, Abbie, shut up! No, I'm not trying out to be a video vixen, for your information. I'm just trying out my new look." She kicks off her five-inch heels and plops down next to me on the couch.

"New look? What's wrong with the old one?"

"What's right with it is the question. So far in my nineteen summers I have had zero fun. Just homework, PBS documentaries and long plaid skirts. And I'm tired of boys not giving me a second glance. Let's face it. I'm about as exciting as a glass of low-fat milk, you know? But no more, Ab. No more."

This really blows me away. Georgette is not exactly a woman of change. "Is this the same Georgette who looked three weeks for a new pair of shoes and ended up buying a pair of loafers exactly like the four pairs she already owns?"

"Yeah, Ab, but that was the old me. I want a new image, a new life."

"But I like your image."

"It's *booor*-ing. When I go to a club, boys don't look twice. I might as well be a barstool or a bottle of beer. Like right before Christmas when we went to Acropolis. I saw a zillion guys checking out your form in that little black dress and I didn't even get one lousy pinch on the ass. Not one."

"Noooooooo, not true. Remember that one guy who bought you those three Sex on the Beach shots? He liked you." That night at Acropolis was crazy—this not-cute-but-not-ugly guy was so up in her business.

"Oh yeah, like he counts. He was old enough to have been my

fourth-grade math teacher. And he told me he just got a 'Slick Willie' haircut last week. Okay, my name's not Hillary and I don't want an old Bill Clinton look-alike. Now if it was Al . . ."

"Al Gore is a fox. Ummmm, those lips! And all those funky Jerry Garcia ties. God, to think a Deadhead actually made it into the White House! It's so surreal, like one of those Dali prints—"

"Good way to get off the subject, Abs. But this illustrates my point. I'm always overlooked like that and I am sick of it. Sick of working at a boring job, pulling my hair back into boring ponytails, driving around in my boring car and sitting here eating boring frozen pizzas night after boring night."

"Georgette, you are not boring! You do lots of stuff." She's really not. I'm not just saying that.

"Like what? Ab, tell me one thing I do that's exciting."

"Umm, you like to go to movies." George does go to a hell of a lot of movies, mostly without me in tow. I get nervous watching other people's dramas; I feel I should be out creating my own.

"Movies are boring," she says with a roll of her eyes.

"You play racquetball."

"Yawn."

"You cook some mean spaghetti and meatballs."

"Snore."

I don't consider George a bit boring, but one look at her face during this conversation and you know *she* thinks she's boring as hell. "Okay, I give up, Georgette. I mean, you are a cool gal—why would I be best friends with a boring person? But boredom comes from within, sweetie. If you feel really boring it'll ooze outta your pores and you'll be surrounded by a little boredom cloud. Kind of like Linus or whoever in the Snoopy cartoons."

"So what are you saying?"

"I guess I mean snap out of it. If it takes fishnet hose and fuck-me heels to make you feel unboring then I say more power to you. But a nice little hobby like mountain biking or basket weaving might do the trick too. Rediscover yourself."

"Amen, Abbie. That's kind of what I'm doing—finding myself. But right now I need to worry about finding my bathing suit or I'll be late for my tanning appointment."

As Georgette dashes into her room, I shake my head in disbelief. This is such a shocker—Georgette is about the most normal person I know and now she's going haywire. I feel like my life is falling around me like that silver and white confetti we tossed at Unity on New Year's. The night I met Franco. Oh God—Franco. Should I call him yet?

After I wish Georgette in all her barfly glory farewell and she tap tap taps out our front door I set up camp next to the phone. Everything I need for a successful phone call is here: bag of pretzels for nervous munching, jumbo glass of ice water for parched lips, compact to check my look, red lipstick for aforementioned parched lips and notepad and pencil for date plans, knock wood. Now all I need to do is call, just dial those seven magical digits. Yep, that's all I need to do.

Fifteen minutes later, I'm still perched by the telly when it rings. My heart skips a beat, but then I remember: Franco doesn't have my number. Damn. It's only Pat. After ridiculing me for freaking over calling Franco, my pal drops the bomb: he wants me to go out with his cousin Chris. I've only met the guy once, like at some party, but all I can say is that the guy is completely not my type. We're talking total Mr. White Bread—cute in that J. Crew–model way but almost too plastic-looking. I tell Pat as much, but he won't take no for an answer. "Three reasons you should go—Chris thinks you're the hottest, he's a blood relative and the guy doesn't drink or do drugs like the rest of your losers." On that last note, I agree to a double date Thursday. I should at least make some attempt to stick to my New Year's resolution; after all, better late than never.

I bid farewell to Pat and dial Franco. One ring, my heart speeds up. Two, I feel sick. Three, I think I'm gonna puke. Then: "Hey, this is Franco. Jane and I aren't here right now but leave us a message and we'll be in touch. Peace."

"Um, hi Franco. This is Abbie at five-five-five, nine-eight-two-nine. Call me." I slam down the phone, freaking in a major way. Who the hell is Jane?

Whoever she is, I hate her.

Chapter 5

The sound of the phone ringing is like a bodyslam, yanking me out of my dreamless sleep. I wipe my drool off the couch pillow and pick up the receiver.

"Hello?" I answer, my voice Demi Moore–husky as a result of my short nap.

"Hey. Is, uh, Abbie there?"

"Speaking." Oh God, it's Him.

"Hey, this is Franco. Calling you back."

"Hey, Franco—Mr. Callin' Me Back. What's up?"

"Oh nothing. Just rolled out of bed actually."

I glance at the digital clock on the VCR, squinting at the kryptonite green numbers. "Isn't it like almost five o'clock?"

"Sure is."

"Oh. So I take it you're not an advocate of 'Early to bed, early to rise'?"

Silence. "Not quite."

"Like others go to bed during 'Letterman' and you go to bed during the 'Today' show?"

"Sorta."

Okay, so he's not a conversationalist. I can deal with it. My dad didn't always tell me I could talk to a brick wall for nothing. I'm putting the quality to good use starting right now. Take the fucking plunge, Ab, you've been freaking over this guy for weeks so any pride you have to lose is already lost. Here goes: "Well, Mr. Night Owl, wanna come over and watch movies or something?"

"Or something?"

He sounds sort of interested. Wrapping the telephone cord around my fingers, I feel like I'm by my grandpa's pond, fishing pole in hand, waiting for a fish called Franco to take my bait.

"Nothing perverse. Like make Rice Krispies Treats or listen to CDs." With a guy as cute and cool as Franco, you wonder if Rice Krispies Treats will be considered juvenile. The moment I suggest it, I wish I hadn't.

"Sounds cool. Maybe you can teach me how to make one of your hats."

"Ancient Chinese secret, my friend. No can do."

"Well, I do have ways to change your mind, you know."

Yep, my bobber is definitely underwater now. Time to reel him in. "Oh really, Franco? Well, get over here and test your powers of persuasion."

"Come get me. I'm without wheels."

Woo hoo, there's gonna be a fish fry tonight! Stay calm, be cool. "I'll consider it, I guess. Where do you live?"

"Second and Glade."

"By Lizard Lounge?" I know the area. A weird bartender who used to work with me worked over there. I learned how to tie cherry stems into knots with my tongue at one of his parties. Bizarre guy.

"Yeah—in Rolling Rock Apartments. Number twenty-seven-nineteen. Ever had Rolling Rock beer? It's my favorite domestic," Franco says with glee.

Oh shit, what's up with the beer reference? Every one of my ex-boyfriends, and I'm talking every single goddamn one, was like a beer connoisseur. I remember this one time I told Parker I had a yeast infection and he said he could totally relate since he drank a lot of yeasty beer. I told him I sincerely doubted he could fully comprehend my deep desire to straddle a cactus just because he'd downed a couple hundred six-packs in his day.

"Well, beer's not really my thing." This is an understatement, really, but I hate to scare him off and all.

"Oh no? What is?"

"I'm a foo-foo drink lover when I drink, which isn't too often. Mai-Tais and Hurricanes are just my speed."

"Oh man, don't even mention speed to me after last night."

"Last night?" I croak, getting the distinct feeling he's not talking about him renting the old movie starring Keanu.

"Yeah. The Chunk concert—I was gone."

"Sounds fun." I can be sarcastic as all hell when I feel like it, but I'm afraid it's lost on Franco.

"Yep. I guess you could call it fun. Hey, do you have a big car?"

"Not really. I have a Kharmann Ghia."

"Righteous. Room for more than two, right?"

"Sure. Why?"

"I don't go anywhere without Jane. Except clubs—she can't get in."

"Uh, Jane?" Pass the Q-Tips. I've gotta clean out my ears. He did not just say Jane-with-a-*J* did he? There's no way a boy I like this much just mentioned another chick, absolutely no fucking way.

"Yeah, you'll love her. So come over. Twenty-seven-nineteen, building twenty-seven. Be here around six o'clock, okay?"

"Okay, uh . . ."

"See ya." Click.

"Later," I reply, but he's already long gone.

I hold the receiver in disbelief. Wherever he goes, Jane goes? What are they, connected at the hip or something? And if he can't bear to part with Janie dearest, then why the hell is he calling me?

"If you'd like to make a call, please hang up and try again. If you need help, please dial your operator." The recorded voice blaring from the phone makes me jump, introducing me to reality once again.

I replace the receiver and head for my closet. Whoever this Jane chick is, I'll be damned if she looks cuter than I do.

WHAT TO wear is such a dilemma. Looking ultracute without looking like you are trying to look ultracute is a lot harder than it appears. If I wear a short skirt to show off my gams, will I look too available? I decide yes, especially since it's thirty-eight degrees outside today. Long skirt and sweater? Too Georgettish, or at least too Georgettish before her fishnet phase. A baby T and jumper? Too '96 for sure.

It's really puzzling. I have a gigantic walk-in closet bursting with bazillions of bodysuits, baubles, boots and brassieres and yet today I cannot find a solitary thing to wear. I am standing in my garden of garments sans clothes, except for my Victoria's Secret undies and the Little Mermaid watch Pat bought me eons ago that I only wear on special occasions. I glance down at it—5:46. I'm supposed to be at Franco's in fourteen minutes and it's probably at least a fifteen-minute drive.

It's 5:53 as I pull out of my driveway. I'm poured into a white T and my favorite Levi's. Black clunky shoes complete the look, which I'm quite satisfied with. Unless Jane turns out to be Elle Macpherson's twin, I'm positive Abbie McPhereson will beat her out in the cute department.

I roll down the windows, crank the stereo and pull onto I-95. A leering semi driver honks as he passes my Molly Ringwald–mobile and I, feeling charitable, blow him a kiss. "You won't be the only boy I blow kisses tonight. Hee hee," I say as I push the pedal to the metal and flip my hair back with my left hand.

By the time the semi looks like an ant in my rearview mirror, I check my watch again. Ariel shows it's 6:03. I turn the radio up a few notches until the bass sounds strong enough to blow up my cheap Jensen speakers. I sing along and bob my head to the beat, feeling like one of those eighties plastic daisies that comes to life when it's around any music or sound. Unfortunately, my stomach feels like it has a thousand of those plastic flowers boogying inside it at the moment also.

Gazing at my car hood, which is the exact same color as Pepto-Bismol, I am reminded of how bad I could use a couple of tablespoons to soothe my somersaulting stomach. I take my eyes off the hood, hoping to calm my tummy. I look at the car in front of me—a red Volvo—and spot a familiar bumper sticker: CASTRATE RAPISTS, IT'S THE ONLY WAY TO BE SURE. God. Somewhere in this city, the exact same black and white bumper sticker is affixed to my ex-love Parker's yellow Honda.

I feel sorry for that bumper sticker and for anything that has to be within forty feet of Parker on a regular basis. He is such a compulsive person. Unfortunately for him and anyone who knows him, his major obsession is drinks that begin with the letter *S*: Salty Dogs, sangria, scotch and Simpatico. And unfortunately for me, he also had an affinity for gals whose first names start with S, as I found out when he started two-timing me with a Hooters waitress named Shanna.

I guess I owe my mom a big thank you, because if she'd named me Sue Abbie instead of Abbie Sue, I might still be with Parker at this very moment. And I'd rather have a molar pulled without novocaine than endure another evening watching football with that egotistical, tobacco-chewing asshole.

My internal Parker-bashing must stop—Rolling Rock Apartments are in sight. My excitement about seeing love-of-my-life Franco is majorly overshadowed by the anxiety I'm feeling over meeting Jane. Is she just a friend? His sister? His girlfriend? A lesbian? All I know about her is that she cohabitates with Franco, can't get into dance clubs and wherever she goes, Franco goes. I'd like to tell her where to go.

I pull into the parking lot and turn left, looking for building 27. Twenty-seven—my lucky number. A good sign? Building 27's straight ahead—big, brown, intimidating. Panicked, I stop in front of a speed bump and turn my rearview mirror sideways. I rub my lower eyelids with my middle finger, wiping off excess liner dust that has settled in the creases under my eyes during the ride over. I inspect my image in the skinny mirror. Didn't I look cute just ten minutes ago? What happened? Knowing it's really too late now for a major overhaul, I grip the steering wheel and step on the gas.

Whipping into a parking space, I rummage through my purse for my trusty tube of red lipstick. When in doubt, put on more lipstick, that's what I always say. As I apply the red ego-booster with a shaky hand, I feel a little better. "This is the moment you've been waiting for, Abs. Franco is yours! Enjoy it," I think as I get out of the car. This is what my head tells me anyway. My heart tells me to get the heck outta here, now. Giving up is no longer an option, though. It's time to move.

Twenty-seven-nineteen—I'm here. I smooth out my Levi's, lick my lips and raise my hand to knock. Knuckles inches away from the door, I freeze. Should I ring the doorbell or knock? I contemplate for a moment, fist in midair. Yes, knocking is more primitive. Sexy. I rap on the door softly, three times fast.

In a few seconds, Franco opens the door. He looks hotter than

I remember—red hair pulled back, black turtleneck, faded Levi's just like mine (fate?), beat-up Docs. And that Lotto-winner smile; um, somebody pinch me.

"Hey, you made it," he says, stepping out onto the porch. "Man, I would invite you in but my place is trashed. Let me just collect Jane and we'll be out of here. Wanna beer?"

I don't answer aloud, just shake my head. I don't even want to attempt to remember the English language right now, I really don't.

"Okay, I'll be out in a sec."

He shuts the door and I'm alone once more. Okay, Ab. "Hi, Jane, nice to meet you." Too mature. "Hey, Jane, what's up, baby?" Too friendly. "Hey." Too rude. *"Hola, señorita."* That might work. Kind of quirky, kind of off-the-wall. Wait—*"Hola, señorita,* haven't I seen you somewhere before?" That way, she has to respond. Ice-breaker. Yep, no matter if I've never seen her before in my life or no matter how much he is hanging on her, the *"Hola, señorita"* line it will be. For sure.

Franco opens the door, Rolling Rock in hand. I raise my brows, looking over his shoulder for the cause of my anxiety attack. Where is the mystery woman?

I feel something damp on my right heel. I look down into the eyes of a teeny-tiny black puppy as the door slams. "Oh my gosh, Franco, look," I cry. "A puppy!" If it's anything that just about slays me, it's a puppy. My first word was "pup," if you can believe it.

Franco's eyes fall to my ankles. "Hey, you cutie." He scoops the dog up and gets licked in the face. Boys who love animals definitely mash my potatoes. I feel that tingle I always get in the pit of my stomach at the moment when a minor crush becomes a major one. Now, if Jane would just walk out the door so I could check out the competition, I could stop sucking in my tummy and relax for Chrissakes.

Franco takes a swig of beer. "Cool car," he says, setting down the dog and walking toward my pink set of wheels.

"Gracias," I answer, looking back at the apartment door. "Soooo, Franco, where's Jane? Aren't we going to wait for her?" I'm trying to sound nonchalant, but I doubt it's working.

Franco is looking at me like I'm in the Special Olympics. "Abbie, meet Jane. Jane, meet Abbie," he says, pointing to the Chinese pug who is relieving herself by a bush about twenty feet away.

No way.

"*Hola, señorita.* Haven't I seen you somewhere before?"

Chapter 6

Cruising with Franco in the passenger's seat, I feel about as tasty as a frosted Pop-Tart. I wish we would pass someone I hate on the highway so they could see me with the beauty that is Franco. Why hello, Lori Hoover, wench who told me my hair was ugly when we were in fifth grade, how do you do? Oh Parker, ex-boyfriend who pawned my VCR while I was at work, check me out now—hot as all hell, Hendrix blaring, hair flying, scorching boy by my side. Too bad you can't join us but, alas, the back seat's full, Park—*c'est la vie.*

We are almost to my pad. Franco's not exactly being a chatterbox, but between Jane's yapping, my rambling and Jimi's wailing, there's almost no way he could get a word in edgewise even if he wanted to. For some reason, my CD and Rice Krispies Treats plans aren't sounding as fun as they did an hour ago. Since this could be my only chance with Franco, I'd like to be able to show him off or at least be seen in public with him. I glance over and see him whispering in Jane's ear, trying to settle her down. He looks back and kind of smiles, revealing this very endearing dimple to the left of his luscious lips.

"So what do you want to do?" I ask as we turn onto my street, Mockingbird Lane, and officially enter my stomping grounds. Franco is scratching behind Jane's ear and Jane's right back leg is doing this spastic jerking thing which looks almost obscene. Franco raises his eyebrows and grins. "I thought we were going to snap, crackle and pop or whatever."

God, he is so cute. "Yeah, that was the plan, I guess. But now I'm thinking I'd maybe like to do something a little more social. There's that one festival thing going on over by Reunion, I think. Or we could drink somewhere and go to the Rhinestone Paste show in Deep Ellum. I don't think it's sold out."

Rhinestone Paste is one of my favorite bands. I used to have a crush on the lead singer when he had bobbed red hair. He was quite angelic—porcelain ivory skin that breaks your heart and eyelashes as long and black as limousines. Then a couple of months ago within a one-week time frame he a) cut his hair off in an uneven style that made him bear a striking resemblance to Shaggy from "Scooby Doo" and b) was talking about *his wife* during an interview on MTV. Double whammy. But even though the crush is officially over, I still love their music.

"The RP show would be cool. How much are the tickets going for?"

"I think it's like sixteen in advance or eighteen at the door." I hate it when people refer to bands by their initials, but I'll let it slide this time. Wonder if he has any cash? Or will he expect me to pay?

"I need to hit the money machine. And we'll have to do something with Jane."

I stifle a whoop of joy. Everyone—and I do mean *everyone*—that I know will be at this show. Thus every friend, acquaintance, ex and enemy I have will be on hand to witness Abbie McPhereson and Franco Richards officially Together-with-a-capital-*T*. That will really fix a lot of people.

I smile and hop out of the car. Franco follows me to the door as Jane gnaws on his ponytail. "This dog loves to chew on anything," he tells me. "Hair, toenails, books, sunglasses, shoes. Man, shoes. The other day I was wasted and accidentally left my black Birks sitting out. The next day the right one was totally trashed."

Franco frequently refers to times when he was wasted or fucked up and this really frightens me. I'm feeling Parker flashbacks majorly and it's scary. "So, Franco, just how often do you get wasted?" I inquire as I unlock my front door.

He bites his lower lip. "Well, I drink at least a beer every day. I'm not gonna lie to you."

I nod and swing open the door, keys on Barbie chain jingling. Beer's not that big of a deal, in comparison to other things. And Lord knows I'm no saint myself. One time I got so wasted that I passed out with my head in the litter box, so I'm no stranger to that shit.

Franco flops on my couch and lets Jane loose. "And I smoke weed probably three, four, five times a week tops. Other stuff, I save for special occasions. You know."

No, I don't know. And I probably don't want to know. But I ask anyway, positioning myself on the couch next to him but not right next to him. I don't want to look desperate. "Like holidays or weekends or what? I mean, what special occasion requires which drug?"

He smiles, showing off perfect Farrah-like teeth. "Okay, Fourth of July I really like to trip—with the fireworks and everything it's just wild. Other times, I don't know. Just like me and the guys will be going out on a Saturday and we'll decide to do 'shrooms just because we really don't get together that often anymore and it's like *the guys* hanging out. That's kinda like a holiday. Or sometimes when Heidi—a friend from my apartments—sells a painting she'll buy us some X to celebrate, but good X is hard to come by these days so it's really not even worth it. The hardcore stuff I really don't do anymore, like Special K and shit like that. I mean, it would be very rare." He looks at me and nods, maybe waiting for approval. I flash him this fake smile. "So what about you?"

Let it be known: I pretty much loathe drugs. They remind me of white trash and trailer parks and fair carnies. And I swore to my-self after Parker-Mr.-I-Can't-Tear-Myself-Away-From-My-Bong-Long-Enough-To-Take-You-To-Dinner-Unless-You're-Paying that I would never, but never groove on a guy who does drugs again. Yet of course the one boy I like happens to be on every substance known to man. My luck strikes once more.

"Well, honestly, I'm not really into drugs. Never really have been, you know? But I'm not like passing judgment on you or anyone else who partakes, they're just not me. At all." I feel like a goody-goody freak. But if you can't be honest at the start, then there's no point in even continuing whatever it is you're starting. That is, if we're even starting something.

"So you've never tried any drug whatsoooooever?" Franco's eyes widen at the thought.

"Sort of. One night I did half a hit of X with Parker but it didn't do anything. I don't really count that, though, because it had no effect on me. I guess it was bad or something."

I remember that night as well as I remember my phone number. A few months prior to the whole experience I had mentioned to Park that I might consider doing X because I heard it was so happy and free and fun. Well, one day he shows up and he's all smiley and proud saying he has something for me that I said I would do with him. Immediately I think he's referring to me making a pornographic movie with him—once he asked if I would make a Movie-capital-*M* with him and I said maybe, not thinking he'd ever take me up on the offer. So I start looking for the bulky video equipment. But instead he pulls out this Ziploc baggie, one of those yellow-and-blue-make-green kinds, with three mondo pills in it, each about the size of my pinkie, as pearly white as a set of new dentures. I panic and say, "What's in zee bag?" even though I knew very well what was in the bag. He came in and told me to relax, we'd just do half a hit so I wouldn't freak out and it would be very low-key and positive. He poured the contents of the capsules, a thin white powder that looked like the powdered sugar on funnel cakes, onto the torn-off cover of the yellow pages, put it in front of my mouth and instructed me to lick it off. As my tongue absorbed the dandruff-sized granules, I raised my eyes to meet his and thought, "So this is what it's like to love someone so much you want to cry." And as we sat on my couch and waited for the drug-induced euphoria that never came, I remember thinking "Parker is so cool" over and over again, my heart teeming with emotion as I held his hand in mine and thought his was my hand to hold forever. Of course, this all happened before he became the selfish, freeloading dickhead that he was in the end.

"So it was bad, huh? The drug or the dude?" Franco turns the TV on. "Cool, you have cable."

I look at the tube and nod. "I couldn't deal without cable. It's like give me my MTV and I'm a happy girl. So, in answer to your question, they were both bad, I guess. The X and my ex, I mean. Although I didn't know it at the time. I thought Parker hung the moon at that point."

"Yeah, I hear ya, I hear ya. We've all had a couple of those unfortunately. They're all cool at first, then wham! Total freaksville. It's like Jesus H., when the hell did you become such a total bitch? It's overnight or something. My last girlfriend broke Jane's legs, that's how much of a psycho that one was."

I look at Jane, now chowing down on my silk sunflower arrangement on top of the coffee table, and wonder how anyone could do her any harm. Jeez, I thought I'd been with some schizos but at least no body parts were broken besides my heart. "How did it happen? And why the hell would she do it?"

"Man, who knows. It's like one minute she's playing with the dog and I'm like asleep, okay? Then next thing I know Jane's wailing and Tuesday's spazzing, going 'Ohmigodohmigodohmigod,' and I jump up and go ask what's wrong and it turns out she's like thrown the dog to the loft ceiling and then when she tried to catch her she missed. Hello, this is a dog, not a goddamn Nerf ball, okay? So I'm like well maybe she's okay and Jane sleeps with us and the whole night she's just whimpering and I can't sleep I feel so bad. Of course Tuesday's sleeping like a baby."

"Of course." Just like Parker would be, the bastard.

"Uh-huh. So the next morning I wake up and I've gotta work so Tuesday takes her to the vet and they're like okay, this dog has a broken elbow and broken hip and that will be eighty dollars for the X rays and nine hundred and sixty for the surgery payable in cash or check at the front counter thank you very much—"

"No way."

"Yeah, that's what I was saying. There was just no way I could come up with it. And the alternative was to put her to sleep and it's like no can do. Tuesday calls her parents who hate me and they say no dice since it's technically my dog. So I pawn my TV, VCR, stereo and Sega which brings in like two hundred then ask my buddy Tim to loan me the rest."

"Did he do it?"

"Yup. Tuesday helped me pay him back since she's the whole reason it even happened in the first place. It really sucked." He sounded bitter as all hell.

"God, I guess. So does Jane have a limp now?" I reach over and feel her Bit-O-Honey-colored legs for any abnormalities.

"Not really. But when she runs she doesn't really run, she hops like a rabbit. Tuesday used to call her Cadbury."

Tuesday. Who has a name like Tuesday? "So what's up with your ex-girlfriend, Miss Day After Monday?"

Franco laughs. "What do you mean, what's up with her? She's psycho, that's what's up with her."

I think the term "psycho" is used a little too loosely in our society. Some of my favorite people were considered a little bit off: Sylvia Plath, for instance. Probably one of the most brilliant writers of our time and thought to be totally off her rocker. My question is: Do any of us really have all our marbles? I'm thinking no. I was in therapy for a few months. The whole reason I started going was because Parker said I needed to be in therapy to figure out why I was so screwed up. Very ironic that once I got into it I quickly realized that my biggest problem in life was having a boyfriend like Parker who always tried to convince me that I was boring and, direct quote here, that I was "totally nothing." Four words: John Travolta Kirstie Alley. *Look Who's Fucking Talking.*

I relate all this to Franco, who's discovered my remote control and is channel surfing like mad. He pauses, "Three's Company" rerun on the screen. "I was in it once. Therapy." Flip. "My mom wanted me to during Zoe." Flip flip. "Felt like damn Gandhi or something." Flip. "Didn't do drugs or really even drink for four or five months after that. Quit cold turkey." Flip flip flip. "Then one day, I guess it was New Year's Eve last year, I had a six-pack and it was a done deal. The next weekend I got blitzed on Long Island Teas and then two or three weeks later I smoked pot at a party and next thing you know I'm back to my old ways."

So Franco was in therapy too. I store this bit of Franco trivia in my noggin with glee. We fatefully share an experience, a common thread. We can have long talks about Freud and Pavlov while cooking generic macaroni and cheese. He'll thoughtfully listen to my rantings on cranky days, nodding and furrowing his brow at the appropriate times, and then analyze my feelings when I'm through spilling my guts. If we start having those little problems that every couple has, like arguing over whether to spend our third anniversary in Brussels or Spain, we will go to couples therapy and bond. And then once we get married we can go to a marriage counselor to make sure we don't become one of those "Can This Marriage Be Saved?" couples from *Ladies Home Journal* or wherever.

"Of course I'd never go back to therapy. Never in a million years. Don't even like to think about it, really."

So much for those long talks over mac and cheese.

"Why's that?" I ask, grabbing the remote control from his channel-flipping fingers.

Franco bites the nail on his right index finger. "Oh, you know, it just got kind of old after awhile, all that 'I'm Okay, You're Okay' crap. Plus I feel like the whole goal of therapy is to be like you don't even need to go anymore because you can counsel yourself. Like I could go in right now and I'd bet money I know exactly what she'd say to me. And since I already know what she'd say, then why spend money I don't have and time I can't waste going in and listening to something I already know?" He recaptures the remote from me and, once again, surf's up, Moondoggie.

Observation: Franco is one of those people you run across every so often that always sound right even if they're not. Ten to one he was in debate in high school. This trait can be incredibly annoying, especially during an argument. My uncle Rudy is like that. Mr. Pro-Life of America—we're talking he makes those militant protesters who chain themselves in front of abortion clinics look like pussycats. And me being Ms. If-You're-A-Guy-Then-You-Definitely-Have-Nothing-To-Say-On-The-Subject doesn't please him one bit. Every family gathering, like Christmas, Thanksgiving, whatever, turns into a battleground with him around, throwing his propaganda pamphlets around the table between servings of mashed potatoes and green bean casserole like there's no tomorrow. One year he was even like, "See that chicken leg? A three-month-old fetus is about that size in the womb, Little Miss Abbie Sue." At the kitchen table. Can you imagine?

"Hey, Franco, are you pro-life or pro-choice?"

"What?" His eyes haven't left the TV screen, now featuring "Beavis & Butt-head." "Where did that come from?"

I explain. One of my most charming (ahem) qualities is how I go off on tangents no one else can figure out. Like we're talking about therapy, Franco uses his debate tactics, this reminds me of Rudy, who reminds me of pro-life, which prompts me to ask him the abortion question. Franco still looks confused.

"I'm pro-choice, but not like go-out-and-protest pro-choice or anything. Just do-your-own-thing-'cause-I'm-minding-my-own-business pro-choice, I guess." He turns his attention back to the tube—Bud Light commercial. "You got a beer?"

The hardest thing I've got is Kool-Aid, so we decide to head to the show where they'll surely be selling the six-point serum. Since it's way out of our way to hit Franco's before the concert, we opt to leave Jane in my room. As soon as I gather most everything from the floor, stick it all on the dresser and shut the door, Jane starts going loco, barking with this high-pitched wail and scratching on my door like it's a bothersome mosquito bite.

"Hey, Franco, would you mind repainting my door before my lease is up?" I say, grabbing my purse.

Franco chuckles, and I wonder if it's a fake laugh. "Yeah, I do need to get those nails clipped, huh? But you bet, I'll be over here painting your door, no problem."

Hint that he wants to see me again? Hmmm. I smile my most high-voltage smile and slam the door behind us.

THE LINE outside Deep Ellum Live curves practically around the building and is full of young, hip-looking people—people who look like they have something better to do—my favorite kind of crowd. I walk to the end of it with Franco, straining to keep up with his loping gait.

A longhair grabs Franco's arm. "Hey, dude, what's up?"

"Not much, man. Not much. What's been going on?"

His friend looks like he hails from Austin, he's straight out of *Slacker* or something. Long straight brown hair, parted in the middle, slightly limp like either it needs a wash or he put hand lotion in it. His plaid flannel is slightly frayed and totally buttonless, revealing a Smitten Kitten concert T. The baggy jeans he wears—probably Levi's—are a couple of sizes too big and hang way down south, like practically to Mexico. A beat-up pair of

Converse suedes complete the look. The shoes kind of throw me. Almost too much of a skater shoe to go with the rest of his look. I would've pegged him as a Birkenstock or Doc type myself, but hey, a little variety is the spice of life. He's pretty cute, actually. I'd go out with him.

As the fellows continue with their meaningful boy-banter—"Would you try that Zima Dry shit for a fiver, Frank?" "No way, man. Pussy drink"—I smile and shiver, semi-waiting for an introduction. It is colder than an ice-cream truck out here. I wish I'd brought my fake fur.

"Well, see you in the pit, man. Later, Sinatra. Later."

I assume this last "Later" is for me and wave. "Why does he call you Sinatra?"

We continue our journey to the end of the line. "You know, Frank Sinatra."

"Oh." I was hoping for more of an exciting explanation than this. I want to know what makes this guy tick, what starts his engine. I crave anecdotes that reveal the true Franco Richards, that give me clues to his soul, that let me know just what kind of fellow this Franco character really is. "Viva la Frank Sinatra, I always say."

Franco smiles and grabs my elbow, steering me around two overweight, goateed thugs in each other's faces, one screaming "No, Eddie Vedder rules!" the other screaming "No, Trent Reznor rules!" at the top of their lungs.

"God, that's a fight in the making," Franco says, releasing my elbow from his firm grasp. Damn.

I look back and sure enough they're still at it. A crowd is beginning to form around the duking-it-out duo. "Yeah, two obvious intellects. Wonder if they've been on 'Jeopardy'?"

Franco glances back. "I think I saw them on there last night, as a matter of fact. They really racked up on that Pearl Jam Philosophies category."

We both crack up on this one, like it just about kills us.

"Hey, Abbie!"

I look to my right. It's Jenni, this sorority chick I used to work with at Darcy Durby's, a restaurant where you have to dress up in costume. She was Cowpatty, the cowgal cocktail waitress.

"What is up, baby doll? You look so awesome!" I screech, running over for a hug. She looks cool—faded jeans and black ballet top, long brown hair pulled back with one of those plastic headbands which would look very grade school on anyone else but still looks good on Jenni. She has one of those Dutch faces—think Swiss Miss—and looks pretty in everything.

"Ohmigod, Chiquita Banana, you look great! Have you lost weight?" she asks in her sororityish way, putting her hands on each side of my waist. "You are a total toothpick!" Sorority girls always say this, just I think so you will say it back to them.

"Yeah, I wish, Jen." I grab Franco's sleeve and pull him closer. "Jenni, this is Franco. Franco, Jenni."

"Cute," she whispers in my ear while grabbing Franco's hand. Her eyes all light up and shit, like she's really excited and all. "Didn't you used to be a duck?"

"A what?" Franco's looking at her like he looked at me that night at the movies when I was asking for his number. Jen's still giving him her movie-star gaze.

"A duck. You know, Delta Upsilon."

"Nope, 'fraid not," Franco answers, glancing around like he's a tad antsy.

An unfamiliar boy joins our trio and puts his hands over Jen's eyes. "Jeeeff," she drones, acting aggravated but grinning gleefully. "Get your hands off my eyes and meet Abbie, my fashion designer friend who used to be Chiquita Banana at Darcy Durby's and her . . . ummm . . . friend, Franco, who's not in Delta Upsilon. Franco and Abs, this is my boyfriend, Jeff Viver. He's not Greek either."

Jeff sticks his multi-braceleted hand out. "Nice to meet you. Forget the Jeff part, everyone just calls me Viver."

"May I call you Viber, you know, as in good vibes?" I ask, shaking his callused hand. This is not the usual type Jenni falls for. The blonde, stringy locks framing a semi-round face, purple and green tie-dye T stretching over a slight beer belly, cutoff army pants, dingy white tennis shoes and cigarette hanging out the corner of a pouty mouth is a far cry from the exteriors of her little frat boy lovahs of the past. Still, he is somewhat appealing if you're into the Grateful Dead thing.

"Yeah, whatever floats your boat." He slings an arm around Jenni's shoulders as his voice lowers an octave. "Anybody wanna smoke some weed? My Bug's right over there."

"Cool, man," Franco replies while me and Jen shake our heads from east to west.

"I've already done too much shit tonight. And I've got a test at eight-forty tomorrow morning," Jenni answers as I say, "No thanks, Viber. But we'll be right here."

Viber kisses Jenni's ear and starts toward the car, motioning for Franco to follow. "Well, dude, let the games begin."

Franco laughs, squeezes my elbow and joins Viber on the journey to the Volkswagen. "Yo, Frankie my man, this is some really good shit," I hear Viber say as they walk off. Lovely.

"So, what is up with this guy, Chiquita? Hot!" Jenni sings. I don't know if she's a singer in real life, but every conversation with her is like a sonata. "So whatever happened to Parker?"

I sigh. His ass seems like a lifetime ago, but it still sucks to talk about it, especially with people we both knew. "Parker is a done deal, like we don't even speak now. I don't know. We had a few good times and everything but he just cost me an arm and a leg. It was like Abbie, you pay for the majority of the bills and the dates and I'll pay for whatever it may be that I'm into at the moment, be it drugs, CDs, aquarium shit—you name it."

She rolls her eyes. "Lame."

"Yeah, that's what I was saying. Plus he was totally hung up on his ex-girlfriend, the one who lives in Minneapolis, and then he smoked pot every day, like alone, for awhile and it was just too depressing to be around him," I confess. Old Parker was a mess, plain and simple, but I was the dumbass for staying with him as long as I did. "All Parker thinks about is Parker, you know?"

"God, it seemed like you two were so happy. Always passing little notes back and forth and everything. We all thought, Man, true love."

Parker and I met at Darcy Durby's. He was a cute kitchen boy—short brown hair, tiny hands, baggy shorts, to-die-for eyes the color of diluted Windex—and I was the fruithead hostess with the mostest and it was all so adorable at first. We sent each other messages like *Do you like me? Circle Yes No Maybe* non-stop. And every time I would see him I was like margarine in a microwave. All the people who worked there were always going "You two are the most perfect couple, I swear," and I would just look at them and smile this little smile that screamed "I know we are hee hee I am loved I am loved I am loved." It was sunshine. It's been like forever since we broke up, yet still, when I am fixing to start my period or I've had a really bummer day, I sometimes pull out the satin blue and green daisy–covered photo album, circa 1972, where I keep all those frayed napkins and flyers and menus and whatever else we grabbed to jot our scribblings of love on during a rough night at work. I take them out, one by one, and read every word, squinting at the Day-Glo purple ink or the tiny grain pattern in the white napkins, wondering which clues I missed, what I did wrong, why I didn't realize that my world was slowly tumbling around my feet like a broken strand of imitation pearls and I was doing absolutely nothing to stop it. Those notes, ranging in length from two lines to twelve pages, are the chronicles of my emotional rise and fall, and when I read them I sometimes cry. I cry not for what was but for what I thought would be. And I cry because as much as I want to forget him, I cannot; not completely. In a small way he is me and I am him, and that is something that is forever.

"Well, although I hate to admit it, I still love Parker, a part of me always will, no matter what bad stuff he did or smoked or said. I can't stand the boy or like him one iota, but a part of me will always hold him dear. We were really happy for a short while. In fact, that was probably the happiest I'd ever been in my life up to that point, during the good times." They were too. I've had happier times since, thank God, and hopefully will have happier times in the future, but with him I was really happy for like three months. Cloud-nine-nothing-you-can-do-can-piss-me-off-because-I'm-in-love happy. "But the bad times were, God, so bad. They were the lowest of the low. I'm talking words can't begin to express."

"That's awful to hear, Abbie, I'm so sorry. When I hear stuff like that and I think how cool we all thought Parker was at first, it makes me scared to like someone, even. It's like, okay, Parker turned out to be, well, Parker and who knows if the same will happen to Viver? They seem sorta made out of the same mold." She shrugs and bites her burgundy lip, looking genuinely troubled. "Jeff reminds me a lot of Parker."

"No, Jen, you can't think like that. They broke the mold with Parker, no doubt. And Viber seems really cool." I squint at the olive Volkswagen, which looks like it's filled with clouds. "Speaking of, what is up with you and Mr. Good Viberations? Not your normal Hello-I-Shop-In-The-Ralph-Lauren-Department type, obviously, but cute. A good change, for sure. How long have you two been a thing?"

She beams, jumping up and down. "Three months, can you believe it? He's just, I don't know. There's something about him. And he's really sweet to me. We met at Liberty's of all places, where I never go but this girl from Alpha Chi was having this party there so I went. And at first with him I was like, no, I don't think so, but then it was like, well, maybe this could work. It's so weird. But I'm really happy. Really, really happy."

Usually people who say they're "really, really happy" actually aren't, they just want everyone to think they are. The truly happy people don't have to go around telling God and everybody just how peachy their lives are, it's just obvious. But Jenni does look positively ecstatic. After all the jerks she's had it's good to see her feeling all warm and gushy inside over a boy who doesn't wear Greek letters on his chest.

We chat a little more as the line inches slowly closer to the entrance. By the time the fellas come back, there are only six more people in front of us.

"Hey," Franco says as he approaches, his eyes a little redder than before he left.

"Hey, baby," I answer, slightly annoyed but grinning. The faint smell of marijuana invades my nostrils and I wince, remembering.

Chapter 7

"Oh Abbie, please don't you ever disappoint us and do drugs. I don't know what we'd do if you turned out like James did. I just don't know."

This is my mom, like every day of my adolescent angst. The boy she refers to is James Cronkite, a boy down the street who's into video games, vo-tech and weed, not necessarily in that order. Mother's best friends with his mother, so who knows how many hours of her life are spent on the phone with Bootsie Cronkite discussing the drug issue. Thus I got to hear about it daily. Joy. So anyways, Mom was forever saying "I don't know what we'd do if you did drugs. I just don't know," but her dreadful tone implied that she and Dad would get maimed by rottweilers or go bankrupt and lose everything they owned if God forbid their perfect daughter Abbie tried a drug. At the time, her little lectures didn't bug me too much because I really had no intention of ever getting high. The crowd I hung out with, the skater/punk/I-wear-black-and-drink-java crowd, for the most part didn't do drugs either, they just drank. And since I wasn't really into that either, I was pretty much a parent's wet dream.

However, my mother, coolest woman alive but queen of the guilt trips, couldn't seem to realize this fact. She acted like at any moment I would go from Miss Wearing-Peace-Signs-President-Of-Art-Club to Miss Roll-Me-Some-Doobage-President-Of-The-Stoners, which was just not going to happen. Even if I were a druggie, those brown moccasin boots the stoner crowd wore were hideous and there was no way in hell I'd be caught dead in them.

Okay, I'm around fourteen and my mom is being a freak and my dad isn't saying much at all, but they both act somewhat holier-than-thou when the substance subject comes up, which is way too often for my taste. My mom always chimes in "Remember, I've only been drunk one time in my life," to which I always respond "God, we know, we know," rolling my eyes like they were roulette wheels. Dad never says anything at this point, so I have a feeling he used to drink some but I don't want to ask. My father is about the biggest hypochondriac on the face of the earth, next to my aunt Judy, so I bet he never got really wasted for fear of a coronary or alcohol poisoning. This is a person who refuses to eat raw cookie dough, the kindest grind in the world, because the raw eggs might carry salmonella poisoning and he could die. Not exactly Mr. Risk Taker of America, but definitely a trip to be around. My dad cracks all my friends up.

Now I'm fifteen and I'm at this all-ages show, I don't remember which one, Fugazi maybe, but it was a very loud and very small and very smoky scene. Someone lights up behind me, and, this being my first time around marijuana, I don't know what's up at first. "What's that smell?" I ask my then-boyfriend Shawn, who ended up coming out of the closet the day after the prom. "Mary Juana," he answered lovingly, like he was naming his first kid, "you dummy." Then he laughed. I laughed too, but for the rest of the concert all I could think about was one thing: a cookie jar.

It was green and white and sat in the kitchen of the house we lived in when I was five years old. I distinctly remembered my dad—*my dad*—reaching in and pulling out the bulging Baggie, the rolling papers, the roach clip, then lighting up with his hippie friends right in front of me, his perfect little daughter. The one he now tells that he never did drugs! I couldn't believe it, so I asked Mom about it the second she got home. At first she was like, "No, never happened," but since I was so certain and could cite details and everything, she finally caved and confessed, providing I promised never to tell Dad that I knew. I kept that promise until I started seeing Parker, who loved his bong more than he loved his babe, and needed a shoulder to cry on. Dad actually was pretty cool about the whole thing, saying it was the seventies when he smoked and things were different then and blah blah blah. Who knows. All I do know is that every boy I've ever loved has loved weed. Every goddamn one.

— — —

"THE SHOW, it was rockin'. Rockin'. *Rockin' Robin—peep, peep, peep,*" Franco sings, reaching over from the passenger seat to stroke my hair.

We are on the way to my apartment after the two-hour-long concert. Franco passed wasted like forty minutes back and has now hit that stage where he's blabbering and on the brink of passing out. He's being extra sweet to me so his drunken state isn't making me cranky. In my experience there are three kinds of drunk boys: mean I'm-gonna-kick-that-guy's-ass types, sweet You're-so-cool-you're-my-best-friend-I'm-serious types and horny I've-got-six-inches-of-throbbing-steel-with-your-name-on-it types. Franco is one of the sweet ones. After his fifth beer he was like, "Abbie, I want you to know I really think you're cool or I wouldn't have come here with you tonight, you know that, right? Right?" and it was so totally nice I was like, Man, I'm loving this guy. But then I think do I really want to get involved with Mr. Drunk One? I glance over and note the half-mast eyes, chin resting on chest, hair in face. Ouch. Why does he have to be so cute?

I turn the radio to the oldies station, crank it and sing along to oldies like "American Pie" and "Goodbye Yellow Brick Road" the rest of the way home. Franco became history around the third time I crooned the Chevy-to-the-levee line, voice slightly cracking. Time for a little internal heart-to-heart action.

Abbie, you dig this boy bad. Like when you look at him your heart beats faster and your stomach does backflips. You laugh at the silly things he says. You get turned on by the way his red, red hair falls in his blue, blue eyes every four minutes and the way he pushes it back with a quick sweep of his right hand. You like how he dances, how he smiles, how he dresses and how he lives. You even love his dog, who has probably eaten your purple Fluevogs for dinner. You have it Bad-with-a-capital-*B*. Yet here he is, passed out drunk next to you while you drive his inebriated ass home. The only good-night kisses you're getting tonight will be the slobbery ones from Jane on the way to Franco's apartment and the one you plant on his forehead after you carry his bod to bed. And this is the *first date*—you know, the one where most boys are majorly on their very, very best behavior in hopes of possibly getting lucky. Hello? What's up with him getting so wasted on date uno? And why do you still like the guy?

I look over at Franco's chest to make sure he's still breathing. He is. A couple of weeks ago I read about this guy in Minnesota or Montana or somewhere—one of the *M* states—who drank like seventeen shots of Cuervo Gold in fifteen minutes to win a twenty-dollar bet and was dead about two hours later. That would suck, alcohol poisoning. I think of how sad that guy's mom must have been, hearing he died like that. I mean, she would've been sad hearing he died no matter how he did it but somehow I would think hearing your kid died from too much José would be a lot worse than if he died in a car wreck or in a drive-by or something. Like if it was an accident you could blame someone else or God or fate as some sort of small consolation. But since it was his fault, who do you blame? And for that matter, who do I blame for my going and getting involved with another drinker? I guess I could blame Georgette for taking me to Unity New Year's Eve. Or I could blame Mrs. Hawkins, my freshman Hatmaking and You teacher, for giving me the skills that allowed me to make the daisy hat Franco was wearing the night I met him. Or I could blame John Thomas, the first boy I really loved, who liked me almost as much as he liked kegs of Miller Genuine Draft, setting the tone for my entire love life. In the end, I must say I can only blame myself. Georgette isn't the one who danced with Franco, Mrs. Hawkins isn't the one who got his phone number, John Thomas isn't the one who wrote *Abbie Hearts Franco* about five jillion times on a shiny new notebook. It was me. I'm the one who got myself into this. Now I just need to figure out if I want to get myself out.

"So, so, so . . . how was it? Details, all of them, spare nothing." Georgette, in Frederick's finest, is sitting on the pink furry toilet seat cover in our bathroom interrogating me while I lather what's left of my Neutrogena bar all over my forehead and cheeks.

"You know, I don't know why, but I always leave this soap in water even though it specifically says on the package 'Do not leave in water' and then it gets all icky and the soap is like covered with this thick waxy stuff that gets under my fingernails. It's irritating."

Georgette's eyes narrow. "No, Ab, what's irritating is that you are avoiding my question totally. What's up? Spill 'em."

I assume she's referring to my guts. Splashing water on my face, I stall for time. I don't want to tell her that Franco was messed up and have her bring up that damn New Year's resolution again. And I know if I give details of the date she's bound to ask if he was drinking or on something and since I don't make a habit of fibbing to my friends I'm not too keen really on telling a bold-faced lie about it. Man, this sucks.

I raise my head from the magenta sink, eyes closed, groping for a towel. "Okay, Georgie, let me go get into my pajamas and I'll come tell you all, and I do mean all, about it."

She hops up, black teddy bouncing. "Yay! I'll go do the hot chocolate thing for us. Meet me in the kitchen."

I go trade my date outfit for flannel pjs and slowly shuffle toward the food room. George, pouring the packets of brown powder into cups of steaming H_2O, tosses me a spoon. "Stir."

"Hey, are you wearing *lipstick?*" I stare at her mouth as I grab my "I Love My Attitude Problem" mug. Lipstick is a necessity in my life too, but not at two-thirty in the morning.

"Yep, to go with my new lingerie. I'm carrying my new image over into the bedroom now."

I laugh, heading for the couch. "Who's there to impress past ten in your bedroom? Conan O'Brien?"

"Very funny. No, I'm impressing me and me only from now on. And if I feel sexier in my lipstick and lace at night then that's what it's going to be. And anyway, who cares? I want Franco facts now." She can be quite pushy at times, she really can.

I take a sip and fill her in on everything that went on, chemicals and all. She is twirling her hair like a madwoman, a surefire indicator that something is bothering my roomie.

"So you came back here, grabbed his dog, took him to his apartment and carried him inside?" she asks, in this no-way voice.

"Uh-huh." Not that I really am proud of it or anything, believe me.

"Like literally carried him over the threshold and dropped him on his bed?"

"Well, more like dragged him. I mean he was kind of walking but not really. Remember that night I got really wasted at Slam and you had to help me to the car? It was like that, only a little bit worse."

"Worse?"

"Well, the thing is, he threw up on the way in," I whisper, almost in hopes she won't hear this detail I'm none too psyched to share.

Her jaw drops, and with the lipstick-and-trash-teddy combo this looks a bit obscene. "No."

"Yes. But not on me."

"On the floor?"

"Yeah, mainly on his shirt and some on the floor. I tried to clean it up but I couldn't find a towel so I used toilet paper and it got all soggy and—God, it really was disgusting. I just took his shirt off and threw a comforter on him and bailed."

"Sick. So, nice bod?" Always one to get to the heart of the matter, that George.

"On a one to ten, what I saw of it, I'd give it an eight."

Her stained lips rise into a devilish grin. "Washboards or no?"

"No, but toned."

"Oh, man, I hate to ask but . . . note or no note?"

I don't know why I do things sometimes—I just do them without thinking about it. Like sneezing, almost; I have no control. "Note," I confess, taking a bite of my pinky nail.

"Oh, Abbie, I knew it." She slugs my right arm and it sort of hurts, too. "Why the hell did you leave a note? What did it say?"

I am famous for leaving notes and calling boys. Even if I say I won't call or leave a note, I usually can't resist. It makes me feel in charge. George is the opposite. She's like, Girls are not supposed to call guys period end of story. The fact I dial boys or ask them out or leave them notes drives her batty.

"Well, I was trying to be vague because I don't know if I still like him or what. I mean I like him but I don't know if I should dig him now after everything that happened. So I just left the concert ticket stub and a note that said something like 'I thought you might want this for your scrapbook. Later, Abbie.' Do you think that sounded lame?"

"No, actually I'm shocked. It sounds a lot tamer than most of your notes. And it gives off that I-like-you-maybe-but-not-for-sure vibe. You didn't put 'Love, Abbie' did you?"

"Hell no. It was definitely 'Later, Abbie.' "

"Praise the Savior for that one. Okay, I've kept my trap shut for the whole"—she squints at the clock on the VCR—"thirty-nine minutes it took to tell the saga. Do you want my opinion?"

With George you know you're getting it anyway, so you may as well just give in. "Let me have it."

"Ab, I will not deny the fact that Franco is very cute. He is," she says real slowly, like I'm reading her lips or something.

"Yeah, he is. And?"

"And he has definitely caught your fancy somehow."

"Yes, to use a seventies term loosely," I say. The girl's in a time warp, as are all my friends. I don't know any phrase that's truly nineties. We're too busy using all the other decades' phrases to make up any of our own.

"More like a fifties term, thankyouverymuch. But my question is, why exactly do you like him besides for his looks? Is it for his job? Oh no, sorry, he doesn't have a job that we know of. Is it because he's in school working toward a degree? Oops, forgot, he's not in school so that can't be it. How about because he fits the New Year's resolution description of not drinking or doing drugs? Ohmigod, forgive me, he does drink and do drugs! Both of them! How about this—I got it—you like him for his sparkling conversation on the way home from Rhinestone Paste concerts, right? Oh, what, he's passed out on the way home and can't speak? Then that's not what's making your heart go pitter-patter. So, baby, tell me, what is?"

I am not in the mood for this sarcastic monologue right now but I sit through it anyway, smirking at all the appropriate places. Why do I like him? That's a good question. I have my reasons, but they're difficult to articulate. "Well, hmmm, I like him because he's cool. Very cool, and that's important to me. And he cracks me up. Like when he talks I actually laugh at things he says because I think they're funny and not just because I'm being polite like I always did with whatshisname. And I like his style, he's got good style. And great fashion sense, like he doesn't wear plaid shirts and ironed jeans like everyone else in this town. And we look really cute together, not Kate Moss and Johnny Depp perfect or anything, but very cute in a hip sort of way. God, I do want him."

Georgette shakes her head. "So the fact he wears combats instead of Cole-Haans is making you overlook the fact that he smoked pot and drank nine beers during your first date?"

I am confused and sleepy and ready to end this conversation. I appreciate her advice and everything—believe me, I do—but sometimes, like right now, she's a bit much to take. All I want to do is curl up and think over what went on tonight and figure out what my next move should be. So I go, "Look, George, put like that, yes, it does sound like I'm an idiot. But you can't program your emotions. I can't tell myself not to like him if I do like him. And I do. I'm not marrying the guy, I haven't even kissed him yet. So there is no point to us stressing about it. I might go out with him again, I might not, who knows. At any rate, I like him and he does drugs and this is a problem but right now I am too tired to deal with it. I'm just really, really tired."

She kisses me on the forehead and goes to her room without a word. This makes me damn sad, the peck on the forehead. Like she feels sorry for me or something. That kiss could probably make you cry, if you think about it long enough.

As I HIT the sheets, I wonder why every boy I like has to have something wrong with him. Aren't there any normal but cool guys in the world? If there are, I can't find any. When I'm worried or tense, I usually count sheep to get to sleep. But tonight when I try to envision fluffy white sheep hopping over stocky wood fences, all I can see are little Francos jumping over a wall of beer cans. After the thirty-sixth mini-Franco leaps over the aluminum hurdle, I sleep.

Chapter 8

"So what's up with Mr. Wonderful? Did you ever get the nerve to call him?"

I haven't even sat down in the damn class yet and already Pat is playing Oprah.

"Yes, as a matter of fact I did." I plop down in the orange plastic chair next to Pat's, purple A-line a-blazing.

"And?"

"And . . . nothing, really. We went out and he is the hottest—it is cardiac arrest when I even look at the guy. I do not lie."

Pat tugs on his wool cap. "Uh-oh. Kind of like when I went out with Joey, that Macy's model, remember?"

I wrinkle my nose. "God, Mr. Ditz, the one with the colored contacts and shaved head? How could I forget?"

A dirty look is shot my way. "Well, Abs, I hope you learned from me that all beauty and zero brains does not make for the most charming of companions, especially if you have to actually engage in conversation."

I roll my eyes. "Pat, look. I know you want me to go out with your cousin and fall in love and get married and have a dog and the whole nine but I really don't see it. I mean, I'll go out with the guy, okay, but I do like Franco. A lot."

He puts his hands up in that I-give-up position. "Okay, okay. So what's so great about this pretty boy?"

"He is pretty, isn't he?" I close my eyes and pause, savoring the saliva-inducing image of Franco's face that's branded in my brain. "Well, he reeks of coolness, for one. And we look cute together. I don't know, you'll just have to officially meet him. He is really, really cool."

"Yeah, Ab, you've mentioned that once or twice. So what *don't* you like about Franklin?"

"It's Franc-*ooooo.*" I bite my lip. "Hmm, well, he drinks. A lot, I think. He was pretty much wasted last night. And he smokes pot, too. I'm not sure exactly what else he's into."

"One word to consider . . ." He fills a piece of paper with *PARKER*, rips it out of his notebook and shoves it in front of my face.

"I know, I know. But I've only had one date with the guy, you know? So who knows how much he does really. I am gonna keep my guard up until I find out for sure."

Pat crumples the paper into a little ball and tosses it toward the wastebasket, missing. "Yeah, probably a good idea. And we already know how much Chris drinks: zero."

"Yes, Pat, I know your cousin doesn't drink and the brownie points have been duly noted in my head, believe me. I mean, I'm not ruling anyone out at this point. I am totally up for grabs. I just have this huge, massive crush on Mr. Franco Richards. Who even knows if it's mutual."

"Yeah, but why wouldn't he like you? There's no way he wouldn't. This whole thing is just freaking me out a little because it's reminding me of the early days of Parker. Remember, he would come over to watch movies with you, me and Stuart and would drink a whole twelve-pack of the Beast in one sitting? And that was in the early dates, when you're usually on your good behavior."

"Don't remind me." Shudder. "But that *was* good behavior for Parker. At least then he wasn't telling me how boring I was or pawning the Sega I gave him for Christmas like two weeks after he got it."

Pat shakes his head. "What the hell did you see in that guy?"

I smile. "The future."

Our conversation is cut short by the arrival of Señor Fredrique, breezing in wearing a basic white T with black vinyl pants. He announces that we have to come up with a theme for our collection by next class, then leaves before we even have the chance to bitch or anything.

I glance over at Pat, who looks pissed. "Did someone tell his ass we're a high school yearbook? None of the big designers have well-defined themes anymore."

"I know, right? This really sucks." I want my theme to be

glamorous, like total fifties. I'm thinking scarf around head, black cat's-eye sunglasses, long cigarette holder housing a red-tipped candy cigarette. I sigh, picturing myself in a long convertible—one of those kinds that looks like a sled—Franco in the driver's seat, arm stretched along the white leather upholstery, hand clamped to my bare shoulder. My scarf is blowing in the wind. Donna Summer is cranked loud. I bend over and stain Franco's cheek with a perfect red lip print and life is good.

"Hello? Hello? Hell-fucking-o?" Pat waves a hand in front of my face, yanking me back to reality.

"God, Pat, chill. I'm trying to concentrate here." I close my eyes to recapture the image, but the convertible is already miles down the road.

I OPEN THE door to my apartment, balancing two grocery sacks in my arms. "Hey, George!" I holler, setting the bags down on the coffee table. No response. Kicking the door shut with my Converse-covered foot, I screech "George!" once more. Still nothing. This is definitely weird, because it's Georgette's day off and she never misses "Love Connection" when she's not in class. And the romantic rerun's on at five, in three minutes.

I check Caller I.D. to see who's called: 12:13, my mother; 1:34, Mimi—a chick George goes to school with; 2:26, a number I don't recognize; 4:13, Franco. Oh. My. God.

I hit play on the answering machine, forcing myself not to fast-forward the tape, prolonging the pleasure of this moment. Franco's first phone message. Documented proof that he exists and he likes me and he knows my phone number and he actually dialed it. First, Mom goes on about some talk show about how to marry a doctor or some shit. Next it's Mimi rambling about some Ethan Hawke movie she wants to see with George but doesn't really know if she really should see it because it might depress her in an I-want-a-boyfriend way. Then George, saying she's at Tiger's getting a tattoo. What the fuck? This is a girl who had a coronary when I got my belly button pierced just two months ago, and here she is getting an accessory that lasts a lifetime? This is practically more unexpected than Franco calling, I swear. Then, finally, *beep:*

"Uh, Abbie. It's Franco." I hit pause, my heart beating a zillion miles a minute. Sitting down on the floor, Indian-style, I breathe through my nostrils, my breath as ragged as a broken fingernail. Just the sound of Franco's voice is having this weird effect on me, like his recorded words are sucking the oxygen out of my lungs and into the answering machine.

Deep breath. Again. Then I hit rewind for a second and push play. ". . . anco. Just calling to see if you wanna come over tonight or something. I was a jerk last night, so if you don't want to I get it. So call me, 'kay? Bye."

I fall on my back and kick my legs in the air. "Aaaaaaaaaaaaah!"

The door opens and a blast of cold air hits my bare feet. "What are you doing on the floor—aerobics?"

I jump up and hug Georgette, hopping up and down. "Franco asked me out! Franco asked me out!"

"Ouch, watch the ankle," Georgette says, pushing me off her. "He really asked you out?"

"Yeah. Ohmigod, I cannot believe you got a tattoo. Let's see it." If my smile was any wider I'd have to tie a red scarf around it to drive it on the road, I'm not even kidding.

She lifts her leg, revealing a big piece of white gauze taped above her shoe. "I know, isn't it wild? My mom is gonna die. Go ahead, but be careful."

Removing the bandage, I uncover a black tribal sun, about the diameter of a silver dollar, still a little bloody. "Georgette, I can't believe this. It is so, so—bad girl. Like not like you at all."

She laughs a throaty laugh, someone else's laugh. "I know. I feel alive, Abbie. Alive!"

"Boy, I'll say." Replacing the bandage, I think about how you think you truly know a person and then when they go and get a tattoo or something you're hit with the realization that you don't know them at all, not really. "I'm fixing to call Franco back and accept his date invite." Hop hop hop. "And you got a tattoo! You of all people. I mean when I heard your message I was like you must be kidding. There is just no way."

"Well, get ready for another shocker. I have a date."

"No. Who with?"

"Rob, the guy who did my tattoo. He's got long blue dreads and a lip ring and he is so cute! And he's in a band."

"What?" George hates dreads. And body piercing. And bands.

"I know, not my type or whatever, but the new me needs a new somebody else, right? He's just—oh, you'll meet him if you're still here. I'm really psyched." She saunters toward her room, sort of shaking her butt a bit. Tattoo the tart and all of a sudden she's got a tremulous tush—I don't even know what's up with that. "Should I wear my new outfit?"

"If you lose the fishnets."

Her door slams and I am left alone, just me and the phone. I'm still clutching the receiver, knuckles white as Casper. It's like I've never called a guy before. I'm so freaked out. Man, I need to just get it over with.

Five—Oh God—*five-five, two*—Pause—*two*—my hands are shaking like a saltshaker over popcorn now—*four*—I'm going to throw up. I'm serious—*three*.

One, two, three rings. What if he's not there?

"Hullo?"

Hyperventilation alert. "Franco? This is Abbie."

His voice perks up, like maybe because I'm on the other end?

"Hey, Abbie! I'm glad you called me back."

"Well, I was happy you called." Understatement of the century, we all know, but I don't want to look *desperate* or anything.

"Wanna come over? I'll make you dinner. To make up for last night. I was a total jerk, passing out on you like that."

"It was no big deal, Franco. Don't worry about it."

"Just say you'll come over and I'll stop worrying."

I pause for suspense value. "I guess," I whisper. I don't know why, but I always do that. Like I'll be totally into a guy and thinking about him for weeks or months or whatever and then when he finally gets around to asking me out, I answer "I guess," like I couldn't care less. The more I like a boy, the icier my response, who the hell knows why.

"Good. We can watch TV." He says this like it's a major social event. Then again, with him, going to the city dump would be a major social event to me, if you want to know the truth.

Chapter 9

"Chicken or beef?" Franco calls, sticking his head out of his kitchen door.

This question throws me. The most Parker ever made me was a helping of Top Ramen, and that was like for my birthday or something. Plus, it'd be hard to concentrate on any question that wasn't true–false with Franco's foxiness punching me in the gut every time he pokes his head out, which he's done like twenty times since I got here fifteen minutes ago. "Definitely the chicken," I call. "You need any help in there?"

"Nope, almost ready. Just relax," he calls, his voice echoing off his empty walls. His place is sparse, no pictures or anything, just the necessities.

Sinking into his vinyl couch, the one I tripped over last night, I think Yes, I am in Franco Richards's house, about to set up Franco Richards's owl-covered TV trays, which shortly will support the food that Franco Richards cooked with his very own hands. This just might be the coolest thing that's ever happened to me. The piece of furniture I'm parked on is not merely a couch, it is my very own island in paradise.

"Dinner is served," Franco says as he emerges from the *cocina*, hands bogged down by a large cookie sheet with a trash bag draped over it. He turns off the lamps—which turns my lamp on, naturally, and I'm sure the sneaky bastard knows it—then lights two short blue candles, one for his tray, one for mine. The lighter's flame flickers as it ignites my candle, bathing Franco's features in a golden light. He looks like a kid in front of his eighth-birthday cake—happy, excited, ready to blow out the candles so he can open his presents. In this case, would the present Franco wants to open be me? I hope not, because none of this package's wrapping paper is coming off tonight. He looks right at me and winks. I return the gesture with my right eye, hoping I look sexy instead of like I have something on my contact.

Lighting perfected. Franco, looking mischievous as all hell, turns around to retrieve the cuisine. "Close your eyes."

I obey, my lids depriving me of the sight of Franco, a cruel and unusual act. I hear a clatter as the smell of poultry wafts toward my nostrils.

"Keep them closed."

Sounds: a clunk, a ting and a swoosh; then again, this time coming from Franco's tray. "Okay, now you can look." I peer down at my tray. The owl's face is almost completely obscured by a large sectional tin full of frozen food's finest: fried chicken, mashed potatoes, corn and brownie. I giggle. A wineglass full of liquid the color of Barbie's Corvette rests above the rather crusty potatoes. I pick it up and sniff.

"Nineteen ninety-seven Strawberry Hill. A very good year." Franco says, mouth full of whatever it is that's floating in a pool of gravy on his tray.

Take a guy like Franco, pouring wine cheaper than the champagne they served at Unity the night we met, and then put adoring me into the equation and you've got one hell of a perfect date. I don't care what we do. We could do nothing for all I care and I'd still be as happy. I'm not even lying.

We hang out for awhile—eating, watching TV, chatting—and after awhile I start wondering if this guy is ever going to kiss me. Other than putting his arm around me he hasn't tried a thing, which is sweet but also kind of frustrating when you are wanting something to happen like I do. And there is no way I am going to make the first move, not knowing how he feels about me for sure, just no way.

"So, want to see my bedroom?" Franco says as he closes his sliding glass door after letting Jane out for a pee break.

"Bedroom?" I croak, hoping my wish for a kiss wasn't intercepted telepathically by Franco and misinterpreted as a wish for a sexual encounter. When a boy asks you to his bedroom on the second date, it's usually not just to show you his rock collection, in my experience.

"Yeah, bedroom. You know, that room with the bed," he says, I think half mocking the way I asked for his phone number in the movies: "You know, I dial seven digits, your phone rings . . ." It has only been three days since that conversation but it feels like forever. It's like my life is like a soap opera and one day goes on for four damn weeks or something. Soap operas, they're the worst. "Well, just so you know, and you might not even have this in mind and in which case I apologize for even mentioning it, but I don't intend to sleep with you tonight. So if that's the reason we're going to the bedroom I don't want to lead you on or anything by saying yes. But I am saying yes because I'd like to see where you sleep."

My face is red, a result of total mortification. Franco just smiles and comes over to the couch, giving me a kiss. Our first—which leads to our second, and our third, and on and on until I lose count. Finally we come up for air. "You make me feel bad, Abbie. Is that the only reason you think I asked you over? Sex?"

I grab his hand. "If this is going to be date rape, just remember two words: Lorena Bobbitt."

He yanks his hand from mine. "Oh man. Why do chicks always joke about that shit? I don't think you comprehend the serious amount of pain we're talking here."

I hate it when guys go off about the Bobbitt thing. It truly pisses me off, and I know there's no use in hiding my annoyance. "Try calling millions of African women and asking them how it feels to be genitally mutilated every year and then let's talk about pain, mister."

His face gets all serious. "Yeah, I know, I know. I was only kidding around. Zoe was really into all that, women's groups and Alice Walker books, stuff like that, so I know all about it. I can't believe that shit still goes on in nineteen-fucking-ninety-whatever, you know? It's crazy, like it doesn't even seem real."

I nod, semi-cringing. "I'm sure it seems all too real to the girls getting tortured, that's what sucks. Who's Zoe? I've heard you mention her a couple of times."

"Let's go in the bedroom and I'll tell you all about it."

— — —

His BEDROOM screams boy: king-sized mattress on floor, stack of *Juggs* magazines in corner, color TV set perched upon a slab of wood balancing on two cinder blocks, clothes covering almost every surface. "So this is where you dream at night," I say, sitting on the end of the mattress, sadly noting his closet door is closed.

This is kind of awkward. We're so new to each other that every experience is charged with this nervous energy, and any scene that involves a bed is that much more intense.

Franco flips on the tube and hits mute, filling the room with a thick absence of sound. He turns off the light and lies down on the sheetless bed. Patting his massive stack of pillows, he goes, "Kick off your shoes and come up here."

Quick thought-flash: What if this guy is a mass murderer and he's lured me here to off me? Or what if he's some sick Uma Thurman–obsessed freak who writes her four letters per day and is going to prove his love by re-enacting the drug-overdose scene from *Pulp Fiction*, driving a needle twenty times longer than the one I got poked with at *Dracula* into my lovestruck heart? God, he's cute.

I smile and kick off my Gazelles, leaving the tube socks on. "So, are you a murderer?"

Franco looks spooked. "Wh-why would you ask that, babe?"

I stretch out beside him, resting my head on the mountain of pillows. Jeez, does he look freaked. "Well, it's just that I know pretty much zero about you."

He brushes the hair out of my eyes, propping his head on his fist. "Come on, you know stuff about me."

"Let's see. Franco Richards file. Good taste in hats. Hates Zima Dry, likes Rhinestone Paste, cool clothes, good kisser," I say with racecar speed. It's like a final exam in my favorite subject or something, and I'm scoring one hundred percent. "Likes Salvation Army, was at Unity New Year's Eve, makes a mean TV dinner, gave blood to get into *Dracula*, threw up on our way in last night."

He looks like a kid who got caught with his hand in the cookie jar: only in this case I guess it'd be the toss-your-cookies jar. "Oh

God, I was hoping I dreamed that part. I am really, really sorry, man. I didn't get any on you, did I?" It's so obvious this guy is full of regret. His eyes are all big and he's not meeting my gaze or anything. You have to feel sorry for him really, with the lowered gaze and all.

"None got on me, thank the Lord, and don't worry about it. Okay, what else do I know about Franco? Address, dog's name, physical description. You don't have a car, you have an ex-girlfriend named Tuesday, you know someone named Zoe and are going to tell me about her. You're going to watch 'Letterman' with me in fifteen, you're not going to try anything tonight, the last four digits of your phone number spell 'acid'—"

"Oh, that reminds me, did you know your phone number spells 'ecstasy'? Nine-eight-two-nine, that's *X-T-C-Y.* Cool, huh?"

I am in bed with a lunatic. "How, may I ask, did you figure that out?"

He smiles, a proud smile. "It's kind of like a hobby, I guess. My best friend's number is five-five-five, *S-H-O-T.* It's perfect for Tim, too, 'cause that's pretty much what he does best, shots." You've got to wonder about a guy with a hobby like this—but then, hey, at least the guy's got a hobby.

"Where do you know Tim from?" I ask, leaning back against the pillows. If you haven't noticed, I ask a lot of questions. Always have. Some people think I'm nosy, others consider me inquisitive. It's probably a mixture of both, truth be told.

"Tim and I go way back. High school buddies, Highland Square."

"Highland what?" I must have misunderstood, he could not have just said Highland Square in Dallas. There is no way my Franco could have made it out of that palace of pretension as cool as he did, absolutely no fucking way.

"Yep, the Highland Square Jaguars, say it loud and proud. Only our mascot was the car, not the animal." He shakes his head, possibly trying to knock the images of the place out through his ears. "There it was like if you didn't dress a certain way, drive a certain thing and date a certain type, you were nobody."

"God, so it must have been rough. Let me guess . . . were you the elusive rebel, the fuck-the-world stoner guy or the *Thrasher*-readin' skater boy?" I can totally see it: long hair, frayed jeans, a big fat J in his back pocket, sticker-covered skateboard under a tattooed right biceps.

Franco tells me the answer is none of the above then goes to retrieve some visuals. He opens his closet slightly but not wide enough for me to check out the wardrobe. "You're going to freak on this, Ab."

He comes back holding a bulky yearbook. "New fact. Franco's graduation date. So are you twenty-one or twenty-two?" I ask.

"Turned twenty-two in December. Capricorn."

"I'm Aries," I tell him, thinking how I can't wait to get home to my *Cosmo* astrological guide to see how the Aries–Capricorn love match is.

"Oh, really? Zoe was an Aries, too." He opens to the index, studying the crammed page intently.

"Who the hell is Zoe? I'm totally dying of suspense over here." This being the third time the girl has been mentioned, my curiosity is definitely piqued.

He smiles, leafing through the pages. "I would show you, but she didn't move here until senior year had already started. Here."

He passes the book over to me, pointing to the dominant photo of four guys. They're all total frat material, wearing identical white Polo oxfords, khakis, braided leather suspenders and Cole-Haans. The foursome is standing in front of a swimming pool, each holding jumbo fruity cocktails, complete with paper umbrellas. I read the caption: "BOYS OF SUMMER. At senior Jodi Myer's coming-out party 'Fun In The Sun,' seniors Trevor Dunbar, Allen Stringer, Joey Ferguson and Franklin Richards III soak in the rays." I blink twice and read it again. My eyes shoot up to the guy on the far right and then to the real Franco, who's smirking. "Oh my God, noooooooo." It is him. A total prepped-out version of the delicious boy beside me in living color, page 38. I look back down, staring at the rich kid grinning up at me like an evil twin or a bootleg rip-off of the original.

"Yeah, wait, it gets better."

He snatches the book from my lifeless hands. My mind is whirling; I'm in shock. I've never given Franco's high school experience any speculation, not even once in the hundreds of hours I've spent dreaming about the guy since our first encounter. Yet never in a million years would I have pictured him as the wealthy type, much less someone whose name ends with "the Third." My Franco is the Franco of no car and nine beers and faded Levi's, not he of braided leather suspenders and coming-out parties. I feel like every perception I've had of this guy is getting chunked into a blender set on puree mode.

"Okay, don't laugh." He sets the book on my lap, hand covering the largest pic on the page. "Ta da." His hand moves upward, uncovering the impossible: Franco, my Franco, tuxedo-clad, garish crown atop short-haired head, arm around sequined, tiara-topped blonde bimbo with silicone tits and a plastic face to match. The enthused two are standing under a large red-lettered banner, declaring them Highland Square Prom Queen and King.

I scream, only half joking. "Aaaaaaaaah! This is too fucking weird!"

He laughs, slamming the book and tossing it on the floor. "I know. It gives me the heebie-jeebies just looking at it. It's like a bad dream."

"But, I mean, what—" I don't know where to begin. The question is, how did he change from that to this in four years? Most boys of that mold are content to remain there forever, going from the in group to fraternities to safe executive positions secured by alumni of said fraternity, then moving on to boys' clubs and country clubs and senate seats. They trade in their proms for Greek formals and their Greek formals for cotillions, but the game remains the same—the game where money equals power and what others think of you is what you think of yourself.

"Yeah, I know what you're thinking. How did I transform from Franklin Richards the Third, the BMW-driving, fraternity-bound, five-hundred-a-week-allowance prom king, into Franco, Mr. Whatever? It was easy." He looks down, and then there's that damn smile. "Summer before college me and all my friends are making school plans and planning rushes and taking big trips to Europe, totally paid for by our mommies and daddies. A lot of people are going Ivy League, to Oberlin and Pepperdine and Princeton. Me and like probably twenty others are going to UT Austin, keeping in mind that Austin is the ultimate party town and the 'rents are just a phone call away if we need more money or the Beemer's down or whatever. Well, the week before rush, I'm talking my fucking bags are packed, the shit hits the fan with my parents and they cut me off totally, telling me to just get the hell out and never come back. I never have, either."

My eyes widen. "What happened? I mean, have you talked to them or anything since?"

"Nope, never. Mom sent me a couple of letters at first when I was living in Austin with Tim but that was like two years ago. I don't even think they know where I am now," he says. The deal is, he doesn't sound sad. I mean, you'd think he'd sound sad as all hell but he doesn't, not really.

"But what did you do that was so bad? Kill somebody?"

He runs his hand through his hair, unbraiding his locks. "Look, I can't really get into this now. It's not you, but I just can't talk about what happened with them to anybody. They're dead to me, they really are." I'm getting goose bumps—his eyes are total rapist right now.

"God, I shouldn't have asked, it's none of my business—" I told you I'm nosy sometimes—I need to just learn to shut up now and then.

"It's no problem, Ab, don't worry about it. If I was gonna tell somebody, you'd be a good choice. It's just part of my past, one I don't care to relive ever again."

I try to imagine life without my parents and tears spring to my eyes; it would be like life without God. "Do you miss them ever? Your parents?"

He nods real slow, glum. "Sure, on Christmas and stuff I miss having a family, a home, but Tim's parents are kind of like my parents now. And I don't have any brothers and sisters so it's not like I'm missing them too."

I squeeze his hand. "I guess I can't really envision it, but it seems like it would be beyond sad for you."

He strokes my hair—how damn sweet is *that*. "You know, it was their choice, and I suppose what makes it bearable is pride.

I'm right, they're wrong and I'll never back down. And since there's never been any doubt I'm my father's son, he's as stubborn as I am. And this thing, this argument, this thorn in his side, is something he feels just as strongly about and will never back down on, either. And my mother is my father's mouthpiece, so the same really goes for her. His thoughts are her thoughts. I don't know, I guess just knowing I'm right makes the pain, the loss, the void go away, at least almost completely."

Heavy stuff, right? As bitchy as I know it sounds—and believe me, I know—I'm thinking, well, a boy with no parents is someone who will really appreciate the love of his girlfriend. Have I told you I can be conniving like this? I can, I'm not proud of it or anything, but I really can. "So what fills that void, the part that knowing you're right can't?"

He points the remote to the TV, hitting mute again, smiling. " 'Letterman.' "

I guess the moment of sharing is over. Gluing my eyes to the set, my brain focuses not on Dave but on the past twenty minutes, still struggling to digest everything. What fills Franco's void is substances, duh. You don't really need to pay a therapist a hundred clams an hour to figure that one out. But I can almost understand why he'd turn to drugs and liquor without having any family to speak of, no solid unit you know will always be there. I think of my own fam: Dad, overprotective and sweet and full of warnings and car tips; Mom, never thinking any boy is good enough for me, always telling me I'm the best designer in the world; brother Jimmy, totally preppy golfer boy who brags to all his friends that I'll be famous someday. They are the biggest fan club anybody could ask for, three people that think I'm the coolest and most talented girl in the world. Without them, I would be lost. I want to help Franco be found. I want him to be found by me.

Commercial break. "So, are you still thinking about my starched-shirt alter ego?" Franco asks, hugging me with one arm.

I laugh, leaning into the embrace. "No, I'm thinking I wonder who the hell Zoe is—my third time to inquire, for those keeping score at home."

Deep breath. "Okay—Zoe. God. I guess she was my first love. She wasn't my first girlfriend or anything, but she's been the only one that mattered. And she is in the middle of this thing with my parents, although she never did anything to them personally. They just use people and don't think about the repercussions and she got caught in their web." He sighs, closing his eyes. Probably picturing the perfect body I'm sure she has or something. "But we stayed together for a couple of years, most of it long-distance, while she was away at college in Portland. She came back summers and breaks, but it just wasn't meant to work out I guess. I still talk to her and see her sometimes. She was my best friend; it's hard to cut out your best friends, you know?"

"Yeah, I know," I answer, feeling a twinge of envy. I hate to admit it, but I'm jealous. Damn jealous. "Parker was like that, kind of. Once I escaped the relationship, I figured out I was his best friend but he wasn't a friend to me at all, which sucked. Like totally sucked. So was it the distance that broke you two up?"

"Ultimately," he says, looking away. He's really broken up over this chick, like he can't even look at me; what fucking luck. "Zoe just . . . she slept with other people up there. She told me about it and everything, which to her I guess made it alright. Her sleeping with other guys was like me drinking every day; we were both trying to make up for the other one's absence. Neither tactic worked too well."

"Love is so confusing." Like right now it's confusing why I just might love a boy who loves his ex, exactly like Parker always did. Just once I want to be the ex who boys can't get over so some other girl can be left to hear about how perfect I am all day. "It's so damn confusing, it really is."

"I know. Like someone can be such a figure in your life, as familiar as your nose or your favorite pair of jeans, and then they're gone, they vanish."

He's so on my level it's spooky, right? "Yeah. And then you wake up and think, Man, somewhere they're waking up too and eating Twinkies for breakfast and brushing their teeth and you're not there for it. Like sometimes I think that about Parker and cry. I prefer to think of him as dead, it's easier."

With a yawn, he says, "Yeah, that's what my parents are to me. Dead as Elvis, six feet under."

He rolls over, fetal position, back to me. "Wanna spoon?" he asks. Sweet as pie.

I cuddle up to him, bods fitting perfectly, and kiss his neck.

"Thanks for tonight," I whisper, meaning the TV dinner and "Letterman" and kissfest and yearbook and Zoe story—all of it.

"Thanks for caring," he answers, voice sleepy.

If only he knew how much I do.

Chapter 10

I wake up, disoriented, full of that feeling you get when you wake up in a Motel 6 or at an all-night party you never made it home from—the where-the-hell-am-I syndrome. Confused, I roll over and ram into Franco, who's sprawled out on the majority of the king-sized mattress and has taken command of all the covers. Ah, Franco. The previous evening hits me like a brass-knuckled fist, and I curl my toes, savoring the memories of the dining, the dissing, the discussing of last night. I wish I could stay here forever, freeze-framing the highlights of the previous evening, but I have to get to school. Squinting, I search the room over for a digital clock that apparently is buried somewhere, thinking if I've missed my class I'm dead. I grab Franco's wrist and bring it close to my face: 6:48 A.M.—shit.

Trying to make as little noise as possible, I hop up and grope for my shoes. Once they're on, I lean over and smack Franco on the cheek, just like I did in my red convertible fantasy only days ago. He looks so angelic, vulnerable as glass, it almost crushes my heart to even look at him. "Bye, baby," I whisper, slipping out of the room.

At Learjet speed, I hurdle Jane and exit the apartment, hauling ass to my car and then speeding home. I hit the bathroom first, brushing my teeth and sticking my hair in a bun simultaneously—one of my many hidden talents. Deodorant spray—left pit and right pit—then refrigerator raid: banana and apple, can of Dr Pepper. I run out of the house in the same jeans and T-shirt Franco and I shared our first kiss in. My new lucky outfit.

Makeup is applied en route to school. Base goes on first before heavy traffic hits, powder is applied on on-ramp, lipstick goes on at seventy miles per hour and mascara gets its chance to shine in the packed parking lot of the Design Institute. Once all lashes are sufficiently lengthened, I check the time: 8:05.

Juggling my breakfast, backpack and notebook, I run through the halls like a kid doing the fifty-yard dash in P.E. Only the holder of my stopwatch is way worse than one of those whistle-obsessed phys ed teachers so often found in elementary school gyms. The one who's keeping tabs on my time is Señor Fredrique, and he looks none too happy when I breeze in the door at 8:07.

"Your theme, señorita?" he asks, standing next to the door like a protective doberman in a black ski bib and turtleneck.

No, this cannot be happening. A glance over at Pat eating his fingernails tells me it is. I forgot the theme assignment. "Can I see your pen, Señor Fredrique?" I ask sweetly, grabbing the Bic from his outstretched hand before he can say no. I scrawl "Abbie" on my banana and place it in Fredrique's palm.

"What is this?" he asks, holding the banana like it's a used maxi-pad.

"My theme. Fruit."

I head for the chair that Pat's saving for me as Fredrique wrinkles his nose in disgust and drawls, "Very original," in this sarcastic way. "Nice move," Pat whispers as I slide into the seat.

"This really bites," I whisper back, thinking there is probably no worse theme in the world than fruit. Pat's is fish, like *My Own Private Idaho* fish, not Long John Silver's fish—way cooler than damn fruit.

Fredrique calls for order. "Okay, okay. I will start by saying the themes are weak. Very weak. My first thought was to give you bad grades and make you redo it, really thinking about it this time." He glares my way. "But then I thought no, the worst punishment I could give you is to make you stick with these themes. No changing them, no turning back. So that is what I am going to do. They are set in stone now. Forever."

A gasp waves across the room, the loudest coming from me. "Now, what I need from all of you is an outline of what you want your collection to say, what attitude it will have, what it has to be. In sketch form, by Tuesday. No loopholes, no gaps. Take the rest of the hour to think about how much your themes lack. Even Versace would have a hard time pulling some of yours off." Is it my imagination, or does he look right at me when he says this? I couldn't blame him really. Fruit for Chrissakes.

Fredrique leaves with a slam and I look at an amused Pat, visions of cantaloupes dancing in my head. "Oh my God, this is not happening. Tell me I do not have to design thirty pieces that have the theme of goddamn fruit. Tell me this is some kind of joke."

Pat leans over and envelops me in a bear hug, cracking up.

"Hello, this is not a laughing matter here, Patrick, and I would thank you very much if you would save your guffaws for another time please."

His hugging body is still shaking with what can only be giggles. "Without this last class I cannot finish, Pat. This is the only damn credit I have left. If I don't pass, I will die. I can't spend another semester at this place. I can't, it's not possible."

"Fruit isn't really that bad. There's no law you have to design one of those sweaters with the jumbo strawberries on it and a skirt with a million little strawberries all over it to match, you know? You'll think of something cool."

I look up at him, pouting. "But what if I don't?"

"Then I'll hire you as my design assistant," he answers with a smirk, knowing full well that I hate to be an assistant anything.

Laughing, I stick my tongue out at him. "Fuck that."

"See, the old you's already coming back. Fruit theme and all, Abbie still rules the world."

The word "rules" of course brings Franco to mind. "No, Pat, someone else has a firm hold on that title. I discovered this last night."

He closes his eyes and puts his head in his hands. "Oh no, let me guess. Frankfurt?"

"It's Franco. Or Franklin Richards the Third, another thing I discovered last night. Let's go to the Commons. This story calls for coffee."

"Oh, shit."

I grab his hand and lead him out the door.

— — —

Pat seems less than thrilled with the perfection of the Franco encounter. I think more worried I'm going to back out of our double date tonight than anything else. I'd never do that to my best friend, no matter how cool I think Franco is at the moment. Plus Sal is being a freak again. Last night, he asked Pat if he sees him in his future and if so, how far. Like he wanted a marriage proposal or some shit. Pat said the last thing he wants on the top of his wedding cake is a little green-eyed monster, eyes darting around the reception to see if there are any boys who might pose a threat.

"It's become like an almost everyday thing with him. Do you love me? Are you happy with me? Do you think that guy's sexier than me? It's like a Buzz Clip on MTV. It was fine the first five hundred times you saw it, but repeat anything a thousand times a day and it gets old real quick."

"Yeah. I love Buzz Clips, though. And you still love Sal. I bet things will get better, you'll see."

He checks his watch. "Look, I gotta run but we'll be by around seven. We're going to the Old San Francisco Steakhouse and a play downtown so please try to wear something dressed up but not too wild. You know how Chris is."

I give Pat a burn-in-hell look. Never have I dressed to please a boy and I have no intentions of starting now. He of all people should know that. "Oh sure, Pat, I'll be happy to change my style for you. Anything you say," I answer in a NutraSweet voice oozing with sarcasm.

Pat looks scared. "Oh shit, forget I said anything."

Armed with plastic, I hit the fabric store to stock up on Valentine's hat materials. My motivating thought is that as long as I'm feeling this love vibe, there's nothing wrong with smearing it all over my headpieces and reaping financial gain from the experience. With sequin-and-satin-stuffed hands, I try to unlock my apartment door while balancing my bundle. It's not working.

I am still jiggling my key in the lock when the door opens from the inside. Georgette is standing in the doorway, clad in an orange bikini, straw hat and sunglasses.

"*Hola,* mon. Welcome to Fantasy Island," she says in this Jamaican voice, sounding drunk.

"George! What are you doing home in the middle of the day?" The bikini, it kills me. Middle of winter and the girl's in a two-piece.

"Sunbathing!" she answers with a giggle, walking back in the living room. "And it's Gigi."

Gigi?

I enter Treasure Island or wherever and find a blue-haired boy lying on a beach towel in the middle of our living room floor, basting under an archaic silver sunlamp. "Gilligan's Island," volume down, is on the tube and Butthole Surfers are blasting on the stereo. George lies next to whom I presume to be Rob and closes her eyes, a half-empty bottle of rum resting at her feet. The dreadlocked one looks up as I drop my bags on the coffee table. "You must be Rob," I say, sticking my hand out.

He shakes it. "The one and only."

I smile and push my hair behind my ears, staring at his lip ring. "I'm Abbie, George's roommate. Hey, aren't you friends with Chris from Soaking Wet Juliet? You look really familiar." And also really stoned, but some boys just have that look.

He nods in slow-mo. "Yeah, I know that dude. We've partied together. But you probably know me from Double Limbaughtomy. You seen us?"

"Hmmm, I don't know. I don't think so, but maybe."

"Believe me, babe, you see us once and you never forget. You need to check us out sometime. With *Jege.*" His lids close, ending our very intellectually stimulating conversation.

"Later, guys." I grab my stuff and go to my room, escaping the *Beach Blanket Bingo* scene in progress. Georgette, a.k.a. Gigi, never misses school, ever, so this is way out of the ordinary. And Rob is like night and day from the cookie-cutter Republican types she usually goes for. I am over even trying to figure her out anymore. Plus I've got better things to think about, the first three on the list being Franco, Franco and Franco.

My bed in the corner, piled with pillows and blankets, beckons. A nap sounds like heaven after the hectic twenty-four hours I've just been through. On the way to dreamsville, though, I spy my journal peeking out from under my nightstand. With as many stories as I've got crammed in my brain at the moment, the book takes first priority. Seventeen and a half pages in the small daisy-covered journal are used to record the events of last night. I leave nothing out—not a glance, a word, a peck on the elbow. Every detail, no matter how minute, is lovingly recorded in my furious scrawl with extreme care. As I write the words, I cannot help feeling like I'm living a bad teen flick lately. After several minutes of deliberation, I decide if there is ever a movie version of my existence, I definitely want Alicia Silverstone to play me. And who would do Franco justice? The only real contender would be River Phoenix, were he not gone now.

I grab an ancient journal from my shelf and flip back to the day River died, so long ago, and read my entry, getting depressed. That was without a doubt the saddest day of that year; my generation's first collective loss, before Kurt or anybody. I suppose my feelings of helpless rage and sadness were not unlike what my mom felt when JFK got shot. Her grassy knoll was my Viper Room; her grieving Jackie O, my sobbing Samantha Mathis. In both cases, a cool guy went before his time. And on many levels the nation is still trying to grapple with both losses.

I slap the book shut and lie down, inserting my earplugs to drown out the Butthole Surfers, which either Rob or Georgette has just turned up to a deafening decibel. A loud silence fills my ears and Franco fills my head, lulling me to sleep.

I'm in Franco's new sports car and we're driving fast. In Vegas. My dad is in the back seat wearing a powder blue polyester leisure suit crooning "Don't Be Cruel" into one of those big fifties microphones. I'm in a wedding veil and yellow raincoat—Franco's wearing camos. All of a sudden, the car starts to shake. Hard. An earthquake? Wow, a big one. Maybe even *the* big one. I didn't know they even had earthquakes in Nevada. The car's shaking violently now—back and forth, back and forth. My dad reaches over and pulls a quarter out of my ear. "Abbie, Abbie!" A high-pitched voice is pulling me out of Vegas, off the strip. "Abbie, wake up!" My eyes pop open. Sunburned Georgette, still sporting orange bikini, looms above me, dangling a tan earplug from her Press-On-Nail'ed fingers. "She's alive! God. I've been trying to wake you up for the past five minutes," she says, landing on my bed with a plop.

I take out my other earplug and look over at the clock: 3:45 P.M. "You've been asleep for like three and a half hours. Rough night last night or what? And what'd you think of Rob? He just left—we're going out again tonight. Isn't he hot? And I haven't told my mom yet so if she calls don't say anything, but I'm quitting school for the semester—if you drop out before the third week you can still get eighty percent of your tuition back. I'm going to get my boobs done with the money from that plus the cash Dad gave me for books. I'm so excited, Ab! But I think all that rum's going to my head now. I have a major migraine working."

Georgette is talking a hundred miles per minute, her voice like a getaway car in a high-speed chase. I swallow, attempting to digest everything she just told me.

"Uh, okay, bear with me 'cause I'm still asleep. Am I getting this right? You're quitting school, like not going for a whole semester, so you can get a boob job for this Rob guy, who I did think was cute but you've only known for two days? Is that what you just said?"

Georgette smiles. "Nope, it's not. I'm not quitting school forever, just for the semester. I mean, I'll still be on schedule if I go to summer school. And the boobs aren't for Rob—he hasn't even seen my real ones yet. They'll be for me. Ab, you know I've always been a freak about my chest, or lack thereof. Now I'll be able to buy low-cut dresses! Have construction workers catcall me! Work at Hooters!"

"Oh God, not Hooters!" I scream, thinking she can't be serious.

"Yes, Hooters. I've always wanted to work there." She adjusts her double-A bikini top.

"Man, you're not kidding." She's not, either. Her eyes are all sincere and everything.

"No, I'm dead serious. I can walk around at hockey games in my Hooters T-shirt and orange shorts, advertising the place.

And I can hang out with the Hooters girls on weekends. Then like probably every day I can have guys come in and buy overpriced beer and hot wings just so they can stare at my chest." She bounces up and down on the mattress. "Sounds like perfection."

Perplexed, I knock on her forehead. "Hello, Georgette—the women's movement? Don't you think it's a tad bit derogatory, the whole concept? Even the name. Hooters, for Godsakes! It's like, I don't know." I'm at a loss here.

"Hooters refers to an owl, Ab, that's why they have that little owl drawing next to the name. Everybody knows that," she whines in this total brat voice. Nails on a chalkboard, I'm not kidding. "And no one's given my body a second glance before, so I'll welcome all the attention. Tall, dark strangers appreciating my bod doesn't sound like such a bad thing to me."

"Exploitation isn't appreciation, George," I say, frustrated.

"Hey, exploit me. I want to be exploited. I'm dying for guys to look at my tits and wish I was their girlfriend. Plus, it's not like I'm stripping or anything. But even if I was, it's my choice. What I do with my body is nobody's business but mine, you know?"

I let loose a sigh of defeat. "Yeah, I know. I'm not saying don't do it, I'm just surprised."

Georgette's eyebrows shoot up. "Hey, didn't Parker dump you for that Hooters waitress?"

Cringe. "Well, he didn't exactly dump me. It was a mutual thing."

"Yeah, okay. But it was over that Hooters girl, right?" George's pushing her tits together, trying to create some cleavage. "Shay or Shannon or something?"

"Shanna. He met her at some bachelor party Steve had there and then started going out with her behind my back. Like two weeks later I figured it out and that's when I moved out, remember?"

"Who could forget? Remember when I came over to help you move your couch and he threw your car key at you and called you a bitch?"

I'll never forget his eyes that day, cold and hard as ice cubes; the key whirling through the air, landing with a clunk on the sidewalk; the door slam, quick and hard, like a hate-fuck with no remorse. "I loathe that asshole. Wonder if he's still going out with her?"

"Let's hope not, for her sake. Hey, I wonder if she still works there? Then at least I'd sort of know somebody."

I slap her leg. She's pushing her boobs together and saying she'll be nice to the girl who stole my maladjusted man from right under my nose and I'm so pissed I smack her, just like that.

"God, Ab, not like we'd be buddies or anything, her being Parker's woman and all. I do have some loyalty, thank you."

We change the subject to happier matters: Rob. She wants me to go to see his band and Don't Play Ball In The House at Weeds tonight, but I tell her I can't because of my double date.

She raises her brows. "Oh yeah, the Polo guy. So are you excited? Or are you wishing it was with Franco?"

I tell her the whole story, quoting from my journal for added detail. She agrees the date was perfect, but looks a bit skeptical. I know the look—that he-can't-be-this-perfect gaze I've given her many a time.

"I mean, he does have some major problems: no real job that I know of, no car, drinks a lot, does drugs. But he is so cool. I think we can work the bad points out."

Georgette looks a bit apprehensive. "Ab, those are some heavy-duty bad points. Not to say they can't be worked through, but it's going to be hard. There is more to a relationship than cool hair."

"I know, I know. But there's no telling what will happen with Franco. It seems stupid to sit here analyzing the situation when there really isn't even a situation to analyze. I guess I'll just see how it goes."

"True. So what are you gonna wear tonight?" She's adjusting her bottom now, twisting around in front of my dresser mirror to check out her butt. The girl's got a nice butt, I'll admit it—a far cry from mine, which is straight out of a rap video.

"Oh, get this. Patrick is like, 'Wear something tame so you won't freak Chris out.' I'm not lying, he said that."

She leans in for a closer look at my face. "Oh man, I know that look. You're going to dress all insane, aren't you?"

I put on my angelic expression. "Who, me?"

— — —

THE DOORBELL RINGS. My moment of glory. I glance at the mirror again—too perfect—on the way to the door. Georgette lurks in the corner of the living room, optimum face-viewing spot. I throw open the door to Chris, Pat and Sal, huddled together on the porch like Siamese triplets. "Hey, guys," I smile, ushering them in.

Chris—in Brooks Brothers tie, denim shirt, khakis and loafers—hands me a bouquet of daisies. My absolute fave. "You look great, Abbie. Even prettier than I remembered. How'd you know green's my favorite color?"

"Psychic Friends Network, man." It doesn't take a psychic to know that Pat's wigging, his face is marshmallow city. Don't think I dressed this way *totally* to spite Pat or to freak Chris out. I actually do like the outfit—it's just that it's a little wild even by my standards. The mucho formfitting chartreuse T-back minidress I designed last semester, chartreuse tights and three-inch chartreuse platforms have transformed me into a human green apple Jolly Rancher, if you will.

I look down at the daisies. How sweet, Chris bringing me flowers. Franco sure as hell has never done something like this, not even close. "Thanks, sweets, the flowers are beautiful. Will you help me put one in my hair?" I coo, turning to look over at Pat with a triumphant grin. He shoots me that I-knew-you'd-do-this-to-me look while Chris carefully sticks a stem in my elaborate French twist. I glare back under my false eyelashes for a second, then turn to Sal. "Awesome pants," I tell him. They are, too—sorta tight and made out of an old American flag, totally complementing Pat's navy pants, white shirt and flag tie.

"Isn't that like illegal or something?" George says, approaching our foursome, smirking like mad. It *is* pretty funny, Pat freaking over the green oufit and all.

"Hey, Georgette," Pat says, sticking out his hand. During the shake, she corrects him on the name. "Okay, er, *Gigi*, this is my cousin Chris. And you know Sal. Chris, meet Gigi, Abbie's roommate."

Chris, done with the beautician bit, extends a hand. "Hey, nice to meet you. I am totally knocked out by your roommate."

Georgette smiles and looks at me, that Man-you-might-want-to-hold-on-to-this-one look. "Oh, you are? Well, she is pretty neato mosquito, alrighty. Look, I hate to meet and run, but somewhere across town a tanning bed is calling my name."

We say our goodbyes and, post-Georgette-exit, everyone kind of looks at each other, waiting for something to happen. I decide to get the ball rolling. "Okay, I'll stick these in some water and then we can be off. What time are the reservations?"

Chris says, "Seven-thirty dinner, nine-fifteen play. Hope you like political theater."

I grin. "As long as it's liberal, I can deal with it."

"Can I take that to mean that you're a liberal?" he says, looking like a kid about to get a measles shot.

"Can I take that to mean that you're not?" I ask, referring to his scared-out-of-his-wits look. God, please please please please don't let him be a Republican, anything but that.

"Republican through and through," he says, semi-saluting or something.

I look at Pat and then back at Chris—they both look positively spooked, who knows if it's the outfit or the political debate or what's wrong—and think that it's going to be one hell of a long night.

We're walking out the door when the phone rings. My heart skips a beat hoping it's Franco. Wrong—it's only Mother. "Hey, Ab. What are you doing?"

"Actually, I'm walking out the door, Mom. It's double date time and we're late."

"Oh, Ab, the preppy guy? I probably don't even want to know what you're wearing. Not the Elvis pants, I hope. Oh God, please tell me no." I could really just record one of these conversations and play it back every now and then to save on long distance charges—she says the same damn thing every time and my responses rarely differ, either.

"Look, I've really gotta go." I look at the gang and throw my hands up, exasperated.

"Okay, okay, Ab. You have on eyeliner, don't you? Because you have my eyes and I'm telling you, we need it."

I roll my kohl-rimmed eyes, having heard this eyeliner speech jillions of times before from her. I'm serious. She has nothing better to worry about so she loses sleep over my cosmetic application. It's pretty depressing; fucking eyeliner, for Chrissakes.

"So, DO YOU like this place?" Chris asks, looking intently at my face. We've just sat down at the restaurant and my Day-Glo self is parked between Chris and Pat, across from Sal. On the way here, Pat let me be in charge of the music, which I guess means he's not too mad at me about the outfit. However, since I'm still holding a slight grudge over this afternoon's events, I popped in this CD he's really sick of and sang along at the top of my lungs. That'll teach him.

"Um, I don't know. I've never been here before," I answer, checking out the menu and hoping they have something other than dead cow. "Do you know if they serve liquor?"

Pat casts a sideways glance of caution. "Oh, remember, Chris doesn't drink," he says in an overly nonchalant tone.

Chris puts his hand on my arm. "But it's cool if you guys do. Hell, I might even have a beer."

Live on the edge, geek. I know it's unfair to think like this but he announced his possible beer-ordering plans like he was telling us he was going skydiving or something. Abbie, be nice—get through this date, I know you can do it.

The blonde waiter approaches and we order drinks, flashing I.D.s, all fake except for Chris's.

After he departs, Chris smiles at me. "So, Abbie, tell me a secret."

"If I tell you, it won't be a secret anymore," I whine in my little-girl voice, a voice Pat hates.

"Well, just a little-known fact about you then."

I think about this for a minute and rapidly realize most of my party anecdotes are about other people. Like the one about how Parker bought his mom a chicken pot pie for Mother's Day and was being serious. Or the time where this vo-tech-looking girl sitting next to me in driver-improvement class kept bragging about her 'vette until finally I was like, "What color is your Corvette?" and she goes, "It's not a Corvette, it's a Chevette." Or when my mom was getting ready to go to her class reunion and sprayed foaming bath cleanser instead of hairspray all over her hair. These are the little-known facts I am apt to share: other people's experiences, not mine.

"Let's see—a little-known fact."

"Yep," he says, smug as hell.

Six eyes land on me, adding to the pressure. "Pat already knows this one, but I had to have rabies shots like a year and a half ago."

Sal shuts his eyes. "Oh man, in your stomach?"

Chris runs a hand over his dark gelled-down locks. "They don't give them to you there anymore, do they?"

"No, thank God. I had to get four huge shots in my hip and then nine in my arm. I really hate needles so it sucked. I was bawling, huh, Pat?"

Pat nods, remembering my hysterics. "I'll say. The whole time they were giving her the shots she was crying and I was holding back her hair and kissing her forehead. My shirt was soaked and she was in so much pain I almost cried."

Chris pats my hand. "What bit you, hon?"

He called me "hon" but I feel nothing. "A damn raccoon. I was tossing something in my apartment trash Dumpster and it just jumped up and bit me, then ran off. Parker kept going 'It's no big deal, I don't know why you're stressing' and then it ended up that I had to get the shots. But I sued the apartment and ended up getting like three thousand and change." Some people hit the Lotto, I get bitten by a rabid animal—my damn luck, I swear.

"And Parker is . . . ?" Chris asks.

"My ex-boyfriend. We lived together freshman year." Maybe this living-in-sin confession will scare off the church boy, who knows. I sort of hope so, I really do.

Pat goes, "Yeah, Chris, get this: he was pissed Abbie would only give him fifty dollars when she got that settlement."

Sal, who's been staring around the joint for the past five, tunes in. "Oh yeah, I remember that. What a jerk."

I smile. "Tell me about it. Okay, Chris, so I told Park I'd buy him some shoes, Vans that were like forty, since he gave a statement in my case. When I got the money, he said he wanted these hundred-and-fifty-dollar horrendous tennis shoes but I would only give him fifty bucks. This is when we were already broken up and everything but still living together. Keep in mind I'd already supported his ass for most of our courtship, buying his beer and cigarettes and food and whatnot—we're talking more than a thousand bucks, easy. Plus driving him around forever while his car was out of commission. So, get this, he has the nerve to say that I am cheap. Because I wouldn't buy him the fucking hundred-and-fifty-dollar shoes."

Perhaps we should change the subject. When I talk about Parker I get bitchy and crabby, thinking about how badly he treated me and how I just let it happen. Right after we broke up, I was all sad and constantly thought of the good times, certain I'd never love again. But since I ditched those rose-colored glasses some months back, it's now more of a pissed-off rage I feel when thinking about him. Which I still unfortunately find myself doing on occasion.

The Baywatchesque waiter arrives with our drinks: Hurricanes for me and Sal, Foster's for the cousins. As he's setting them down on little white napkins, I turn to Chris. "So, what about you? Let's hear your secret."

"Well, you'll probably laugh." He picks up the Foster's like it's a bomb or something, all delicate and shit. "Even Pat doesn't know about this one."

This catches Pat's interest. "What, man? Have you gotten drunk before and not told me? That's it, isn't it?"

Holding up his mug, Chris chuckles. "Nope, that's not it. One beer's always been my limit."

"So what is it?" Sal asks, leaning his chin on his fist.

Chris looks over at me and bites his lip. "I'm mimophobic," he mumbles.

"You're what?" I ask, leaning closer to his mouth. I need another Hurricane for this one, I bet.

"Mimophobic," he repeats, more clearly now.

We all look at him blankly. Like what the hell's a mimophobe?

"Fear of clowns."

Pat is the first one to bust, quickly followed by both me and

Sal. We're cracking up and Chris looks a little hurt. "See, I told you you'd laugh." He takes a big gulp of beer.

"I'm sorry," I say, wiping my eyes, hoping to God I don't lose the false lashes. "You're being serious, right?"

"As a heart attack." The laughter subsides, everyone wanting details.

"So when did you discover you have this fear-of-clowns thing?" Pat asks, trying hard to keep a straight face. Who can blame him for laughing here, really? Phobia of goddamn *clowns.*

Chris loosens his tie. "Uh, I guess it was when Mom and Dad took me to Disneyland. I was like fourteen at the time and this clown comes up behind me and starts juggling. I didn't know he was there and I was just walking along, my dad videotaping the whole scene. All of a sudden I feel something on my back so I whirl around and here's this guy with a painted face juggling these milk bottles. I didn't even think—I just grabbed one of those bottles out of the air and hit him in the face with it."

"In the face? Mr. Nonviolence himself?" Pat asks, stunned.

"Yeah. And from then on I just noticed any time I was within, say, fifty feet of a clown I felt this pure, red anger—an uncontrollable feeling—something animal, something dangerous. For instance, if someone locked me in a room with a clown I swear I'd kill him." He looks like he could, too. Scrunched-up face and all; it's really kind of creepy.

I giggle. "This is the wackiest thing I've ever heard. Can you go to the circus or anything?"

"Yeah, if I'm far enough back. But I can't get too close to the front or I just lose it."

Sal fishes the cherry out of his Hurricane and pops it in his mouth. "It just seems weird that it's a real phobia. I mean, do a lot of people have it?"

Chris nods, solemn. "A lot of guys named Steve have it, oddly enough."

"What?" Fucking *Steve*, for Godsakes?

"Yeah, I'm not kidding. It's common among guys named Steve. Steve Martin has it. Stephen King has it. And Steven Wright has it. And those are only the famous Steves."

Sal and I look at each other and explode with giggles.

"Does the *v* or *ph* spelling have any effect on whether a Stephen will get it or not?" Pat asks above our guffaws, peeling the label off his Foster's.

Chris laughs. "Not that I know of, nope. Did you know that when—oh, shit." He looks like he's just seen his parents having sex. Or Bozo the Clown.

"What is it?" I ask, setting down my cocktail. Something is definitely wrong here.

"It's the Robinsons from my church. They just came in." Eyes glued to the door, he slowly pushes his beer across the table to Pat.

"So? What are you doing with your beer?" Pat inquires, confused.

The Robinsons, still waiting for the hostess, catch sight of Chris and approach the table. He stands, extending a hand. "Hi, Mr. and Mrs. Robinson. Hey, Staci. What a surprise." His voice sort of cracks on "surprise"—a total Peter Brady "When it's time to change, you've got to rearrange" moment. I'd sure like to rearrange myself the hell out of here, with Chris pushing his beer away like a lameass.

Mr. Robinson, a big guy in a cheap suit, says, "Fancy meeting you kids here. Having a nice time?" He glances down at the drinks, eyes lingering a little too long.

"Yes, yes sir, fine time. This is Sal, Abbie and my cousin Pat. We're getting ready to go to a play, the one at the Arts Center."

Our waitress approaches, balancing a stacked tray on her shoulder. "Pardon me, please."

The Robinsons move aside and Chris sticks out his hand again. "Well, looks like our food's here. It was good to see you. I'll look for you Sunday."

They wish us well and head back to the hostess stand. After our waitress leaves, Pat breaks the uncomfortable silence. "So what the hell was that all about, Chris, pushing your beer over my way? Who cares if they see you with it? It's not like you're getting drunk or anything."

Chris looks down. "I know, it's stupid. I've just been so worried about what everybody thinks of me for so long it's hard to break the habit. Plus, I know the Robinsons, they would get the wrong idea if they saw me with that beer. I should've never ordered it."

This whole scene is a turn-off to me. Not the fact Chris doesn't really drink—I actually like that. It's just that he is so worried about what these people will think of him for having one lousy beer. What about that "Judge not others" scripture? Did the Robinsons overlook that one? From the way Mr. Robinson checked out the drinks on our table, I'd say he did. That's one thing I like so much about Franco, he doesn't care what anybody thinks. He's his own man. And Chris, obviously, is not.

"I'm going to the ladies'," I announce, needing a break from the double date action.

"I'll hit the boys'," Sal says, following me to the lavatories.

"Well, Chris really likes you. He hasn't taken his eyes off you the whole time we've been here," Sal whispers once we're out of earshot.

"Really?" I respond, not thrilled.

"Yes, haven't you noticed?"

"Well, I guess," I say, as we approach the bathrooms.

Right before we go our separate ways, Sal grabs my arm and whispers, "Have you noticed Pat looking at our waiter?"

"Noooooooo," I say, trying to convey in one word that he's being a complete idiot.

He looks around the dining room. "Well, it's just that once he told me he likes blondes. And of course I'm not blonde, I'm brunette. I don't know, I just noticed him staring at him a few times. And he *is* a knockout."

"This is getting ridiculous, Sal," I say, bladder getting fuller by the second.

"I don't know. I'm having a bad skin day too. I'm getting a zit. I can feel it."

He points to a faint red spot on his cheek that's practically nonexistent. "Sal, listen to me. You have perfect skin, okay? And you are so cute. Pat is in love with you, he wouldn't be with you if he wasn't. The only risk you run of losing him is by excessively acting so insecure and jealous. And you truly have no reason to act like that at all."

"Did he tell you that? That I was insecure and jealous?"

I sigh. "He didn't have to."

He frowns and goes back to petting the invisible zit.

"Look, Sal, I'm about to explode. Meet me at the table."

After I pee, I wait a few moments to make sure Sal has done his business, allowing extra time for his zit evaluation. When I'm certain the coast is clear, I surreptitiously hit the pay phone sandwiched between the boys' and girls' rooms. After kissing my quarter for good luck and dropping it in the coin slot, I dial Franco's number—*A-C-I-D.* Please please be home. Somehow knowing his whereabouts would make all the difference right now, but by the third ring I know it's not going to happen. The machine picks up and I slam down the receiver. I refuse to leave a message since he hasn't even called me yet today.

I fish another quarter out of my bag and call in for my messages. Maybe he's called and has already left. At the beep I punch in my code, two-one-three, and wait for the tape to rewind. It begins to play: *beep beep beep*—me punching in for the messages just now. Our only phone call.

"Fuck it," I mutter, heading back to our table. I glance back at the pay phone, silently cursing it and Franco and my empty answering machine tape.

I feel even worse when I slide back into my seat than when I left it five minutes ago. Chris looks over at me, starry-eyed, and goes, "I really hope we can do this again." He really said that, no lie.

THREE HOURS later, we're on my doorstep. Pat and Sal wait in the car, fighting about Pat's alleged crush on the guy who played the young Bill Clinton in the play. "Well, I had an interesting time tonight," I say, meaning it.

Things got better after the restaurant. The play, *Gen and Willie*, turned out to be liberal and was really good. All the way home Chris and I debated over whether or not Bill should have ever been elected. Even though I didn't agree with most of what Chris said, I respected the fact that he was intelligent and knew what he was talking about. Not to mention the fact he's a damn good debater, like he was practically swaying *my* opinion, for Chrissakes. And since words excite me beyond belief, this was a major brownie point for Chris.

"Hey, me too. I had a great time."

It's the moment I hate—that moment you're like are we going to kiss or aren't we? Given the beer episode and everything I know about the guy, my money's on the no-kiss option.

Chris leans over and plants a kiss above my eyebrow, then one on the bridge of my nose. "So would you like to go out again? Just the two of us?"

With the good-debater and forehead-kisser combo working, he cannot be denied. "Sure, that sounds like fun. Give me a call next week."

This bigass grin takes over his face and I feel like such a bitch for not really liking him as I turn the key, waving with my free hand. As soon as the door is shut I dart to the answering machine, heart full of hope. The red light is blinking so I push play.

Beep beep beep. Me calling in for the nonexistent messages, how depressing. Then George telling me she's at Rob's. Then no more messages, meaning Franco hasn't called. And if you think I'm fucking calling him, you're crazy. You really, really are.

Chapter 11

"So he called me like six times over the weekend, talking about you."

"Did he?"

"Yes," Pat continues, "six, maybe seven . . ."

It's Monday morning. Pat and I are having coffee in the Commons after finding a note on Fredrique's door saying he was snowed in on his ski trip and couldn't make it in until tomorrow.

". . . and I am telling you, Chris likes you in a big way. I mean, he's holding off on calling because you told him to wait until next week, which is now this week, but he is really pumped over the romantic possibilities here."

"Hmm. Well, great, I guess." I honestly wish I liked the guy more than I do, it's just one of those things. I think even if Chris wore different clothes or had longer hair, I still wouldn't really be as into him as I am Franco. Like if you don't really like oatmeal, you just don't like it—no matter if you sprinkle it with cinnamon or sugar or whatever. If you're not into oatmeal, you're just not into oatmeal. And I'm not into oatmeal. Or Chris, its human equivalent.

Pat looks at me, coffee cup next to lips, expectant.

"Okay, I like him and everything, Pat, although the beer thing was weird. He's cute and sweet and a really good talker . . ."

"And I know how you are about words," he says, giving me this knowing look. He knows me damn well, he really does.

"Yeah, but Franco he's not, you know? Franco's all I can think about these days."

Pat runs a hand through his hair and takes another gulp of coffee. "I should've guessed this Franco would ruin things. So have you seen him this weekend or what?"

"Nope, he's out of town," I answer, although I have no idea where he is and am going ballistic over the fact he hasn't called since I saw him Wednesday. Five days. I know we're not like boyfriend-girlfriend or anything but to not call someone for five whole days is a dick move, plain and simple.

"Oh. Well, Chris likes you a lot. A lot more than Sal liked me this weekend," he says into his coffee cup.

I touch his arm. "What's up with you and Sal? Don't say anything about this please but outside the bathroom he was asking me if I noticed you staring at our waiter during dinner. Then we both know what went down at the play, him spazzing over the young Bill."

"He really thought I was trying to go backstage to get the guy's phone number when all I was doing was going to the john. Jesus. We pretty much fought all Friday and Saturday, but things seemed better last night." He shrugs, a who-knows gesture. "So what'd you do this weekend?"

A jerky change of subject, but I get the hint. He doesn't want to talk about love troubles at the moment. Since I don't either, I decide to leave out the details of what consumed the better part of my weekend: depression over Franco's non-call. "Saturday night George—pardon me, Gigi—and I went to Twenty-one twenty-three."

Mouth full of donut, he garbles. "That meat market? How was it?"

George wanted to try out her look—black spray-painted-on spandex dress and spiked heels—at a club. And she really did get hit on more than usual, but mainly by geeks. Pretty much all the guys there were nonevents, with a few exceptions. I make a face, thinking about the loser who asked me if I was tired because I'd been running through his mind all night. Guys who say shit like that depress me, they really do. "My mom always tells me hot boys don't hit on us because they're intimidated, which sounds like a crock. I mean, you're a boy, tell me—why is it that geeks aren't intimidated by girls like me but cute boys are?"

He waits a few seconds before answering. "I'd say it's because geeks basically have nothing to lose."

I nod, thinking of the countless lameass nerds who have

developed crushes on me over the years. "I guess. So things are looking up with you and Sal?"

"For now. But anything could happen."

"Yep," I answer, thinking of Franco. "Anything could."

Home in front of the answering machine again. Two messages: one from George, at the plastic surgeon's office getting her consultation, and the other from Chris asking me out for tomorrow night. No Franco for the fifth day in a row. I am really sick of this shit.

Chris's machine picks up: "Hey, this is Chris. I hope this is Abbie. I'm at work so leave a message and I'll call back. Bye, Abbie." Man, sweet. I leave a message accepting the invitation and telling him to call me.

Abbie is an idiot. Here she has this guy bringing her flowers, spending mondo bucks on her and leaving personalized outgoing messages for her on his machine and she's not even caring. Instead she's brooding over a boy who has spent probably four dollars on her ass and hasn't called in over a hundred hours. So very like her.

This is it, I'm sick of being blown off like a damn wallflower. If he's dissing me, at the very least I deserve an explanation. And I intend to get one if it kills me.

I pound on Franco's door with force, like a cop knocking at the door of a drug house. Jane starts yelping and I can hear the TV on in the living room, the bings of a game show bell coming in loud and clear. How could he just be sitting there petting his dog and watching television as if nothing is wrong? I bang on the door again, infuriated. After Parker, I said I'd never chase after a jerk again. Yet here I am, doing just that. Shit. I kick the door in disgust. I wish I didn't like Franco. Kick. I wish I was in love with Chris. Kick. I wish Franco would open the goddamn door. Kick kick kick.

Before I have a chance to perform my I-wish-I-never-met-Franco kick, Franco, wrapped in a blue bedsheet, opens the door. Rumpled hair, crust in eyes, dried saliva in corner of mouth. "Hey, what's up?"

What's up is that you haven't called me in five days and it's three in the afternoon and you're still in bed and I need to know what the hell's going on.

I smile. "Oh, nothing much, just in the neighborhood."

"I was asleep. Come on in."

I follow him to his room, which looks about the same as it did Thursday morning when I left. He lies back down and I sit on the edge of the bed, petting Jane.

"So what have you been doing?" I ask, wondering if he plans to just go back to sleep or what.

He closes his eyes. God, does he not want to look at me or what? "My friend Byron from California flew in Thursday night. He's loaded—he works for a television station down there. He was in for this convention and had this killer suite at the Anarole. We're talking like three hundred bucks a night. So we get this idea to pretend we're Raoul and Doctor Gonzo from *Fear and Loathing in Las Vegas . . .*"

I do love that book. Hunter S. Thompson kills me, he really does.

". . . doing mescaline, acid, cocaine, uppers, downers—the whole shebang. We rented a convertible like they did in the book and watched *Viva Las Vegas* and one of those Las Vegas travel videos about twenty times each. The next best thing to being there."

"Whoa," I respond. So he was too wasted to call. At least he has a reason, I guess. A weak one, for sure, but a reason nonetheless. And he was with his best boy friend, not like he was screwing around on me with another chick or anything. But then again, what kind of dumbass would he be if he did tell me he was with another girl, even if he was?

"So Byron left last night and I've been crashed out ever since. What time is it, anyway?"

"I think it's around three."

He yawns. "Oh shit. Listen, I hate to be rude but I've gotta catch some more z's before Tim picks me up for work at four-thirty. I am seriously a zombie right now."

"Work?" Knock me down. The boy has a job.

"Yeah, well, it's kind of embarrassing, but I sell my sperm a couple of times a week. I'm also maintenance man for this place whenever they need me. Plus I work at Joe's Liquor like one or two days a week."

A stockbroker he's not, but at least he's employed. If you can call it that. "So you give sperm? That's interesting."

He looks down at his hands, possibly blushing—it's hard to tell. "Well, it's good money, twenty-five a time. And I do it for other reasons too, but it's kind of a long story." He pauses, maybe debating on whether to tell me the kind-of-a-long-story or not. "So, on the nap action, you're welcome to join me. In fact, I'd love it if you did. I've missed you a lot and told Byron all about you."

Franco told his best friend all about me, Abbie McPhereson? He was hanging with his homey from crossfuckingcountry and—okay, he didn't call—but he did tell him all about me. And now a nap invitation. I translate this to mean that he wants to mug, which is fine by me. I lie next to him, gently kissing his cheeks and his nose and his chin before planting one on his lips. Franco kisses back and puts his hand on my back, slowly trailing it down to my butt. I kiss harder but after probably sixty seconds he stops responding. I pull away, confused, noting that his breathing is regular and his eyes aren't opening. He's asleep.

I try to just rest and enjoy the nearness of Franco, I do, but a tiny voice immediately starts chattering in my head, making sleep impossible. When the little "Why the hell are you here? This guy hasn't called you all weekend and now has fallen asleep seven minutes after you arrived" voice has grown into a full-fledged scream, I get up and leave. Franco doesn't stir when I depart.

George is in the living room when I get home, leafing through a stack of magazines. "Oh good, you're home. I'm about to go to Rob's for the night." As I approach, she unfolds a centerfold of a blonde Miss September with cantaloupe breasts. "What do you think of these, Ab? Too big, you think?"

She has really lost it. "Well, I hate to make a judgment call about something of such importance without thinking about it first. Can I sleep on it and tell you tomorrow?"

George nods and continues to study the centerfold. She must think I'm being serious.

Without telling her about Franco or asking how her consultation went, I go to my room and fish under my bed until I find the empty TV dinner tray I swiped from Franco's Thursday morning. I hold it in my lap, looking at my reflection in its silver surface. Some of the mashed potatoes that were stuck to the sides have gotten all crusty, flaking to the bottom of the tin. Not unlike my hopes for me and Franco, getting all dried up and floating to the ground, like pennies down a well or meteors from the sky. Flaking away to nothingness.

I lie down on my bed, cradling the aluminum pan like a baby, until the voice in my head goes away, the one that says boys like Franco will never care about anyone but themselves and I'm the stupidest girl in the world to hope they will.

When I sleep I dream that Parker and I are on a railroad track. I kiss his eyelids and hold his callused hands and tell him he was my first love but not my last, and then he dissipates like a morning fog. And finally for the first time I am free of him and all boys like him. In my dream, I am free.

After the nap I'm ready at last to tackle the Runway Collection assignment I avoided all weekend. What attitude will my clothes have? I think the sick-of-boys-who-would-rather-be-with-their-friends-getting-messed-up-than-being-with-me attitude would be good. But I know it's time to forget all of the Y-chromosome types and get down to business. My future career is on the line here.

I get out my sketchbook and start to lay out some plans. I'll create clothes with colors named pumpkin, plum, grape, mango. All fruit names. That's a start. Deep, rich colors inspired by some of the nation's finest produce departments will abound. I draw a few lines, mind whirling. The attitude is carefree. Miami. Bright, bold, in your face. Donna Karan with an edge. This is good. My hand can't keep up with my mind: the ideas are flowing like beer at a keg party.

I close my eyes, seeing it all. Carmen Miranda hats on the runway, like the one I wore at Darcy Durby's when I was

Chiquita Banana. Boys with shaved heads and purple and green body paint modeling grape-print boxers. Dried fruit as accessories. White little dresses with big green apples all over them. Lots of sheer, inspired by grapes' skin.

No waify models on my runways. And no pale faces. Tons of blush, vats of red lipstick, false lashes like I wore with Chris the other night aplenty. My line will be about glamour with a sense of humor—Audrey Hepburn times Janeane Garofalo. Fun sophistication, nothing that takes itself too seriously.

As I bury myself in my work, I remember how much I love design and how damn good I am at it, two things I've almost forgotten since meeting Franco. Here and now I make a solemn vow to get back into myself and quit worrying about boys in general, something I've been doing way too much of lately. After all, I don't need a boy to be happy. Nope. I return to my pad and get lost in my drawings.

The phone jingles, yanking me back to reality. I drop my pen, wondering if it's Franco. After the second ring, I pick my black pen up from the floor and draw another sure stroke, letting the machine pick up the call.

Chapter 12

"So you ready to discuss your concept?"

"Extremely, incredibly, absolutely. You should check out all the ideas I have, Pat. Last night I spent four hours on it and it felt more like four minutes."

"It's so cool when that happens, when time flies," Pat says. We're in class, it's Tuesday morning and I feel like a new woman. A talented one who won't put up with anybody's shit.

"Guess who I have a date with tonight? Your cousin," I announce gleefully.

Pat smiles, proud-like. "I know, he told me. He said he tried to call you last night to set the plans but you weren't home or something."

"I got his message this morning. I'm calling him right after class to figure out what's up."

He brushes a stringy lock out of his eye. "Yeah. I think he's scared you were blowing him off maybe. I'm happy you're not. He's really a good guy."

"I know," I say, looking down at my *Abbie Hearts Franco*–covered notebook. "I know."

Fredrique cruises in, sunburned. "*Hola*, class. We won't be meeting for two weeks, so you can devote all your time to doing whatever it is you plan to do for your collections. I suggest maybe designing something in this time frame, but look where that got me." He narrows his eyes and pauses. "For now I would like you to get up one person at a time and explain your concept. Show us what the collection has got to be. Slowly, so I can take proper notes." So he can gather ammunition to annihilate us, I bet. He finds a chair in the back and I hop up, wanting to get mine over with.

Behind the battered podium, I present everything I worked on last night, getting more excited with each unveiled sketch. Everything sounds even better than I remember it sounding yesterday. My illustrations, while rough, have an energy that jumps out at you from the page. By the time I show the last design—mango feather jacket over peach-and-mango-striped top—I am feeling pretty damn conceited. I rule this school.

"Well," Fredrique says when I'm done, beady black eyes piercing into mine. I smile, preparing for the praise that's bound to be next. I'm a bridesmaid waiting to catch the bouquet, a kid on parade sidelines anticipating a shower of suckers and mints. "I don't intend to be embarrassed at this show, but that's exactly what will happen if all of you have followed McPhereson's lead. This isn't high school art class and we're not just playing around. This is real life, a real show, real designs. And in this case, real disappointing. Needs work, and a lot of it. You may be seated."

His bitter words wrap around my heart like twine, each syllable strangling my ambitions and hopes. Fredrique's speech is an amoeba, sucking me dry of every ounce of happiness and confidence in my being. Tears blur my vision as I scurry to grab the papers I so painstakingly poured my guts onto last night. I should say something, anything, defend myself, tell him . . .

"Where do you get off? Are you blind or something? Abbie's designs are hands down the best around." My eyes dart up and land on Pat, jumping out of his seat and bellowing loudly. A rush of love hits me as I listen to my best bud defend my honor.

Fredrique smiles and puts his fingers together, steeple style. "Let's hope not. And I'll take your little outburst as a sign you would like to go next."

Pat glares at him for a minute, then looks over at me with a sympathetic shrug, like "What can I do?" I smile, grateful for his efforts. Salty tears drip onto my gums as I sink into a plastic chair, sketches pressed tightly to my chest. What someone else thinks of my designs shouldn't determine how I feel about them or about myself. But somehow Fredrique's words have convinced me that I absolutely and totally suck. The bastard.

— — —

"So THEN HE told me I should just throw away my shit and start over," I say in between bites of spaghetti. Chris and I are halfway into Official Date Number Two, which would have never come to pass if he wasn't Pat's cousin honestly, and I'm filling him in on Fredrique's evil ways.

"What's this guy's number? I'd like to ask who died and made him King," Chris says, his expression somewhere between sympathetic and angry.

"Yeah, no kidding. So then I started practically bawling right there. I just about lost it, I was so upset," I screech, voice carrying all over the damn place. I'm quite loud at times. I really am.

"I wish I could've been there to hold your hand." Chris smiles and pats my arm. For some reason this statement annoys me. It sounds too whipped and maybe even a bit wimpy coming from his lips. I feel bitchy even thinking this, but the annoyance prickling my brain is real. Why is it that a potential dick like Franco could say "Hey, babe, bring me a beer," and I'm swooning, but a nice guy says he wants to hold my hand and I'm annoyed? Jeez. I need some psychological help.

"You'd hold my hand? Thanks, that's sweet." I grin at Chris and feel even more guilty. "Where was I? Oh, yeah. I'm crying almost and sitting down in my chair and then all of a sudden Pat gets up and starts freaking out on Fredrique, totally standing up for me. He is just the sweetest."

"Yep, my cousin the rescuer." He takes another bite of lasagne and swallows, not one to talk with his mouth full, Mr. Manners. "He's forever been that way. When we were in first grade he always won this thing called the Friendly Frog Award for being so nice all the dang time. I remember I was really jealous because I wanted to win bad but I never did, not once. If he wasn't helping some old lady down the stairs, he was putting a Band-Aid on some kid's skinned knee or something. I think the whole family expected him to be a doctor or a dentist. Or maybe a priest. But never, ever, a designer."

I give him a look, one of those don't-put-down-my-life's-ambition-if-you-wish-to-be-spared-a-kick-in-the-shins glares I'm so famous for. Chris starts stammering wildly and loosens his tie.

"Uh, not that a designer is anything bad or anything. I think it's a really neat career and all. I do, really, it's creative and it's . . . uh, you know, it really requires a lot of artistic talent. You, for instance, have a tremendous talent—it's obvious by the designs I've seen you wear, like that dress you have on right now. And vision, you have to have a lot of vision, um, about what people will want to wear a year from now. Almost a psychic thing, really, when you think about it . . ."

He is totally trying his darndest here to kiss my butt so I decide to let him live. "Okay, you're off the hook. And don't worry, you're not the first to say 'fashion designer' like that, like—and don't get me wrong, a lot of people do this—but you said it like it wasn't a real profession. Like how a little kid says 'liver.' Or that's how I took it, anyway."

He takes a big gulp of water, Adam's apple hula-dancing against starched collar. "I didn't mean it like that, Abbie, you know I didn't. I have a lot of respect for your talent. I was just telling my mom on the phone today what a good designer you are. I'd like you to meet her someday."

"Oh really?" He's telling his mom about me? And wanting to introduce us? Not a good sign. I've told my mom about him, don't get me wrong, but that's different. Girls usually tell their mothers about who they're dating. Guys don't. But that's me being stereotypical—I'm sure some guys tell their moms about girls they like. Or maybe girls they really like. But does Chris really like me, enough to tell his mom about me and my design abilities? And want to introduce us, when she lives in damn Michigan or somewhere? A look into his moony eyes tells me yes.

I feel a little sick. "Would you excuse me?"

"Sure—you okay?" Chris asks with wrinkled brow.

"Yes, something just didn't agree with me, I guess." I hop up and flee to the bathroom. I am having major guilt pangs here—for wishing Chris was Franco, for getting irritated when he says sweet things, for feeling panic instead of pleasure when I look into his adoring gaze.

I push open the bathroom door and go to the mirror, staring at the face of a heartless wench. As I apply more lipstick, I try to talk myself out of this sick feeling I'm getting. Maybe I need a plan. Okay, Abbie, give Chris a chance, at least until the date is over. You aren't comfortable with his niceness because you've never had a sweet guy before. There's not really an attraction, this is true, but he's really into you and maybe he'll grow on you, in time. This is the kind of guy your mother would love. The type who would never go five days without calling you. The type who wouldn't get wasted drunk at a concert. The type who wouldn't pawn your VCR. The type you should like.

I smack my lips and kiss the mirror, leaving thin red lines of wax on its shiny surface. The little voice in my head is right. I know it, and I vow to give Chris a chance for the rest of the evening. This is a guy who won't screw me over like the rest of the jerks I've dated. A boy with a car, a job, a future, a huge crush on me! And of course I'm not excited about him, but that's just me being stupid. Do I want the loser with a substance problem who doesn't call or the nice boy with a career who takes me on dates? I've always been known to pick the loser in this scenario. But not this time. I'm going to like Chris if it kills me.

"So I HAD a really interesting time tonight," I say under a sky full of stars. I'm not lying, it was interesting and all, but more in the way a documentary is interesting. Chris is a black-and-white documentary and Franco is a Technicolor feature flick.

"Yeah, me too. The movie sure was good. Whew. You really know how to pick 'em, Ab." It's that awkward end-of-second-date moment—a step above the end-of-first-date one we shared Thursday. Now you know you're probably going to kiss but you don't know if you should start or wait for him to initiate it or just shake his hand and forget the whole thing.

"Well, time for the good-night kiss," I trill. None too subtle, I know, but I'm hoping that kissing Chris will spark a feeling in me that's been missing in action thus far.

"Oh? Is it?" He leans in and our lips touch tentatively. As the lip-lock gets heavier, I wait for a tingle. A bang. Something. Anything.

Nothing.

I pull away and smile, cursing my hormones for remaining inactive. It was a good enough kiss, not too much or too little pressure, but I could've been kissing my brother for all the excitement it wrought. "Chris, thanks for tonight. It was fun."

He nods eagerly and his voice lowers an octave. "I wish I could stay over and snuggle with you. You could be my teddy bear."

There's that annoyed feeling again. I laugh nervously.

"But I know we can't do *that*, so I'll just have to dream about you tonight instead," he whispers, the starlight bouncing off his gelled locks.

I laugh again, wishing Chris would just stop talking because his every whipped word is grating my frayed nerves. My annoyance, coupled with enormous guilt for not falling in love with him, is giving me one hell of a headache.

After our goodbyes, I slam the door and dash to the machine. No messages, meaning no call from Franco. Realizing I'm being pathetic, I pick up the phone to make sure it's in working order and of course it is. Too bad I can't say the same for my brain.

Two IN THE afternoon and I'm still in bed, not because I'm tired but because I have no reason to get up. My designs reek, so there's no point in working on them. Franco still hasn't called, so I have no date to prepare for. And talking to Georgette will just mean having to vocalize my feelings about Chris and hear a lecture. Or worse, having to check out the latest set of knockers she's coveting. The only thing that seems worth dragging my butt out of bed for is food, and last time I checked, the cupboards were a bit on the Mother Hubbard side. I close my eyes again and try to go back to sleep. The ringing phone prevents this from happening.

Please be Franco please be Franco.

"Hello?" I answer in a voice I hope sounds somewhat seductive.

"Hey, Ab, something in your throat? You sound weird."

Not Franco. I go back to my normal tone and tell Pat something must be wrong with our phone. He asks me to lunch but, even though I'm starving, I decline due to lack of *dinero*. My student loan check still isn't in yet. He says he'll bankroll if I give him some Sal advice. Apparently, shit hit the fan last night and he threw a Rubik's Cube at him. Rubik's Cube? I didn't even know anyone still owned one of those relics. I'm about to be polite—like "No, I can't let you pay" or whatever—but my stomach growls so ferociously I forgo the niceties and tell him to get the hell over.

I THROW ON some overalls and twist my hair into two baby braids, clasping the ends with yellow plastic barrettes decorated with a duo of ducklings. When Pat knocks, I am staining my lips with dampened cherry Kool-Aid mix, a trick I learned in some teen magazine.

"Hey, baby. You're looking very grade two today," he exclaims, kissing my cheek.

That being the look I'm going for, I grin. "And you look very much the fifties father this afternoon."

He does, too. He's the picture of 1952 as he plops down on my couch in light yellow Boy-Scout-Den-Leader button-up shirt, navy Dickies and black patent leather mailman shoes. Pat dresses like my ideal man, like even when he's just kicking it, the boy looks together. When people ask us if we're a pair, which happens just about always, Pat always says yep, we're a pair of freaks. That just about kills me every time.

"Why is it that we're still trying to capture the past in our wardrobes?" I wonder. Like whatever happened to dressing for the future?"

I tip my head to the side and ponder, plopping beside him. "Who knows, baby doll. Maybe our past is our future. They say history always repeats itself, like a broken record. Or my dad during a lecture."

Pat cracks up. "Does your dad still repeat himself like he always used to?"

My dad notoriously gets totally hooked on one phrase and can't stop saying it for days, until another one takes its place. I tell Pat how my mom called me a couple of weeks ago and said they went on a road trip with her sisters, who are both divorced, and Dad kept going "To keep a man, you've got to keep his stomach full and his balls empty" over and over. Like she said he repeated it about a hundred-something times.

Pat's jaw drops. "Your dad did not say that."

"Uh-huh, he did. And what's sad is that is pretty much his

philosophy on the subject of boys. Of course, he'd never say as much to his virgin daughter or anything."

"Nope, never. You were pretty much the perfect little girl, though, right? Wasn't Parker your first go at ball-emptying?"

Grossed out, I slap Pat's arm. "That is such a disgusting way to put it. I can't even believe my dad says that. But, yeah, Parker was the first. And I was like eighteen, which was ancient compared to the rest of my friends. And I've still only slept with two guys—Parker and Michael—and I'm almost twenty. That's one every ten years."

"I think I need some salsa in my bloodstream to continue this conversation. Let's go."

Two enchiladas and one margarita later, Pat and I have passed the sex topic and are still hooked on topic number two, Fredrique. Ever since he railed into me the other day, I've been totally depressed. I mean, it's one thing if an ex-boyfriend thinks you suck or something—like who cares, plus that gives you all the more reason to succeed so he can open up *W* or watch "Entertainment Tonight" or go in Neiman-Marcus and see your name plastered all over the goddamn place. Like if I'm tired and don't have the strength to finish a design or something, I just think of Parker's face when he's looking at my kickass dress on the racks. Or better yet, his face when he's ringing up my twelve-hundred-dollar dress as a damn cashier. That fuels me. But if your instructor thinks you reek, particularly if he's the instructor of the only class you have left to get your Associate's, it's another story.

We bitch about Fredrique through the whole main course. There's loads to say. Take a guy like Fredrique, bitter and all, and put him in a position of power—you're basically screwed. Like he wants us to be taught *about* him, not by him. Maybe I'd be the same way, who knows. You take away people's dreams and they're completely fucked, they really are.

Pat signals to our big-haired waitress and points down to his empty glass, the international I-need-another sign—a sign I'm a little too familiar with after countless dinners with Parker, most of those dinners and I-need-anothers paid for by me. But Pat, unlike Parker, usually never has more than one drink—especially at lunch.

"Could your alcohol consumption have anything to do with Sal and the story you still haven't shared with me?" I ask, pointing to his glass.

"In a word, yes. But first tell me what's up with you and Chris."

I feel weird talking about Chris to Pat since he's his cousin. Like it's one thing if I call my cousin Russell "trailer-park," but if someone else calls him that it's like that person's dissing my family and that's just not cool. Plus, it's not like Chris and I have any sort of future together with me feeling like I do. Nausea is more likely than nuptials when it comes to me and Chris at this point.

"Well, okay, here's the deal. He's like too nice or something. It sounds stupid, but it really turns my stomach. Like I'd say jump and he'd say how high, that type of thing. And he's a great guy, don't get me wrong . . ." My voice sort of trails off. Like I don't even know what the hell I'm feeling, how can I articulate it?

"But?" Pat's brows shoot up and I know he wants to know all the details but I can't tell him. I just can't. Like I cannot with clear conscience tell Pat that Chris and I went to this movie and I was like, "So on a one-to-ten, what did you think?" and he goes, "Oh, probably a seven-and-a-half." And I said, "So it doesn't rank up there with the very best, huh?" and he goes, "No, it doesn't rank up there with you." It sounds bitchy, but that little exchange really made me think, Damn, this guy is whipped already.

"I guess I just need more of a challenge," I say with a shrug, picturing Chris and his Moon Pie grin. Pat's disappointed because he says he's tired of seeing me with losers and druggies and moochers, a trio of words that just about covers all of my ex-loves. But if it's not there, it's not there. I wonder aloud if it's still there with Sal.

Pat scratches the top of his head. "I've been pretty happy until recently. You know—good friends, alright job, school's going okay, supercool boyfriend. But now the supercool boyfriend isn't being so supercool anymore, and I don't know how to handle it. So I'm reduced to drowning my sorrows at La Casa Taco. Depressing."

I flash back to my bathroom meeting with Sal at the Old San Francisco Steakhouse, when he was freaking out over the waiter and Pat's supposed obsession with him. "Is it still the jealousy thing?"

"Yep, but it's gotten worse. Like he doesn't even know I'm here with you right now. I told him I was going to the library."

I shake my head in disbelief. "Why would he care if you were out with me? Your best friend? It's not like I'm going to attack you between the enchiladas and sopapillas, for Godsakes."

Big Hair approaches and sets two margaritas-on-the-rocks on our table. "Did I hear someone say sopapillas?"

I smile, my gaze going from her Aqua Net–covered 'do down to the drink I didn't order. "Oh, I didn't want anoth . . ."

"I'll drink it," Pat says, sliding the glass his way. "And we just need the check."

Oh man, two more margaritas? "Looks like I'm driving the Bug home, thanks to Sal."

Pat tosses his tiny red straw on the floor and tips cocktail number one to his lips, draining the glass in like five seconds. "Yep, Sal. As we were saying, he's even jealous of you, which is beyond stupid. I mean, you two are friends, right? But he's jealous of anyone, including you, who has the one thing he doesn't: blonde hair."

"Oh my God, whatever. Hello"—I grab my right braid and tug—"does he think this is natural? It's not. But if it bothers him so much why doesn't he go buy a box of that L'Oréal shit and be done with the whole thing?" Sal is one insecure nutcase, he really is. Kills me.

"Because he is a totally gorgeous brunette and would look ridiculous as a blonde and he knows it. But the thing is, he is a beautiful, beautiful boy. Is he not? But I tell him one time I like blondes and all of a sudden his self-confidence is out the window and he's convinced I'm going to dump him for the next Brad Pitt who comes along," he says, tipping the now-empty cocktail number two skyward to get every last drop. "It's like, please, give me a little credit here."

"Amen, Patricko," I say, pounding my fist on the table. Sal's making the guy drink out of an empty glass, for Godsakes.

He looks at me intently. "You'd never do that to me, would you, Ab? Be a jealous freak like that?"

I look at him and shake my head from side to side, braids slapping my cheeks. "Nope. I never, ever would."

Two pillowy brown sopapillas covered in a mountain of powdered sugar break our gaze. "Here's the bad news," Big Hair says, setting the check in front of Pat and walking away.

I dig in, looking up at my lunch partner. "No, here's the bad news. We have somewhere *muy importante* to be as soon as we leave here."

He looks scared. "Not the drugstore, Ab. I'm telling you . . . Sal would look awful as a blonde. Remember when Marisa Tomei went blonde? Some people just shouldn't be blondes."

"Not the drugstore—the liquor store. I have this sudden urge for a bottle of cold duck, and you're buying," I say. Bratty as hell.

"Cold duck? Three-dollar nectar of the gods? What's the celebration?" Pat's got this confused look. It's really depressing, him with those empty glasses and that confused gaze. I'm not even kidding.

WE'RE IN THE parking lot of Joe's Liquor and Party Goods and there's Franco, behind a pane of glass, ringing up an old man's bottle of whiskey. Am I a stalker? I feel a little *Fatal Attraction*-ish sitting in Pat's Bug, watching Franco in action. But at the same time I'm mesmerized. The mere sight of Franco is a drug, sending me into a euphoric state. "Pat, should I go in?" I whisper, although there's no way Franco could hear me even if I was shouting.

"Yes, we're both going in," Pat says, scratching his eyebrow. He always does this when he's annoyed, and it doesn't take a genius to figure out who the cause of his annoyance is this time. "We haven't driven twenty minutes for cold duck to just not go in. You're not backing out of this one. Plus I want to meet the guy."

I crouch down in the driver's seat and dig through my purse for my compact. "Do I look okay? I feel sick."

"You look cute. Stunning. And whatshisname's not too dressed up anyway, so I don't know why you're worried about it."

I peek over the dash and take in his pulled-back hair, his Adidas shirt, his tattered jeans. "He is breathtaking," I murmur, my pulse racing.

"Okay, you're drooling. We're going in now before you have an orgasm or something." He swings open the door, hops out and turns toward my crouched-down self. "Well?"

I glance in my compact one more time, inspect my teeth for any hint of the Mexican feast that my stomach is currently digesting and I'm good to go. "I'm coming, I'm coming."

I hop out of the car, trying to look nonchalant in case Franco's watching. A thousand voices run through my brain as we approach the door. "Oh, Franco, I didn't know this is where you worked!" "Hey, Franco, we're just in the neighborhood." "Is it true Joe has the coldest and duckiest cold duck in town?" "Franco, why the hell haven't you called me?"

I push open the door, Pat right behind me. Jangling bells announce our entrance. Franco looks up, flash of recognition crossing his perfect features. "Hey, Abbie! What's up?"

I give him a little smile, an "Oh, Franco, imagine meeting you here!" grin. "Hey, Franco, how's it going?"

He comes out from behind the counter and gives me a hug, glancing over at Pat curiously. "Long time no see, huh, babe?"

We break the embrace and I put my hand on Pat's forearm. "Yep, it's been a couple of days, hasn't it? Have you recovered from your *Fear and Loathing in Las Vegas* weekend?"

"Barely, just barely." Franco looks at Pat and Pat looks at him. Major testosterone tension, I can't even tell you. Franco—clueless to Pat's sexual preference—is definitely jealous, so I skip the introductions. Might as well keep him guessing.

"Well, we just need a bottle of bubbly to celebrate a very special occasion. Can you point the way?" I ask, my voice total Zsa Zsa.

"Sure, sure—are we thinking Asti, for the very special occasion? Or cold duck, for the sort of special occasion?" he asks, leading us to the back. His jeans show him off well, and I am fully enjoying the view. Pat, behind me, puts his hands on my sides, in a mock-boyfriend way. I'm loving this.

"Well, Pat, what do you think? Is it a sort of or a very kind of special?" I ask, my voice as effervescent as the champagne we're purchasing.

"Hmm." He scratches his chin, pondering, and then pulls one of my braids. "Any occasion with Abbie would have to be considered very special, don't you agree, Franklin?"

Franco smiles, eyes shifting from Pat's face to mine. "I'd say so, definitely. Asti it is, then?"

"Yes, Asti it is, Frankfurt," Pat answers, putting his arm around me as we follow Franco to the register. We are both milking this encounter for everything it's worth. If Franco had just called me, simply picked up the phone, he would have been spared this jealousy-inducing scenario. But no, he had to ignore me, to blow me off . . .

"That'll be nine seventy-five," Franco says, placing the bottle into a tall brown bag and avoiding eye contact with both me and Pat. Jealous, no doubt about it.

Pat hands him a ten, grabs both the bag and my arm and turns toward the door. "Hey, guys, your change."

I twirl around, illuminating his dazed expression with my thousand-watt grin. "Keep the quarter and call me with it." It kills me how I came up with that. Fucking brilliant.

Tiny bells jingle as Pat and I exit arm in arm, off to celebrate our very special occasion—me finally giving Franco a taste of his own medicine. When we get to the car, Pat holds the bottle tightly by the neck, lifts it above his head and then slams it down on the hood of his Bug: Captain Stubing christening the *Love Boat*. White suds shower both us and the car as we explode like the bottle of Asti into hysterical giggles.

While Pat unlocks the car, I bend down to retrieve a chunk of dark glass from the soaked concrete and slip it in my pocket. Even though we're certain Franco is watching, neither Pat nor I look up before driving away.

Chapter 13

There are these White Supremacists on a talk show I'm watching and they're making me so mad I want to punch out the TV screen. But of course I hold back because without a television set I would have no form of entertainment whatsoever. Lord knows I have no dates. Friday evening and still no call from Franco. I haven't spoken to him since the liquor store encounter. And Chris has phoned three times but I'm dodging his calls. His last message on the machine, left about an hour ago, said "Phone tag, you're it!" If "it" means a girl who has no date with Franco and wishes Chris would quit calling, then I guess he's right. I am it.

George breezes in, wearing one of my latest chiffon numbers—very ballerina. Her newfound fashion sense and lack of sorority girl clothes is frightening. She's starting to look a little like me.

"Okay, poll time. These, or these?"

She holds up two pictures of nude chicks. Both girls have had their own heads amputated and replaced with little Georgette faces much too small for their naked bodies.

"Oh my God, are those your ninth-grade homecoming pictures? You still have them?" I grab Boob Exhibit A and laugh. Freshman George has the mall bangs working and, no way, pink and blue eyeshadow on. The small-town cosmetics, coupled with the out-of-proportion bod, is hilarious. "You have to give me one of these, George. They're cracking me up."

She snaps the picture I'm laughing at out of my hands, heaves a big sigh and rolls her eyes. "Gigi, Gigi, Gigi! How many times do I have to tell you, Abbie? Please try to help me on this one, please."

I unsuccessfully try to hide a bratty smirk. "Okay, *Gigi.*"

"Thank you. And it's the breasts you're supposed to be checking out, not my little homecoming heads. They're just on there as a point of reference. So you can imagine how the boobs will actually look on me."

"Are you going to get your head shrunk too? These bodies are about ten times the size of your head. Hell, the boobs alone are like six times the size of your face," I say with a laugh. She's really lost it, we're talking bonkers here.

"God, Ab, be serious for one second." George looks pissed. "It's not like I had pictures that would actually fit the bodies. Not everyone has a million pictures of herself like you do."

Ouch. She hit below the belt on that one, as I have probably twenty-plus photo albums stuffed with pictures of me, George and all my friends, past and present. I try to look solemn. "Okay, okay, you got me there. So let's see them again."

She gives me a dirty look, clutching the pics to her chest.

"I swear I won't laugh this time. I promise," I say, hoping I'm up to the challenge. She hands me the first picture apprehensively. I try to think of something sad so I won't laugh. Fredrique bitching me out. Franco not calling. My grandma dying. Parker living.

"Hmm. These seem a little big to me, Geor—I mean, Gigi. How the hell could you balance these for the rest of your life?" I'm not exaggerating. They're bigger than your average grapefruit for sure. Maybe a little smaller than bowling balls, but not much. Too big.

"Yeah, those are probably triple-D size. I don't know. I just kind of think if I'm going to do it I might as well go all the way," she says with a shrug.

"Well, yeah," I say, thinking she has gone completely nuts. "But you have to think about function also. I mean, when you go buy a new car you're not like 'Hell, I'm going to get that hugeass boat over there because if I'm going to buy a car I'm going to go all the way.' You think, 'Hey, I want what's going to fit my needs. The smaller little Rabbit might not be as big as the seventy-eight Cadillac, but it's the more desirable vehicle in my opinion.' We need to start thinking like this about your boobs. Biggest does not equal best, you know?"

"You may have a point," she says, rubbing her chin like we're discussing world peace or something. "Those *are* too big. In fact, they belong to one of those Barbie twins, I forget which one. Probably not a good idea, since I hated Barbie when I was little. What do you think about this set?"

As she hands me the next picture, I feel like we're talking about snow tires or something. Buying body parts like you'd buy groceries makes me a little nervous. I squint down at the boobs before me, trying to picture them on her bod. "Hmm, well, these are better, I guess, but still maybe a little big for your frame. Wouldn't you say they're a bit jumbo? I mean, what are they, D's?"

"Yeah, probably. But D is where I draw the line on minimum size. My mom's a C and she's not really that big. D is definitely the smallest I want them." She looks past my shoulder, probably seeing herself serving buffalo wings to a group of businessmen at Hooters. I hate damn buffalo wings, I really do.

"Earth to George," I call, waving my hand in front of her face. "I'm afraid I'm not going to be much help on this one. You probably need to talk to your doctor."

She smiles, a snooty little grin if I've ever seen one. "I just did. The surgery is March seventeenth. And he said I just need to figure out how big I want them by then."

March 17 is only about a month and a half away. Which means the fashion show is only about three months away, and graduation is right after that. If I even graduate. "Oh, man, I need to get out of here. I keep thinking about Fredrique and the fact that a tasseled hat is not going to be on my head any time soon unless I join the Shriners. It's making me really depressed."

"Abbie, we talked about this yesterday. You just need to talk to the dean next week and get it straightened out. Fredrique can't flunk you. You're the best."

I nod, not convinced. Compliments coming from friends or family don't count because they are totally biased. "Well, whatever. If I'm the best, why hasn't Franco called?"

She sighs like she's terribly fed up with the whole subject. "God, we've been through this too, Ab. He probably thinks Pat's your boyfriend after the way y'all acted in the liquor store. You should just call him."

I shake my head violently. "No way. I'm not calling him. I went out of my way to visit his work and when I was there I told him to call me. I even left him a quarter, for Chrissakes. He has no excuses not to call." Why should I be the one making all the effort here? I'm like the glass of beer after a shot of whiskey, forever the chaser. I'm ready to be the chasee for a change.

"Well, what about Chris? He's called a couple of times. I mean, I know he's no Franco in your book but he's making a lot more effort. And you won't even talk to the guy."

She's right, he has called. But why is it that boys you like never call, and boys you don't won't leave your ass alone? Never fails. "I don't really like Chris. I mean, it sounds lame but the guy is too nice. Like too whipped. And the attraction is really not there."

George rolls her eyes sympathetically—every female I know can relate to the "too nice" syndrome, her included. "Yeah, well, I'm the last person who should be giving you guy advice. Rob hasn't called all day and we're supposed to do something tonight. He hasn't called, huh?"

Hate to be the bearer of bad news, but: "Nope, only damn Chris."

Her eyes light up as she pushes her tits together. "We should go do something tonight. Just you and me. To hell with these guys. We're too good for them anyway. We're women of the nineties. We don't need a guy to be happy. Who cares if they call? I mean, we're not going to waste our whole evening sitting around waiting for their asses to call us. Nope, no waiting by the phone for us . . ."

The phone rings and we both dive for it. Georgette grabs it first.

"Uh—hey, Chris." She looks over at me. I mouth the words "I'm not here," shaking my head vigorously from side to side. She gives me a thumbs-up.

"Nope, you just missed her. I have no idea where she is. But I'll leave her a note that you called, okay?" Her voice is all sincere, we're talking Academy Award here.

She nods while he responds. "Okay, so you want the message to say 'Phone tag, you're still it'? I can do that. Talk to you later.

guy." Why can't it just be Franco and not Chris? I feel guilty as hell sitting here while George out-and-out lies, but I really can't talk to Chris right now, I just can't. George slams the phone down and asks what's up with the phone tag. I tell her don't ask.

A HEAVY metal band is wailing loudly in the center of Samurai, the place we decided to come to drown our sorrows. George, dressed in new black leather pants, is fitting right in with the weird mix of hardcore headbangers and gay boys slugging sake at the bar for the campiness of it all. I, on the other hand, in Donna Reed–meets–Judy Jetson frock, am looking a little out of place. My five-inch platforms make me tower over everyone else and the music is migraine city.

"They have dollar Kamikazes," George yells over the pounding bass. "You want one?"

Kamikaze. The first drink I had with Franco. "Yeah, why not?"

We get the drinks and find a spot at the bar. A wiry weasel-looking guy approaches.

"Hi, I'm Clifford," he squeaks. "Clifford Jones." He has the wrong last name, I'm not even kidding. His cardigan, button-up shirt and khaki pants are total Mr. Rogers. A baseball cap and big glasses complete the geek's look.

I smile. "I'm Abbie and this is Gigi."

He glances over at George and then back at me. "I like your hair," he says in a high, whiny voice.

"Thanks." My hair is nothing spectacular. It's cut in a straight blonde chin-length bob, parted down the middle. Not something many people comment on.

"I'm a—I'm a hairdresser. And your hair is cute. I like it. I like it."

I laugh and wonder if this guy is for real. Is he repeating himself to be funny, or is he really nutso? "Thanks," I say for the second time, wondering when he'll be exiting the area.

"It's cute. It goes like this"—he pushes his hands against his cheeks—"and like this"—he pushes his hands against the top of his forehead and the bottom of his chin—"and it looks good on you."

Georgette kicks my ankle and we exchange a This-guy-is-a-total-freak look. "Well, thanks a lot, man. I'm glad you like it."

He nods vigorously, glasses jiggling. "I like it. It's cute. I'm a—I'm a hairdresser."

You're a—you're a psychopath.

Georgette to the rescue. "Look, Ab, over there. Well, if it isn't old Frazier from San Antone. It's been ages, hasn't it? We must go say hello."

"Frazier? From San Antone? You gotta be kidding. It's been—how long has it been? Seems like forever." This is an incredibly true statement for we know no Frazier from San Antone. "Let's go say hi."

George grabs my arm and yanks me her way. "Nice to meet you, Clifford!" I call as we migrate toward fictitious Frazier.

"I like your—I like your hair," he hollers, wiggling his fingers toward me and my boring bob as George and I make a quick getaway from his psycho hair babble.

"What the hell was up with that guy?" George whispers, dragging me toward the dance floor.

"Who knows. I am a freak magnet, I swear I am." I am, too. Everywhere I go, freaks are drawn to me like moths to a goddamn flame. I don't know why. I look around for cute boys on the dance floor, quickly noting that there aren't any. All of the many longhaired fellows around me have heavy metal hair. I look up at the stage, thinking maybe there'll be someone to look at in the band. All I see are five guys with big hair and bigger egos.

"The bass guitarist is checking you out," Georgette says as we get down to the cheesy cover tune.

I look up and, sure enough, the bass-wielding one is sizing me up. He's holding his instrument between his legs and is crouched on the stage like a tiger about to pounce on his prey. I just pray I'm not the prey he'll be pouncing.

He winks at me and I look away. Any boy who wears more eyeliner than I do is out of the question for me as far as romance is concerned. "Maybe I should just join a convent," I say to George, disgusted.

She laughs. "Yeah. I can see it now: Sister Abigail, she of no worldly possessions, none, which would mean kissing your extensive shoe collection goodbye. And wearing the same black and white outfit day in, day out. And replacing the pics of hot men you tape above your bed with snapshots of Pope John Paul the Third."

"You're right, it's probably not happening." The song ends after a painful drum solo and the singer announces a fifteen-minute break.

"Want another drink?" George asks, tugging on her wedging-up leathers.

"Yeah, as long as we stay away from the guy who likes my hair." I trail her to the bar. When we're almost there, George twirls around and pushes me in the other direction, obviously not wanting to be seen by somebody.

"What's up? Did you see Joe or something?" I whisper while being shoved toward the other bar.

"No, but it's almost as bad. Don't look over there, but Sal is sitting at the bar with a guy and the guy is not Pat." Drop-jawed, I immediately turn around and crane my neck for a glimpse.

Georgette slugs my arm. "God, did I not just say 'Don't look over there'? Jeez, let's be just a little more obvious about it."

"I just can't believe it." I surreptitiously glance over there again. Sure enough, it's Sal sitting very close to some boy who has overdone it with the hair gel this evening, Chris times twenty. "What's up with the gel?"

Georgette puts her hair in her face to shield her stares. "Yeah, no kidding. He's not that cute, huh? Maybe he's a cousin. Or a friend."

I roll my eyes. "Yeah, and I'm a virgin. I mean, let's get real here, George. Sal has his hand on the guy's arm. And the guy just whispered into Sal's ear. Has your cousin Clark ever whispered into your ear?"

"No, but if he had to tell me a secret he might and it wouldn't be weird."

We watch as Gel Boy whispers into Sal's ear, an ear only Pat is allowed to whisper into, for a second time. A high-pitched giggle, which sounds more like it should be coming out of a fifth-grader's mouth than Sal's, ricochets across the room as Sal throws his head back in laughter at something Gel Boy said. Seeing Pat being betrayed like this calls for another round of Kamikazes. Should I go over and say something to Sal? I mean, before he sees me first, which would be even more awkward? But what do I say? "Hey, Sal, who's this guy whispering into your ear? And where is Pat tonight, you remember—your boyfriend? Does he know you're out with another guy? And correct me if I'm wrong here, but aren't you the one who has a heart attack when Pat even so much as looks at another boy? What's that about? And what is up with this guy's hair gel? The glare's bad enough to make a person go blind." A damn no-win, that's what this situation is.

The bartender sets our drinks before us. "On the house, ladies. From the gentleman at the end of the bar. He said something about liking your hair."

Why me?

We down our free shots and look back at Sal, who is clumsily feeding Gel Boy sushi with wobbly chopsticks. "I cannot watch this anymore, George. Let's get out of here before they fuck on the bar."

As MY nonexistent luck would have it, the one and only message waiting for us when we get home is from none other than Pat, and there is just no way I can call him after what I just saw. If I'm the one to tell him about what's up with Sal, he'll only end up hating me for it and I'll in a weird way be the cause of their breakup and I just can't handle it, not now. I explain this theory to George as I wash the evening's cosmetics off my guiltyass face.

"Hold the phone—you wouldn't be the cause of anything. Sal is the one out with another guy, not you. You'd just be reporting it," George cries, mouth full of toothpaste.

"True, but you know how when a few years ago they released that study about how movie popcorn is made with coconut oil and has about a hundred fat grams or whatever? That night, I was so pissed at Grant Shaw, the newscaster. For like a week I wouldn't watch Channel Four because I knew I'd see Grant

Shaw's toupeed ass on there, and he pissed me off. Notice I wasn't mad at the study or the popcorn itself or even at myself for loving the fattening stuff. Nope, I was pissed at Grant for ruining one of my greatest pleasures. Because I knew as soon as he uttered those words I'd never be able to eat movie popcorn guiltlessly again. It would never taste as good to me, now that I knew what I did. And I also knew in my heart that every single tub of corn I order until the day I die will remind me of Grant Shaw. And his red ties. And his toupee that looks like a damp squirrel. That realization made me sick."

Georgette, leaning over to spit, stares at me with that annoyed glare of hers, quite like the one I usually reserve for Grant Shaw. "And how does this relate to anything?"

An exasperated sigh escapes my lips. "Hello, anybody home? Don't you get it? I'm Grant Shaw. And Pat is me and Sal is popcorn and Gel Boy is coconut oil. So I (Grant) report to Pat (me) that his boyfriend Sal (popcorn) is getting it on with Gel Boy (coconut oil) and he'll react the same way I did, by being pissed at Grant Shaw, who in this case is none other than me."

"God, you need subtitles to have a conversation with you lately, I swear," she says, slugging my arm. She's quite sarcastic when she wants to be. "Why is it that when you go out you always see people you don't want to see, but you so rarely run into people you'd like to see? Like why couldn't it have been Rob and Franco that we ran into instead of your best friend's boyfriend with another guy?"

Franco. The weight of his name is like a boot in the face. "Oh man, I want to call."

George, knowing I mean I want to call Franco and not Pat, darts to the living room to guard the phone—its porcelain edges curving like a road to paradise, its twelve buttons begging to be pressed. "I refuse to let you call Franco, Ab. He hasn't called you all night, so why the hell should you call him?"

"I haven't called him all night, so why the hell should he call me?" I know she's right deep down. I shouldn't call his ass. It's just so hard for me not to, when it's totally what I want to do. That's my problem, always doing what I want instead of what I should.

She steps away from the phone, defeated. "I'm going to bed. Do whatever you want."

I plop on the floor and pull the phone down with me. Why won't he just call me, like me, kiss me, be my boyfriend? In a desperate whisper, I turn to a higher power. "Dear God, there are millions of boys on the planet, so why can't just this one measly one fall for me? Is it too much to ask?"

I stare at the phone—half expecting it to ring, knowing it won't—and wonder what it really is I'm praying for.

Chapter 14

When I wake up I'm feeling so blue it takes me like forever to motivate myself to get out of bed. There's a note from Georgette on the table: *Hey Ab, Went shopping for Wonderbra! Drinks at Henry's later? Joe the Elephant is playing!! Rob sucks—time for a replacement!!! See ya at 4! Gigi.* The dots on her *i*'s are not dots but microscopic hearts, filled in with neon purple ink. George has never dotted an *i* with a heart in her life. Or used exclamation points after every sentence, for that matter. Perhaps she's possessed? I'd get out the Ouija board and consult it, had I a Ouija board. Instead I crumple the note and toss it toward the trash can.

I miss.

I don't know why, but for some reason my missing that shot into the trash can makes me cry. Tears stream down my cheeks before I even realize I'm upset over it. I stare at the crumpled wad of paper resting next to the trash can and sob. It's alone on the floor, just like me. Alone. And the whole reason the paper isn't cavorting with the rest of the pieces of paper in the trash right now is because I suck so bad at basketball I can't even make a lousy basket into a trash can.

Basketball is just one of the things I'm lousy at. Most sports are hopeless for me, even though I'm tall and all. I can't sing either. When I used to sing with the radio in my dad's van, he'd sometimes turn down the volume and ask, "What'd you do with all that money?" And I'd be like, "What money?" And then he'd say, "The money you should have spent on singing lessons," cracking up. You know you can't sing when even your dad admits it.

I'm a slob, too. Laundry eludes me. It's hard enough for me

to gather all my stuff and trudge it down to the cleaners. When is the last time I even did laundry? My brow wrinkles as I try to remember. It's been a couple of months, I think. After that B.Y.O. Condom party at Ulysses's. I was totally hung over and the Laundromat was the last place I wanted to be, but I was down to clothes I hadn't worn since ninth grade and didn't have the cash to cover bulk laundry services. So there I was, surrounded by stale, sticky air and the pungent aroma of bleach. The swoosh, swoosh of the washers and whir, whir of the dryers was making me feel even more nauseous. And when all was said and done that day, I'd spent three hours and twenty-four bucks on twelve loads of laundry I didn't end up folding until like three days later. And by that time most of them were so totally wrinkled I just threw them back on my floor until I could afford bulk, where the lady folds them and irons them and everything.

I'm so lazy, it makes me sick.

I sit like this for an hour, maybe longer, thinking of all the reasons my life sucks. I go through every one of my bad qualities, from indecisiveness to inability to pass calculus. I mentally list my physical imperfections: the hips a little too broad, thighs even Suzanne Somers couldn't master, the zit on my chin. I'm going through all the guys I've ever liked who didn't like me back, one by one, when the phone rings.

"Hello," a dejected voice answers. Mine.

"Hey, is Abbie there?"

"Franco?" Instantly my tone changes from funeral home director to kid on Christmas morning.

"Yep, that's me. What's up for tonight?" He's all cool as hell, like we already have plans or something.

"Um, nothing definite yet. My roommate said something about Henry's, but I'm not sure." Like I wouldn't drop any plans for Franco, who am I kidding here?

Franco groans, like someone just kicked him in the shins. "Henry's is lame on Saturdays, man."

"Yeah, that's what I told her." I lie. I have no idea if it's good or not anymore, honestly, because I haven't been there in ages. It sucked the last time I was there—total cover band, cheesy guys—so Franco's probably right about it being lame.

"The Iguana has a beer special going on tonight and a pretty cool band. You wanna go? My friend works the door so he'll probably get us in free. And it's right down the street, so we could walk." Maybe it's just me, but I swear to God Franco sounds positively weirded out. Probably thinking I'll turn him down for Pat or something. Sometimes boys are so predictable.

"Who's playing?" I ask, not wanting to commit quite yet. Let him think I have plans with Pat, serves him right for not calling.

"Double Limbaughtomy. You heard 'em before? They kick ass."

Shit. Rob's band. "I've never seen them, but I know a guy in the band. Rob?"

"No way! You know Cradle?"

"Cradle?" Who the hell is Cradle?

"Rob. Cradle, that's what we call him. I've known that guy forever." Small world. Of all the people for him to know, it has to be George's ex. I can't wait to tell her—she'll really flip.

"Why do you call him Cradle?" I ask, collecting information for future conversation with George.

" 'Cause he's a hardcore cradle-robber. Get it? Cradle Rob." He chuckles, I don't. "That shit cracks me up. One time he was going out with this hot chick, very blonde, and I go to Cradle, 'How the hell old is that girl?' and he goes, 'Well, we're going to the freshman prom next weekend,' and dude was serious!" What a pervert. We can only hope George didn't sleep with the fucking virgin surgeon. "Not college freshman, high school freshman. He likes to break them in, you know?"

"No, I didn't know, not until now." Thank God she's looking for a replacement for his child-molester ass.

"I thought that was pretty much common knowledge about Cradle. How do you know him?" Franco asks. Jealous, maybe?

"Uh, he came over here once. And I've talked to him on the phone a couple of times." I refrain from mentioning that he came over with and called for George. Might as well make him wonder.

He laughs. "You're a little old for Cradle, aren't you? I didn't know he dated girls who could get into rated-R movies without a parent."

The boy is officially out-of-control jealous deep down, I know it. "We didn't date. He was going out with George, my roommate, but she's dating this other really hot guy now." False, but if he's friends with Rob he might let this fact slip, which would be a point in George's favor.

He tells me to ask George and Hot Man to go with us. I don't say it, but I'm thinking that it would be hard for them to attend since one of them doesn't even exist. Instead I go, "Well, she really has her heart set on Henry's, I think. And she and Rob just stopped seeing each other so it might be weird."

"Yeah, might be a bad scene. But you want to go, right?"

If he knew how much, he'd think I was psycho for sure.

I MEET HIM at seven. George freaked when I told her about Rob. Not sad-freaked, more oh-God-that's-too-weird freaked. She modeled her Wonderbra for me and I have to give credit to whoever designed the thing. It turned her nonexistent chest into a hot fudge sundae—her boobs were two heaping scoops of vanilla ice cream and the black lacy bra was the hot fudge. She said she met a guy at Macy's and he's taking her to dinner. He's like an accountant or something, which may mean she's over the wild boys stage. But when I asked her if I could go back to calling her Georgette, she said no. So who knows.

I'm wearing a Boy Scout shirt and jeans. I was going to dress trendier but decided against it, not wanting to be inconspicuous at the Iguana. The crowd there is kind of a mix of post-BMXers, soccer players, people who used to be in bands and now incessantly talk about forming one and people who work in or have worked in record stores. This covers probably ninety percent of the crowd. The other ten percent, probably the category I'd fall into, are people who come for the cheap drinks and/or the band. So the trick is to dress kind of soccerish but not like you're trying to look soccerish. It's tougher than it sounds.

When Franco opens his door, I see he has pulled off the look perfectly. A gas station jacket that used to belong to Bob, white T, jeans and Docs. Hair down, pushed behind his ears. Painful.

"Hey, Bob," I say, pointing at the name tag on his jacket.

"Hey." He pulls me into a hug. Jane is nipping at my ankles and a little of Franco's beer spills on my back.

"You look very pretty tonight," I tell him, walking into his pad.

"And so do you, Den Leader." He covers my right sleeve with his hand. "What's your troop number? Quick."

I laugh, not knowing the number but knowing for sure Franco is smashed. "Uh, fourteen?"

"Wrong," he says, uncovering the number. "Troop Eleven!" I glance at the red and white patches on my yellow sleeve. One one. January 1! The official day I met Franco. Wonder if he's making the connection also?

"Eleven. You know what that is?" he asks, putting his hand on my side.

"Whaaaat?" I smile, thinking I am so psychic.

"How many beers I've had tonight. Eleven." He walks over to the couch and grabs the last beer of the Coors Light twelve-pack. "You want it?"

I hate beer. I've told him I hate beer. I can tell you everything he's ever told me about himself, and he can't even remember that I hate beer. "Yeah, I want it." I pop open the can and take a swig of the lukewarm piss. "Ready to rumble?"

"Yep, let's go." He grabs my hand and leads me out the door.

I wish I was drunk.

Two hours later. My wish came true a few shots back and Franco is taking full advantage of the coin beer special. Since the word go he has been really touchy tonight. Putting his hand on my arm. Brushing his leg against mine. Touching my cheek with his fingertips.

"Eyelash," he says after the cheek touching, holding his thumb out for me to see. "Thumb or index finger?"

"Thumb." I used to do that all the time when I was little. The deal is that when one of your eyelashes falls out you put it on your index finger and press it against your thumb. Then you guess which finger the lash will stick to, and if you're right you get your wish.

"So I'll take the index, I guess." He presses his fingers together and releases. My stray eyelash is on his index finger.

"Your wish comes true, your wish comes true," I sing.

He closes his eyes and squeezes my knee. I wish I could read his mind and know what he's thinking, just for this instant. But of course the eyelash landed on the index finger, not the thumb, so I'm in no position to be making wishes, even if it is just to know what Franco's wish is. His lids open. "Let's do it again, so you can have a wish."

"No can do. We don't have a fresh eyelash," I say. Franco closes his left eye, yanks one of his lashes out and hands it to me. "There. You can have a wish now."

He just pulled out one of his eyelashes for me. So I could have my wish. And his hair is falling from behind his ear and the collar of his gas station jacket is turned under and his seventeenth beer is almost empty and he is looking at me and I think that maybe this is the coolest moment of my life. It absolutely kills me, I swear. An eyelash. Such a little gesture, but God, what symbolism. Adam's rib created Eve. And Franco's lash is creating me. I close my eyes to make a wish, but I'm so happy I can't think of one.

It's maybe an hour later and Franco has his arm around me. I'm ecstatic. Rob, on break, just brought us two shots of Cuervo and when he made the toast, he goes, "To youth." Whatever, Mr. Dating-a-Fourteen-Year-Old. Franco and I just look at each other and crack up, then down the shots and bite into lime wedges. Only someone who has done too many tequila shots understands why its name sounds so much like To Kill Ya. It's harsh. Not as harsh as the sound of the band going into their second set, though. Franco likes them and George told me they were cool, but I'm sorry, Double Limbaughtomy is too Black Flag for me. I don't want to hear any more. I'm ready to go home with Franco. Because I already decided like thirty minutes ago that I'm going to have sex with him tonight.

It was after the eyelash incident. I still had the tiny hair on my index finger, thinking that this is the only guy in my whole life who's ever done something like that for me. Once Parker pierced my nose, and I thought that was special at the time. Like it symbolized my total trust in him. In retrospect all it symbolized was him raping my nose like he raped my emotions and raped my life. It can in no way compare to this. And Parker can in no way compare to Franco.

I looked over at him and put my finger up to my right eyeball, placed his lash in my eye. I guess that's when I knew.

"Something in my eye," I hollered over the music.

He kissed my eyebrow. "Rum drink is my life?" he slurred, repeating what he thought I'd said. I didn't correct him.

Except for Franco forgetting I hate beer and having to listen to three hours of the none-too-soothing sounds of Double Limbaughtomy, the night's been perfect. We just stepped into his apartment, still drunk but slightly coming down.

"I'm spending the night," I announce.

Franco smiles. "Very cool."

I raid his closet for suitable sleepwear and find a big T-shirt and pair of boxers that will do the trick. Not that they're going to be on my bod for long. Franco's feeding Jane in the kitchen and seems kind of nervous, talking to Jane in this too-loud voice. I guess it's awkward because I know that he knows we'll probably have sex and he knows that I know it too. But since we're not talking about it, it makes it even more of a nervous scene. What can you say, though? "Hey, Franco, I want to fuck your brains out tonight." Doesn't really blend well into a conversation. Guess the only option is to pull a yellow pages, let my fingers do the talking. Or is that do the walking? I always forget.

I climb under the covers and Franco comes into the room, stripped down to his boxers, and closes the door. "Jane, you know," he says, pointing to the shut door.

"Yeah, I know. Come here." I pat the spot next to me.

"Don't hog my favorite pillow, McPhereson," he says, yanking the pillow from under my head while he crawls in beside me.

"We'll share." I put my head beside his and then we're kissing. His hands are everywhere: my breasts, my butt, my thighs, my hair. Mine start exploring him too and then he's on the brink, condom in place, when I panic.

"Wait a minute," I gasp, my voice wobbling.

He lifts his face from my ear, breathless. "What, baby?"

"I'm about to sleep with you. Have sex with you," I say, completely freaked.

"You are?" he says, all mock-surprised. I ignore him.

"So I'm about to waste a finger, because now when people say 'How many people have you been with?' it will be three instead of two, practically a whole hand," I ramble, just picturing it now. "Which means soon I'm on my second hand, and next thing you know I'll be on my toes and other appendages."

Franco's tongue is in my ear again, making it harder to concentrate on what I'm saying. I manage. "And I don't know who your third-grade teacher was. Or who you got your first kiss from. Or even what your favorite kind of pizza is. I don't know any of that."

He starts kissing my neck again and goes, real low, "You want to know that?"

My neck is my weakness and he knows it. I squirm around and whisper, "Yes, I do. I mean, you don't even know my middle name, for Chrissakes."

More kisses on the curve of my neck, hands squeezing my tits. "What is it?"

"Sue," I moan.

His mouth moves lower. "Okay, Mrs. Oyler, grade three." Lower. "Tori Spencer, first kiss." Lower. "Pepperoni." Lower, he's there.

"Pepperoni?" I squeak.

He looks up from between my legs and says, calm as hell, "You?"

"Cheese," I gasp, thinking who gives a shit about the damn three fingers, I want him.

He moves back up to my face. "You're incredible. Cheese? Over pepperoni?" His voice is total seduction, like he's talking dirty instead of talking pizza.

"Pepperoni makes me sick," I murmur, feeling him against me. Wanting more.

"Oh, Abbie Sue," he whispers. The clown-covered birthday card I got my baby cousin last week flashes through my brain: *Now You Are One.*

The phone is ringing, jarring me from a deep sleep. I squint over at Franco's digital clock: 8:43 A.M. The sound of his voice breaks the silence. "Hey, this is Franco and Jane. Go ahead and yak, we'll call you back." New message since last time I called. Then: "Hey Franco, this is Tim. I know your ass is still crashed but I'm off to Austin in about five to see Lulu. Ran into Cradle at the Romper and he said he saw you with some chick. You score? Saw Heidi out there too and she said to remind you about the acid party or whatever next weekend. So that's what I'm doing, always a man of my word. I'll come by to pick you up around three tomorrow, so you better be up."

God. "You score?" Thanks for making me feel like a total slut, I think, getting up to go to the bathroom. I throw on the boxers and T-shirt, in a tangled heap on the foot of the bed, in case Franco wakes up before I get back. I'm not real comfortable with him seeing the total package while he sits in bed, covered up. Plus I have a zit on my back that's really embarrassing. Hopefully he didn't see it. But, then again, oh well if he did.

I brush my teeth with a squirt of his toothpaste on my finger. Even though I've had all, and I do mean all, of Franco in my mouth, there is something gross about using his toothbrush. Stupid, I know, but I've always been like that. I'll have to bring a toothbrush over next time. Hell, if there even is a next time.

I spit in the sink and my stomach cramps up, like I might need to go to the bathroom. But I'm sorry, I will not go number two in some guy's bathroom I've just started dating. It's like what if he has to go right after me and grosses out? Or if the scent drifts into his bedroom, waking him up? I'll just have to hold it.

Leaning in close to the mirror, I notice an attractive red spot under my right eye. Great, another zit. Pretty soon I'll be like the perfect poster girl for Oxy or something. Or maybe I could be the official face of that pizza Franco and I were talking about last night, right before we had sex.

And that's another thing. We've had sex now. I look down at my hand. Three fingers, three boys. I remember in ninth grade Maura Branson told me she'd been with two guys and I thought she was such a ho. Now here I am on my third damn finger. What does that make me?

I tiptoe into the living room, being extra careful not to wake Franco or Jane, and fish my foundation out of my purse. Sad I'm applying base at nine on a Sunday morning, but if Franco gets up I hate for him to see me at my worst, on big-blemish alert. Crawl back into bed, hug the edge of the mattress. Franco stirs and kind of snores. Should I move back and lean against him? Or put my arm around him? God, I wish there was a book like *How to Act the Morning After You're Slept with Someone for the First Time.* Best-seller material, for sure. Then at least there'd be something to consult when you wonder if you should fold his boxers you wore last night and leave them on his dresser or if you should take them home and wash them. Or if it's rude to use his shower without waking him up and asking. All of these questions are very much on my mind as I sit here, very quickly realizing there's no way in hell I can go back to sleep. I look at the clock again. 9:03. Wasn't I supposed to do something today?

Then I remember. Chris—I told him I'd go to church with him this morning. Shit. I think it starts at 10:30, which gives me plenty of time. And really, it's going to take a lot of awkwardness out of things, me being gone when Franco wakes up. Maybe even a blessing in disguise. I slowly get up, trying not to wake him. Last night was great, perfect, but now it's morning and we're sober and we're officially lovers and I feel kind of weird. Maybe even a little slutty, even though it's not like it's a one-night stand or anything.

"You score?" His friend's voice echoes in my brain. Maybe that's all it was, really. A score. A scam. A notch in Franco's belt or whatever. It felt like more, but then that's what I thought with Richard Zachary, too, and look how that turned out.

Richard Zachary was a very cute boy I met right after the Parker breakup, when I was all fragile and thinking all guys were Satan and basically just a walking, talking brick wall when it came to the opposite sex. He had on this Adidas shirt the first night I met him, black and white, and looked very Italian, very Beastie Boyish. I told George I wanted him right then and there, and we started calling him "Italian Boy." She'd see him and give me reports: "Italian Boy sighting at Brewery last night." He went out a lot, to the same places we went to. He had curly black hair, a cute smile, was a good dancer. He seemed perfect.

It took a couple of weeks to start talking to him. The first thing I asked him after our initial introductions was what his middle name was. Zachary. Richard Zachary. Even the name sounded made up, like too cool or something. And he was wearing a red polyester cowboy shirt and white flared jeans that first night we talked. We danced, and he kept saying "Do you have a shovel? Can you dig it?" and when I told him he was a Beastie Boy he said I was a Beastie Girl. Aaaaaah.

He called me Abbie Sue and went dancing with me at this after-hours place, the Romper, the place the guy who just called Franco was at last night. We went to my car and talked. He'd only had one serious girlfriend and was twenty-one. He was a translator for some big company. He had lived in Europe for a year. And he seemed very into me but didn't even try to kiss me or anything; total gentleman. When I dropped him at his car, he took one of my deposit slips that had my number on it and said he'd call or put money in my account, one of the two. We laughed and I was in lust, major.

He called the next day and we went to the drive-in the following weekend. We had a dreamlike date, ate dinner at a truck stop and visited this milk factory I love. It has big sixties cows painted all over it and the cows are wearing polyester and go-go boots. The factory has been my all-time favorite place in the city since I've lived here. We kissed in front of the bell-bottomed cows and I felt I might burst with happiness.

He asked if he could spend the night and I was like okay, but no sex. He tried but we didn't do anything really. I did start to go down on him and that's when he told me that the last blow job he had was five months ago, from a guy. But he wasn't gay, he assured me. Or bi. Thanks for sharing, I said, pretty pissed off. He then tells me he's fucked up, probably because his mom tried to have sex with him when he was fourteen. I was like, "Your mom what?" It was pretty upsetting but I tried to be understanding. It wasn't his fault after all.

We just went to sleep after that and the next morning I was very cool, asking him about the blow-job-from-a-boy thing and thinking, Well, maybe he was just experimenting. He again assured me it was just a one-time thing and he was drunk or whatever. Okay. I told him I'd see him later at Unity.

Well, I did see him later that night and he was being a total jerk to me, like I can totally comprehend why the nickname of Richard is Dick. And I went up to him and was like, What is your deal? And he said, Listen, I'm really fucked up and you don't want to get involved with me. And I was like, What? I really like you! and he looked me in the eyes and goes, Listen, just fuck off. He told me, Abbie McPhereson, to fuck off! No one had ever said that to me before. And this was a guy I had kissed in front of the bell-bottomed cows. Had shared family secrets with. Had, hello, slept in the same bed with the previous night. I couldn't understand it.

A few minutes later, I tried to talk to him again and he told me once more to fuck off, this time with a little more venom in his voice. Great. I started crying and found George, filling her in on the situation. She couldn't believe it and said he was like Dr. Jekyll and Mr. Hyde. Then I went to the bathroom to repair my makeup, which my tears had wrecked, and Richard Zachary comes up to George and goes, Keep your friend away from me, she's psycho.

I'm psycho? When she told me that, I was like consider the fucking source.

So that's what was up with him. But I thought we really had something cool and, hell, would maybe have even slept with him eventually since I liked him so much. And it turned out he was a total freak who didn't bat an eye when telling me to fuck off and didn't care one iota that I had shared my favorite place with him or told him about the coolest dress I ever designed. He didn't give a shit when it came down to it but totally acted like he liked me at first. Emphasis on "acted." So that's how I know things are not always as they seem. And if you take something at face value, usually you're going to get screwed in the deal one way or the other.

I slip on my jeans and look at my fingers again. Parker, Michael, and now Franco. Almost a whole, entire hand of lovers. Maybe I'll wear gloves to church. It might ease my guilt just a little bit.

Once I'm dressed and have folded Franco's boxers and T-shirt, I check the mirror. I looked a hell of a lot better last night but am not too hideous. And you can barely see the zit under the concealer, unless you're looking real close. Which he won't be, probably, since he'll be half asleep if I decide to wake him up to say goodbye.

Should I just forget it and bail, leaving him to wonder where I went when he gets up? Like throw in that mystery factor? Or should I say goodbye and have to think up something lame to say, anything to deflect the conversation away from the incredible sex we had last night? Again, someone should write a book about this. They'd get rich, no question.

After a couple of minutes of contemplation, I decide to wake him up. If not, I know I'd leave a note and that would stress me out even more, trying to figure out what to write. "Hey."

He sort of jumps when I say this and looks up at me with frightened eyes.

"Are you like, 'Who the hell is in my house?' " I ask, for lack of anything better to say.

"Yeah," he mumbles. "The alarm go off?"

"No, you want me to set it?" I've had sex with this person, I'm thinking.

"No." He closes his eyes.

I grab his hand to kiss his fingers. I should say something, but what? After a few seconds of contemplation, I opt for the ever-safe "See you later."

"Yeah, later." He rolls over, I guess to go back to sleep. Without even a kiss goodbye.

Two hours ago I was in bed with Franco in his boxers and now I'm sitting in a pew with Chris and his dad, having donned my Sunday best. Talk about culture shock.

Chris keeps looking over at me and smiling. I know he likes me, and this makes me feel really sad. Especially considering what just happened with Franco. I smooth my dress with my white-gloved hands and sigh when he gets the nerve to put his arm across the back of the pew about halfway through the sermon. I stare at the words of the Bible before me so hard they start to swirl all over the page like little eyelashes, a million dreams waiting to come true.

Then Chris goes up to give a prayer and something weird

happens. I feel an unexpected attraction toward him, which totally surprises me. He is in front of the congregation in this starched white shirt and I think, for the first time, that he is really hot. His eyes are closed and he's holding hands with two other people and he's praying aloud into this microphone and I feel something in the pit of my stomach, that something I feel when I start to like someone.

Chris is a boy who has faith in something, and I guess that's what's drawing me in. This very public display of his faith proves how much he's into it. How much he believes. He's probably one of the few people I know that believes in anything anymore. It's like out of style or something to have faith. But he has it and doesn't care who knows it. Refreshing, really. And Pat's cousin and all. I really should give the guy a break.

I continue to stare, trying on this out-of-nowhere feeling like a new pair of shoes. When Chris does finally open his eyes, he looks directly at me.

Chapter 15

Driving down the street I used to live on, the one my parents still live on, I think how weird it is to be back in the place I grew up. The houses in the neighborhood seem smaller and the roads seem narrower, but I guess it's me who's done the growing. Somewhat depressing, really. I am not about to ruin this Friday with any of the melancholy thoughts being back in Tulsa usually provokes. So I turn up the radio, sing along to a song I don't know the words to and step a little harder on the gas until my old home's in sight.

Even though I've come back to visit every few months in the almost two years since I've inhabited it, my first glimpse of the chocolate brown A-frame always makes me do a double take, like I'm seeing a chick who looks familiar but I'm not sure where I've seen her before. When you live somewhere or are surrounded by something your whole life, you don't always see it. You look at it and everything but never really see it for what it is. It's like that with people, too. Like just a few months ago at Christmas I noticed for the first time ever that my mom's eyes are this really pretty green color. She was taking off her makeup and I was sitting up on the counter next to the sink and it was the first time I ever really noticed her eyes before, how green they are. I always thought they were hazel, like my brother's. But there I go again, being melancholy. I must stop before I start crying and ruin my eye makeup, a thing Mom would be sure to comment on.

I see her peering out the kitchen window as I pull in the driveway. She runs out the front door before I even get a chance to put on the emergency brake.

"Abbie, I thought you said you'd be here by five," she hollers as she swings open my door and pulls me out of my bucket seat.

"Mom, I said I'd try. But as usual I got held up. Pat had to talk to me and we've been in this big fight for the past couple of days so I had to go over there. I'm not that late, am I?" My words jumble together as I take note of many things: that the garage window my brother's baseball knocked out last summer is still broken, that Mom's dressed in her usual sweatshirt and jeans, that she looks depressingly skinnier than I do.

"If you'd wear that watch I got you for Christmas, you'd know," she says, enveloping me in a hug. She buys me a watch every Christmas, knowing full well I never wear watches with the exception of the Little Mermaid one on occasion so I can always have an excuse for being late.

I hug her back and tell her I need to get my stuff out of the trunk. "You are just going to freak when you see this luggage I found at the thrift, Mother." It's cream with big black daisies printed all over it, Samsonite circa 1960 or something.

"Oh my gosh, Abbie. How much?" No matter what you show my mother, that is always practically the first thing out of her mouth—"How much?" Maybe it's her bargain shopper ways. I don't know. But the cheaper you say you got it for, the more she likes it.

"Get this, it was like nine ninety-six for the entire set. Big suitcase, medium suitcase and carry-on. And wait 'til you see the lining—bright orange satin."

"No!" she gasps.

We drag my stuff in and I immediately pop open the bag to prove I'm not lying. "And it's not even ripped or anything."

"What a find!" She turns her attention from the lining to me. "Did you get it at the same thrift you got that dress?" Nose wrinkled, she looks me up and down.

"No, this is from Salvation Army, thankyouverymuch." The pink polyester ultrashort maternity frock is not my mother's speed, which is exactly the reason I wore it.

"I wish you'd wear some of that stuff I got you for your birthday, Abbie. Like that one pantsuit, the navy one. That looked so adorable on you."

"Mother, I told you then and I'm telling you now, it's not my style. You should be happy I even have a style. Most people don't." This song and dance is damn old, especially since I'm a designer, for Chrissakes.

She leans against the bar and runs a manicured hand through her blonde curly bob. "I want you to have a style, Abbie. Mine."

I roll my eyes. We always have some variation on this discussion within five minutes of my arrival. She hates what I wear, even if I designed it, but should know by now I'll never change. Nonconformity makes her nervous, I guess. I react in the way I always do: by changing the subject. "Soooo," I say, plopping down on a dining room chair. "Pat and I are made up again."

Mom pulls a chair next to mine. "What is going on with you two? Every time I call it's Pat said this to make me mad or Pat's not talking to me for that. He doesn't seem that threatening to me."

I laugh at the thought. "Pat's not threatening whatsoever, very much of a pacifist. It's just that maybe we're too much alike. I try to confide in him about Franco and Chris and he gets all high-and-mighty on me, freaking out for no reason."

She nods thoughtfully. "But there has to be a reason. Chris is his cousin, right?"

"I guess that's a big part of it." I cross my legs and swing my right foot back and forth. "He feels a loyalty to him or something, which I understand. But I have no commitment to either one of them so I don't feel like I'm doing anything wrong by dating them both. I mean, I haven't even talked to either guy for two days."

"But Pat thinks you're being sneaky by dating them both?" she asks, leaning over to run her fingers through my hair. Jeez, her obsession with my appearance annoys the living hell out of me, I swear it does.

"Yep. Said I'm being dishonest. But I'm not, really I'm not. I'm just being unattached." Pat went ballistic earlier in the week when I told him I slept with Franco, like said I was this awful person for leading two boys on at the same time.

She grabs my left hand. "No ring on this finger, am I correct? Until there is one, I say just have fun. When you meet the right one, you will just know."

"That's what I'm saying, Mother. But Pat's acting like it's some cardinal sin or something. I don't know. I feel kind of bad not telling them, Franco and Chris I mean, about the other one, but neither relationship is that serious really. Who knows. Pat apologized today and said he's really on edge, with the Sal situation and all." I fill Mom in on what's going on with Pat and Sal, wrapping up with the time I saw him with that other guy at Samurai.

"Don't say anything; he'll only resent you for it. But what a jerk that Sal sounds like." She sighs, looking down at her watch. "It's seven-thirty. Your father should be here by now, but with that promotion he's always working late. And Jimmy, he's never here anymore now that he's a senior. It's always 'Be back later, Mom' and me not knowing where the heck he's going. When I do get an explanation out of him, it's usually a lie anyway. And he's been going over to this girl Kelly's house all the time and any time I ask him about it he says 'You're being an idiot, Mom' or something like that. You don't think he's done it, do you?"

"It? As in *it*?" The thought of my brother having sex makes me a little queasy. Kind of like picturing your grandma having sex, only a little worse.

"Yes, you know, sex. I mean, you don't think he has, do you?" Her voice gets quite squealy at times, high-pitched as all hell.

"If he's had the chance, I'm sure he has. It's not like he's not thinking about it a lot. I doubt he's reading those *Playboy* mags for the music reviews, Mother." Hello, Mom: cluephone for you.

"I know that, Abbie, but surely he hasn't done anything with anybody yet. I mean, I can't see how he would even know what to do." She shakes her head back and forth. Whatever dream world she's in, I hope I never go there.

My eyebrows shoot up. "I'm sure if you spent twenty-four hours a day thinking about how to do something, you'd damn sure figure it out. And he's seventeen, right? I think the national average is sixteen. So technically he's above the average age."

She cringes. "Oh God, let's not even talk about it. It kind of makes me sick. But when you see him later, try to find out for me." Mother is forever trying to get me to pump Jimmy for information and then pass it on to her. Maybe I used to do it when I was like twelve and couldn't stand him, but now I'd never spill something he told me in confidence. She knows this but always asks anyway when she thinks he's hiding something from her. Knowing he'd had sex would just make her sick, yet knowing he's hiding something from her makes her sicker. A mother who wants to know every detail, this is my mom. Jimmy always says she has no life so she has to live through ours, which is remarkably true. Ever since he's said that, when someone asks me to describe my mom, the word "vicarious" always comes up.

Just as I'm about to go into my ethics speech about invading Jimmy's privacy, Dad breezes through the door. "Hey, Ab, are you tired?" This is his standard greeting. Never "How you doing?" or "Long time, no see," always "Are you tired?" Always. Every time I see my dad in his dark suits and starched shirts and crazy ties, I am struck by how gray his hair has gotten lately. It only enhances his boyish good looks, but in my memory his hair is thick, brown and unruly. The silver in his hair makes me sad.

"No, Dad, I'm not tired. Are you?" I say, pushing my hair behind my ears. It's always great to see him—I'm such a daddy's girl at heart.

"Beat. Be right back." He loosens his tie and heads to the bedroom, calling for Cardigan, the family cat. Notice we didn't hug. We never do. Physical affection makes Dad nervous. Except for sex, which Mom says he still wants all the time. Another subject that kind of grosses me out.

"Does it ever make you mad that he talks to the cat before he talks to you, Mother?" I ask, genuinely curious. My therapist had a field day over this trait, believe me. Fucking bizarre, talking to cats and all.

"That's just your father, Abbie. He feels weird showing his affection to those he loves, so he shows it to the cat. He's strange. You need lipstick." As I've said, Mom has this odd obsession with my appearance—especially my lack of eyeliner or lipstick, whichever the case may be. Drives me nuts.

"Mom, I'm not going to Buckingham Palace. I'm home."

"Ab, for me, please. You look dead without it, trust me, you have my lips." She gets quite persistent about cosmetics. It's easier to just apply them without argument or you'll be hearing it all day. Let's pray she's got a shade that won't clash with my polyester, that's all I can say.

We're eating sandwiches in front of the TV when Jimmy walks in. Every time I take a bite, the bread gets covered with a thin line of hot pink wax, which I then consume in the next bite. Pass the lipstick, *por favor.*

"Hey, Jimmy, what's up?" I cry, mouth full of sandwich.

He high-fives me, looking very cute in plaid button-down, jeans and baseball cap. "I didn't know you were coming this weekend, Ab."

"Yep. You gonna be around?" I ask, grabbing him in a hug. Just because Dad doesn't hug anybody doesn't mean Jimmy won't, I hope.

"Yes, Jimmy, are you going to be around?" Mom pipes in, in a tone that implies he better be.

"Maybe. Party tonight at Kendra's," he says, rolling his eyes. I wonder if they give some sort of Eye Rolling 101 course in high school, because everybody does it like two hundred times a day at that age.

"You better not be drinking," Dad garbles, mouth full of pretzels.

"Yes, I mean it, Jimmy. I heard Ty is selling you guys beer at that gas station, and all I can say is I better not find out you're buying any," Mom says, trying to sound all reprimanding but not quite succeeding with her dog-whistle voice.

"Mom, shut up. I'm not drinking," Jimmy answers, none too convincingly. Did I mention that my parents aren't big authority figures? Like Jimmy regularly tells Dad to fuck off in fits of rage and never gets grounded or anything. My parents hate for anyone to be mad at them, even their children. Which of course means we could pretty much get away with murder, a fact my brother takes advantage of way more than I ever did. Which makes me a little bit jealous.

"Guys, give the guy a break. He's a senior." I smile over at him and wink. Since I moved out, we have a very different relationship than when we lived under the same roof. Like I don't wish him dead anymore and he doesn't read my diary to his friends, that sort of thing.

"Yeah, I'm a senior." He grabs a pretzel off Dad's plate and leaves the room.

"Raising him is so different from raising you, Abbie," Mom says, wringing her hands. I told you she's into the parenting thing too deep. "I don't know if it's because you're a girl and he's a boy or what, but it's just like night and day. We never know where he's going or what he's doing."

"Or who he's doing." I smirk.

Dad pretends he doesn't hear that comment. I know he heard, though, because he kind of clears his throat and turns up the TV, even though it's on a commercial. Mom goes, "Oh, Abbie, you don't think he is, do you? You have to find out for me."

"If you want to know, you ask him," I say, scarfing down another wax-coated bite.

"Believe me, I have. He won't tell me." There she goes with the hand thing again, wringing them like a goddamn bell.

I picture Franco. "Listen, Mother, some things about your kids you're just better off not knowing. Like there's plenty of details about me I spare just so you can sleep nights."

Mom raises her eyebrows and looks over at Dad. "Oh God."

Dad glances her way and hits the volume once again. "Where's Cardigan? Caaardigan, come to your daddy."

I GET so dizzy from all the comments that bounce back and forth in this household but are never directed at the person they're intended for, I swear. Mother wants to find out something about Jimmy so she pumps me, Dad can't say what he wants to say to me so he talks to the cat, Jimmy doesn't really talk to anyone at all for fear it will get back to Mother. Me, I just sort of keep my mouth shut. I'm scared that if I open it too much I'll get sucked back into their communication cycle, one that took me many months of therapy to break.

I just had lunch with one of my and Pat's best friends from high school, Shawn. I dated him for like five minutes sophomore year. He's the one who came out of the closet to us the day after the senior prom, which was like two years after Pat did. Not that everybody didn't already know Shawn was gay. It was never a big deal with me, him or Pat being gay. Most of my friends are. Hello. I'm in fashion design. Some people are sensitive to that, like don't stereotype fashion designers as being gay. Well, it's okay to stereotype most teachers as being literate, right? It's the same thing. Something about being gay really enhances one's sense of fashion. I totally believe this. And who cares if you're gay or straight or white or black or whatever? If you're a good designer, you're a good designer. Design knows no gender or sees no color or any of that shit. Now I sound like a T-shirt logo or something. Being in Tulsa does that to me. I don't know why. Maybe because almost every car you pass has a bumper sticker on it, like the whole place is very into these little catchphrases. It's annoying. Contagious and annoying.

So, anyway, lunch with Shawn. He's very much the happy boy, in his sophomore year working toward degrees in theater and mass communications. When I last saw him many months ago, he was very into this fraternity thing but has since been blackballed for his sexual preference. Such a crock of shit. They talk about brotherly love and friends forever but when they find out one of their brothers is homosexual their whole tune changes. Or such was the case in Shawn's fraternity, anyway. My friend Keith got blackballed for the same reason by a major frat at OU. This was after he had gone through all this hazing and even had the Greek letters tattooed on the inside of his ankle. It's like, since you're kicking me out, will you pay for my tattoo removal, too? Really makes me sick.

Anyway, so it's been awhile since I've seen him and he looked majorly cute—the gay ones always do, right? I totally filled him in on Pat and Sal, leaving out Sal's infidelities, and then told him what's up with the Franco and Chris situation, wanting to get the famous Shawn perspective. Almost immediately, he said he can't figure out why I would like Franco, except for his looks.

"Not that that's not a good enough reason. When I went out with Vince, it certainly wasn't for the size of his brain," he said knowingly, running his fingers through his curly red bob.

I relay all the things that are cool about Franco, only they sound somewhat insignificant when I vocalize them. And then I tell all about Chris, who sounds almost too good to be true. "But of course, the nice guy does nothing for me," I say with a shrug.

"Nothing for you? Sounds like he'd do anything for you," Shawn answers, totally missing my point. Then the hand through the hair again. A guy like Shawn, he's always running his hands through his hair. If my hair was that perfect, I'd be touching it all the time too probably.

"No, I mean, like nothing for me chemistry-wise. I have developed a slight attraction but it's only slight. Franco has me in a frenzy. And he cracks me up."

"Looks go away, Abbie. Look at Denny."

Denny was Shawn's first boyfriend, who on last sighting—Christmas—had shrunk to like a hundred pounds and had these really dark circles under his eyes. His first love was Shawn, sure, but his true love is coke, the thing that broke them up.

"Denny is a sad case, Shawn. Could have been a movie star with all those good looks, and turned into a skinny, shivering wreck."

We gossip about who in our class has married who and who has gained weight—the stuff all high school buddies talk about when getting together after being apart for any extended period of time. When we exit, Shawn tells me he knows I won't take his advice, but that I should ditch Franco and stick with Crisco.

"Chris sounds like a better investment for your love and energy," he says, fingers encased once more in those damn gorgeous curls. "But you're getting this advice from someone chasing after a cute freshman stagehand at the moment, so take it with a grain of salt."

THE PHONE rings at like eight o'clock. It's a usual Saturday night at the McPheresons'. Dad is at the bowling alley, trying to win this jackpot thing they play on Saturday nights. Jimmy's at some party, probably swigging beer or getting laid, anything to piss Mom off. Mother's napping in front of the TV in her bedroom, probably having nightmares of what Jimmy's doing at that party. Me, I'm fixing my face for an evening out. Blush always gives me fits, and tonight is no exception. It's either too dark or not dark enough. And I'm supposed to go to Sponge Club in an hour with Shawn, and since I'm sure we'll see tons of people from high school, I need to look slamming as hell.

I throw down the blush brush and pick up the receiver, hoping the noise didn't wake Mom up. "Hello?" I snap, annoyed by the blush interruption.

"Abbie?" a boy—not Shawn or Pat—asks. Who else knows I'm here? "It's Franco."

Franco? "How'd you get this number?" I ask, quite excited. His first long-distance call to me! Like he's actually *paying* to talk to me now.

"Georgette gave it to me," he says, voice all low. "You busy?"

"Sort of." I want it to seem that I'm a chick with a very busy social calendar. Like I'm on the other line with Madonna right now, but I can talk if you make it snappy. "What's up?"

"Uh, just sitting here," he sort of whispers. Jane's yelping in the background. "Wanted to hang out with you tonight."

"Really?" It's our one-week anniversary since the first sexual encounter. Nothing seems different but nothing seems the same either. I'm sure he feels it too.

"Yeah, any chance of you coming back tonight?" he asks in a—get this—hopeful tone. He's actually pinning his hopes on my arrival, it's like too much.

I twirl the phone cord around my index finger. "Not really. I think I'm coming back tomorrow, though. If you want to do something."

"Tomorrow's that acid party, which doesn't really seem like it'd be your thing." Voice as dejected as an old balloon.

"Nope, doesn't seem like it would be," I answer, slightly bitchy. Like he might as well just tell me he doesn't want to see me tomorrow, that's definitely what he means.

"But tonight, I really would like to be with you tonight," he whines, but in a sexy way. "I've been thinking about you all day."

"You have?" I think about him all day, every day, but him thinking about me is another thing entirely. Like he's actually sitting there and thinking about me, Abbie McPhereson. "What have you been thinking?" I ask, wondering if he's been thinking thinking or masturbating thinking.

"Um, just, you know, thinking I want to see you."

"Yeah, how long has it been?" Six days, I already know. Six long days.

"Couple of days, right?"

"Yep. A couple." Six could be considered a couple of days, I guess.

"So, noooothing I can say can persuade you to come back early?"

It's a six-hour drive. It's seven now. I can call Shawn and cancel, write a note to my family and be on the road in fifteen, which would put me there by a little after one. "I really don't think there's any way."

"How 'bout Jane? Here Jane, come tell Abbie you want to see her." I laugh as he calls the dog to the phone. She doesn't bark or anything, just breathes heavy. Like an obscene phone caller or an out-of-shape runner.

The dog persuasion does me in. "Okay, okay. I give up. I'll be there after one."

"You will? Cool." He sounds damn excited and all, he really does. "Be careful."

How thoughtful that he told me to be careful. Like he's really concerned about my safety, maybe even like a boyfriend would be worried about his girlfriend making it okay. Without labels placed on our relationship, it's hard to know where I stand with Franco. So little comments such as these give a girl like me encouragement.

It's almost one-thirty in the morning when I pull into his apartment complex. I have to be crazy to drive six hours to see a boy who is not even officially mine yet. I've been beating myself up about it since I got on the interstate, but I never felt low enough to turn back. I just kept on trucking and turned the radio up a little louder. Somewhere around the state line, I blew a speaker, which only reinforced my need for a new distraction in life. That's the third speaker I've blown in the last six months.

Knocking on Franco's door, I feel slightly spooked. What will I do if he isn't even here, after I've driven three hundred–something miles? Just go home? Cry? Kick his door down? I don't want to think about it. Because when I do think about it the thought of him not being here at one-thirty on a Saturday night doesn't seem so unlikely.

He's here. I hear him coming to the door before he actually opens it, fumbling for the doorknob. "Hey, baby, you made it!" He's in a two-piece blue-and-white-striped pajama set, the kind most grandpas wear. His red hair is tousled and Jane nips at his heels as he ushers me in. His right hand grabs my elbow, his left grips a bottle of whiskey. "You wanna drink?" He kicks the door shut and holds up the bottle slightly, swaying a little to the left.

I smile, justifying everything in my mind. It's Saturday, the universal party day. So he had a couple of drinks before I got here, so what? Just because I'm not drunk doesn't mean he can't be. The prickling annoyance I feel is just because I've been on the road for six hours and am exhausted. Nothing else.

"Um, nope. What I really want is a kiss." I lean over and plant one on his lips. After a couple of seconds, he pulls away. "I need to get fucked up real quick. My buzz is just sort of drifting. But then I'm all yours. You sure you don't want one?"

I stand up—this is all I can take. "Look, obviously I'm taking a back seat to your whiskey, even though I've spent six damn hours in the driver's seat of my car trying to get here to see you. I really can't deal with this right now, especially considering the fact that even though we're sleeping together, a major deal, I don't know whether to call you my boyfriend or date or fuck. And since it's so important for you to catch your buzz or whatever, it's me who's doing the drifting. Right out your door." My voice gets louder with every word, kind of like my radio on the way to Dallas. Franco looks at me, scared. Like he's seen a ghost or something.

He grabs my arm, I guess to stop me from leaving. Which I'm not even attempting to do yet. "Hey, don't go." He sets the bottle down and cradles me in his arms, making me cry. "Don't cry, Abbie. I'm an asshole, ask anybody. I don't mean to be, I just am." His confession is making me cry harder. I'm tired and hurt and confused and the only thing I can do is bawl. His blue and white stripes are getting more soaked by the minute.

He puts my head in his hands and kisses my forehead. "Baby, you are the coolest girl, you know that? And I want you to be my girlfriend, if you'll have me for your boyfriend. Will you? Be my girlfriend?"

Tears are still streaming down my face, so I don't say anything for a minute. Finally I croak out a yes and he carries me to his bedroom. He doesn't bring the whiskey along.

Around three-thirty, when we're on the brink of sleep, the phone rings. "Want me to answer it?" I whisper.

"Nope, machine's on," he answers, half asleep. He squeezes me tighter and kisses my shoulder. Sweet.

Franco's message blares after the fourth ring, then a low female voice fills the air. "Frankoney Baloney, what is up and where are you? This is Zoe. Like I told you the other day, I'll be in town Friday. And a bunch of us are going to that thing Saturday at Orange Tape so you better be there. I wish you were home, you're the only one I can call this late. Talk to you later, sweetie."

Franco stirs and squeezes me again. I know he heard every word. And even though he's officially my boyfriend, something about Zoe's message keeps me up for over an hour. It was her voice. When Zoe spoke, she did so in a way that implied Franco was still very much hers.

Chapter 16

"So that's three eggs scrambled with a side of toast? You want hash browns, grits or biscuits with that, sir?" the smoker-looking waitress asks.

Franco's hangover is as big as the waitress's hair, so big he can barely speak. He just sort of grunts a response and I translate. "Hash browns, he wants hash browns."

Another grunt.

"And coffee. Black?" I look over at Franco to make sure I've accurately deciphered that one. He points his thumb toward the sky. "Black."

When the waitress is out of earshot, I speak. "So you really feel like shit, huh?"

"Slightly. We were partying at Harley's until I called you, then I went home and practically killed that bottle of Jim Beam." It takes him about a year to get this out. I'm not kidding.

"Yeah, you were pretty much gone when I got there." I remember the "I need to get fucked up real quick" episode but refrain from mentioning it again. A dead horse and all.

"I barely remember you getting there. I know we had an argument, sort of, but it gets hazy after that." He shakes his head, then gives a half-smile. "You're not still pissed at me, are you?"

I reach over and brush a strand of hair out of his eye. "Nope. Everything was resolved, really."

"I was being a dick, right?"

I nod slowly, thinking this might be the understatement of the year. "In a word, yes. But you were a very drunk dick, so at least you kind of had an excuse."

He rests his chin on his fist and grabs my hand. "I'm sorry

about that, Ab. I was really happy to see you last night, I mean really glad, and I screwed it all up."

"Nothing was screwed up. I still had a good time and everything. It was cool."

Franco hops up and crawls in next to me on my side of the cramped booth. I'm enveloped in fuzzy flannel as he hugs me tight. "I'm still sorry about anything I did last night. You drove that long way and all I did was fuck it up."

"It's alright, Franco, really. It's fine," I say into his shoulder as he tightens his embrace.

"Hate to break it up, lovebirds, but food's here," Looks-Like-A-Smoker Waitress sings, setting down identical platters heaping with eggs and hash browns in front of us. "Thanks, Madge," I say, reading her name tag.

"You kids look like my kids used to after a night of partying. Not that I would know what they look like now after one of those nights—I never see them," she says, rubbing her hands on a stained, frilly apron.

Franco is already inhaling his eggs as I smile at Madge, feigning interest.

"Your boyfriend looks a little like my Johnny," she clucks, leaning in for a closer look. "My boy's hair never got that scruffy, but the nose is the same. Roman nose, my husband always called it. God rest his soul."

I gulp. Not only is she rambling incessantly, she's calling Franco my boyfriend. A title, despite everything said last night, I have yet to utter when referring to him.

"Madge, can you get me and my girlfriend some ketchup?" Franco garbles, mouth full.

Me and my girlfriend? Does he remember his drunken question of last night?

As she trots off to fetch the condiment, Franco elbows my side. "Had to save you. Eggs are getting cold."

I smile at him and scoop a forkful of the runny eggs. Suddenly I feel too sick to eat. His girlfriend. What if Franco was just kidding or something, reacting to Smokin' Madge calling him my boyfriend? Or just saying it like a figure of speech? This is all incredibly possible. But why would you refer to someone who seriously wasn't your girlfriend as your girlfriend if you didn't slightly wish she was? You wouldn't, not unless you were just being mean. But there's no way he could ever be that cruel. Is there?

"Eggs good, girlfriend?" Franco asks, looking over at me with a tranquil grin, like he's called me that a zillion times before.

"So is that what I am now? Your girlfriend?" I croak, trying to sound light and funny, in case it's all just a big joke.

He bites into a toast wedge and looks down at his plate. "If you want to be. I mean, I asked you last night, right?"

A huge smile takes over my face. The totally sober (albeit hungover) Franco Richards wants to be my boyfriend. Mine, all mine! "Right," I say with a nervous titter.

He intertwines his left pinky with my right one. "Okay, girlfriend," he says, putting extra emphasis on the last word. He draws it out real slow, prolonging the pleasure I'm deriving from hearing it roll off his tongue.

"Okay, boyfriend." I cannot even wait to tell Georgette.

We continue like this for awhile, just eating, pinkies connected. The after-church crowd starts filing in a few minutes later and the restaurant gets louder and more crowded. I barely notice. That is, until I spot Chris and fam walking in. I disconnect my pinky from Franco's frantically, trying to plot my next move.

"Whassup?" Franco looks up from his plate.

I put my hand over my face in a lame attempt to disguise my identity. "Um, just this guy I know just walked in."

He points to my shielding hand. "Someone you don't want to see, I guess?"

"Sort of," I whisper.

"He one of the suits?" he says, looking around inconspicuously.

"Yes. The one, shit, who's waving." Chris has spotted me and is waving wildly.

I feebly return the gesture and nudge Franco to do the same. Chris says something to his dad and brother, who also wave, then bounces over in his usual loping gait.

"Hey, Abbie. What's up?" His *GQ* apparel just reminds me of how totally thrashed Franco and I must look—me in day-old outfit, Franco in flannel and Levi's. Chris eyes Franco curiously.

"Hi, Chris, how weird to see you here. This is Franco. Franco, Chris. Chris, Franco," I say, I'm sure sounding as weirded out as I feel. They shake hands and Franco goes back to his eggs, none too concerned. Chris gives me this look like, Who is this guy?

"Nice to meet you. So are you guys friends from school?" Chris is trying to sound composed and casual, but his hurt expression betrays him. I'm such a total bitch.

"Nooooo. Not exactly," I answer in falsetto, knowing that he knows we're not.

"Well. Why don't you just give me a call this week," Chris says to me in this forced way.

I smile guiltily. "Okay, this week. I'll do that."

"Uh, nice to meet you." We both look over at Franco, shoveling in the last of his eggs.

He looks up with a bemused expression. "Same here, dude. Try the eggs, they're awesome."

Chris smiles and goes, "I might do that. Sounds like we just might have the same taste."

Franco's too entrenched in buttering his toast to get this last comment, but I sure do. I open my mouth to say something, anything, but there's nothing really to say. I reach out to brush his arm, but Chris recoils from my touch. "See you around, Abbie."

As he walks off to join his family in nonsmoking, I feel like such shit. My nerves are as scrambled as the eggs I've barely touched.

"You okay?" Franco asks, nudging my elbow.

"Yeah, you know me." I sigh. "Built for guilt."

ON THE WAY back to Franco's, empowered by my new "girlfriend" moniker, I ask the question that's been nagging at my brain since last night. "So, what's up with Zoe coming into town?"

He pushes his hair behind his ears and fiddles with the radio knobs. "She'll be here for a week and a half, starting Friday. I'm picking her up. From the airport, I mean." His voice is all freaked out, like someone trying to talk his way out of a speeding ticket.

"That's cool," I say, forced-happy, even though it's really anything *but* cool.

"Yeah, she really needs a friend right now. A lot of shit is going on with her family," he answers, still messing with the radio. Quite like he's messing with my mind.

"Really?"

"Yeah, like some really major stuff with her dad."

"Her dad?" I know I'm freaked when I'm like cheerily repeating everything someone says to me like a parakeet on Prozac.

"Uh-huh. Her dad fuckin' hated me, man. He's a college professor, the kind of guy who owns no TV."

"Oh, shit." The mere concept of possessing no TV is enough to send me into hysterics.

"Yeah. Zoe doesn't have one either."

I have this vision of Zoe and how she's probably this crunchy-granola girl who doesn't wear makeup or shave her legs and spends her nights sipping cappuccino and reading Proust in various dimly lit coffeehouses around Portland. I hate her already.

"I don't know how one survives without TV," I say, sneering, sort of in a put-down-Zoe way.

"Ask Zoe, she can go on for hours about it," he declares, fishing in his pocket for a cig.

The kind of girl who owns more than one loofah and wears vanilla extract as perfume, I bet. "I'd like to meet her," I say, hopefully sounding nonchalant.

"I don't think she'd be up for that. She's really hard to be friends with right now, with everything that's going on. And she's never been too big on meeting my girlfriends. Like it would be cool to hang out or whatever in theory, but in reality it could never happen. She couldn't deal." He closes his eyes and sucks on his cigarette, long and hard.

I turn up the radio a notch, trying to drown out the doubts bombarding my brain. Does he want to be alone with her, is that it? Is he even going to tell her I exist? Is he ashamed of me, is that why he doesn't want us to meet? I could ask him all of the above, sound like an insecure freak. Or I can be adult about it.

trust that he won't dump me for her. Know that if he did dump me he wasn't good enough for me in the first place.

"That's cool," I say for the hundredth time today.

"Yes. That's cool, girlfriend." He closes his eyes and leans the passenger seat back to a reclining position. I wonder if he'll still call me that when Zoe gets here.

LATER THAT night, much later, we arrive tardy to this show in Deep Ellum Franco's dying to see. On the way in, he wants a shirt but doesn't have enough cash after paying our cover and saving some for beer, so I spot him five bucks and he becomes the proud owner of the XXL garment. It has that *Mad* guy, Alfred E. Neuman, on the front, with Smoking Hips, the band's name, on back. Not too spectacular, but neither is the band really from what I remember of the last time I saw them. The stage in the middle of the warehouse is empty, meaning they haven't started yet. Everyone's sort of milling about, checking out everybody else. I have on this very cool thrift store dress that's pink with silver toasters all over it and feel very hip. Over in the corner I see this one girl I kind of know, Bethann, who has the coolest clothes in Dallas, I swear, and she's wearing this green sweater with fake fur around the neck and looks so awesome. Franco's in the same thing he's had on since this morning, the flannel, but still looks adorable. Looks like his are hard to fuck up. I catch Bethann sizing him up so I put my hand on his arm and smile like, He's mine. She smooths her fur and smiles back like, I know. At least one thing's established.

Franco's jonesing for a beer and they're only selling them upstairs. We go over there and this big burly guy with a matty goatee is like, Can I see your I.D.s? and Franco gets his out but I discover my fake one is in my jeans back at Franco's apartment. So the bouncer won't let me through, even though I assure him I'm twenty-one as of last March 31, adding two years to my age. He looks at me like, Yeah, right, and refuses to let me up there, no matter how much I plead or how far I stick my bottom lip out in a cute pout. Franco says he'll be back and that I should circulate. I tell him to find me, then circle the room.

Immediately, I run into Ulysses from school, standing alone

against the wall. "What's up, baby doll?" I holler, thrilled to see him. It seems like forever since we've been in class, even though it's only been two weeks.

"Abitha, what's up?" He engulfs me in a timid bear hug, careful not to rumple my frock.

"You are looking so retro," I trill. His polyester patchwork button-down shirt and stove-leg pants with ragged-bottom hemlines are total seventies. We're not such great friends, more like great acquaintances, but I swear the guy's wardrobe just about kills me every time.

"Baby, you know I'm just a disco diva trapped inside a male model's body," he says, striking a pose.

"Whaaaatever! Are you growing an Afro or what?" His curly locks are looking bigger and nappier than they were the last time I saw him.

"Yep," he answers, stroking it like a kitty. "I'm going to let it grow 'til spring break, then shave it off."

"Very R.E.M. of you," I tell him, cracking myself up.

The lights go down and everyone starts screaming. "Why does everybody always yell when the lights go down?" I yell.

"Because the whole reason they came was to see who else is here and they can't do that in the dark. They're screaming in protest."

I crane my neck to look upstairs. In the bevy of over-twenty-one-ers up there, Franco would be impossible to pick out from this angle.

The music starts up, spotlights flood the stage and at once people start moshing. "We'll never find our dates now," Ulysses screams into my ear as the jostling begins.

"Nope, we won't." I latch onto his arm as a sea of movement washes over us, like water beginning to boil.

THE SHOW'S over by the time I see Franco again. His damp flannel is half tucked, half untucked and his hair is plastered to his head. The T-shirt I pitched in on is slung over his shoulders.

"You look like you've been through the wringer," I laugh. He does, too, but still cute as ever. Almost cute enough to make me forget I'm pissed he didn't even come look for me during the entire show. It's not like I could come up where he was without an I.D. or anything, and though I hate to admit it I spent about half the show craning my neck looking around for him.

"Yeah," he says, kissing my cheek. "I saw you from upstairs but I knew there was no way I could get to you, with this crowd."

I guess that sounds plausible, I think as I hug his damp self hard. "Well, luckily I saw a boy I know. He just left, or you could meet him."

He nods. "Saw one of my ex-girlfriends, Jennifer, and she bought me a couple of beers."

Great, how many Zoes and Jennifers does the guy have? "Is she still here?" I ask, looking around the emptying amphitheater.

"Nope. She and her man bailed before the first encore, that's when I hit the mosh pit. They were going to some after-party. I got the address but it sounds pretty lame." And her man. Thank God.

Given the fact that I look and feel like I've been run over by a Mack truck, a party full of strangers and ex-girlfriends doesn't sound too appealing. Even if it was the happeningest party in the world, I don't think I could handle it right now. "Some freak stage-dived onto me and ripped my dress. See?"

I hold up my wounded sleeve, freshly ripped at the seam.

"It just adds character to it. More hardcore."

I grab Franco's hand and pull him toward the exit. "So it's weird we didn't see each other the whole show," I say with a tinge of regret. Since I came here with him, I would have liked to be seen with him for more than five minutes.

He squeezes my palm. "Yeah, but we got to socialize. And we'll see each other all the time now anyway, since we're boyfriend–girlfriend. Might as well mingle."

In my opinion, one of the perks of being part of a couple is having a permanent date for concerts and parties and clubs. But it sounds like Franco is thinking we'll just split up as soon as we hit the door somewhere to "socialize" when we go out. Wrong.

"So you're gonna ditch me, now that we're together?" I say in a half-joking voice as we approach my car.

"Ditch you? Who said anything about ditching you?"

I climb in and unlock his door. "Well, you said we'll always see each other now, so we need to socialize when we're out . . ." I start the engine.

He slams his door. "Yeah, socialize. You know lots of people. I know lots of people, and we're the kinds who don't have to be around each other twenty-four hours a day to know the other one cares. That's what's cool about us."

We're an official "us" now. As I pull on the interstate, I look over at him and down at my dress and we look so cool, so vintage. Just like the kind of couple I've always wanted to be half of. And so what if he wants to socialize at clubs or hang with his ex-girlfriends? He's coming home with me, nobody else. And that's all that matters, really, when you think about it.

Chapter 17

I meet Pat for lunch Monday and the first thing he tells me is that Chris is absolutely out of his mind freaked about the breakfast encounter. Like that's a big surprise. As guilt bombards me, I decide I absolutely have to call Chris and end it, whatever the hell there is to end. Last week, sure, I felt that twinge of something, whatever it was, for him in church but in retrospect I'm sure it was probably just me psychoing out over sex with Franco. I think Pat's somewhat bummed about me not marrying Chris, but I have to think of my needs here, no one else's.

On the way home, Patrick has to stop at Arrow to pick up another sketchpad. We're ambling down the school supplies aisle when who do I see coming toward me in an Arrow red vest but my first post-Parker boyfriend, Michael, who now goes by Mickey according to the name tag above his heart. Or rather the place his heart would be if he had one. Oh God, months since I've seen the guy and my pulse still takes off, who knows why.

"Michael Tyner, what is up?" I say, since he's passing right by us and it's not like I can just not say anything. And I look pretty cute today so I am kind of enjoying the reunion.

"Abbie! Man, I thought that was you. How goes it?" He looks pretty startled as well. If I was working at Arrow I certainly wouldn't want to run into Parker or somebody, no way. I haven't seen this guy since last summer, the summer he dumped me for his skateboard. He looks exactly the same as he did then, only his face seems a little rounder. Like he's put on about ten pounds, probably thanks to the many post-skating six-packs he consumed weekend after weekend.

"I'm great, getting ready to finish school," I say in that seeing-an-ex voice, like my life is so much better than yours hee hee hee. "This is Pat."

"Hey, Pat. I remember hearing about you. Mickey, an old friend of Abbie's." He says "friend" with a leer, like probably remembering me naked or some shit. I'd remember him naked, too, if there was much to remember. And there definitely wasn't.

The shiny tag on his chest features the title *Assistant Manager.* Whoo. Glad to see my exes are climbing up the corporate ladder. "So, you worked at Arrow long?" I ask, tilting my head.

"Yeah, about eight months. Ever since I got out of skating, right after I last saw you. Just got promoted last month." He points to his name tag with pride, like I care.

"Congrats. You must be honored." This is from Pat, who remains totally straight-faced while saying this, a feat that deserves respect.

Mickey shifts his weight from foot to foot, looking pretty uncomfortable. It's pretty depressing, that red vest and all. "Well, yeah, it's kind of a big deal. I might make manager in a year or two. That's the big bucks."

An overhead speaker crackles and a nasal voice goes, "Management assistance on aisle three, price check."

Mickey shrugs apologetically like, Duty calls. "Well, guys, gotta run. Great to see you, Abbie."

We half hug, like I hug my dad, and he disappears down the aisle.

"That was Michael, as in the Michael I dated and slept with right after Parker. Remember? The Republican I never introduced anybody to," I whisper to Pat when he's out of sight.

"Oh man, *that's* him? What the hell did you ever see in that guy?" Pat asks, clutching his sketchbook.

"The future," I answer, somewhat embarrassed to admit this even to my best friend, fully aware of how asinine it sounds.

"What the hell does that mean, exactly? That's what you always said with Parker, too. 'The future, the future, that's what I see in him.' What is the future?" Pat says, scratching the top of his ear.

"The future is us happy together after boy finishes school, after boy stops smoking pot, after boy does all the shit he's always promising he'll do. The future is him keeping all his promises, how it'll be when everything's perfect. But of course with Michael, his future was that he was going to finish his Bachelor's and then go to law school to be a judge. And his reality is that he's assistant manager at Arrow. So go figure."

Pat puts his arm around me as we walk to the checkout stand. "Freak, you really need to forget that future forever and start being with these losers for the present. You'd be a lot better off."

Michael, on aisle three, looks up and waves. I wave back, thinking Pat is so right. I would be a hell of a lot better off.

Chapter 18

Fredrique and his new lip injections stand before the class, looking surprisingly placid. "Welcome back after your little siesta. Only twelve and a half weeks left, eleven and a half if you subtract spring break, so that's almost three pieces a week you need to be sewing. But first I need to okay the designs. So let's go. And by the way, yes, my lips are killing me, so let's make it snappy."

I'm camped next to Pat feeling sick to my stomach. My new sketches aren't as punchy as the first, due to Fredrique's unbridled abashment two weeks ago. But, flipping through them, I guess they're not God-awful either. Just less splashy, less me.

Pat goes first and Fredrique is surprisingly silent through his presentation—even when Pat shows his draft of an aquarium purse with a live goldfish swimming around the bottom. When Patrick is finished, Fredrique just purses his collagen-crammed lips, scribbles something in his notebook and tells him to be seated.

I look over at Pat like, What's up? and he shrugs. It's a one-eighty from how Fredrique was acting a couple of weeks ago—almost too good to be true, really.

Then Christy and Ulysses go—their sketches are good, not anything spectacular—and Fredrique reacts in the same way, sort of stone-faced and diplomatic, just nodding and scribbling thoughtfully before sending them back to their chairs without a word. I figure I might as well jump on this bandwagon while the getting's good, so I hop up as soon as Ulysses returns to his chair and head to the front.

"Miss McPhereson," Fredrique says as I'm starting to show my first sketch.

Great. He doesn't talk to anyone else all morning just so he can save his strength to bitch at me. "Yeah?" I answer, on the defensive.

"Sit down, please," he mumbles while applying a fresh coat of Chap Stick.

What the hell? I haven't even started my presentation yet, and he's already banishing me to my seat? "Wha—Why . . ." I start to protest, but he cuts me off.

"There's a package for you in the office that might be of interest. Please sit down. You can get it after class."

He looks down and scribbles something else in his notebook, then hollers, "Next!"

I go back to my chair, dazed, everyone's eyes upon me. Pat nudges my side. "What's up with the package?"

I don't answer because I have no idea. Maybe a letter telling me I'm kicked out of class? That seems the most likely theory, considering Fredrique wouldn't even look at my new sketches. Why would he waste precious time on a student who's not going to be around much longer? I bury my head in Pat's shoulder, destitute with despair. A letter like that would mean I can't graduate this term. Which would mean I am destined to be a loser for life. All those tired Generation X stereotypes personified, right here—slacker, shopper, Prozac popper. I always said I wouldn't be one of those people—the kind who whine and cry and quit and cry some more until Tabitha fucking Soren comes and interviews them for a twentysomething talk show to be aired on MTV three times a day. Now that prospect doesn't seem so unlikely. Seven failed fashion designers picked to live in a house with no closets and have their lives taped. One would have a disease and there'd be a country-singer-slash-designer and I'd be the codependent one whining about my alcoholic ex-boyfriends and how I would've been so great had I just graduated from the Design Institute. Then I'd be a cult hero for all losers, sort of the Beck of the design world.

God.

By the time Fredrique finally tells us through swollen lips that we can go, I'm beside myself. Pat pulls me to my feet.

"Let's go find out what's up with the mystery package," he says cautiously, like if he talks too loud I might break into a million pieces.

"Okay," I whisper. I follow him down the hall, numb, my head brimming with visions of the staples of my soon-to-be future: bounced checks, broken dreams, ramen noodles, 48-hour utility-cutoff notices.

"I am so completely screwed," I mutter, already tasting that damn Top Ramen.

Pat, I guess still pretty startled, rubs my back in little circles. Sad circles, depressing even, round and round and round until I feel even worse. Then he goes, "Baby, don't freak out. Everything is cool, everything is just fine."

But nothing feels fine and as I enter the frigid office and stare into the blemish-free face of Alison Simone, a girl who truly fits her name, I wonder if anything will ever be okay again.

"Hi, Abbie McPhereson," she chirps in her cheerful way, swinging her blonde pageboy over a padded shoulder with the flip of a bejeweled hand. "What can I do for you?"

You can fuck off and die, I think, but instead say, "Um, I need a package—it's supposed to be here for me."

While she saunters to the mail room like a fucking princess, I go over my theory. If it's thin, there's no need to open it—it's my ticket out of here, no doubt about it. If it's thick—maybe a collection of college catalogs for places that take transfer students, compiled by Fredrique out of the goodness of his nonexistent heart? That's the only possibility I can think of. I consider voicing my fears to Pat, share the scare, but here comes Alison around the corner, with big, bulky envelope in hand.

Catalogs. My heart sinks, my throat contracts. I could kill the bitch, I swear to God I could, with that fucking pageboy and all.

"Here you go, Abbie. New Bloomie's catalog, special delivery?" she titters, eyeing the package curiously.

"I'm sincerely doubting it," I answer, snatching it from her perfect claws.

Pat scurries after me as I fly out the door, running his hands through his hair like a madman, like practically pulling it *out* for Godsakes. "What do you think it is?" he says, monotone as hell, while I let it fall to my feet with a thud.

"Too cumbersome to be a letter of suspension," I whisper tentatively. I'm fucking out of here, show me to the goddamn door. My head fills with the perfect early nineties soundtrack to this scene: "I'm a loser, baby, so why don't you kill meeeee . . ." Over and over and over and over, that line, hypnotic as hell.

"Like they'd ever suspend you, please," Pat says, none too convincingly if you want to know the truth.

"Please, my ass." The song in my head's making it hard to speak. Not to mention the tears pressing the back of my eyeballs, ready to fire-hydrant any minute. "Pat, the guy would not even look at my sketches today. All I can think of is that it's like a lot of college catalogs for places I should transfer. It's not too heavy, but those things are usually pretty thin. That's really all it could be."

"Whatever, you're being crazy." A guy like Pat, he'll say you're being crazy even when you're not. To be nice and all.

We both eye the package on the ground for a couple of seconds.

"Well, the only way we're going to know is if you open it," Pat says, waiting for me to do something, anything, anything at fucking all.

"I know." My eyes don't leave the bulging brown envelope at my feet, stuffed with God knows what.

"Well then, let's see what it is," Pat says in a cheerleader voice, I guess trying to motivate me into action. He bends down and picks up the parcel, holding it out to me.

"Here goes nothing." With trembling hands, I tear it open gingerly, like you'd open a love letter you want to save forever. But it's anything but love I feel as I work up the nerve to peer inside.

"Well, I'll be damned," I mutter.

"What? What is it?" Pat asks, leaning over with impatience.

I hand him the package, totally confused. He pulls my tear-stained sketches from last class, the ones Fredrique tore apart and I subsequently trashed, out of the envelope.

"So does this mean he likes them now?" Pat asks, looking at me with bewilderment.

It's a question only Fredrique can answer. When I go to hunt for him a few seconds later, he and his lips are nowhere to be found.

— — —

"B FOURTEEN."

Georgette and I sit in a smoke-filled bingo hall and try to get rich. All around, chainsmokers in Happiness Is Yelling Bingo shirts are vying for the same goal, armed with Day-Glo Dab-O-Inks and lucky rabbits' feet. As for George, she's got her good luck Chia Pet, a gift from accountant man Gene, a.k.a. Geek.

"Isn't it quirky how he got me a Chia Pet? Unexpected from a CPA. Sort of whimsical or something," she told me on the way here, after revealing dick size and income. Both were pretty big, alrighty, but not big enough to compensate for his tiny personality, in my opinion. I told her so, but it fell on deaf ears. She's smack-dab in the middle of that murky trying-to-make-herself-like-him stage and there's no pulling her out of it.

"O sixty-nine!" the announcer calls.

"BINGO!" an elderly woman at the other side of the hall screams. A variety of under-the-breath curse words are muttered from bitter bingo-goers around the room, including us.

"Shit. And that's my favorite number, too," George says with a smirk as the floor attendant verifies the old bag's winning card.

"Yep, I bet. But Geek doesn't seem like the sixty-nine type, sorry," I say, tears sliding down my cheeks. My eyes are totally watery because of all the damn smoke in here. You like have to smoke to play bingo; I think it's a rule or something. Kind of goes along with that white-trash image, I guess.

"You never can tell," she says, pointing at the Chia Pet. "And he's not a geek, Ab. Give him a chance."

I had given him a chance last night. He came over for dinner and was all "Oh I looove your designs, Abbie" in this schmoozy way but was wearing a polo, Dockers and loafers, the most boring outfit on earth, and in my head I was like, Yeah, whatever, sure you do, that's why you're oozing with such style. But I was trying to be cool so I asked him about his work and he went on for forty-five minutes about some CPA exam he'd aced that puts him in this genius category, like I care. Then he called George "Puddin." Not Pudding, which would have been horrible enough, but Puddin, minus the *g*, which is much, much worse. And he was being serious. She is so much better than him. I cannot even begin to tell you.

"Next game, Kriss Kross," the bingo caller screeches.

"Speaking of, whatever happened with Chris after that breakfast thing?" Georgette asks, dabbing all her free spots.

I drop my Dab-O-Ink and put my head in my hands. "Oh God, I've gotta call him."

MAYBE IT was bad karma—me not calling Chris equals us losing at bingo. I don't know. But whatever the reason, we did lose at bingo last night and I am calling Chris today. Right after I call Franco, who I haven't talked to since Monday after the freaky sketch experience with Fredrique.

He asks me to go see a movie at the drive-in with him tonight—totally retro—pajamas, snacks, the whole nine. And he sounds so happy to hear from me, like he's playing Sega with Tim and totally stops the game so we can talk. When I hang up, I'm so elated from the great conversation with Franco that the Chris call doesn't seem so scary.

"Hello?" God, does he sound happy. Like top-of-the-fucking-world happy and I'm about to crush him like a bug.

"Chris? This is Abbie," I say, feeling like hell. Why did the guy have to sound so damn happy when he answered, like he'd just won the lottery or something? That happy voice and all, jeez.

"Hey, what's going on?" Mean voice. God, does *that* make me feel like shit.

"Uh, nothing. I was wondering if you want to come over and watch our shows," I say tentatively, twirling the phone cord around my index finger until it turns as red as the heart I'm about to break. "You know, so we can talk."

Silence. "What's there to say?"

"Chris, don't be like that. Please. I'd really like to talk to you. Okay?"

"Okay. I'll be over there by seven." Suddenly his voice sounds positively hopeful, and this makes me feel even worse than when he sounded pissed, to tell you the truth.

I go put on the dress he's most likely to hate, a red and blue polyester number, to make it easier on the guy. It's always better if the one breaking up with you is wearing an ugly outfit, in my experience. So I put on the polyester, throw my hair in two little braids—which Pat told me Chris hates—and wait.

At six forty-five he shows and gives me this hard hug like, Thank God you've come to your senses. I sort of halfheartedly hug back and he goes limp. I know that he knows what I'm going to say. He pulls away and looks at me.

"So."

"So." I hold open the door wider. "Come in." We have a seat on the couch and I stammer for a minute, the speech I'd rehearsed already erased from my memory. I completely suck at this. I've only broken up with one guy in my life and even that was a disaster, me trying to give him money and all. Like paying him off not to like me anymore or something.

"Listen, Abbie, save it. I know about Franco. I've known about him for awhile. Your best friend is my cousin, for goshsakes," he stammers. It's almost like I have on clown white or something, he's that pissed. I look down, remembering Pat's You-owe-it-to-them-to-tell-them speech.

"And I kept thinking that one day maybe you'd look at me and think, Here is my future," he continues. "But you didn't. You just didn't."

My head snaps up. "Pat told you about my future thing too?" Glad to know every little thing I tell my best bud goes straight back to Chris. Who knows what the hell else he told him. Oh God, if he told him I had sex with Franco or something, that would be too much.

"Don't be mad at Pat. He was only trying to help me win you over." He tilts my chin up with his fingers and his voice gets all low. "Because he knows how much I liked you. Like you."

Torture, plain and simple. I look back down, like I cannot meet his gaze during this exchange, there's just no way. "I know, and I like you too. You're the best. And believe me, I wish things could be different. They just can't, with me and Franco and all. They really just can't." I look up at him and see pain behind his blank expression. For a second I wish I could be into him instead of Franco. And we could be together and go to dinner with his dad and he'd leave personalized outgoing messages on his machine for me and bring me flowers and I'd always know what to expect. But that's the trouble with me, I like the unexpected. And Chris delivers anything but that.

He leans in to kiss my forehead—salt in the fucking wound, let me tell you. "I know, Abbie, I know they can't. But I'll miss hanging out with you."

"We can still hang, Chris," I say, pressing my lips against his smooth cheek. "We're friends, doll. And friends are forever."

The door swings open and George breezes in, Geek in tow, totally oblivious to the tense scene they just missed. "Hello, why isn't the TV on? Our show started five minutes ago."

They plop on the floor in front of us and turn on the tube. It's the first commercial break before we make any introductions.

EVEN IN my flannel pajamas buried under a thick blanket, I'm still freezing at the drive-in. "Maybe pjs weren't such a good idea," I wonder aloud.

"No shit," Franco answers, teeth chattering. "Think we should turn on the heater?" We decide to do that and, even though the sound is harder to hear, things are much more toasty in minutes. Franco is wearing yellow old-man pajamas, a fetching cotton shirt and pants combo, and looks too cool for school. My plaid flannel ensemble complements his look very nicely. The first flick is almost over but we've missed most of it so we decide to chat until the second one starts.

"This gang movie is supposed to be good, right?"

"Uh-huh. But I tell you right now, one racist comment from anybody in this joint and I'm going off." Franco nods over to the pickup next to us, full of obnoxious rednecks seemingly more interested in their Schlitz than the screen.

"Damn, you sound vicious. I mean, I'm against racism too, you know, don't get me wrong. But you sound for real. Like you might kill somebody or something."

"I've already had to once," he says slowly, looking out the window. Then he glances over at me and laughs. "Just kidding."

I join in his laughter but feel a little uneasy. Great, is he a murderer too? I am such a freak magnet, it really would not surprise me a bit, this is what's sad about the whole thing.

Franco leans over, breaking my reverie. "Hey, girlfriend, my little Hat Gal." I look into his eyes and think. No way is this the face of a murderer. I'm getting much too psycho these days. Like it's to the point I can't even take a joke.

I lean over and give Franco a kiss and he kisses me back, and by the time we look up the movie's already on, which makes our drive-in experience even more fifties. Somewhere after the thirtieth on-screen drive-by shooting, I fall asleep on Franco's shoulder, just like my mom used to do on my dad's when I was little. As the credits roll, Franco kisses my forehead to wake me up. When I open my eyes and see him there, I think this must be what it's like to be truly happy.

The next day, I have to deliver my once-a-semester fashion column to the *Dallas Gazette* by one and of course I wait until ten to even start the thing. Right off, I gush about Bethann's fake-fur-trimmed sweater at the Smoking Hips show. Then I flip through the past month's society pages I've stashed under my computer for more inspiration. I'm tempted to discuss pajamas as fashion, citing last night's drive-in experience, but I hate to seem like I'm glorifying myself or gloating about my cool life, which is of course what I would be doing, primarily for the benefit of Parker since I know he'll read it. I opt instead to go on for three paragraphs about the Southern belle dresses three debs are sporting in a pic in last Friday's paper. It's like, Why do these dresses still exist? Why aren't hoop skirts illegal? And why the hell don't you just carry the staff as an accessory to complete the Little Bo Peep look? I'm sure this will piss many Buffys and Muffys off, but that's why the paper pays students to write this weekly column—controversy. Any reaction—even hatred—is a good reaction when it comes to the alternative press, Mike, the editor, told me after my first column's batch of hate letters came in. It's an adage I take great comfort in, since outraging people is something I do exceptionally well.

Franco calls as I'm typing the final draft and I ask him if he wants to run errands with me. He says yes, so I pick him up on the way to the paper.

Have I mentioned that I'm a bad driver? I am, extremely, like my insurance is sky-high and they probably shouldn't even let me out on the streets. It's not that I don't know how to drive. I do. It's just that I'm easily distracted. By anything. Cute boys driving past, bad song on the radio, Big Gulp about to spill in the passenger seat. Any of these things is enough to divert my eyes and attention from the roadway, which has caused some problems for me in the past. Parker hated my driving. Even though I drove his ass everywhere, he was always muttering shit like "Great, you missed another turn" or "Gaaaaaawd, Abbie" in this really annoyed tone when I would slam on my brakes or something. Now I'd be like, "Whatever, get the hell out and walk if you don't like the way I drive," but back then I was very into Parker and eager to please. So I would feel inadequate and try my hardest to be a better driver, which in turn just made me more stressed and if anything worsened my driving.

So my driving has always sort of been an issue with boyfriends past. And on the way over I'm thinking Franco hasn't said a word about it yet, so I'm going to observe his body language on the ride to the *Gazette*, looking for signs of annoyance.

I honk and in a few seconds he and Jane hop in the car. "Hey, baby!" Franco calls, kissing me on the cheek. Jane is spazzing, running all over the back seat.

"Hey, sweetie, what's up?" I respond, my voice full of hormones. Franco is in a white T-shirt and old Levi's and I just want to jump him, he looks so cute.

"Not much, girlfriend," he says. God, I love it when he calls me girlfriend. "Just talked to Tim. He's coming over around four but I can hang with you 'til then."

I smile, looking for clenched fingers or rolled eyes as I peel out and lurch onto the expressway. No dice.

"So Zoe's in tomorrow, right?" I ask, attempting cucumber status but probably missing the mark.

"Yep," he answers, twisting around to pet Jane.

"That's cool. Do y'all have any plans?" I'm trying not to be nosy but these questions have very much been on my mind since the Frankoney Baloney message last weekend.

"Uh, not really. Well, sort of." He's still petting the damn dog, like he can't even look at me, for Chrissakes.

"Sort of?" I turn the radio up a notch.

"Yeah, but not anything major." He still can't look at me. I swear he can't. It's obvious he doesn't want me to know of his plans with her, and even more obvious that I'm not included in them. Time to retaliate.

"Well, you know that guy Chris you met at Eggs It that morning? He's been calling, really freaking out, since he saw me with you. So I guess I might see him, let him know what's up with us." Never mind the fact I did this last night and that he hasn't been calling at all. There are no rules in the trying-to-make-someone-jealous game, a game I perfected during my Parker period.

"That geek who liked you? In the suit?" Jane is licking his face and most of his attention is on her. Doesn't seem jealous in the least.

"He's not a geek," I protest, trying to add fuel to the fire. Pointless, since there are no fires of jealousy whatsoever raging in Franco's eyes. I'd have a better chance of making Jane jealous.

"Okay, whatever. Can I see your column?" That's cool, him wanting to see it. Parker wasn't the least bit interested in reading my shit or seeing my fashions or any of it. Which now I can see translates into him not being interested in me, since my clothes and my words are me. Back then I was such a dumbass—it's really embarrassing to remember some of the shit I put up with, it honestly is.

I open the glove compartment and hand him a copy. "Remember, the key word here is bitchy. My pen name is Polly Ester, isn't that a riot?"

Franco reads for awhile, chuckling at appropriate moments. I peer over at his face, all intent and everything. He really looks interested, he truly does. I'm pretty excited. It's like we're entering a whole different level now. Finally he looks up. "You know what? Zoe hates those Southern belle dresses too. She had to wear one in *Gone With the Wind*. In high school. I remember her saying she wished they didn't exist."

I could say the same about her.

I STARE AT my printed column, top of page eight in the Sunday edition. Even though I've read it probably ten times already, it's always a thrill to see my words ritualized in print, kind of like seeing my designs on somebody else. Private thoughts that were floating around my head nine days ago are now in the homes of 250,000 Dallasites. Such a trip.

The usual excitement I feel, however, is dampened by one major factor: Franco. The bastard hasn't called since last Friday, the day perfect Zoe landed from Oregon. Am I irrational to expect my boyfriend to call at least once a day, especially if his ex-girlfriend's here? I don't think so, but either I'm expecting too much or he's giving too little, because I am not a happy Hat Gal at the moment.

Let's say I haven't spent all week sewing like a madwoman to get him off my mind. Or that I haven't eaten four pints of Ben & Jerry's in the last four days. Or that I haven't thought incessantly about what he and Zoe are doing. Or that I haven't had Mom hang up and call me back on three separate occasions to make sure the phone's working. Let's for a moment pretend none of this has happened. I would still be extremely pissed at Franco. But since it all very much did happen, I am an even deeper shade of pissed.

And to top it all off, neither George nor Pat have been here for moral support. George drove to Austin with Geek, probably getting to hear how wonderful he did on the CPA exams another trillion times. And Pat's with Sal in Houston celebrating their fourteen-month anniversary. So here I sit, alone, just me and the silent telephone. Quite possibly going crazy. Most definitely going to bitch Franklin Richards III out the first chance I get.

Chapter 19

"It was damn Valentine's Day Friday and he didn't even call, Pat," I whine Tuesday afternoon on the way to Liberty Park. Pat's taking me there in an attempt to cheer me up, which is totally sweet. You have to love a guy who will hang with you when you're depressed without once mentioning PMS, you really do.

"Well, lots of people hate Valentine's Day. Like Fredri— Fucking bastard, learn to fucking drive," Pat bellows, honking at some guy in a Toyota who just cut him off. "Jeez. Okay, look. Fredrique even canceled class he was so depressed. Maybe Frank, like Fredrique, chooses not to celebrate it." He speeds up to catch the Toyota, flipping him off on the pass.

"Okay, hello, Fredrique has no one and Franco has me," I whine, looking over at my reflection in the side mirror. I'm cute enough and all, I really am. I have no clue why Franco wouldn't be proud to be with me. "Usually people with partners rub it into single people's faces this one day of the year. 'We like each other, we found each other, we have somebody and you don't.' And I didn't even get one lousy conversation heart, much less have the opportunity to flaunt my taken status to others. That would have been slightly hard to accomplish when your boyfriend is nowhere to be found and hasn't called since Friday, you know?"

Pat slides into a parking spot and jerks the emergency brake. We look forward and he points straight ahead. "Abbie, your merry-go-round awaits."

The apparatus to which he's referring sits in the middle of the park, sandwiched between the twisty candy cane slide and the rusted teeter-totter. Jumping out of the car, I see it—its chipped blue paint, the slightly lopsided base—and feel a tug of longing. I look over at Pat and break into a run.

He first brought me here in the June before freshman year, right after we moved to Dallas. I had just been dumped by Cunningham, BMX boy who went by his last name to be sophisticated, after only dating him two weeks and was pretty much depressed. So Pat told me he'd take me to his new favorite spot in the whole world to cheer me up. And that spot was the merry-go-round at Liberty Park.

It was funny, what he said that day. I remember he told me to sit in the center of the thing, in the middle of all the iron bars. And then he started spinning it around, faster and faster, for what seemed like forever. Until I felt nauseous. And when he stopped and the thing came to a halt, he goes, "See, something actually can spin faster than your life right now." It was cool, the way he said it. Like, Now the merry-go-round is under control, and your life soon will be too. In the year and a half since then, this merry-go-round has twirled many turns with one of us in the middle of it. The time Pat and Jay broke up. The day Parker threw my keys in my face. When Pat and Sal had their first fight. Any time our problems make us feel like we've lost all control, we sit on this thing until our equilibrium is lost along with it.

I hop on, sitting Indian-style in the center, and grip the two bars nearest me. Pat grins. "Ready?"

I squeeze my lids shut, feeling a bit nauseous already. Why couldn't the sonovabitch just call, would five lousy minutes kill his ass? I take a deep breath, then respond: "Ready." When I open my eyes again, the world is a streaky blur. The whirring in my ears is the sound of motion, my own, like a jet taking off into the sky.

As I KICK in the door after my uneventful class Wednesday, I curse myself for letting a male dominate my moods. Why should my happiness depend on another's actions? Why can't I just be happy for the sake of being happy, and to hell with Franco and whoever else should darken my day? It sounds simpler than it is, unfortunately. Even though I want to slap myself for doing it, I check Caller I.D. before even hitting the bathroom. And there it is: 555-2243. 3:45 P.M. I glance over at the clock: 5:16. One hour and thirty-one minutes since he called. The message light's blinking, but my bladder is about to explode. I go pee and weigh my options.

He's called. Either he's going to act like nothing's wrong, like he hasn't ignored me for twelve whole days, and just be like, What's up? Or he's calling to say he and Zoe are back together so they can not watch TV together and discuss foreign films and the sexual impact of *Lolita*, shit like that, for the rest of their days. It makes me tired just thinking about being that sophisticated. It's like how do Zoe and all of those coffee shop people have the energy to put on their berets and go to those experimental theater groups and read all those dreary books they're always discussing? Plus brush their teeth and wash their faces, normal stuff? It seems it would be hard to fit day-to-day tasks in your schedule if you had to keep up with the Zoes of the world. Like, Sorry, George, I can't drop off the phone bill payment—I've got a poetry reading, a "Kill Your Television" rally and then a "Hemingway: Genius or Junkie?" discussion group at Java Joint tonight. Whatever.

I have a certain respect for a person who can live her life like that, but there's no way in hell I could ever do it. Nor would I ever want to, for that matter. But maybe that's what Franco wants: Zoe. Or a Zoe replica, which there are plenty of in Dallas. If that's the case, I'm definitely not the girl for him. And maybe that's what he wants to tell me, why he's waited so long to call. I flush the toilet and head to the answering machine to hear the verdict.

"*Beep.* Hey, Abbie, Franco here. You haven't called in awhile, just seeing what's up. Zoe left today, just dropped her at the airport. Call me when you hear this, okay? Jane misses you. And Happy Valentine's Day, better late than never, right? Bye."

I rewind and play it again, hoping to figure out what the hell he's trying to say the second time around, to no avail. Okay. "You haven't called in awhile, just seeing what's up." Why would *I* call *him*, knowing his ex-girlfriend is in town and probably staying with him? "She left today and I just dropped her at the airport." So she's no longer here, I guess it's cool to call Abbie with Zoe out of the picture. And he picked her up from and took her to the airport, scene of a million teary goodbyes. Did he cry when she left? Did she? And "Jane misses you." What about him, does he not miss me? Or is he just talking through Jane—doesn't want to reveal his own feelings so he projects them through his dog, like Dad does with the cat? And my belated Valentine's greeting—acknowledgment that he actually did know the day existed and did not call me on the holiday of love. "Better late than never," my ass.

I play it a third time before calling him back. I dial quickly, anxious to hear what he has to say when he's talking to me directly and not to a machine. Let's face it, it'd take a real dick to break up on a machine. So maybe he's waiting to tell me person-to-person about his reconciliation with Zoe. If there was one, which there probably was, given the fact he never once called while she was here.

"Hello?" He still sounds the same at least. That is, what I can hear of him over the loud beat of my heart.

"Hey, Franco, this is Abbie," I say, trying to be cool. Like I couldn't care less.

"Abbie, long time no hear," he says, just like nothing's wrong. "What's up?"

"What's up? What's up? How the hell would I know what was up, since I haven't talked to you since last Friday?" Okay, so I lost it a little bit. But my God, twelve days?

"Huh? Ab, you're not pissed, are you?" The guy sounds totally taken aback, which kills me. I mean, if you didn't call your girlfriend for twelve days you would slightly expect she'd be pissed, right? "I told you Zoe was coming in, I told you that weeks ago. And I also told you she was going through a lot of shit with her dad right now and she probably wouldn't be up to meeting anybody, did I not tell you that?"

Ohmigod, he does not sound pissed, somebody tell me this is a joke. *He*'s pissed at *me*? When he's the one who hasn't called for twelve days? I'm fucking speechless, I really am. "Yeah, but . . ."

"So I did tell you that. And you knew she was here, right?" he asks, his voice getting louder and madder and louder and madder.

"Yes, Franco, but . . ."

"So you knew why I wasn't calling and I called the moment I got in from the airport, so what's the problem?" He sounds pretty damn defensive for a boy with nothing to hide, I'll tell you that much.

"The problem, if you would let me finish," I say—I told you I could be quite sarcastic when I want to—"is that you told me she was coming in town but you never said anything about ignoring me for twelve whole days, one of those days being Valentine's Day."

"Ab, I told you she was going through a lot of shit right now," he says, exasperation oozing all over the damn place. "It's not like I could just go, 'Oh, Zoe, sorry about your uncle molesting you and your dad not believing you. I am really interested, but can you hold that thought? I need to go call my girlfriend.' Abbie, it just wasn't possible."

I look over into the mirror and note I really look like shit right now, bags under my eyes and everything. Good thing I dye my hair because I'd bet anything Franco's making me go gray. "So you're telling me in twelve days"—I pause to do the math—"which equals two hundred and eighty-eight hours, you couldn't find one minute to call me?" I've got him there, I really do.

"No, I'm not saying that. I'm sure there was one minute I could've called, and I thought about it, really I did. But last week we went to Zoe's grandparents' in Houston and didn't come back until Monday. And I had to work at the liquor store until nine and then I just crashed. I mean, I guess I should have called, but I really thought you knew I was with Zoe. I never thought you'd be pissed." His tone conveys the fact that he thinks I'm being a jealous freak here. Maybe I am. I don't know, but you just don't ignore someone for twelve days—that's just not cool.

"Okay," I say, taking a deep breath. "You knew I knew you were with the love of your life, famous Zoe from Portland you bring up always, and you really thought I wouldn't be the slightest bit jealous or uneasy about that?"

He sighs, this long, skinny hiss. "Listen, Abbie, if you don't trust me, there is no point to continuing this relationship. If you don't trust someone, there is nothing there."

Is he trying to tell me we should break up or something? "I

trust you, Franco, but you have to admit the details on the Zoe thing are sketchy. You've never really even told me the full story on why you broke up."

"What does it matter? It's something I can't really talk about, I've told you that. And you know how much I like you, Abbie," he says, voice turning total Hershey's. Is he kissing ass because he feels guilty? I mean, did they fuck or something? "I can't deny that Zoe was a big part of my past, she was. But that's exactly what it is: past. You're my now, you know? And Zoe influenced a lot of my views, molded me in a ton of ways. But she isn't a goddess, and she isn't perfect. And she wasn't for me. That's why we're not together anymore. And we could never be together probably."

"Why not, though, Franco? I mean, when you talk about her, your whole voice changes. Like you're talking about this thing so cool, you can't waste your normal voice on it," I tell him. It does, too, I'm not lying. "And you get this look. A look like love, I guess. And that's what scares me."

He coughs, this uncomfortable little cough. "Look, Abbie, I will always love Zoe, but not love love like you're probably thinking. Love for like, I don't know, maybe a shirt."

"A shirt?" I look over into the mirror again. God, I really need some concealer or something. It's depressing, those dark circles and all.

"Yeah, your favorite shirt, the one you used to wear all the time. It fit great, was so comfortable, looked cool on you, went with a ton of your pants. Everyone always said what an awesome shirt it was. But one day, or more likely over the course of many days, the shirt didn't seem so great anymore. Maybe you washed it with the wrong thing or it got torn or just started looking dingy from too much wear. For whatever the reason, you just wore it less and less, until you couldn't imagine ever wearing it again. But it's still in the back of your closet, and every time someone tells you to throw it out or give it to Goodwill or something, you refuse. Because even though you wouldn't wear it anymore, you still love that shirt. Not for the shirt itself, probably, as much as for the memories you have of the great times you had wearing it." He pauses for breath. "Do you know what I mean?"

I nod into the receiver, thinking of Parker. "Yeah, I truly do."

"So will you not be mad at me anymore? Let me take you out to dinner. I still have Tim's car from my airport run, so I can drive for a change. Anywhere you want. Deal?" He sounds so sweet. Maybe I am being a freak, who knows. I get so crazy when my dad gets jealous, like asking Mom where she's been and who was there and so on, and possibly I'm doing the same shit. Like it's inherited or something.

"Deal," I answer, sticking my tongue out at myself in the mirror. I really need some concealer. I'm not kidding; I look about a million years old.

We end up going to Pepe's, my favorite Mexican joint, for quesadillas and margaritas. Franco's acting pretty normal, like all kissing me and telling me he missed me, the whole damn nine. I was nervous before he got to my apartment but once I saw him it was totally the same, really. I'm happy to be with him and everything—he looks hot, he's being cool—but I'm still a bit hurt. I mean, how much can you really like a person to not call them for twelve days? Like I'm not sure of anything anymore. I'm studying him for a sign. Is he looking at other girls? Not paying me enough attention? Engrossed in his thoughts, which are probably thoughts of her? Nothing seems out of the ordinary, though. Same old Franco. We talk about nothing for awhile, just bullshit stuff, but pretty soon, the topic turns to Zoe. I mean, I'm dying to know what's up but am afraid of looking like the jealous freak here. So I wait for him to bring it up, which finally he does right after the food arrives.

He tells me she wasn't so perfect, like she did have her faults. More than Parker ever said about Jan, that's for sure, like the girl could do no wrong. So Franco tells me she was always bitching about him smoking cigarettes. Always, in this belittling way, like calling him "trailer park" and stuff like that. And when she was in school in Portland, while they were still going out, she was sleeping around on him up there. Like a lot, which I already knew. But then he says he didn't even know for awhile, so here he was going up there to visit and he's sure all these guys he was being introduced to as her boyfriend were just laughing their heads off. Like, Sure you're her boyfriend, I fucked her two days ago. Which sucks. But when she told him about it, he remembers she said she didn't sleep with anybody she wouldn't want to be the father of her children. Like that was supposed to make him feel better about it, how selective she'd been with her partners. He just felt totally betrayed and lied to, that's all.

So that was the beginning of the end, he says. They'd already broken up once, majorly, after the deal with his parents. But then they got back together and he thought it'd be forever after all they'd been through. But he was wrong and it wasn't, which is really for the best.

Fresh margaritas are set before us, hopefully strong enough to loosen Franco's tongue about the big mystery link between Zoe's breakup and what happened between him and his parents. "So, the big blowout with you and your parents was about Zoe, right?" I inquire, hopefully not prying.

"Yeah. It was a big deal, the watershed event of my life, definitely."

"One thing or a series of things?" Why won't he just tell me? I am his damn girlfriend after all. Not knowing is definitely driving me nuts, especially since he's always hinting around about it and shit.

"One thing." He takes a big drink and closes his eyes. Tell me tell me tell me. "Basically, we were seventeen, the condom broke and she says she's late. For what? I said, like a dumbass. Pregnant. She's so pro-life it's not even funny. I tell her I'll support her no matter what. But she ended up going with the abortion, our parents got involved and it was just this huge mess. I haven't talked to my father since, if that gives you a clue of how major it was."

I don't know what to say, so I say nothing and just reach over to squeeze his hand tight. He's still looking out the window, at what I'm not sure. God, an abortion. And some major shit went down, so bad he can't even tell me or talk to his dad ever, and here I am freaking out because he hasn't called, so goddamn petty. He squeezes my hand back and together we look out into the darkness, saying nothing at all.

— — —

SATURDAY NIGHT is my night with George, the first in weeks. She's been with Geek almost twenty-four/seven lately, and I've either been freaking over Franco or hanging at his *casa*, so neither of us have been at the apartment much. The fishies are feeling neglected, I guess, because one of the clown loaches died today. George swears it died of loneliness.

"We need to be here more, to talk to them," George says, flushing the fish corpse down the toilet.

"I've been feeding them every day. I don't get what's wrong. That's the second one this month." Death always depresses me. Like when a fish dies, I start thinking about the time my dog died and next I think of how would I go on if one of my parents died and then I think about how weird it'd be if I died and next thing you know I'm teary-eyed. Georgette bounces back quickly from these funeral services, however, so my attention is diverted from death to more dire matters: boobs.

"Okay, here's the deal," she says into the mirror, applying eyeliner. "I got this Polaroid camera and two rolls of film. We go into a strip bar and explain I'm getting ready to get my boobs done and can we please snap a few photos, for ideas. Then we snap, snap, flash, flash, and it's done. We're free to enjoy our evening."

"Are you crazy? They don't let you have cameras in those places. It's illegal, I think." I sort of humored her at first, looking at the *Playboys* and all, but she's really starting to scare me with the boobspeak. I'm not kidding.

"No, not for our purposes. This is research," she says, looking down at her T-shirt. Probably envisioning the knockers she'll soon be sprouting. "I can see it being illegal for some pervert who's going to jack off or sell them or something, but this is strictly an academic endeavor."

God, I love her, I do, but what a naive bubblehead she can be sometimes. "Hello, Georgette, how the hell will these people know we're not going to sell them?"

"Look at us, Abbie, they won't think we're trying to sell them," she pleads, giving me her most innocent gaze in the mirror. "I mean, please, we'll give them our word."

"Oh, I'm sure our word is good as gold in one of those

places," I say, rolling my eyes. The girl's gone crazy, it's really frightening me. "It's never going to work."

She turns from the mirror to look me in the eye. "Ab, tell you what. We'll try it at one place, and if they kick us out we won't try anymore. I just need a little field research. Pleeeeeeease? I don't want to go by myself. And Gene won't set foot in one of those places, so he's out. Abbie, I'm begging here."

Take someone like me, nice and everything, and I'm always giving in to some crazy scheme. "Alright, alright. But I'm telling you, it's not going to work."

"Thank you, thank you!" She hugs me tight, hopping up and down. "Red Beaver, here come Gigi and Ab!"

Just like Design Institute receptionist Alison Simone, Red Beaver totally lives up to its name. It's an old barn that's been converted to a gentlemen's club. Green neon boobs flash on and off above the door, making the burly bouncer look like a martian every five seconds. He's total Wolfman Jack, like he was born to do this job. "Evening, sweetmeat, you here for amateur night?" he growls as we approach. "That's Thursdays."

I try not to cringe while Georgette giggles loudly. "Oh, amateur night, no, not us. What we're—I'm—actually trying to do is get some pictures of your girls. For research."

"No cameras, little lady. No video cameras either," he says, looking back at me, scratching his snarly beard. Like I'm hiding a video camera down my pants or something, please.

"Uh, it's not for anything perverted, not that this is a perverted place or anything—that's not what I mean," George stammers, punctuating every other word with an annoying giggle. "It's just that I'm getting ready"—her voice drops an octave—"to get my boobs done. And I need some ideas."

He looks at her chest and laughs. "I tell you what, doll, the only idea you need is this one: the bigger the better. You tell your doc that and you'll be just fine." He guffaws again real low, like he just cracks himself up.

"Can we get out of here?" I whisper to George, who's still looking hopefully at Mr. Disgusting. I'm really getting the creeps. Places like this aren't exactly the perfect setting for a night on the town or anything, you know?

"Well, how much is the cover?" she inquires. "Maybe we could just check it out."

Bouncer adjusts his jeans jacket and lets out a brawny belch. "Ten apiece."

Georgette twirls around to look at me pleadingly. If she thinks I'm paying to get in this place, she's crazy. "Hell, no, we are not paying twenty dollars to look at fake boobs when we can pay five for a magazine and see the same shit!"

"They're not all fake," Georgette protests.

Bouncer clears his throat. "Yes, they are, little lady. But plastic's fantastic far as I'm concerned."

I roll my eyes and grab George's arm, yanking her away. "Let's go."

"Remember, Luscious Lips, you and your new titties come back on a Thursday night soon. So you can test the merchandise!" Mr. Disgusting calls as we head to the parking lot. I'd like to kill his ass, I really would.

We get into the car as fast as possible and lock the doors. "That," I say, "was a total nightmare. What an asshole!"

Georgette looks toward the barn, which casts a green glow over her face. "Wonder how much you get on Amateur Night?"

I wait for her to laugh but she doesn't. Refraining from gracing that question with a response, I peel out of the gravel lot, crank up the radio and sing at the top of my lungs.

Chapter 20

Around four, two hours after George and I dragged in from our Girls' Night Out, the ringing phone jars me from a deep sleep.

"Hullo?" I croak, not fully awake.

"Hey, Hat Gal, Hat Gal," a drunken voice slurs. Franco.

"Franco? Where are you?" I ask, waking up damn fast. He can be rude, sure, but he never calls this late. Something must be wrong.

"It's not important," he says, sort of laughing. "Just called to say I'm glad you're my girlfriend."

It's sweet, him calling to say that, even if it is such an ungodly hour. "So are you drunk?" Rocket scientist, I know. But like I said, I'm asleep and everything.

"Yep, pretty drunk," he whispers, like he doesn't even want me to hear.

"Do you even know what time it is? Who are you with? Is Tim there?"

"Nobody, I'm with nobody, and it's late. But I just wanted to tell you that. That I'm glad, you know, glad you're my girlfriend. That's all." He hiccups.

I sit up in bed. "Do you need me to come get you? Where are you? You're not driving Tim's car still, huh?" I ramble, probably making little sense.

There's a long pause, and I'm afraid Franco's passed out on the phone. "Franco! Franco!" I holler, in hopes of reviving him.

"I gotta go," he whispers. "I'll call you when I'm back in town."

Back in town—where the hell is he? "Back in town from where? Franco, where?"

He hiccups again. "But I'm glad, remember. Okay? I'm real glad. Bye-bye."

In a daze, I check Caller I.D. a few minutes later: "4:07 A.M., Out of Area." I plop down on the couch and point the remote toward the TV. An infomercial for Psychic Friends Network lights up the room, promising "unequaled advice and direction in love and life." I look over at the phone and back at the screen, thinking, Should I? God, I am now officially pathetic. It doesn't take a psychic to tell me that.

Franco confuses me so. Calling at four, piss drunk, telling me he's happy I'm his girlfriend. Out of Area. Where the hell could he be? I mean, sweet he told me he's happy and all, that was cool. But now, like what if he's driving and gets a D.U.I.? He had Tim's car. And he said Tim wasn't with him. When he dropped me off this morning, everything was fine. I felt really close to him after the Zoe talk and all. But now he's calling me getting me all scared and confused and I don't know what to do.

I remember once my therapist told me to rate the following things in order of preference on a piece of paper: when someone makes me sad, when someone makes me angry, when someone makes me happy. Real fast I wrote, *happy, mad, sad*—I'll take mad over sad any day of the week. When I handed her the paper, she crumpled it up and threw it in my face, telling me they're all bullshit, no one can make you feel a certain way. You're in control of your emotions, she said, looking me straight in the eye, and don't you ever forget it.

A soap-star-turned-psychic with a bad toupee comes on to share his near-death experience, confessing how his psychic friend saved him from the clutches of death. I think it'd probably take more than a psychic buddy to save me from the clutches of Franco at this point. As Soap Star continues his tale of tragedy and triumph, I drift off into a restless sleep.

OVER SUNDAY brunch—cold pizza, Ding Dongs and Dr Pepper—I fill George in on the Franco call. She agrees it's fucked, him not telling me where he is, even. I swear, I cannot figure him out. Which is probably why I'm with him, truth be told. Like a dumbass, I like the mystery men. George tells me she's finally getting bored with Geek, thank God. No mystery there. It's like, Can you tell me one more time what you made on those C.P.A. exams? I've forgotten since the last five hundred times you told me.

And even the sex sucked, she says. Like he had no fucking clue. I haven't even told George or anybody this, but the sex thing with Franco is really weird. Like we don't have it too often.

"Like how often are we talking?" George leans in once I confess, eager for the dirt. I rarely share sex secrets, even with her, so this is a treat.

"Um, like we haven't had sex in seventeen days. Since two weeks ago last Thursday. It's starting to get kind of weird. I didn't really see him since Zoe was here or whatever, right? But then I saw him and tried to initiate it, but he just wanted to fool around. Which is cool and everything, but it's like, Is he not attracted to me? Or what? And then Friday I was going to put a movie in his VCR but there was already one in there." I pause, remembering. "*Blow Me Blondes.*"

The tape affixed with a bright yellow sticker, black lettering, three words. I saw it in a flash—pow pow pow—and then I just thought, What the fuck is going on? Am I not good enough to get off to, you have to rent the fucking video? No pun intended or anything, but my God.

Georgette gasps, and I know this is freaking her out. It's freaking me out. "Ohmigod. No way."

"Yeah, I know," I say. I mean, frankly it gets worse. I debate telling her, like I don't want her to think I'm dating a freak and all, but I'm sick of keeping it a secret. "While he was fixing the toilet in some lady's apartment I was sort of straightening up and I found this wadded-up T-shirt of mine all stuck together next to the couch. And it doesn't take a genius to figure out what's making it stick."

When I saw that T-shirt, basic ribbed Gap I left over there one night, I held it for a long time, feeling the dried cum flake beneath my fingers. Like the mashed potatoes flaked off the TV dinner tin I took from that date with Franco. I had so many hopes that date: he seemed so into me. But now, what's going on? I masturbate too, don't get me wrong, but I don't choose it over sex or anything, not like he apparently does.

"Oh God." She takes a big bite of pizza, eyes wide as pies. "But masturbation's normal really. I know I do it."

I just masturbated this morning if you want to know the damn truth. "But if you're masturbating in addition to having a normal sex life, fine," I say, frustrated. "But if you're masturbating instead of having a normal sex life, isn't there a problem there?"

She taps her fingers on the table. "Well, think about his job."

I picture him in a white room, the white T-shirt, the white cum. "I know, that's another freaky thing. He's jacking off into a cup every weekday afternoon, so is it like he's too tired to have sex? But if so, how can we explain *Blow Me Blondes?* Obviously he had enough energy to stain my shirt."

She laughs, pulling her hair in a ponytail. "It is kind of strange. But seventeen days really isn't *that* long. Some people go a month without having sex. Or longer."

Some people, okay—but not me and Franco. We should be like goddamn bunnies, not Bundys, for Chrissakes. I just don't get it, like it makes me very insecure. Am I not cute enough? Is my butt too big? Do I need lacier underwear? The questions thunderstorm around my brain like so much rain. "I can see it after they've been married fifty damn years. Not when they've just been having sex for four weeks or whatever."

She laughs, looking down at her boobs. She does that all the time now; it can be quite annoying. "Next time you're over there, just rape him. Maybe he's waiting for you to take control."

I bite into my third Ding Dong of the morning, making my butt just that much bigger. "Maybe I'll do that, just rape him," I say with a shrug. "But who the hell knows when the next time I see him is gonna be."

Franco calls later in the afternoon, still Out of Area. I'm gone to Pat's so he tells the machine, not me, his whereabouts: Graceland. Took a bus because he's missing his dad, he said. Depressing, really. I went with George once. It was funny, cheesy as hell, but I doubt a peanut-butter-and-nanner sandwich would taste too good alone. Franco asks me to pick him up at the station the next day. When he hangs up, he really sounds like he's going to cry. I swear to God he does.

After I play the message a couple of times, I call my own dad, who's in the middle of a basketball game. I know he wants me to let him go so he can watch it, but I make him talk to me about nothing until halftime anyway.

Fredrique's in one of his usual moods again, I see as I walk in the door Monday. The swelling in his lips has gone down but has been replaced by a scowl the size of Texas. "I was informed this morning by the administration that some of you"—he looks around the room—"have been complaining that I don't do enough teaching. Not enough lecturing. Not enough tests. Well, guess what, kids, the only test you'll face in the real world is if your collection can hold its own on the runway. And as I said the first day of class, I take Runway Collections, the name of this course, to mean that you must create a collection for the runway in order to pass."

He rises from his chair, hands clenching the sides of his desk. "Now I don't know who's been bitching to the administrators. Nor do I care. I am going to tell you all the same thing I told them. When I cancel class or let you out early, which I do often, this is not to mean you can just go play or dance or whatever it is that you do with yourselves. It means I am giving you time to work on your collections, which I hope all of you have been doing. You should have nine complete pieces done by now to be on schedule." I look over at Pat and raise my eyebrows. I have five pieces started but none completed, and I know he hasn't done much more than me.

"But just to please the higher powers that be, you all need to bring in one of your designs, completed, on Monday. Not the muslins, either—the real thing. I also need to see accessories, shoes, anything you've designed to complete the look. Though I hate to, I will be grading you on this. And no late work will be accepted." He stares at me for a second, probably remembering the theme-banana fiasco. "Are we understood?"

"Yes," we groan in unison.

All I need is another grade to fuck up. My parents aren't going to help pay for another semester and I already owe a million dollars in student loans as it is. Whoever went to the administration about not having *enough* class must be off their rocker.

"You have the rest of the week to work on this. I will be holding a lecture class"—he rolls his eyes—"Wednesday and Friday for those feeling slighted. It is optional, and if less than five people are here at eight sharp the lectures will be canceled." He snatches up his notebook and opens the door. "Class dismissed so you can work on your projects," he screeches into the hall, probably in case whoever reprimanded him is listening.

A MELANCHOLY Franco's been very affectionate since I picked him up thirty minutes ago at the Greyhound station downtown, a scary little building that reeked of urine, one I hope never to visit again. We're swinging by Tim's to pick up Jane before going to his apartment. "So I finally get to meet the infamous Tim," I say, patting Franco's hand on my knee.

"Yeah, you'll love him," he says, kissing my elbow. "He's the best."

The boy opening the door of the run-down duplex is just the sort of guy I expected Tim to be. Black hair, shaved close to the skull, pretty but vacant blue eyes, beer belly peeking out under a shrunken concert shirt. A foaming beer's in his right hand, a yapping Jane's at his ankles. "Hey, dudes. What's up?"

Franco high-fives Tim as we enter the trashed environment. Beer cans, clothes, pizza boxes, ashtrays and newspapers cover every inch of available space. Snow globes and shot glasses line the bookcases, which are overflowing with paperbacks, textbooks and a few incomplete sets of encyclopedias.

"Abbie, this is Tim," Franco says, pointing to him with a wink. "Tim, my friend Abbie."

I stop staring at my surroundings long enough to shake Tim's hand and get pissed about the fact I was just introduced as Franco's friend and not girlfriend. Is he hiding the fact from his friends, too? Like the only time I'm allowed the privilege of being referred to as his girlfriend is in private and in twenty-four-hour diners?

"Hey Jane, hey baby." Franco scoops Jane up and pretty soon

is covered in dog saliva. He does adore that damn dog—more than he adores me?

"Have a seat," Tim says, knocking the junk covering the couch onto the floor. I smile at him and perch on the corner of the rust Early American monstrosity. "You guys wanna smoke?" he asks, pulling out a bong.

I pass on it but Franco nods and they smoke for awhile. Each puff of pot smoke and gurgle of bongwater drives me further and further into depression. Since the whole Parker ordeal, I really can't be around the stuff without getting down. So by the time we finally gather Jane and say our goodbyes, I'm not in the best of spirits.

"What's wrong, Hat Gal?" Franco asks as we pile in my car.

"Nothing," I say, slamming the door. What the fuck. "Well, something. What's up with you introducing me as your friend in there? And not your girlfriend?"

He looks at me like I'm on crack. "You are my friend as well as my girlfriend. And 'girlfriend' seems really sexist."

"Sexist? Why the hell would it be sexist?" I ask, voice rising to Mom levels. "You are distinguishing me from your other friends by calling me your girlfriend. Like I'm a different sort of friend, you know? But when you don't call me that, I'm thinking, 'Does he not like me or what?' It's upsetting." My voice breaks. I told you this sex thing has really made me insecure. Like maybe I should change my name to Sal or something.

"God, Ab, I'm sorry. It's just that Zoe always thought it was sexist," he says, grabbing my hand. "Like I was bringing attention to the fact she was a girl when there was no reason to. A gender thing."

"Oh," I answer all cold. Lovely Zoe again. I'm aware everyone has exes by now, we're out of high school and all, but do I have to hear about them every damn day? I certainly don't bring up Parker every five seconds. I might think about him but I certainly don't talk about him all the time, especially in front of Franco. It's rude.

He squeezes my hand. "Baby, I'll call you that from now on. I mean, I like calling you that."

I nod and we drive along for a few miles in silence. His

sweater got permeated with pot smoke back at Tim's, and now the smell's wrapping around me like a noose. I roll my window down and flip the heater on.

Jane, almost asleep in Franco's lap, lifts her head in response to the brisk breeze swooshing through the car. Franco clears his throat. "Whatcha thinking about, Ab?"

"Just thinking about my ex," I say. I am, too. Like how could he have a wonderful girlfriend like me and then just want to get high all the time and forget I exist?

Franco strokes Jane's head. "What'd yours do to you?"

So I tell him the whole story—the countless nights Parker blew me off for his bong and the smell permeating my clothes and how I locked myself in the bathroom and cried, all of it. He rubs the back of my neck and says he feels really bad for smoking in front of me, knowing about everything now, and that he'll be more considerate next time. So we go in his apartment and lie on the bed with all of our clothes on. Jane's scratching on the door and I'm thinking, Is this another night of nonaction? But then Franco goes in the bathroom and comes out wearing the daisy hat I made and we just have the most incredible sex ever, sex that makes you cry.

Wednesday Franco's at the liquor store until nine so I come home for the first time in two days to get some clean clothes and watch TV with George and Chris, who still comes over for our shows despite our couplehood not working out. We're getting the lowdown on the dumping of Geek when all of a sudden George says something, like I can't even repeat it because I'm not really listening, and Chris starts laughing hysterically. I tell them to shut up because the commercial's over but they keep on giggling and giggling. Then George jumps up to go to the bathroom and comes back wearing a fresh coat of lipstick and I think, Hmm, what's up with that? As soon as the show's over, I go back to Franco's and we don't get out of bed until Thursday afternoon. When Franco finally crawls into the shower to get ready for the fertility clinic, I whisper, "*Blow Me Blondes*, eat your heart out!" and laugh and laugh.

— — —

EARLY FRIDAY I come home after Franco trots off to do his maintenance stuff and there is a boy I've never seen before sitting at the dining room table with Georgette. He's wearing this I-Heart-McDonald's shirt and frayed jeans. His blonde bob is slightly wavy, like hair that's just been taken out of tight braids, and frames a cute-in-a-little-boy-way face. Hot Boy Alert.

"Hey, Georgette. Hey, McDonald's," I say, wishing I'd bothered to put on some eyeliner before coming home.

"Hi," Georgette says, avoiding eye contact. She fucked him, I can tell, and this really freaks my shit out because she is so anti-casual-sex, like she never even had sex with Cradle Rob. And they at least dated, you know? "Steven, this is Abbie. Abbie, this is Steven."

"So how do you two know each other?" I ask in this overly cheery way, grabbing an apple from the bowl on the table and having a seat. Georgette shoots me a dirty look, like Please don't make this any worse.

"We met last night at Freezer Burn," he drawls in this surfer voice. "Gigi's cool, man."

Georgette squirms a little and I go, "Yeah, she is. Man."

We all look at each other for a second in silence, then Steven leans back in his chair. "You seen my boxers, Gigi? I looked on the floor by the couch, but I didn't see them."

Georgette giggles, turning three shades of red, as we all look over at the striped couch. The scene of the crime. Three empty condom wrappers, orange, dot the carpet. At least they were safe, I guess. "Nope, haven't seen them," she says really fast, like an auctioneer. "Ab, you're supposed to call Pat ASAP. And Steven, I better get you home. I've got class in about an hour."

Even though I could torture her further and say something about her not being in school this semester, I decide to return Pat's call instead. "Well, guess the phone's calling my name. Nice to meet you, Steven. Have fun in class, Gigi."

She gives me a This-guy-is-clueless smile. "Oh, guess who I saw at Freezer Burn last night? Sal. With that guy again. But I didn't say anything to Pat when he called."

I put a hand on my forehead and feel a headache coming on. "Maybe I won't call him, then." When I get in my room, I kick my shoes off and lie down. George having sex with a cute, dumb boy—quite a shocker. She's always been a little insecure, hence the boob job, but she's really becoming someone else entirely. I should talk to her about it, figure out what the hell's going on.

"You wanna go out this weekend?" I hear George asking Steven as they leave the apartment. "That way I can still say I've never had a one-night stand."

Chapter 21

Reality hits Sunday when I don't have one complete outfit done and have less than twenty-four hours to figure something out. Franco's still in bed when I slink out of his apartment, feeling guilty as hell for spending practically the whole week over here partying and playing house when I should be a responsible adult and finish my projects and do my laundry, shit like that. The problem is that I don't feel like an adult at all, probably because every time I talk to my mom she reminds me what an irresponsible kid I still am. And me playing hooky all week at Franco's really proves her right.

I stop by the fabric store on the way home, hoping to get some sort of inspiration. The closest thing I have to finished is this brown trapeze dress—I just need to finish the zipper—but it really needs something, I'm not sure what. I hit the crafts store next door and think, Leaves, that's it. Big old green leaves around the neck and bright yellow stockings on the legs would make for an untraditional banana-inspired look, sure to be the talk of the town. Especially if that town is Food Town, my next stop.

I walk directly to the banana aisle and grab a bunch, making a big to-do over which to pick in case anyone is watching. "Man, these look really fresh. But these . . . it's hard to decide which are fresher." An old lady in a double-knit pantsuit swiftly selects a bunch of celery from the bin next to mine and scampers off, casting me a curious sideways glance as I ramble on. See, the deal is that I need not the bananas but the stickers on the bananas. The little red ones. I'm going to cover a pair of platform shoes in them to accessorize the dress. But the trick is how to go about the thievery without a manager-type questioning my actions. Plan A is to act crazy. And so far it seems to be working.

"Do you guys wanna come home with me?" I say to a bunch of bananas in my left hand, while swiping its sticker with my right and placing it in my purse.

"No, we don't," I say in a falsetto voice, then set the bunch back where I got it. I repeat this about fifteen or twenty times, changing the dialogue every few times for variety. I figure I need forty stickers to cover two size-eight shoes, so I'm halfway there. Then I spot a uniformed kid in green, sixteen tops, coming toward me. An employee. I cross my eyes and turn the volume up on my Adam Sandler voice.

"But Mr. Banana, won't you come home with me?" I coo. "I promise I'll be good."

"Uh, ma'am, um . . ." The employee lurks a few feet away, hesitating. I look at him with one eye, the one that's not crossed.

"What, mister? Can't you see I'm having a private conversation here?" My theory is that while most people will mess with a thief, very few will mess with a loon. My aunt Janice is crazy, so maybe it runs in the family, who knows. It's coming awfully easy, whatever the reason.

"Um, just checking to see if you need anything," he says, averting his eyes and shifting his weight from foot to foot. His acne-plagued face gets even redder as I give him my best crazy glare.

"No, I don't." I spin around, then set the bananas on top of my head. "Do you need anything, Mr. Banana?" I clear my throat and cross my eyes as hard as I can. "No, *gracias*, señor," I growl in a really bad Spanish accent.

The stockboy or whatever he is sort of backs off, looking very freaked. "Okay, miss, just checking." He turns around and sprints down the aisle, probably to tell the others that some crazy lady's loose in the produce section.

I start plucking the red stickers off really fast, one after the other, until every banana's bare. Now that I'm a known loony-toon, I can steal in solace. They won't take some crazy lady to jail for stealing stickers off bananas. If I'm questioned any further, I'm going to say I need them for my letters to my grandmama in heaven 'cause I ain't got no stamps. The heaven thing plus the bad grammar should convince them not to book me. I'm too sad and stupid. But I never get the chance to act out my plan because no one dares speak to me as I leave. They just stare.

"That's the banana lady," my clerkboy friend says in a stage whisper, nudging his clerkboy cohort as I stroll out the door, eyes crossed as hell.

THE PHONE'S ringing when I get inside and it's Pat, perturbed that I haven't called him all week when he's left twelve messages. "Sorry, sorry, I've been at Franco's," I say, transferring the swiped stickers from the inside of my purse to the door of the fridge. They'll be safe here since we have no food and rarely go near the thing anymore.

"George told me you were at Franco's when I talked to her, but that was like Thursday," he says, sounding semi-hurt. He's really quite sensitive, I swear. "Then yesterday some dude named Steve answered. Is he the geek?"

I close my eyes and picture the I-Heart-McDonald's boy that George is still hanging with, a beautiful image. "Nope, he's a new one. Cute, but I get the feeling it's like, It's a pretty house—too bad nobody lives there."

"Not a brain surgeon, huh?" Pat jokes, chuckling.

"Hardly," I say. I've talked to him a few times since that first encounter and it's like he's totally the kind of guy who'd study for a drug test, that fucking stupid. "Hey, have you done your piece for tomorrow yet?"

"Just about done with it. I've got to finish with the rocks and it's finito."

Rocks? "Did you say 'rocks,' as in 'Love on the'?" I crack myself up, I swear I do.

"Yes, you Neil Diamond freak, and that describes my love to a T," he says. "But that's all you're getting out of me. I want it to be a surprise."

"Okay, whatever. But mine can't be, because I need your advice on it now." I give a detailed description of my concept. "I mean, it's more detailed than the sketch—the original draft was just a trapeze dress I called 'Kiwi,' for the color and the fuzzy brown material. But now that it's something tangible, it definitely screams for more. So I decided to go for the banana thing because it's brown like the top of a banana but not obvious like me coming in with a yellow tube dress and going, 'Hello, this is the unimaginative banana dress, give me an *F* please.' You know?"

He doesn't know, probably, but he tells me he does to get me off the phone. He's late for his job at the bookstore. "Buy me the new *Vogue*, please," I plead, since he gets a thirty percent discount. He tells me he will, so I kiss into the phone in lieu of saying goodbye.

I GET UP late Monday, as usual, and dash around the apartment trying to find my other black boot. Thank God I had the good sense to gather my assignment in a garment bag by the front door last night, or else I'd be twice as stressed.

"George, have you seen my other boot?" I holler, opening her door to an unslept-in bed, still made and everything. Guess she's at Ronald McDonald's. Either that or in a ditch somewhere, but someone would have called me if she was in a wreck.

It's fifteen to eight and a twenty-minute drive, so I give up the hunt for the boots and slip on my Mary Janes. They look okay with the little-girl dress I'm wearing, but it's almost like it's too much: overkill. I was hoping to contrast the schoolgirl-uniformishness of the outfit with the hipness of the boots, but oh well.

I haul ass to school, applying makeup en route. It's five after as I slide into class, bogged down by garment bag, purse and bag of banana Laffy Taffys. Fredrique isn't even here yet, meaning I risked my life getting here for nothing. I collapse into my usual seat, out of breath.

"Breakfast of champions," Pat says, pointing to my Laffy Taffys.

"Yep. Great shirt." I touch his oil-stained mechanic's shirt in awe. "Real grease and everything, right?" His style kills me, it really does.

He nods with pride. "Yep. Pennzoil ten-W-forty. It was my grandpa's."

"Let's see your project," I say, starting to unzip my garment bag, but Pat stops me.

"Fredrique just said no one better give any sneak previews. He went to get Mr. Bradley. I guess he's gonna have Bradley sit in during our presentations to prove we're actually getting grades. Someone must have chewed his ass out major, because he's all freaking out. But he'll be back in a second."

At that moment, Fredrique glides in, wearing a peasant blouse and bell-bottoms, Bradley in usual fake Armani hot on his heels. "Okay, everybody, Señor Bradley is going to observe this presentation, which you will be graded on." He puts extra emphasis on the "graded on" part, pulling out a seat for Bradley in the back of the room. Mr. Bradley kind of waves, like a prom king in a hometown parade.

"Now, we will go in alphabetical order, starting with *Z* and going to *A*, and you will have three minutes to show your piece. I'll be looking for presentation techniques discussed in our lectures." He pauses again, smiling at Bradley. We all look at each other like, What lectures? Fredrique is really laying it on thick, I'm serious.

"Think of this as a test. Because every piece of fashion you create is a walking test score of its designer." Fredrique titters. He sounds nervous probably because that last statement made absolutely no sense. Then he calls the first person up, Rick Zambini, like he's calling a sheep to slaughter.

Maybe it's because Bradley's in the room, who knows, but for whatever reason Fredrique is being very cautious with his reactions, very not himself. Rick's theme is skeletons and his piece is a black dress with white bone shapes sequined on the top, like an X ray. In normal mode, Fredrique would have more than likely made some catty remark about whether this is a dress or a Halloween costume. But this morning he just looks over at Bradley, nods and says, "Very imaginative, Señor Zambini. Exciting concept, bones. You may be seated."

It continues along that vein, boring, until Pat goes up. All hell breaks loose, I swear. His dress is turquoise, tight, with big orange goldfish sewn all over it, everywhere. Then he has sewn a clear shower curtain material over the entire dress, creating that aquarium illusion. Around the high neckline he's stitched bright green neon piping, like those necklaces you buy at the circus that glow. And around the bottom of the dress, right above the knee, are hundreds of those bright orange aquarium rocks in a big row. I look at the thing as he's pulling it out of the bag and I'm thinking, My God, he just totally blew everybody else out of the water. Or the aquarium. Everyone else must be thinking the same thing because there's a buzz then a murmur and then a small roar as we all gather round it.

"Here is what I call the Swim Dress. Dressy enough for a formal affair, quirky enough for a nightclub, it is versatile, whimsical, and, most importantly, unforgettable," Pat says in his cheesy D.J. voice, cracking up. He holds up the sandals for us to see. They're made of this printed canvas that has that fluorescent sign all over it that says *Gone Fishin'*. It's an ornament everyone has had at one time or another, even if they've never owned an aquarium, and I smile at my bud's ingenuity.

"Bravo!" I holler, and everyone claps.

"Order! Order!" Fredrique hollers, losing his cool momentarily. "Settle down, settle down." He clears his throat and looks at Pat. "Very creative, very unique, señor. You may be seated."

As he walks back to his chair, there's a new strut in Pat's step, like he knows he officially rules now. I'm proud to be sitting next to him. "You are so awesome. I cannot believe you did that in a damn day!" I whisper, thinking my dress really sucks now.

"Try four days. One of the benefits of being in a fight with Sal and having your best friend ignore you," he says, sticking his tongue out at me. "Lots of free time."

Even though he said it with a smile, I hug him to make up for all the calls I never returned and all the times I've blown him off for various boys over the years. "You know, guys come and go with me, but you're here to stay. Even if I never call your ass. And even if your dress is better than mine."

He kisses my forehead and tells me his is in no way, shape or form better than mine. I'm flattered for a sec until I realize he hasn't even laid eyes on my dress yet. No one has but me.

I pass out banana Laffy Taffys before my presentation because I've found your grade usually improves if you have a gimmick or gift for the audience that somehow ties in with what you're talking about. Banana dress, banana taffy. It was either that or banana nut bread, and there was no way my ass was going into the kitchen for Fredrique's sake. The other option was back to Food Town for more bananas, but I wasn't up to more dramatics. So taffy it was.

"A dress for the lady on the go and in the know, a statement that says, 'I'm bananas about fashion and I have sex a-peel'—the Banana Dress." I pull out the fuzzy frock dramatically, pausing for a moment. "The look is completed by bright yellow tights"—I hold them up for a second—"and shoes that can handle any sticky situation." For drama, I pull out the shoes extra slowly from the garment bag, adding to the suspense. A slight gasp goes through the crowd as they inspect the Andy Warholish sticker-covered platforms. Pat claps, but he's the only one.

Fredrique clears his throat. "No more clapping, please. Very interesting, McPhereson. But spare us the puns next time." I look at him expectantly while he glances over at Bradley and sighs. "Nicely done. You may be seated."

I got a kind word out of Fredrique finally, for the first time. I drag my stuff back to my seat and breathe a sigh of relief.

DINNER, Franco and I, Wednesday night. He tells me he and Tim are going to Lubbock for the weekend to see Marcia Pastry, not considering my feelings a bit. I mean, he doesn't even ask me to go or anything. Not that I want to go anyway, really. Just a zillion boys and girls getting high and bobbing their stockinged heads to the beat of some shitty surfer band. But it would have been nice to be asked.

After four rum-and-Cokes, Franco's pretty drunk, but a good drunk—all smiles and kisses and corny wisecracks. He's kissing everywhere—my eyes, my hair, my ears—as we wait for the check, and I'm thinking tonight will be the night for some major sex, no doubt about it.

But now the prospect of an orgasm not induced by masturbation is looking more and more unlikely as Franco nods off in the passenger seat next to me on the way home. When we get to his *casa*, I half walk and half drag his butt to the door.

"What's up?" he asks, totally disoriented.

"Home sweet home," I answer, trying to get his key to fit in the lock.

"Okay." He leans against me and rests his head on my shoulder. Jane's barks and yaps ring out into the air as I kick the door open.

"Hey, Jane." I guide Franco back to his bed and dump his fully clothed body onto the mattress with a plop. Jane jumps up next to him and starts licking his face, but he doesn't stir.

No sex for Abbie tonight.

After taking Jane for a walk around the complex, I make myself at home in the apartment. First, I grab some chips from the cabinet. Then the phone takes priority—first George and then Pat. Neither are home. A quick flip through the channels proves just as unfruitful. Despondent and bored, I start rifling through his drawers in search of a magazine or book or something, anything, to keep me occupied. That's when I see it.

A letter.

Addressed to Franco in Austin, a woman's flowery handwriting. No return address. Postmarked like two years ago.

Should I open it? It'd be a violation of privacy, definitely, but then again wasn't a part of me violated tonight? Taking Franco to dinner, thinking we'd have an intimate evening, and then having to tow his tanked ass to bed—wasn't that in a way a violation of my hopes, my expectations?

Maybe not. But I pick up the envelope anyway and take it over to the couch. Perhaps it's nothing—an overdue notice from a landlord, or a letter of recommendation from an employer. Then me reading it wouldn't be so wrong, really.

I drop it on the couch and go check on Franco and Jane. They're both out cold in the center of his mattress. I close the bedroom door softly and resume my perch in the living room. Then slowly I remove the letter from its envelope.

One page, handwritten, on plain white paper. My eyes dart to the bottom of the page: *Love, Mom.* Oh shit. Not exactly an eviction notice from an angry landlord. The right thing to do here would be to fold the letter up, stuff it back in its envelope and stick it in the drawer where I found it five minutes ago. But of course with all the questions I have about Franco and his past there is no way I'm going to let this puzzle piece slip out of my hands. I begin to read.

Dear Franklin,

First of all know that I love you and always will, no matter what roads you've taken or will take on life's journey. But there are a lot of things you've done that I will never understand, no matter how long I agonize over it or how many tears I cry. And I know there are many things that your father and I do that you will never understand. Our beliefs are strong and you know that on many points your father is unwavering. Especially this. And even though I'm afraid this will mean losing you, I still stand by your father. What you did disgraced not only us but everything we as a family represent. But nobody's perfect, and we've all made our mistakes.

Remember the day you left—how I cried and cried and you told me you loved me but were in no way sorry? I think that's the saddest moment of my life. That you could look at your mother, see her tears that you alone caused, and tell her you weren't sorry. That did, and still does, break my heart, Franklin. I don't know if you still feel the same. It's been over a year and there's been no word from you, none at all. I hired an investigator, without your daddy's knowledge, to make sure you were still alive. And that's how I got this address. Don't worry—I won't try to contact you. You said you never want to talk to me again and I respect your wishes. Even though you may not believe it, your dad and I do love you, despite the things you've done. And we will always be your mother and father—just as you will always be our son, one we still love very much.

Love, Mom

I hold the letter with trembling hands. What could Franco have done that was awful enough to constitute this sort of reaction from his parents? Rape? Murder? A million felonious acts dance through my mind as I fold the letter up and place it back in the drawer.

Quietly, I tiptoe into the bedroom and crawl in bed. Jane snores loudly as I place my arm around Franco.

"What did you do, Franco Richards?" I whisper into the darkness, wondering if I will ever know.

SATURDAY. I tell this whole story to Georgette on our way to Club Clearance. When I get to the part about the letter, I just give her a summary since I can't remember it verbatim. "So the letter was like, 'What you did was so awful, you disgraced the whole family, we'll never understand it but we still love you.' I mean, what could have been so bad?"

George shakes her head. "I don't know, man. Was it like a mean letter? Or a 'We still love you, come back home' letter?"

"It definitely wasn't a 'Come back home' letter, that's for sure. Franco's no Prodigal Son. It was like, 'We'll always love you but we stand by our beliefs and can't forgive you' type thing. But forgive him for what?" The possibilities have been flying through my mind all week—child molester, serial killer, rapist, you name it.

"Have you asked him about it at all?" George says, checking her lipstick in the rearview.

"The next morning I sort of did, but it is so obvious he does not want to talk about his parents. He just clams up. I mentioned I had a dream about my parents, like hoping he'd say something about his, and all he did was go, 'With me, it'd have been a nightmare,' then kiss me on the nose. Not quite the wealth of info I was hoping to obtain, you know?"

"That is too weird!" she exclaims, pulling into the lot. "I mean, you almost have to wonder if he killed somebody or something. But then Franco isn't really the Jeffrey Dahmer type, right? I can't see it."

"Maybe he robbed a store or something like that," I say, turning off the engine. Some gas station or something when he was drunk. "What's scary is that this is my boyfriend and I know so little about his past. I could tell you more about his wardrobe than his history, and that's pretty sad."

"Well," George says, getting out of the car, "you haven't been dating that long. Some people don't really open up right away. At least he's not totally blowing you off, like Steven."

Steven's on our shit list right now. He's the perfect-looking guy George shacked up with the other night—the stupid one. Even though she is way smarter than him and he wants to be a race-car driver when he grows up, she is still pissed he hasn't called in three days. She's like, "How dare someone that stupid blow me off!" So we are out tonight to find new boys to take our minds off the old ones.

"I.D.s please," Door Boy asks, checking out our bods before he checks our birthdates. I smile and snatch my fake one from his fat fingers. Georgette follows and soon we're in the middle of the writhing and raving—people smearing Vicks VapoRub on their hands, boys in old-lady wigs, girls with tongue rings and couples making out in front of the bathroom. I grin and look over at George with a sigh of relief. I'm totally in my element here—this is home.

Pretty soon, both Steven and Franco are practically forgotten as boys begin buying us drinks and we just get into being together.

"George, you look awesome tonight," I tell her in the bathroom. She's in my black pants and tiny mohair sweater and boys are really freaking over her this evening.

"God, so do you, Abbie," she says, kissing my hair. Pat let me borrow the fish dress he made. Paired with big platform shoes and goldfish barrettes, the dress really is a head-turner.

We look at ourselves in the mirror and smile. We're experiencing that conceited drunk where you think you look better than you probably do and just can't get over how damn hip you look.

"God, you really look good, George," I say for the second time, poking her belly button.

"Fuck Steven," she says, rolling her eyes. "And Franco, well, he's so cute who cares what wrong he's done? It's not like you're going to marry the guy."

I close my eyes and take a deep breath. Like who knows if I will or not? Every boy I date, I think about it eventually. What's the point of dating someone if you never hope it will progress into something more? But for me to vocalize this would be suicide at this point, like George would completely kill my ass.

"That's true," I say, picturing myself in a daisy-covered veil, Franco in daisy hat beaming by my side. "Franco is just for fun."

She smacks her lips together. "See, they both start with *F*. Franco and fun."

"Yeah," I say, running a hand through my hair, "and so do *fuck* and *find*. As in fuck Steven and find cute boys to hang with."

She casts one more admiring gaze into the mirror—the girl does look good. Damn good. "Let's go," she calls, voice of confidence. I hate to see her once she has the boobs. I really do.

We leave the bathroom and spot two cute ones by the main bar. "Okay. Operation Lost in effect," I whisper, pointing to the two longhairs.

"Cool," she says, heading in the opposite direction.

I wait a minute and then approach the boys. "Have you guys seen a brunette, about five eight, in an itty-bitty white sweater pass by here?" I ask with a perplexed look on my face.

"Nope," the blonde in the plaid jacket says, tilting his head. "You lost?"

I smile and grab his arm. "Sort of. Do you guys mind if I hang here a second and look for her?"

The dark-headed one in vintage Hawaiian shirt goes, "No, go ahead. Now what's she look like?"

"Really cute, brown hair past her shoulders, little white sweater, black pants, red lipstick. Her name's Geor—er, Gigi."

"Gigi?" Plaid Jacket asks. "And what's yours?"

"June." I don't know why I just lied about my name, probably because these guys are cute but definitely scammers. The fact they don't know my real name makes me feel like I have a little control in the situation.

"Like June Cleaver?" Hawaiian Shirt asks.

"Or like June eleventh, my birthday?" Plaid Jacket asks, taking a swig of beer.

I laugh like they are both soooo funny and look around again. "So, you want a drink?" Plaid Jacket asks, putting his hand on my shoulder. I cough loudly, which is the signal for George to join us.

She runs up and screeches, "Hey, what's up?"

Plaid Jacket looks her up and down and goes, "So this must be the mystery woman. Just asking your friend June here if she'd like a drink."

"Oh, June, I've been looking for you forever. I am so totally out of breath from circling this place!" The girl is good, you have to admit. Calling me June and all.

"You want a drink?" Hawaiian Shirt asks, holding up his beer and looking at her.

"Sure, thanks, rum and orange juice," she says, holding out her hand for a handshake. "I'm Gigi. And you are—?"

"Todd," he answers, total Rico Suave.

Plaid Jacket grabs my hand. "And I'm Mark. So what are you drinking?"

"Hurricane, please," I say with a smile.

We hang with them awhile and even though I love Mark's plaid jacket, I keep thinking about Franco and am not even into Mark's stories about his songwriting and his therapy and his resemblance to the late Kurt Cobain. George looks as equally thrilled with Todd's impersonation of Jerry Seinfeld, so after our second drink we bail.

"Well, I've got to be in the office by eight tomorrow," I say, glancing down at my nonexistent watch.

"Yeah, we better be going," George says with a frown, like it really pains her to leave.

Mark asks if he can walk us out and I say no, that I have to go to the bathroom on the way out so we should probably just say our goodbyes here.

He asks for my number, June's number, and I think about saying no but the plaid jacket is really cool and he's been pretty nice. So we try to find a pen but can't and it's like this big ordeal but then finally we find one and he hands it to me with a napkin. And I'm about to write my real number down but then I think, Wait, I have a boyfriend, and at that precise moment Mark reaches over and grabs my ass so I write down 555-8737, the number for Dial-A-Psychic, and hand it to him without even feeling a trace of remorse.

Chapter 22

Fredrique tells us Monday that he's going to be in New York City for a week trying to gather up some big names to come to our fashion show. He writes all the prospective spectators' names on little pieces of paper and throws them around the room. As they fall around me like snow, I can't help but think of the confetti that fell on me at Club Unity the night I met Franco. That was practically two months ago. And now he's my boyfriend and I'm almost out of school. It seems like a dream. Tears prick at my eyes as I look over at Pat, who has Todd Oldham's name in his hair.

"What's up, buttercup?" he asks, looking at me with concern.

"I'm just thinking how cool it is when everything ultimately comes together, when you get everything you want," I say, practically bursting into tears. I must be getting ready to start or something, all bloated and weepy and shit.

He nods. Todd's name falls to the ground. "Yeah, it's weird how things usually do turn out. But here we are. Graduation doesn't seem such an impossible dream anymore, me and Sal are doing better, I've got all these great friends."

I beam at him. This is one of those moments I know I'll remember forty years from now. Like for one second, this very moment, everything seems okay. "Isn't it great?" I croak, overwhelmed.

He looks at me and nods solemnly. "It is. It really, really is."

THE WHOLE week is like that, little perfect moments. Franco buying me daisies Tuesday for no reason. Georgette and I looking through our respective photo albums from high school. My mom and I really connecting on the phone, talking about my future. Everything is so flawless that I decide to have a slumber party Friday night to celebrate.

Everyone I invite shows up. There's George, George's friend Mimi, Pat, Sal, Chris, Franco, Franco's friend Tim and me. We're all sitting around the coffee table eating pizza and drinking wine coolers, deciding what to do next. Everyone has suggestions.

George: "Let's go to Hooters." Mimi: "How about Orange Tape?" Pat and Sal: "Turn on MTV." Franco: "More beer!" Tim: "Anyone got some weed?" Chris: "Who's up for Twister?" Me: "Truth or Dare! Truth or Dare!" Since I scream my suggestion loudest and am the hostess of the evening, I prevail.

"I hope you mean the old documentary and not the game," Pat whines.

"Who wants to watch Madonna go down on a bottle of Evian? Of course I mean the game, dummy," I say, punching him in the arm. It is my party after all.

This comment is met by a chorus of groans. "Who's first?" I ask, turning off the television.

Franco pats my knee, looking damn cute as always. "Not me, baby," he says, between light pats. "Count me out."

"You have to play, Franco. It's a slumber party," I insist. My God, ask them to play Truth or Dare and they act like I'm asking them to sign over their first child or something. One of the reasons I'm being so adamant is I figure this is the perfect opportunity to ask Franco about his parents without him thinking I'm being too nosy or whatever. Like if I ask him as a truth question, I might get just that—the truth.

Franco looks over at Tim and rolls his eyes. "Okay, whatever."

"Good," I chirp, happy to have my way. "Who's first?"

"I'll go," George volunteers. Since she's changed her name to Gigi, the girl certainly is an adventurer. "Don't we need a bottle or something to spin?"

"I think you're thinking of Spin the Bottle, Gigi. This is a different game," Chris says with a smirk. Seeing Chris has been cool, like he's totally over me now, I think. This is the first time Chris and Franco have been together since our little talk—you can't really call it a breakup, I guess—and surprisingly it's been quite pleasant. A guy like Chris never causes waves, it's against his nature. And Franco couldn't give a damn about Chris's ass one way or the other.

"So I can just pick whoever I want?" she asks, all innocent. "Okay, Chris. Truth or dare?"

"Truth," he answers. No surprise there, really. He's not the type to be removing his boxers on a dare, that's for damn sure.

George pauses dramatically. "Okay, truth: Have you or have you not ever had oral sex?"

Oh shit, I knew she'd ask something sexual. As you can imagine, Chris turns positively strawberry and squirms around for a second. "Uh, can I pass on this?"

Pat laughs, probably dying to know the answer to this one. "No passing. Just answer the question."

"Yeah," I say, wanting to know myself. "Answer the question."

Pretty soon the whole table's chanting "Answer! Answer!" causing him to blush all the more.

"Yes, I have," he blurts out, obviously embarrassed. Does that still qualify him for virgin status? I wonder.

"Well, well. I'm learning new things about my family members every day," Pat says and everyone laughs. He looks over at me, like raised eyebrows and all, I guess wondering if I'd given him a blow job or something. I look back squinty-eyed, like Hell no, as Chris chooses Sal.

"Truth or dare?" he asks, skin still slightly pink.

"Truth," he says, smiling sweetly. He wouldn't know truth if it knocked him upside the head, I think.

"Okay. Have you ever cheated on a boyfriend before?"

Choke. I start coughing major on this one and look over at George, who's white as a damn sheet. Wonder if Chris knows about Sal's infidelities too? Between coughs, I stare at him intently, wondering if he's going to crack. He looks down demurely and then over into Pat's eyes. "No, I've never cheated on a boyfriend before. Of course not."

"Why would he cheat when he has a man like me at home?" Pat says in this deep voice, kissing him on the cheek. We all crack up and the awkward moment fizzles, thank God. But what nerve, that low-down dick.

"Okay, Tim," Sal purrs through his deceptive, lying lips. "Truth or dare?"

"Dare," he answers, rubbing his swelled belly. In my experience, when someone asks for a dare, he or she is just begging to perform a sexual act or take off his or her clothes. Since I have no desire to witness Tim doing either, I'm not exactly thrilled about him choosing the dare option.

"Okay," Sal says, rubbing his damn cheating chin. "I dare you to kiss whoever you think is the most desirable person in the room."

Great, please don't let it be me. I try to get an ugly expression on my face, then put my hand on Franco's. Surely he wouldn't pick me, with my hand on his best friend's hand and all.

He looks around the room slowly, still stroking his burly beer belly. "With tongue?" he asks, raising his eyebrows suggestively.

Everybody groans, like "Oh shit."

"Yep," Sal says with a big grin. He's safe since he's obviously not Mr. Motorhead's speed.

"Right on." He leans over to Mimi like he's going to kiss her and her eyes widen in terror. Then he leans over to Franco. Then George. And then me.

Grabbing my chin, Tim says, "And the winner is, . . ." then he lays one on me. Three seconds of torture, as far as I'm concerned. I push him away and he has this look on his face like, See what a stud I am? and I look at him like, Yeah, whatever.

I glance Franco's way, hoping to see some jealousy in his expression, but he's high-fiving Tim and laughing. Yeah, crazy with jealousy, that's him. He catches my gaze and kisses me on the cheek. "That's my girlfriend," he says proudly, like I just won the New York City Marathon or something. Everyone laughs and then the moment I've been waiting for arrives. My turn.

"Franco," I say, looking him right in the eye. "Truth or dare?"

Please say truth please say truth.

"Truth." The boy can read my damn mind, that's why we're such a good pair. I smile, noticing the frown on Mimi's face. I bet she wanted to see Franco naked, which is definitely a sight to behold.

"Okay, here goes," I answer, taking a deep breath. Should I or shouldn't I? The couple too many coolers swooshing through my bod tell me yes. "Um, why do you not talk to your parents?"

There's a slight pause. Franco's eyes narrow, the room falls silent and I know I've fucked up. Fear pricks at my inebriated brain as I look at his eyes. They're full of something, maybe even hate. "I really can't believe you, you know that, Abbie? I really fucking can't," he spits, jumping up. He grabs his olive jacket from the coatrack and storms out the door with a slam.

Tim, his ride, gets up sheepishly. He looks over at me, a hard look. Boy, did I fuck up. "Uh-oh. Sorry, guys," he says, sprinting out the door to catch him.

Everyone looks over at me, like waiting for an explanation. Should I run after him, stay here, what? I want to take it back, erase the words, make it all better—but I can't. Not ever.

Sunday morning, it's like I'm sitting here sewing like Betsy Ross, totally depressed. Who cares if I've sewn seven pieces since yesterday or that I've only slept two hours since the party or that I've eaten two half-pints of ice cream in the past three hours? Nothing seems significant since I made the stupidass comment at the party. Why did I do it? I know he doesn't talk about his parents, refuses to discuss them, yet I ask anyway. And in such an insensitive way. What did I think, that he would spill his guts in front of such a large group of strangers? Like, "Oh, Ab, I won't tell you in private but I'd be happy to tell the intimate details of my life in a party setting"? I am such a complete fool.

I left him a message on his machine yesterday, apologizing profusely and basically telling him that I suck for asking him such a private question in such a public place. But he hasn't called back, and I hate to call again. Maybe I'll write him a letter. Or design a hat in his honor. Desperate times call for desperate measures, and this is a desperate time if I've ever seen one—like there is absolutely nothing I can do.

Pat calls and listens to me bitch. He tries to tell me it's not as bad as it seems, that if Franco and I really had something great it would take more than this to break us up. Pat totally doesn't understand where I'm coming from here. To prevent an argument, I tell him to change the subject. He does, to Sal. They're getting along a lot better, he says, and didn't they look happy at the slumber party? I cringe, thinking of how Sal goes, "No, I've never cheated on a boyfriend before," all sweet and innocent.

But what can I say to Pat? Your boyfriend's a cheater and a liar, and he's making a fool of you? I've already screwed up one relationship this weekend—I'd rather not demolish another. So I just tell Pat that yes, he and Sal did seem awfully smiley and I'd love to discuss it further but I have a splitting headache and I have to go now.

I lie down and shut my eyes. My pounding temples are the sound track for the images that have taken over my brain: Franco high-fiving Tim. Franco giving me flowers. Franco asking me to be his girlfriend. Franco wearing my daisy hat. I try to nap, but even sleep brings me no solace. The dreams I have are of Franco, and in them he never picks dare.

Chapter 23

The doorbell rings around six, waking me from a light sleep. George is over at Mimi's so I have to answer it. Groggily I get up and look through the peephole. Franco.

I swing open the door. "Oh God, I am so sorry."

He gives me a little smile and hands me a warm pizza box. "Hope you haven't eaten," he says, pulling two candles from his leather jacket and placing them on the coffee table along with the pizza. "I'm here to call a truce, baby."

"I'm the one who should be doing the apologizing, not you," I plead, practically crying, as he wraps his arms around me. I thought I'd never feel his arms around me again. I really did.

"Well, I acted like a jerk, just walking out and not calling you back. But I thought you knew how I felt about my parents," he tells me, all low, pressing his lips against my forehead. Like Chris used to. "I can't talk about it, you know? And it's nothing personal, it's just that I truly cannot get into it. It hurts too bad."

"I know and I'm so sorry I even—"

"Wait, let me finish," he says, looking down at me through his perfect tousled hair. "The thing is, I thought you knew how I felt. So I was really pissed when you asked about it in front of a crowd of people I barely even know. I like couldn't believe it. But then today I started thinking that maybe you don't know how touchy the subject is. Like I've avoided it with you but never made it totally clear how much I just do not want to talk about it."

"Franco, I knew it wasn't your favorite subject, I did," I cry, brushing the locks out of his eyes. "And like I said on your answering machine I am so completely sorry about asking it. I was drunk and stupid and have felt like total shit the entire weekend because of it. I really have."

He kisses my forehead again, slow and sweet. "I'm sorry I acted like such a freak."

"And I'm sorry I pried into something that is so none of my business." God, is that an understatement, I cannot even tell you.

We kiss a long, sweet kiss and hold each other tightly. The pounding that's been in my head all weekend is drowned out by the pounding of my heart, strong and true. And as we tumble onto the couch everything becomes okay again, like I find the antidote for this entire hellish weekend in Franco's tender embrace.

MONDAY MORNING, nothing can bring me down. I'm still high off the incredible evening Franco and I shared—the roll of the thunder, the glow of the candles, the thrill of his touch. If I didn't have a million things to do, I'd be content to just lie in bed and go over the previous night frame by frame all day long. But that's not happening for three very major reasons. One: It's the first day of spring break, which means no Fredrique for seven more days. Two: It's Boob Day, which means George's wait for Hooters employment will soon be over. And three: It's St. Patrick's Day, which Franco and I have agreed to observe this weekend, after George recovers a bit.

Clad in my most comfy green T, I drive my roomie to the hospital in a daze. The weekend, torturous as it may have been, did take my mind off George's impending surgery, which has been really stressing me out. I mean, what happens if they screw up and make one bigger than the other, like an A and a D? Or if that saline dealie breaks inside her once we get home? Or if she ends up looking like Pamela Anderson Lee? You could drive yourself crazy thinking of stuff like that, you really could.

I glance over at the passenger seat. George is completely freaked, like out of her mind, not so much because of the surgery but because of what her mother's going to say. The whole way over, she's been going on and on and on about how she's totally terrified Mommie Dearest will find out, especially since she used her tuition money for the surgery. Plus lied about being in school all semester, telling her mom all about these nonexistent classes and projects and exams. I can't imagine any mom being too thrilled by that.

I pull off the interstate onto Ross Avenue. The hospital ahead looks like a big cathedral—St. Saline's, I think with a smile. Whipping into a parking space, I pat Georgette's knee. Everything will be fine, I tell her, even though I'm probably freaking out more than she.

We enter the waiting room and George has to fill out about a million forms. She's all shaking and shit. "This one says if I die they're not responsible!" she gasps, shoving the paper in my face.

I don't look up from my *People*—I'm trying to calm her down by playing it like I'm not worried in the least. "Don't be a nut, George. They say that any time you're under anesthesia. When I got my wisdom teeth pulled, the doctor made me watch a video that told me that. So it was like I had to hear it from someone's mouth and not just on paper, which was a jillion times worse."

"Glad to see you're so concerned, Ab," she says, pissed. "It's only my life we're dealing with here."

I look up and into her frightened deer-in-the-headlights eyes. "This anxiety is normal. It'd be odd if you weren't psychoing out right now, you know? Just chill and in a minute you'll be on an I.V. and then you'll sleep. And when you wake up it'll be Dolly Partonville and the whole thing'll be over."

She drops her pen on the clipboard with a clang and closes her eyes. "The whole thing'll be over."

"Yep," I chirp, looking back down at my magazine.

"Georgette Hanson?" the nurse who's just entered the room bellows.

"Right here." George gets up and hands the clipboard to the lady in white. I follow.

"Sorry, miss, you'll have to stay in the waiting area. We'll come and get you when the little lady's done," the nurse says sternly, looking at me.

I grab George and give her a hug. "You are gonna be okay, baby, alright?"

"Alright," she mumbles into my shoulder, not letting me go.

I pull away and look into her eyes. She's actually going

through with it. I can't believe it. Like someone says they're going to do something, most times you don't believe them. Because most people don't do shit they say they're going to do—they just talk about it and never do it. Hence the expression "Talk is cheap," I guess. But here she is, following her dream. As fucked up as her dream may seem to me, at least she has the balls to follow it. "Listen, the next time I see you this will all be over and you'll be good as new. Okay?"

"Okay." She nods, looking like she's on her way to the electric chair. Then she and the nurse disappear, the green door closing with a thud behind them.

"Good as new," I call.

THAT OF course was wishful thinking—she's not good as new when she makes her way out of the hospital. She can barely even walk. The doctor told me she'd only be semiconscious for awhile so I need to make sure I force her to take her antibiotics and pain pills. On the way home, I keep looking over to see a difference in her body but since she's all bandaged up and slumping over, her baggy T-shirt doesn't look much different than it did on the way over here. She's moaning and groaning something fierce, and I feel totally bad for her. I'll take my padded bra over this any day, I think as we pull into our apartment complex.

There are tulips from Chris waiting on our doorstep, but Georgette's too out of it to appreciate them at this point. I drag her into her bedroom, concentrating my hardest on not dropping her limp body. As I tuck her unconscious self into bed, I experience a weird déjà vu, then remember that I've been through this same song and dance with Franco on a couple of occasions. Only with him it's alcohol and not anesthesia that's the culprit. I'm coming to realize there is very little difference between the two.

MY FLORENCE Nightingale act is still in full effect the next day. Franco just called from the liquor store. He wants to see me when he gets off work but as much as I'd like to see him I can't exactly leave Georgette in her time of need. She's still barely even coherent and says her pain is excruciating. I tell him to call me later and maybe we can get together tomorrow.

"On your TV night?" he gasps, overexaggerating his surprise. "I must really be scoring brownie points with you lately if you're willing to skip your favorite shows for me."

Wrong. "Franco, you must be on K. I'm not skipping my shows for anybody. What I mean is that you can come over here and watch TV with us if you want to."

"I'll be hanging out with Tim most of the day. Is it cool if he comes too?" I haven't seen him since the Truth or Dare day. God, he probably thinks I'm the biggest bitch or something.

"If I get the okay from George it's fine with me. That is, if Tim doesn't think I'm too much of a freak after Friday night," I tell him, hoping he'll tell me what Tim's said.

"No, he knows what's up, baby," he says, laughing. "Plus he did think you were the hottest person in the room, remember."

I picture his puckered lips, his pregnant belly. "Don't remind me. Okay, so call me later."

"Will do. Bye, girlfriend."

I love it how he calls me that. He doesn't say it in a gay way, like how the nellier boys at school punctuate every sentence with "girlfriend." He just says it in a normal way, like how I call my mother "Mom." Like it's the most natural thing in the world.

George is feeling better so Franco and Tim come over to watch our shows the next night. I briefly lay down the ground rules—no talking except on commercials, etc.—and we turn on the tube. On the second commercial break, George shows us her new breasts. They're kind of bruised and there's a little scarring around her armpits but otherwise they look pretty good. Since she has to pull away a few layers of bandages to show them to us, the guys aren't getting into it as much as they probably would if it wasn't such a clinical situation. So the viewing's not like awkward or anything. It's hard to comprehend that the things are actually attached to George's body. It's like looking at a set of Michelin snow tires on a bicycle—they just don't seem like they fit. But I guess they'll take some getting used to.

The whole rest of the time the boys are here, Tim keeps sneaking glances at George. I get the feeling I'm no longer the most desirable person in the room by his standards. And this is just fine with me.

— — —

SUNDAY is my belated St. Patrick's Day celebration, and Mimi has come over to baby-sit George so I can hang with Franco. The only reason I insisted we observe the holiday at all is because St. Paddy's has always been one of my faves. In addition to me looking particularly awesome in green, I adore having the opportunity to pinch cute boys at random. So it's with particular glee that I put on my chartreuse dress, the one I wore on my first date with Chris, this afternoon.

I arrive at Franco's to find not only is he not wearing green, he's wearing nothing at all. As I inundate him with pinches he tries to tell me his eyes are green, which is such a lie, and this only intensifies my attack.

"Stop! Stop!" he cries, running into his bedroom. He comes out a few minutes later with a white shirt and green plaid golf pants on. "This green enough for you, girlfriend?"

"Okay, you're off the hook," I say, hopping up and down. "Let's go rent a movie. Something Irish." So we go rent a leprechaun horror movie and then I pinch two boys in the grocery store as we scout for green goodies. We end up with mint chocolate chip ice cream, green apple suckers, lime Popsicles and green beans in our shopping cart. Our final stop is Joe's, Franco's work, for stuff for margaritas, the only green drink I can think of besides green beer, which grosses me out.

The movie sucks but the campiness of it is more important than the quality so it cracks us up. With each margarita the scenes get funnier and funnier and by the end of the movie we are giggling so hard our sides ache.

"Let's watch it again! Let's watch it again! Can we, Mom, can we?" Franco teases, jumping up and down in front of the TV set. I throw a pillow and miss, hitting Jane instead of him.

Franco comes over and plants a kiss on me and soon we're in the bedroom. When the Jolly Rancher dress is off and he tries to pinch me for my greenlessness, I tell him my eyes are blue-green. He seems surprised by that, the color of my eyes. For a moment I am struck by how many little things he doesn't know about me. And how many I don't know about him . . . hell, that's a whole different ballpark.

Hours later we're still in bed killing the rest of the margaritas and I can't stop kissing Franco: his forehead, his elbow, his knee. This so far is probably the best day I've spent with him. It's not like the day's events have made it spectacular; it's more the mood that's rendered it so special. I can't remember ever feeling closer to a boy than I do right now to Franco. I know he has a lot to learn about me, and me about him. But I finally feel like I'm on the road to knowing Franco Richards, the real him—his true self. It's a great feeling—that knowledge.

Things never felt this right with Parker, not even close. He was the end-all be-all of my existence for such a long time that it sort of freaks me out, connecting with someone who's not him. It's like the closer I get to Franco the freer I feel of Parker, if that makes any sense. And Parker is someone I never thought I'd be truly free of. It's like since we broke up I'll hear a song, and it'll be a group he listened to and for a moment I'll think of him. Not really *thinking about him* thinking about him, like wanting him back or missing him or anything. Just remembering that he liked the group. It's as if he's in my head and he'll never leave, no matter how long we've been apart or how much all my friends hate him. And perhaps that's what happens when you love someone. They remain a part of you forever, whether you want them to or not. Maybe ten years from now I'll see a leprechaun poster somewhere and think of this day with Franco and remember little things. How his hair is falling in his eyes right now or how Jane is snoring so loudly it sounds like a buzz saw—simple things that sound insignificant but are anything but that to me.

"Tell me a secret," I say to Franco, snuggling against his side.

"A secret? Let's see." He reaches over to grab his margarita, of which he takes a big gulp. "What kind of secret?"

"Just something I don't know about you," I say. Like what's up with your parents, maybe? "That leaves a lot of ground to cover, huh?"

"Yeah, it kind of does," he answers, all sighing. "You go first."

"Okay, a secret?" I pause for a moment, thinking. I don't really know what to say here. Most secrets are secrets for a reason. I don't want to go blabbing or anything. "Okay, I got one. I got one. When I was like in fifth grade, during summer vacation I was snooping through some stuff, you know how kids do, and I found this videotape hidden in this wooden box. It was a Beta, this was before they came out with VHS tapes I think. And the girl from across the street was over so we pop the tape in the VCR and it's my mom and dad having sex. Like a porno."

He gasps. "You are lying."

"No, I swear to God. And what's sick is that we watched the whole thing. I remember we had it on fast play, which was like fast forward but you could still see everything, and there were my mom and dad going at it and my mom going down on my dad at this accelerated rate. I don't know why the hell we watched it."

Franco cracks up. "God, what a nightmare. Did you ever tell your parents about it?"

"Oddly enough I did tell Mom, years later. She just about died, as you can imagine. I'm sure she told my dad I saw it, but he and I have never discussed it."

Franco shakes his head. "Man, that'd be weird, watching your parents do it. It's like we all know how we got here but the idea of parents actually procreating sort of sicks everyone out. I can't even imagine my parents doing it."

The mention of his parents instantly clams me up. I'm not about to make the same mistake twice. "It isn't one of my fondest memories, believe me."

"That's probably an understatement. Let me get us another margarita and I'll give you one of my secrets. I have a feeling we'll probably need a cocktail to get through this one."

I feel a twinge of fear. A drink is needed to swallow his secret? Maybe it's something I'd rather not hear. As he hops up to fetch our margaritas, I lean against the wall and pull the sheet up around my shoulders. Whatever he tells me, I can handle it. After all, nothing he could tell me is worse than I've already speculated. I'm quite sure of that.

Franco comes back in a few, 'ritas in tow. "Okay, here goes," he says with a gulp. His expression is really freaked, like scared or something. I close my eyes. He's a murderer, he's about to tell me he's a murderer.

"The Zoe deal. She had an abortion. I told you that part. But what went down was, she's totally pro-life, right? And there was no way she was getting an abortion, no way. But the deal is, she's black. And my dad is racist. As hell. Like he's in the Ku Klux Klan." His face is red and he looks over at the wall, at nothing. I can't believe this story, it's crazy. The Ku Klux Klan, for Chrissakes. It's too much, it really is too fucking much.

"So I tell Dad everything, like I might have a kid or whatever. And he goes fucking ballistic, ends up paying off the family so Zoe will have an abortion. They were getting death threats and shit by this time, like they really had no choice. And so I never spoke to my dad again, ever," he tells me, squeezing my hand so so tight. "And then I started selling my sperm right after. Since I killed one kid against my will, I might as well try to help someone else have some. You know?"

I don't know, not completely. This is insane. I thought he was a murderer, and he's giving life daily. I thought it was him who was fucked up, but here his dad is in the damn Ku Klux Klan. Goddamn soap opera, it really is.

I take a deep breath and reach out to Franco. I've been so insensitive, asking him about it in a damn game of Truth or Dare. It's no wonder he's afraid to get too close or that he's turned to substances for solace. If my family had betrayed my trust like that, I don't know how I would possibly survive.

Yet, he has. He's here, living and breathing, a walking testimony of his own strength. Through all of this hell, he's made it—on his own terms. And he trusts me enough to share his story. I squeeze him tighter and kiss his temples. The puzzle of my mystery man is falling into place, piece by piece. And what's resulting is one perfectly complex boy who's just for me.

Chapter 24

"So all I'm saying, chickadees, is you best get cracking because you've only got six weeks," says Fredrique. As he pounds his fist on the podium, his belled sleeves slap the metal with a swish. "Six weeks."

I look over at Pat in horror as he puts his head in his hands.

"The week before spring break, I went to the Big Apple and lined up a few more big names to come to the show. One of the most prominent costume designers in film, an old schoolchum of mine, is flying in for the occasion. He's looking for a few apprentices to start after school's out, so if you play your cards right, you just might get a job out of this deal." My eyes light up like a marquee. I can see it now—me, trotting down a taxi-filled street in cutting-edge outfit and ultraglam shades on my way to a big, important job on Broadway where I make glorious costumes for famous stars and frequent glitzy cast parties and always receive long-stemmed roses at premieres from my equally brilliant boyfriend. Ah, the life.

Pat's boomeranging hand in front of my face brings me back to reality. "Hello, anybody in there? Fredrique said we can be off to work on our projects. But obviously you were off somewhere else."

"Yeah," I say, the stars of Broadway still shining in my eyes.

He groans. "Don't tell me. Francoville?"

"Nope. New York, New York," I say with a smile, bending down to collect my furry purse from under the plastic chair.

Pat melodramatically rolls his eyes. "Oh shit."

I hop up and down. "I mean, would it not be the coolest? Costume design for a couple of years, make some contacts. Then introduce my own line, maybe open up my own shop eventually in SoHo or the East Village. The world is at our feet, Patrick! A famous costume designer who needs apprentices will be in the audience. And you and I both know we're the two best designers in here. It's like too good to be true or something. New York! Can you not totally see it?"

He smiles a slow grin. "New York. Damn, you know it's always been my plan. To get anywhere in fashion, I think we both know it's where we're gonna have to be. But God, two months?"

"Why not?" I can see it. I really can. Studio apartment, taxi rides, Central Park. I push open the exit doors and harsh sunlight hits me like a fist. "So, Pat, what are you thinking?"

"Man, I don't know. I'm just sort of freaking." He looks it too, running his fingers through his hair like mad. "I've always wanted to go there . . . in theory. But when we start talking about it for real, it's a different story. Like what about my car? My boyfriend? My apartment?"

I tell him he doesn't need a car in New York. Anything else—boys, apartment, clothes—he can get there, easy. I'm excited. I really am. New York is someplace happening. A place I could happen, too.

I'M OVER AT Franco's after class and he asks me if I want to go with him to donate sperm, like I go all the time or something. Of course I say yes in about half a second, since I've never gotten such an invite before and who knows how long 'til I'll get one again. So now I'm in this elevator on the way to the third floor, home of the Family Planning Fertility Clinic, with Franco by my side. Tim's not with us—he's making a cake for his mother's birthday party tonight. Whipping batter instead of whipping tool, so to speak.

The whole donating-sperm thing is a big mystery to me, especially since Franco and I haven't made love much lately. I reach over for his hand and squeeze it. Maybe inviting me here is his way of explaining his low sexual appetite. Every time I initiate sex lately he's just not into it. I won't get into specifics here, but use your imagination. A girl just knows. And this girl definitely knows that Franco hasn't been grooving on the sex action these days. But what she doesn't know is why the hell he hasn't been. Is it her who's the problem or is it him or what?

But there I go again, thinking of myself in the third person. I must stop doing that. The elevator doors slide open and Franco leads me to a surprisingly normal looking office, suite 305. I have a seat on the cobalt blue sofa while Franco checks in, and consider once again how weird it is that Franco gives sperm when we so rarely have sex. It's not that I'm a nympho or whatever, it's just that the whole situation strikes me as a bit odd. Like, what's the thing that differentiates really good friends between boyfriend-girlfriend? The answer is one thing and one thing only—sex. When the sex goes away, you tend to question the status of the relationship. Especially one as new as ours. And thinking about this problem in the waiting room of a sperm donation center makes it all the more strange. Franco looks up from the clipboard he's signing and smiles at me. I return the gesture, wondering what's going on in his head if this is what's going on in mine.

"Do they not give a drug test?" I whisper, thinking there's no way Franco could have passed.

"Nope, not initially," he whispers back, looking around the waiting room—I guess to make sure no one is within earshot. "They do test for STDs though. And they ask you if you do drugs on the questionnaire. I always check 'no.' "

"What if they find out?" I ask, picturing babies with birth defects and Franco behind bars and all kinds of horrors.

Franco shrugs. "If they suspect you're on something, then they can give you a drug test. And they can drop you from the program on the basis of your test results."

"It seems a bit dangerous," I say, biting my lip. "I mean, couldn't you screw up someone's kid?"

"Naw," he says, shaking his head. "If pot did anything, every child from the sixties would be fucked up."

I disagree, but say nothing for now. A couple of minutes go by and a nurse calls Franco's name. He pats my knee then ambles over to this door and disappears behind it, just like Georgette did last week. I read some lameass mag, *Forum* or something, but it's not too stimulating when I'm thinking about what Franco's doing and the nurse keeps looking over at me and the canned music *deer-neer-neers* all around me. When Franco comes back fifteen minutes later he is without any new appendages, unlike George. His face is slightly flushed and he has this dazed look, a look I've seen before. It's his I've-just-gotten-laid look—only he hasn't, not technically.

"So, read any good magazines?" he asks, punching the 1 button in the elevator.

"I should be asking that of you," I say with a laugh, nonchalance the ultimate goal here.

"My magazines?" he says, scratching his chin. I wonder if he washed his hands. "Sure, there were some good ones. They try to keep a fresh supply, so the donors don't have any, you know, problems. And there are videos."

"Videos? Like with a capital *V*?" I say, borrowing a phrase from Parker, who used to attach capital letters to all things pornographic. Books-with-a-capital-*B*, said he when I opened up my Christmas present: a three-pack of erotic paperbacks; a real gift from the heart. Who says diamonds are a girl's best friend? They haven't read *This Wife's in Heat*, I'll tell you that much. Parker certainly knew how to literally put the ho in my ho ho ho, this is for sure.

"Capital *V*? More like capital *P*—porn for all walks of life. Gay porn, animal porn, Siamese twin porn, interracial porn, fat girl porn, run-of-the-mill porn, all of it."

"What the hell is animal porn?" I ask as the elevator doors swoosh open, thinking he's got to be joking.

"I haven't ever watched it or anything, honest, but it's called *I Love Ewe*, like *E-W-E*, not *Y-O-U*, and it's about some farmer and his sheep, I think."

What a lovely thought that brings to mind. "That is so sick! What'd you watch?"

"Magazines only today. Really the quickest way to get off is just your own imagination," he explains. Wonder if he thinks about me ever? "Fantasy is always a million times more erotic than the fake shit you see in pornos."

We pile into my car and crank the radio. While he's fiddling with the dials, I hesitantly go ahead and ask, "So. Do you ever, you know, think of me? While you're in there?"

"Yeah, sure I do," he says, looking over at me with a smirk.

"Like what? Do you think about?" I croak, slightly embarrassed. Not like I'm fishing for compliments or anything—I truly am curious.

"Um, let's see. Me touching your body, all over. Your boobs. Us, like together. You with a Great Dane."

"What?" I scream, slapping his leg. He thinks about me while jacking off but rarely wants the real thing—what's up with that? I cannot figure this guy out. He's a total mystery, I'm serious.

The moment I've been dreading since the first time George even mentioned the implants arrives: the Hooters meal, the one we have to eat so she can pick up an application. Being served by tan girls in short-shorts the color of construction cones is not my idea of a fun time. Yet here I am and here they are and Georgette is way into the whole thing, just smiling and laughing and chumming it up with our waitress, who thankfully is not Shanna of Parker-and-Shanna fame. George has on this low-cut number for the occasion and it reminds me exactly of the time she pasted her little prom heads to those *Playboy* centerfolds, I swear. I simply cannot get used to the boulders on her body and have been doing double takes all day, not unlike every guy within a ten-foot radius in this joint. The constant leers and jeers coming our way are making me slightly fidgety, but Georgette is taking to it like a sponge. I bite into another buffalo wing and tell her to hurry and fill out the damn application, which she does, thank God. Before I even have a chance to finish my celery garnish, fortunately, the application is handed over to the manager, and me, George and her boobs are out the door.

"Well, it's time for fate to intervene," she says, pressing her crossed fingers to her swollen chest.

"Yes, baby, whatever will be will be. Or in your case, perhaps we should say whatever will *D* will *D*," I say with a laugh, referring—duh—to the new bra size.

Georgette cracks up and we're off, leaving the restaurant and its owl sign in a cloud of dust.

Saturday I'm sitting on Franco's bed watching "Saturday Night Live," him at my side and Jane at my feet. I'm totally worn out from sewing, which I've been doing nonstop for two days. Franco has been an absolute saint—modeling my stuff, making me pizza rolls, tiptoeing around me if I'm engrossed in a piece. With his assistance, I've managed to complete seven pieces and am totally where I should be on production now. I kiss his shoulder in gratitude. He really has been a prince, trying on my banana dress and all. He's the best, the absolute best. A few seconds later he proves that statement right, so right, four days since the last time.

Chapter 25

My birthday—the big two-oh. I've decided to throw myself a party to commemorate the blessed event. That isn't the only thing we'll be celebrating, either—Georgette is now an official Hooters employee, with her own shorts and everything, as of yesterday. Her first day on the job is tomorrow, and she's already tried on her outfit at least four or five times—like a kid before her first day of school or something. Let's just hope she doesn't wear it to the shindig, which is going down at Spaghetti Hole, my favorite restaurant in the world, at six o'clock. I made the reservation for a party of eight: me, Franco, George, Pat, Sal, Chris, Mimi and Tim. Outfit of choice is a short silver frock I designed last semester—simple yet decadent, I think the teacher called it. As I apply thick strokes of fifties liquid eyeliner over muted silver shadow, I wonder what, if anything, Franco got me for my birthday. Butterflies flutter in my tummy at the thought but my mind's a blank. He's never gotten me a gift before, not really, so it's hard to predict what he'd select for his girlfriend on her day of birth. Something personal, like lingerie, or practical, like a toaster? With him, anything is possible, which is exactly why I like him so.

We meet at the restaurant and hail, hail the gang's all here—no absenteeism whatsoever, to my immense relief. I am bombarded with gifts of all shapes and sizes as soon as I sit down at the head of the table. "You guys, you know you didn't have to!" I cry, this big grin taking over my face.

"Yeah, whatever, shut up and open," Franco says, shoving a big purple package in my face. As I shake the box back and forth and up and down, everybody chuckles and groans. "Hurry up, open it!" Pat says, throwing a wadded-up napkin my way.

"Okay, okay," I answer, ripping the wrappings off in a frenzy. I let out a squeal of delight as the box top comes off. "Oh man, thank you!" I grab Franco's neck and squeeze. Levi's Big E jeans, the kind I've been coveting forever. Black Converse, shoe of champions. And a plastic packet of two white aspirin-looking pills. I hold it up and look at him, question marks in my eyes.

"This new vitamin, for energy. You're supposed to take them in a club, before you dance or whatever. For a boost. We can do them together."

What a doll, a complete doll. I bounce up and down in my seat. "Thank you, thank you! I absolutely love it, all of it!"

Everyone around the table breaks out in spontaneous applause as Franco and I share a birthday smack. And to think I was worried he wouldn't give me anything at all! How paranoid I am.

I open the rest of the gifts: Elvis magnets from Sal, unisex fragrance from George, bottle of cold duck from Tim, hardcover *Catcher in the Rye* from Chris, Chia Pet from Mimi and original fish-print jeans from Patrick. I shower the crowd with kisses before we order, then look around the table as my friends debate the concept of Chia: pet or pastime? How fortunate I am to know these guys. My arm wraps around Franco. He's passionately insisting Jane's way better than a Chia Dog and his eyes are sparkling and his hair is falling in his eyes and my heart hurts, he's so perfect.

"Jane's tongue is an alarm clock, wakes me up every morning. Let's see your Chia Dog do that," Franco says, pounding his fist on the table.

"Hey, hey," protests Mimi, a die-hard Chia fan. "Let's see Jane grow foliage all over her body."

"She does. It's called fur," Pat pipes in, cutting into a hot loaf of bread.

"But the Chia Pet doesn't have to be potty-trained," I point out.

"I'll drink to that!" Tim says, pointing to the approaching waitress and her trayful of drinks. She dispenses full wineglasses to everybody but Franco. In keeping with the conversation, he's drinking a Salty Dog, the cocktail Parker put on the map. Pat *bing-bings* his fork against his goblet and proposes a toast.

"To Abbie—cool girl, great designer, perfect friend." The clank of our glasses kicks off a dinner straight out of a beer commercial. You know, the ones that show a big group of people laughing and eating and everybody's cute and one chick invariably has big boobs—that would be George—and it's like, Yeah, whatever, no scene's that perfect in real life. Yet here we are smack-dab in the middle of one. On my birthday, no less.

Then the bill comes and with a jolt I'm reminded that this is no television spot. For if it were, the dashing, adoring boyfriend would pass his gold card to the waitress with a flourish, wanting nothing more than to pay for his girlfriend's birthday dinner. Instead, Franco sheepishly hands me three crumpled one-dollar bills, one for each of his drinks perhaps, and goes, "Sorry, babe, can you spot me?"

Normally this wouldn't bother me. I mean, after all my unemployed and/or moocher boyfriends, I am plenty used to footing the bill. But on my own damn birthday? You're not supposed to pay for shit on your birthday, that's like a law or something. Obviously one Franco's unfamiliar with.

I try not to look pissed as I extract three twenties from my wallet. Discretion is key since I'm not wanting to advertise the fact that Franco isn't treating, especially since I'm essentially living on student loans at the moment. Me paying for dinner would just give George and Pat more ammunition against Franco, and I don't want it thrown in my face later. So I plaster a grin on my face and pretend everything's cool as Franco kisses my forehead.

"So what now?" I ask once the bill's settled.

We decide to continue the celebration at my apartment. On the way, we stop so Pat can purchase supplies for Jell-O shots—"the must-have birthday drink," he tells us, high-fiving me. Who am I to argue?

Once concocted, it takes about thirty minutes for the red liquid to solidify in the Dixie cups on the top rack of my refrigerator. It doesn't take quite that long for them to take effect on me.

My mind soon flies out the window, just like my nineteenth year. I look around for Franco and realize I haven't seen him since my first shot, some twenty minutes ago. I long to hold him, but the faces around me aren't his.

"Where's Franco?" I giggle, hugging Patrick.

"I think he said he was going outside with Tim," he answers, kissing my ear. "To smoke or something."

I exit the apartment and see them in Tim's Toyota, surrounded by billows of marshmallowy smoke. The thump thump of Tim's stereo can be heard from my doorstep, but the music isn't quite distinguishable. But then again neither are they, really. It could be anybody I've ever dated in that car, getting high and bonding with another on his own damn girlfriend's birthday. Parker, Michael, Franco—fill in the fucking blank. I opt not to disturb them and return to the party, my party, and do a couple more shots. Each one that goes down my throat is the equivalent of each notch I turn up the stereo in my car—drown the frown. And, just as my speakers often blow out from too much volume, my body soon cries uncle and passes out.

I WAKE UP the next morning on the living room floor, silver dress twisted around hungover body. Squinting over Pat's elbow, I make out the time: 6:48 A.M. My pounding head serves as alarm clock, unfortunately one without a snooze button. I shake Pat, trying to revive his lifeless form.

"Pat, wake up. We've gotta be in class in an hour and fifteen," I croak, practically choking on my morning-after breath. I'll never be able to eat Jell-O again, no question. Let's hope when I get old I'm not shipped off to one of those retirement villages, because I'm pretty sure Jell-O is the requisite staple of all residents' diets in places like that. I'd be forced to starve to death.

When Pat finally opens his eyes about ten years later, I hit the bathroom and stand under the hot spray of the shower, waiting for the Tylenols I just popped to take effect. They never do, so I'm still pretty much a shivering wreck twenty minutes later when the hot water runs out.

A bare-chested Pat's in my closet when I stroll in wearing only a towel. "What the hell are you doing?" I shriek, clutching the terry cloth a little tighter and hoping it's covering the essentials. Ohmigod, this is completely embarrassing.

He grins and puts a hand over his eyes. "Don't worry, I didn't see a thing. I'm just trying to find a shirt to borrow. Mine totally reeks."

I shove him. "Well, get out while I find something to put on, please. My body hurts too bad to take being a peep show."

"Okay, okay," he says, shutting the door behind him. When friends see you naked—or semi-naked, in this case—it's always weird because you never really imagine what a friend looks like nude. A teacher, a movie star, even the guy who works in the yogurt shop—sure you might picture these people in the buff and it'd be no big deal. But a friend, that's different. Kind of like picturing your brother naked—something best left to the imagination.

I'm sure I'd give the matter more consideration if it didn't pain me so to think at the moment. My head feels like a hunk of ground round being pummeled by a meat cleaver. I jump into my new Franco jeans and a black turtleneck before exiting the closet.

"All yours," I say to Patrick, who's sprawled out on my bed. I'm pulling my hair back into a ponytail when he comes out like three seconds later in my 7-Eleven uniform shirt.

"I've been dying to wear this forever," he says, running his hands through his hair. "Reminds me of my ex-boyfriend—open twenty-four/seven."

"Ha ha," I say, all bitchy since it's such a bad joke, one he tells every time I wear the thing, swear to God.

We get to class and it sucks because Fredrique's in this really bad mood and he's telling us that *WWD* might be at the show to research a story on up-and-comers so there's all this extra pressure and everyone is just schizing out, like this one girl next to me practically starts crying because we only have five weeks left and there's so much to do and what happens if we don't get finished and flunk? It feels like a million cockroaches are square-dancing on my forehead, tiny little pound pound pound pounds, and this doesn't exactly improve matters.

When there's five minutes left of class this guy comes in and hands Fredrique a pink slip of paper. Fredrique glances down at it, rolls his eyes all melodramatically and says, "Certainly, certainly," then throws the paper on his desk. "McPhereson, see me after class."

Oh, shit. What the hell have I done now? I look over at Pat and he widens his eyes like, Whassup? And I shrug like, Who knows? Because I totally don't know. The pink slip of paper has got to be about me or for me, but God only knows what the damn thing says. Probably that I'm being kicked out for being too hungover or something. The way my luck's been lately, I'd believe it.

Fredrique wraps up his forties fashion influences speech and we're dismissed. I approach his desk, praying he's not going to be a dick about whatever it is. "Urgent message for you. Might as well get them to install an answering machine for you in the office, it'd save us all some time and trouble."

I smile sweetly and snatch the message out of his hands. Who the hell would call me at school? When I have a phone and operable answering machine at home? I unfold the paper hurriedly.

Black ink covers the tiny page—big flowery handwriting. Probably Alison Simone's. *Do you like me? Circle yes, no, maybe. Happy birthday. I love you, Franco.*

Ohmigod, how sweet. I read it again and hand it to Pat. "This is the coolest thing ever."

He reads it and looks up at me with a smile. "Wow. Maybe he feels bad after his disappearing act last night."

I grab the message and clutch it to my chest. "Who cares about last night! It says 'I love you'! A message like this is straight out of a Harlequin. Like this does not happen in real life. At least not to me." I jump up and down, hugging Pat. I really cannot believe it. This shit happens to other girls—skinnier ones, prettier ones, luckier ones.

"At least one relationship is going good. Sal was being a freak to me this morning; who knows what his deal is."

As Pat embellishes on the Sal situation on the way to the car, I completely zone out. The Shirley Temple-esque cockroaches have been replaced with dozens of harp-toting angels, beaming around my head like rays of sunshine, playing songs of love.

— — —

I APPLY another layer of mascara and look up in the mirror at George, who's wearing a slightly rumpled Hooters shirt. "Franco's in Austin with Tim and I don't even feel like going out."

"All the more reason to go out. Your man is out having a grand old time and you're sitting home on a Saturday night applying a mud masque or some shit? That's definitely not the Abbie I know. Plus, my first day on the job—we've got to celebrate that too. You are going."

She's right, I know, but I really am not up to it. Since the I-love-you message, I cannot even look at another boy. And the thought of a lot of cheesyass freaks hitting on me is not a motivator, it's just not. "Where do you want to go?"

We decide on Club Two, this sort of half-gay, half-straight dance club downtown, and an hour later we're dressed to the nines, ready to face the world. I'm in a black dress Pat made me last semester and George is wearing this bustier thing that's like probably illegal in some states. But she looks great in a cheesecakey sort of way. As she applies yet another coat of lipstick, I start thinking about how probably every shirt Franco owns has lipstick on the collar—mine. The thought is a soothing one, but not soothing enough.

"I miss Franco," I whine, running my fingers through my hair. I really do too. Bad.

George rolls her eyes. "Don't start, please. But speaking of, let's take those vitamins Franco gave you. My first day of training totally wore me out. So they couldn't hurt, right?"

Taking something he gave me, kind of like he's here or something. "Not a bad idea. Maybe that will make me miss him a little less, if I take one."

"Swallow and it'll be like he's here," she says, cracking up, obviously referring to something sexual that I rarely do anyway. I offer the obligatory groan and go to my room, returning seconds later with the vitamins.

"Now or later?" I ask, waving them in front of George's face. She looks really good, her boobs all out to high heaven and all.

"Later, when we can wash them down with a cocktail, preferably one purchased for us by cute boys." Hard to believe this is the girl who just three months prior was sipping O.J. no ice, in her "Little House on the Prairie" dress on New Year's Eve. Seems like three years ago, so much has happened since then.

I smile and stick the plastic package of vitamins down her cleavage. "For safekeeping."

She takes it out and shoves it in her purse. "Let's hope they wouldn't be safe there," she says, heading out the door.

THE CLUB IS wall-to-wall people, most everyone totally cute and fucked up. A drag queen runs into me as I make my way to the bar. " 'Scuse me, hoooney," he slurs, pinching my cheek.

"Oh shit, I hate arriving at a place where everyone's already wasted," I grumble, but George's attention has already been diverted by a guy in a gas station shirt leaning against the bar.

His friend, cuter than Gas Station but in lamer *Want Female E-Mail* T, comes up to me and goes, "Hey, babe, what do you want to know about me?"

I consider saying "When you're leaving" but decide against it, opting instead for "What kind of a drink you're buying me," because I'm poor and can already tell I won't be able to handle this place sober.

He smiles a lazy grin. "Anything you want, baby."

"Singapore Sling," I answer, because it sounds so fifties that I'm hoping it'll prompt this boy into a search for a more nineties chick. One with whom he can discuss cyberspace and the Internet.

"Singapore Sling. I like that. Very retro," he says, turning toward the bar.

So much for losing him to a cyberspace chick.

I tap George's head, which is thrown back in mid-giggle. "Vitamin, please."

She digs through her purse and tears open the clear packet. "Bottoms up," she says, placing the tablet on her tongue and sipping the drink Gas Station just handed her. As soon as E-Mail returns, I follow suit.

"What are you taking?" he says, eyebrows raised.

"A vitamin." I leave out the part about it being a vitamin my boyfriend bought for me, because I figure he might be good for another drink.

"Yeah, right," he says with a chuckle. "So what's your name?"

"Alison Simone," I answer, feeling instantly better.

"Alison Simone, I'm Mike Webster."

"Well, great to meet you, Mike Webster."

"Same here, Alison Simone. What a great name. And it fits you to a T."

It's going to be one of those nights.

MAYBE twenty minutes later the room starts cartwheeling and I feel this rush of raw energy, like a locomotive is swooshing through my body. I stumble and hold on to Mike for balance. "Oh, man, I'm gonna throw up."

He grabs my shoulders and stares into my eyes. "Your pupils are so fucked."

"I can feel my hair growing," I say, falling back against a stool. I look over at George, whose knuckles, clutching the bar, are just as white as mine.

"Oh my God, what's going on?" she says, bending down to the ground. Seconds later, her shoes are covered with vomit.

Gas Station is scrambling for napkins. Mike is chanting, "Don't throw up, don't throw up" in my ear, a mantra, but I feel like that's exactly what I'm going to do, any minute.

"It's too much, it's too much," I whisper.

"It'll calm down in a second. Ride it out, ride it out. Isn't it great?" Mike says, his face a swirly pinwheel of color.

George looks up at me as Gas Station wipes off her shoes. "What the fuck is going on?"

Mike reaches out his hand. "Ecstasy—isn't it the best?"

Puke shoots out of my mouth, all over his outstretched palm. He's like, "Oh, shit," and tells Gas Station to watch me while he goes to wash his hand off.

George grabs my arm. "I love you—you know that, right?"

"I love you too, man," I tell her. I do, too, so much. "What is happening? What is happening?"

"I guess Franco gave us Ecstasy," she says, her eyes wide and wild.

"Must be some guy," Gas Station says, clutching my arm.

"Must be," I answer, trying to make sense of something while everything is swirling and swooshing and railroading through me like a roller coaster.

The next three hours are like a dream—nothing seems real exactly but everything freaks me out because it's too now, too intense. Gas Station and Mike hang out with us pretty much the whole time, happy to be along for the ride. One of Mike's friends gives him a jar of cherry VapoRub and he keeps holding it under my nose, sending my sinuses into another universe. George and I get talked into going to this after-hours place, the Romper, to dance. It didn't take much coercing on the boys' part because suddenly dancing is about the only thing I want to do. That and tell George I love her, which I'm doing practically every three minutes.

We enter the Romper's dark and murky environment, thankfully coming down a little bit from the X—enough to be semicoherent, but still fucked up to the point of being totally blitzed. The guys go find the bathroom and George and I head to the dance floor.

A girl comes up to me, her features swerving like a race car. "Abbie?"

"Yeah?" I say, grabbing her arm as another wave of the drug crashes through my body.

"Remember me?" she says, blonde hair glowing. "I'm Kay."

"Kaaaaay," I repeat, singing her name like a nursery rhyme.

"Yeah, Parker's girlfriend. Remember, we met once at Mudslide?" The only word I catch is "Parker." My first love, boy who dumped me for Hooters waitress, boy I haven't seen in practically a year.

"Parker," I repeat. She did not just say "Parker."

"Yeah, he told me he just saw you here." She smiles a perfect smile and all I feel is panic, total panic.

"Parker?" Oh God oh God. "He's here?"

"Yeah, in the bathroom I think." She grabs my arm. "Are you okay?"

The fact that Parker is here is too much. My balance becomes history as I buckle under the announcement of his presence. I grab Kay's shoulder for balance before twirling around to tell George the news. "Parker is here," I screech, my tone and expression implying something much, much worse is going on. Like a total "Kennedy's been shot" voice.

"Parker Parker?" she asks, jaw dropping.

"Yes," I slur. Parker is here, oh my God. My heart is taking off. This is so much worse than seeing Arrow Mickey, I cannot even tell you. "And this is Kay. His girlfriend."

"Oh shit," she says, looking into my eyes, and I know she knows how fucking freaked I am. "Hi, Parker's girlfriend, I'm Gigi," she says, holding out a wobbly hand.

"We're on X," I blurt out with a nervous titter, hoping this will satisfy Kay's curious glances.

"Yeah, that's what Parker said," she says, smiling. I'm thinking, How the hell does Parker know I'm on X? but my dilated pupils might as well be a billboard advertising my drugged state to everyone in the joint.

"So he's in the bathroom?" I say, scanning the dance floor for his ever-present baseball cap. I don't want to see him, yet that's all I want to do.

"Yep, I think so," Kay answers, shaking her bod to the beat. "Oooh, I love this song."

"Me too. See ya later," I say with a wave, dragging George off the dance floor and toward the bathroom. "Parker is here."

"Abbie, don't say anything you'll regret," George whispers as Parker comes out of the bathroom, right toward us. He's ball-capless and is dressed like a video store employee in white oxford and khakis. His once-shaved head is covered in gelled brown locks and his complexion looks slightly ruddy, like he now perhaps frequents a tanning bed.

Seeing him is awful and torturous. I'm thinking I loved this motherfucker and he didn't care—he just didn't. And here he is at a club, living and dancing and gelling his goddamn hair and he hurt me, he still hurts me.

"Parker, whassup?" I holler, enveloping him in a hug.

"Hey, Abbie, how's it going?" he replies, all casual. Like I'm doubting he's freaking right now. The bastard doesn't give a damn.

"Fine, we're on X." This has been my unimaginative reply to every question directed toward me all night. My heart is beating so fast too fast too much.

"No shit you're on X. Listen, Ab, first of all I just want to say that I'm not going to pay you the money I owe you."

What a nice greeting. As if I ever thought I'd see a cent of the cash I'd loaned his ass like almost two years ago. "I wrote that off long ago, Parker."

"Yeah, well, I just wanted to tell you," he says with a shrug. The light of the dance floor bounces off his gel. Just like Sal's guy, Gel Boy. Maybe all pricks wear gel, it's like a prereq or something.

"Okay, it's cool," I tell him, all smiling. Why am I still nice to this person? Because I care, I always will, even though I don't want to. "No hard feelings. So what's been going on?"

"Just waiting tables," he says, rubbing his eye. "You know, keeping busy."

"So are you still in school?" The entire ten months we were together, Parker was in and out of school, directing his energies instead toward dodging student loan agents and coming up with ingenious reasons professors should let him out of their classes after the official drop date.

"Nope, not this semester. You're getting ready to graduate, right?"

"Yeah, in about six weeks. And then I'm probably going to move to New York, to work under this guy who designs wardrobes for movies."

Parker chuckles. "No offense, Ab, but you don't know shit about movies."

Parker is this major movie freak. Granted he probably does know more about film than I do, but what does it matter? One thing about Parker, he never misses an opportunity to put me down. I haven't seen his ass in a year and yet here he is, cutting me down in the first sixty seconds of conversation, even though he's a waiter and I'm a designer and I'm finishing school and he's dropped out! Although it defies logic, he totally has this power to make me feel like I'm zero and he uses it every chance he gets.

"Well, I don't know a lot about movies, I guess, but I do know clothes."

"Yeah, you do. I've seen your hats around town—really cool."

"Thanks, man." A compliment from Parker, somebody get on the phone to fucking Ripley's!

"You saw Kay, right?" His girlfriend. She's pretty nice, she really is, holding me steady and all.

"I saw her a minute ago. She's cool."

"We broke up like two months ago but we're still super tight." He looks over at the dance floor. "I dig the shit out of that girl." As he glances at me and sighs, the unspoken rest of that line—"but I don't dig the shit out of you, Abbie"—rings through my ears loud and clear.

"So you're friends?" I ask, tilting my head. What I feel isn't jealousy, it's more like insecurity. Like he's friends with that ex, why not me?

"Oh, God, yes. Great friends," he says, nodding real fast, like *of course.*

"Too bad we couldn't have ended up friends," I say, even though he treated me way worse than a friend ever would through most of the relationship so us as friends is an unrealistic concept.

"With us, it was a money thing." He scratches his damn pretty eye again. I fell in love with that Windex-eye, I'm thinking.

"It was never a money thing. It was a respect thing. You didn't respect me so we could never be friends," I say, voice rising. Just the fact that he totally blew off the hundreds of dollars he owed me is only one of many things he did to prove my lack-of-respect theory.

"No, I think I respected you," he answers with a shrug. "But it was a long time ago, who cares now?"

Unfortunately, in my wasted state, I do. But there is no point in arguing with Parker whatsoever. All of the apologies and explanations I'd like to hear fly out of his mouth will never, ever come—I might as well just accept it.

"True." Change of subject would be nice now. "So how's your sister?"

He smiles his damn perfect baby-teeth grin. "Great, she's rolling. In a sorority and going to college. And Jan's doing awesome too, in grad school in Minneapolis."

Jan being the ex-girlfriend before me, the one he never got over.

"You are so still in love with her." He is, too, it's obvious.

He shrugs. "With us, it's just right."

Another thing to bring Abbie down. As if I didn't hear enough about Jan's ass while we were a couple, I have to hear about her during this brief encounter too. It's like every single thing Parker can think of to piss me off, he's cramming into this conversation.

I refuse to sink to his level. George is pulling my sleeve, like "Let's go," and I see Mike and Gas Station lurking by the snack bar behind her. "Well, Parker, you were my first love, and I'll always care about what happens to you," I say with finality. Reciting our epitaph.

"Thanks," he says, avoiding my gaze. Not "I care about what happens to you, too" or even "You were special to me also," just "Thanks." Why I expected more from a boy who pawned my VCR, I'll never know.

"See you later, Park." I feel slightly sick. Seeing him will always be weird, my mom told me when we broke up. She was so right.

"Okay, good seeing you." Then, in this ominous tone, he goes, "Remember: Stay away from movies."

I bite my lip, waiting for his next rude comment. But I guess he's fresh out. As he heads off to the dance floor, I lean over and kiss his cheek.

"You did not just kiss him!" George says, pulling me away off him.

"Yep, I did," I admit in a little voice. I loved that boy and he really didn't even care at all, he didn't. "I kissed him goodbye. As in *goodbye.*"

She squeezes my arm as her eyes widen. "Thank God, a year later, we get some closure on that fiasco. Good riddance."

Gas Station and Mike approach, handing us Styrofoam cups of orange juice. "So who was that guy?" Mike says, nudging my side.

"Nobody," I answer, the corners of my lips curling up in a smile.

Chapter 26

"Don't even say a word," I holler, swinging open Franco's door, "because I've got a helluva lot I need to say to you."

I cannot believe he gave me drugs without telling me, I cannot fucking believe it. And then who do I see but Parker, the last person I want to be fucked up around. I kissed his cheek, for Godsakes, when sober I would have just been like, Kiss my ass. It's humiliating, it really is. And I didn't even know what I was getting into at all. Franco lied and deceived and there's no excuse, just no excuse.

A look of surprise takes over Franco's features as I walk in. "What the hell—"

"Nope, not a word. Because I need to tell you a story first. Sit down." I place my hands on his shoulders and push him on the couch. He wears a startled expression but remains silent. He's scared, fucking terrified.

"Once upon a time," I begin, sweet as all hell, "there was this cool girl named Tabitha. Patient, nice, even-tempered, she'd do just about anything for anybody. Especially her boyfriend, Franklin. Oh, yes, she thought he was the shit. Hanging out with him and his buddies, buying him trinkets, paying for his meal on her own damn birthday—not much she wouldn't sacrifice for the guy. And what does old Franklin give her in return for all this sweetness and light? A bit of honesty, you ask? Why, no, honesty's something this fellow's not capable of, not even close. Nope, instead of giving his girlfriend the truth, he feeds her lies. Two lies, big ones, in tablet form. 'Vitamins,' he says. 'For energy,' he says. Then he bounces out of town and she and her roommate decide to go dancing. Feeling a bit sluggish, they pop the birthday pills for a boost. But instead of the pick-me-up they were expecting, they get a throw-me-across-the-room. 'Ecstasy,' boy who's hitting on them declares, 'isn't it the greatest?' Is that what it is, Franco? The greatest? Because it sure as hell didn't feel like the greatest to me, unless we're talking the greatest load of bullshit anybody has ever subjected me to. Giving me drugs and telling me they were vitamins! I could've taken them at school! While driving! Given them to my mom, for Chrissakes! My God, have you no shame?"

With each syllable, my voice, along with my anger level, escalates while Franco's posture deteriorates. By the end of my tirade, he's slumped over like a sack of potatoes. I stare at him, wild-eyed. "Well?"

He lifts his head and looks at me sheepishly. "Well, I told you they were for us to do together."

This guy kills me, he really does. "Pardon me if I didn't follow your strict orders. But hell, why should I take anything you say literally when you're spewing forth these blatant lies?"

He looks back down. "It wasn't like a lie, really. I mean, it was, I guess. But I wanted to surprise you."

"Well, guess what, you succeeded on that note. I was real fucking surprised when the drug ravaged my body and there I was not knowing what the hell was going on." Puking on some guy's hand, kissing Parker's cheek, practically falling on his damn girlfriend—surprise sur-fucking-prise.

"It wasn't supposed to be like that," he whispers, taking his hair out of its ponytail. "That wasn't my intention."

"Wasn't your intention! Well, it wouldn't have been my intention to be in a car wreck and die but that could have happened if I took the pill thirty minutes sooner. My God, we're talking something major here, Franco!" I grab his chin to make him look at me, see my pain.

"Abbie," he pleads, gaze piercing. "I swear to God I didn't mean any harm. I should've told you, yeah, but I can't change the past. I'm sorry."

"You're sorry," I repeat, all slow, like I'm speaking to a kindergartner. Damn, that's practically how I feel here. "And that makes everything okay, right?"

"No, it doesn't. But I don't know what you want me to do

here!" he yells, I guess getting fed up. *He*'s fed up? How's that for irony? "Look, I'm sorry. I don't know what else to say."

Neither of us says anything for a minute. Then, Franco: "Did you at least get off?"

At that moment—of course, my luck—a strand of hair falls in front of his eyes and all at once he looks succulent enough to eat with a spoon. He is the picture of a reprimanded schoolboy; sparkle of mischief gleaming in his eyes, bratty smirk playing on pouted lips. Even though I try hard not to, I laugh. "You are a bastard, you know that?"

"I'm sorry, Abbie, I swear," he says, pulling me down beside him. "The plan was that we would do it together. I never thought you'd do it with George. Or I would've told you."

I give him my famous squinty-eyed glare. "It's no excuse. I seriously could be dead right now." I could, too. I mean, not knowing you're on a hardcore drug like that and swimming or driving or walking out in the open or something—I'd be fucking gone.

He smiles. "But you're not."

"But I could be."

He puts a hand to my heart. "It's still beating."

"No thanks to your ass," I say, slugging him on the arm.

"You still love me?"

Pause. "I hate your guts when you do stupid things like this."

He kisses my forehead. He knows how I love that, fucking conniver. "Then you love me. You only hate the ones you love, right?"

I roll my eyes as he again presses down harder above them. "I guess."

Franco covers my mouth with kisses. "I'm sorry, Abbie, don't be mad. It was stupid—I should have told you. I'll never lie to you again, no matter what."

"You so owe me," I whisper menacingly, kissing the tip of his nose.

"I'll do anything you want me to, Ab," he says, squeezing me tight. "Anything at all." For the next several hours, I force him to make good on that offer.

Chapter 27

Two red, puffy eyes meet mine when I rush into class Monday morning, late as usual.

"Who died?" I ask, grabbing Pat's arm. "You look like hell."

"We broke up," he chokes, not looking at me.

"You and Sal?" I gasp. Finally, see ya, dick. "Oh my God, why?"

"He cheated on me." He looks down, visibly upset. "Can you believe it? I'm in shock. I really am."

"Oh, Pat. I'm sorry." An image—Sal with Gel Boy at Samurai—stabs my brain. As much as I hate to see his pain, I'm glad Pat's rid of him. He could do so much better.

"Yeah, well, so am I. Not that we had the perfect relationship by any means, but my God, the betrayal! And here he was always accusing me of shit when he's the one running around on me!"

I pat his shoulder. "So how'd you find out?"

"He leaves, supposedly off to yoga, right? And I'm finishing up that orange jumper, the one that wants to have wider sleeves I was telling you about, and don't have to be at work for a couple of hours. So I think, Hey, I could go for some food. But, you know me, I have nothing in the house. I'm like, Okay, I'll run to the store and nuke a sandwich or something. So I pull into QuikTrip and see his car, or actually first see his dented bumper, which is attached to his car. I really don't think anything at first because maybe he's grabbing some juice or something before his class. I walk in and spot him in the corner, on the pay phone. His back is to me, right? So I think, Hey, I'll surprise him or whatever. So I tiptoe over and I hear him, you know how his voice carries, and he's like, 'Yeah, I can't wait to see you either, these three days without you have been hell.' And dumbass me still doesn't even get it. I'm thinking maybe he's talking to his teacher or something, I don't know. But then he goes, 'Yeah, I love you too, honey,' so, without thinking, I grab the phone out of his hands and next thing you know I'm screaming 'Who the hell is this?' into the phone and the guy on the other end is asking me the same question. Meanwhile, Sal has whirled around and seen it's me and instantly crumbled into these wet, sloppy tears. So I'm like, into the phone, 'This is his boyfriend, goddamn it,' and the dude's like, 'Who? I'm his boyfriend. Who is this? Where the hell is Sal? Put him on the phone,' so I, still not really believing this is happening, throw the phone in his face. 'Your boyfriend wants to talk to you,' I say, then storm out of the store."

Serves Sal right, it really does. I play surprised for Pat's sake. "Oh my God, no! What did he do?"

"He did his usual, crying and freaking out. 'Let me explain,' he says, slamming the phone down. But what's to explain? I get into my car and go home, of course he's right behind me the whole way, and when we get there it's this big scene, like he didn't mean to hurt me but he's always worried I have someone else and then this guy started liking him and he didn't mean to do anything, it just happened," Pat explains, running his fingers through his caramel locks for about the hundredth time. You really have to feel sorry for the guy. "And I have you and a job and a talent and he can't deal with the time I spend away from him and it's my fault, really, because my first love is fashion and not him and he's sick of competing with my friends and my designs and my job. So, basically, I'm to blame for the whole thing and he wouldn't have had to find another man if I had been more, done more, said more . . . who the hell knows. He was blubbering on and on and I was just like, 'Get out, get out,' because I was getting madder and madder by the minute. Well, of course, with him nothing is simple and he can't just leave, let it at least sink in. No, he has to continue to blab out these lame-ass reasons why I'm the one at fault, not him, no sirree, and finally I just blow up. 'For the past year,' I tell him, 'I have put you on a pedestal. Endured your many mood swings. Reassured you that no, I wasn't cheating on you. Indulged your little jealous rages. And have I ever accused your ass of anything? Not once. I was too busy being the accused. But who was the one actually running around on whom? Who should have been the recipient of the accusations, the questions, the third degrees? Sure as hell not me.' I told him all this, loudly, as I threw his ass out the door. And you know what I said before I slammed it shut?"

I shake my head. There are lots of things I would've said, sure, but then I didn't love the guy. "No clue."

He smiles for the first time today. "I go, 'From now on, baby, I'm sticking to blondes.' You should've seen his face."

A malicious giggle escapes my lips. "That was such his weak spot, the blonde thing. You really know how to hit 'em where it hurts, honey."

"So does he, man, so does he." Pat shakes his head in disbelief. "Once he was actually gone and I heard his car puttering off, it kind of sunk in. I don't have a boyfriend anymore. A year of my life down the tubes. All of the good times we had flooded my brain all at once, in short, sharp flashes—like jabs. Our ski trip. Him taping paper hearts to my car on Valentine's. Kiwi, who I'll probably never even see again. And I loved that damn cat."

Fredrique breezes in, cutting Pat's confession short. His lavender fake fur jacket lands on the floor with a whoosh as he pounds a clenched fist on the podium, commanding attention. "No offense, but I certainly wouldn't be wasting my energy on talking if I had a full collection due in less than four weeks," he drawls cattily, narrowing his eyes at the thirteen frightened faces before him.

Less than four weeks. And I still have fifteen pieces to finish. The light at the end of my tunnel, once so bright and blinding, grows dimmer with every minute that ticks by. It's time to forget life's distractions—Franco's head-games, George's boob fixation, even Pat's broken heart. The only thing that matters is graduation, finishing the damn collection. I don't care if my hands cramp up, if my body gives out from exhaustion, if I retch at the mere sight of a fruit stand until the day I die—I'll be ready for the runway in time if it kills me. There are clothes to construct, models to line up, songs to select, fabric fittings to conduct—the multitude of tasks before me buzzes around my head like a hacksaw, easily drowning out Fredrique's rambling. I close my eyes and concentrate on the humming sound, which no longer signifies my tasks but my future. I visualize a big oak tree. It has a thousand tiny branches, many of which are snapping off at an alarming pace. The sharp objects that are severing them from the tree aren't blades, but voices. Familiar ones. "You are nothing," Parker says. Snap. "You have no talent," Fredrique drivels. Snap. "They're vitamins," Franco lies. Snap. "You don't know shit about movies," Parker quips. Snap. The voices jumble together, the tree gets slimmer, the buzz grows louder. Finally a single tear rolls down my cheek, my nerves snapping like the branches of my future.

"What's wrong?" Pat whispers, nudging my elbow. I open my brimming eyes and focus in on Fredrique, who's waving a piece of broken chalk like a godmother's wand.

He can break all the chalk he wants, but I refuse to let that bastard break me.

A WEEK AFTER Fredrique's freak-out lecture, I get my ass in gear.

MODELS WANTED
If you are as cool as my clothes are, call to be part of my Design Institute runway debut in three short weeks. Low pay, high glamour.
SIGN UP NOW!

I tape a bright orange flyer to Highland Square High's bulletin board. Franco's alma mater. The school is straight out of an Aaron Spelling production: zillions of rich kids in convertible Beemers with zit-free faces off to fast-lane places. The exact look I'm going for is everywhere I turn: glammy waifs, Ivy League–bound prepsters, ex-cheerleaders lost without their pom-poms. People who look like they wouldn't be caught dead in my wacky fashions displaying them for all the world to see. Throw off the audience by draping my duds on hunky swim team members and student body presidents, that's what I want to do. Show that the clothes work on "normal" people, not just supermodels or club-kid types who usually grace runways these days. It's a risk, one I hope will pay off.

I hang by the bulletin board for a minute but school's over and no one's around. These halls give me major flashbacks, even though I didn't even go here. High school was hell. Everyone thinking I'm a freak, lesbian or anarchist just because I had a tattoo and nose ring. Two years later, those same people who hated me run up to me in clubs when I'm home for Christmas to hug like we're long-lost friends and show me the rose on their ankle or their belly button piercings. Fucking stupid. Someone, I forget who, once said that if you're popular in high school, that's usually like the highlight of your life. And if you have a hellish experience like I did, it only makes you stronger and prompts you to achieve future greatness. Too soon to say if that theory's true or not, but it sounds pretty on the money.

Next stop: Bill's Music, to select the sound track for the biggest day of my life. Although it borders on cheesy, all the tuneage I pick is fruit-related. Lemonheads, Mighty Lemon Drops, Cranberries, Chiquita Banana song, and "Copacabana" (rhymes with "banana," that's why).

"Do you think this is lame, all fruit songs for a fruit-themed fashion show?" I ask the unibrowed clerk ringing up my purchases. He's been helping me for the past hour and has heard the whole saga of my future being on the line.

"People dig gimmicks. Hell, you could pass out cups of fruit cocktail at the door and get away with it if you're good enough," he says, not looking up.

If you're good enough. The statement ricochets through my ears as I hand him my cash. Am I? Good enough? Not according to the high school bitches way back when. Not according to Parker, who used to define my existence. And not according to Fredrique, who holds the key to my future in his hot little hands.

But a lot of people believe in me—Franco, Pat, George, past teachers, my family. And most of all, I believe in myself. I know I have more than it takes to make it. Now if I can prove just that to a roomful of people three weeks from now, my life will be set.

— — —

"I CAN'T stay long." I kiss Franco's cheek and slam the door behind me, noting the uncharacteristically clean apartment. "I have about a hundred things I should be doing right now, and I am not even kidding."

What to the rest of the world are minutes have become to me *minutes I should be sewing*, enabling even the tiniest break to plague my tired self with guilt. I wouldn't even be here now if Franco hadn't been calling me incessantly for the past two hours. He misses me, he hasn't seen me in four days, what will an hour hurt? When I have so few left—two hundred and eighty-eight, to be exact—an hour away from my sewing machine could do some damage. But I acquiesced, more out of desire to shut him up than to see him. Since the X saga, even though we've made up and everything, things have been slightly different with us. I'm more removed—translation: not calling every day—and he as a result has all of a sudden transformed into Mr. Attentive—phoning, begging to see me, wanting to get serious. It's like he caught a glimpse of what he could lose and it scared him. He's on probation and kissing my ass is his community service.

"What a nice greeting." He grabs my waist and pulls me in for a kiss on the mouth. Jane licks at my ankles, slightly tarnishing the romantic moment.

"Sorry, I'm stressed," I tell him, head pounding. Understatement of the year, that one was.

"I've missed the hell out of you," Franco growls, scratching my chin with his new goatee.

"Looks like you've been busy in my absence—growing facial hair, cleaning your pad, washing Jane." I bend down to pet the pug's shiny coat.

"Yeah, new dog shampoo. Smell my hair? I ran out of mine so I had to borrow Janie's. Works good, really." I take a whiff of his locks, their aroma an odd combination of apples and flea powder.

"You are so crazy, you freak," I laugh, sinking into the couch. "So I only have an hour, two hours max."

He nods, all smiles. "So what do you want to do?"

Stupid question, seeing as I haven't seen him in four days. When we're done, maybe thirty minutes later, Franco takes a deep breath and goes, "I want to go to New York with you."

"What?" I gulp. Surely I misunderstood.

"I want us to move together. To New York."

I search his mouth for a smirk, his eye for a twinkle—any sign he's kidding. He's not. "Man, this is big. I mean, us moving in together would be a major thing in itself, but moving to New York together?"

The thought gives me chills, and I'm not sure if they're of the good or bad variety. I look over at him, my eyes full of questions.

He strokes his chin. "Look, Abbie, when I was in Austin a few weeks ago I did some thinking. You've really been there for me. And a lot of times I've treated you like shit. That day you drove back from Tulsa and I was wasted—that was a dick thing to do. You've driven my ass around, listened to my shit, taken care of me when I've passed out. On the way home, I was tripping and Tim goes, 'You know, Abbie's really cool. Try not to fuck it up.' And it just hit me. You are so cool and that's all I'm doing, fucking it up. Like you've told me your plan is to go to New York and it's like we haven't even talked about what's going to happen to us. We haven't even talked about it."

There is a desperation in his voice that's familiar, and I realize with a jolt the reason it sounds familiar is because it's the same tone I've taken with my boyfriends so many times before. This is why I love you, this is why I want you, don't leave, please, stay, stay. It's a song I know by heart, but hearing the words come from a mouth other than my own feels strange, like the first time I saw Franco wearing my daisy hat. First, the recognition: that hat, those words—could it be, are they? Yes, they're mine, all mine. Only they're Franco's too. The hat perched upon his perfect head, so grand; the words spilling out of his mouth with such sincerity—as much his as they are mine. He possesses them like he plans to possess me by moving to New York, following my dream instead of searching for his own.

"I don't know, Franco," I say. "What's there for you?"

"What's here for me? When you're gone?"

When I'm gone? I didn't even think he'd care. I really didn't.

and now this. I don't know how to feel. On the one hand I'm like, It would never work. I'm going to New York for my career and having Franco along would only slow me down. And why does he want to go in the first place? Is it because he wants to be with me, or does he have some other agenda? But on the other hand I'm like, Wow, he really wants to move cross-country with me. Like flattered. Maybe the X thing did make Franco wake up and clue in to what a dick he's been to me. And he's finally realizing how much I love him and how much he loves me.

I take a deep breath. "Franco, you have a life here. Friends. Your weird jobs. Jane. An apartment. If you give up everything for me, I'm worried you'll only end up resenting me for it. You have to follow your own dream."

"How can you say that?" He kicks the sheet off, revealing his nakedness. Symbolism of his present vulnerability; an infant fresh out of the womb? I can't be anyone's mom anymore. I'm having a hard enough time parenting myself. "You are my dream, baby. I love you. I want to live with you. I want us to go pick out a lamp together and buy it. Pay our bills together. Go hang out in Greenwich Village. Ride the subway. Give pennies to bums on street corners."

He wants us to pick out a lamp together and buy it! Ride the subway! Give money to homeless people! I can't believe he's saying this, it's like too weird. If he had said this a month ago, I would have been orgasmic. But now, while I'm still sort of excited by each syllable that spills from his perfect mouth, the happiness is clouded by doubt. Will it work out if we move together? Things would be so much less scary and lonely in a big city with Franco by my side, that's true. And maybe I'd be more liberated in my job search and designs if I had that safety net of a loving supporter at home. There are definitely two sides to the coin. But if Franco did make the trek with me, there are some major issues that would have to be resolved beforehand.

"Franco, you don't know how happy I am to hear you say all this, really you don't. I mean, the whole four months we've been dating I have done nothing but love and love your ass, you know that. But things are changing, honey. I'm on the brink of something big. In New York, my career has to come before anything and everything, including you. Things wouldn't be the way they are now. I've been putting you first, even when you don't do the same for me. And that wouldn't be the case in New York. It just couldn't be." I reach over and give his hand a squeeze, hoping he's really hearing what I'm saying.

"I know, baby. I know. I have taken you for granted. I know that. And I know I have some things of my own to work out. But we can work our problems out together. I'll help you with your designs. And get a job bartending. Maybe try my hand at acting or something. Hell, you can be whatever you want in New York. And I just know I can do anything with you next to me."

I grin, on one level so happy I can barely breathe. But I have to be realistic, keep everything in check. "Okay, baby. I admit it does sound tempting. But if you can do anything with me by your side, how about we start with not bringing this up until after the show? It's too much right now, with everything going on. But after the show, we'll talk. I promise."

"You've got a deal, Lucille. New York, here we come! I am so psyched. Abbie McPhereson, you are everything," he declares, stretching out his arms for a hug.

I am everything. Everything. Parker's poisonous words ricochet off my brain once more: "You are nothing. Nothing. Nothing." Now I have a boy who says I am everything, absolutely everything. And he wants to move to New York with me and come to my shows and gallivant through the avenues with me arm in arm. It's a big step, but are we ready to take it? I don't know. I really don't.

Some questions: Would Franco be wasted all the time in New York like he is here? What about the sex problems, will those carry over state lines? Would he give sperm there too, to help deal with the Zoe guilt? What will we do with Jane? We can't really take her, but could Franco bear to give her away? And what about my career—could I really put it first, with Franco by my side? Could I break this destructive pattern and finally put myself and my career before him?

Despite all the potential problems, I allow myself to feel a twinge of excitement. Things would be easier with a partner in crime, they really would. I wouldn't have to worry about finding a boyfriend there because I'd already have a hot one in tow. And then I could channel my looking-for-a-boyfriend energies into my looking-for-a-job endeavor. And Mom and Dad would feel a lot less scared about me going if I had a protective boyfriend watching over me, they really would.

Franco's voice interrupts the twister of questions swirling around in my head. "Well, Ab, how 'bout it?"

I look at Franco's outstretched arms for a moment and leap into the void, sealing our fate with a kiss.

Chapter 28

Pat's about as far along as I am in our project—which is to say, not far enough—and since misery loves company, this news brings temporary relief. Eight days left and I still have to finish up two pieces—the hardest, of course—and meet with models and get with the D.J. doing the mix for me and God who knows if I'll make it. Fredrique canceled class until the show rehearsal but said we're welcome to stop by and chat anytime before noon because his acupuncture is at twelve-thirty or something. A man who has needles stuck in himself voluntarily is not someone I'd choose as the keeper of my fate, yet that's exactly what he is. As much as I dread the encounter, I'm meeting with him in moments.

My clammy palms clutch final sketches and the backpack holstered over my shoulders houses one of the swooshier skirts in my collection, almost exactly the color of yams. I'm not sure what I'm doing here. It's not like I need Fredrique to answer a question or write a letter of recommendation or anything. No, what I'm looking for is something more intangible—a vibe, a feeling, a hint of what my future holds. Fredrique pokes his head out of the doorway, wearing a plaid beret and a scowl. "McPhereson?"

"Yes?" I am positively terrified. It's not like we're all that close or anything.

"Come in," he says, giving a thin smile. "I can see you now."

His tiny office looks different than I'd imagined. Cluttered desk, piled high with back issues of *WWD* and *Vogue* next to a Barbie-shoe-covered phone. Tattered pages torn from magazines featuring Cam, Fredrique's favorite model, cover the water-stained walls. There's not a single instrument of torture in sight. Fredrique's voice interrupts my search.

"So, what can I do for you, McPhereson?" There's that thin grin again, a snake's smile.

I uncross my legs nervously. Damn, this guy makes me nervous. My palms are sweating all over the freaking place all of a sudden. "Well, I was just hoping you could give me some, uh, guidance."

"On your collection? As I explained to the class last week, I'll be happy to give technical advice but all criticism on style must be reserved for the day of the show. What is it now, nine days away?" he says, going into a Joker grin. Probably thinking of my failure.

I look up at the calendar hanging lopsided above Fredrique's beret. "Eight."

He purses his pudgy lips, then smiles. "Yes, eight. Well, as they said in the eighties—or was that the seventies?—'Eight Is Enough.' Or is it? Guess we better get cracking or we'll end up as washed up as Adam Rich."

"Yeah, I guess." I shuffle through my designs, racking my brain for a question to pose. Fredrique clucks his tongue impatiently. "Um, I'm not even sure what I want to ask here. I guess I'm scared, in light of your first reaction to my sketches, that I won't do well on this final project. And if I don't do well on it, and consequently fail this course, that means I don't finish school. And I can't not finish, you know?"

He nods his head, prodding me to go on.

God, might as well go for it. I certainly have nothing to lose at this point, him holding my future in the palm of his damn hand. "So, I don't know, I guess what I want to hear from you is basically that I don't suck. Every time I go to sleep, I have nightmares of not passing. When I work, it's like I can barely sew a stitch because every stitch is one stitch closer to failure." My voice breaks. "Fredrique, I guess what I'm saying is I need your help."

He sighs through the steeple his fingers have just formed. "My help."

My pulse is really racing now, out of control. "Yes. Please, maybe you could just look these over—I brought these sketches and this dress . . ." As I fumble with the buckle on my backpack, panic seizes my brain. What am I doing? What was I thinking, coming in here?

He holds up a hand. "Stop, McPhereson."

"But I—just a minute, I've almost got it." I gnaw the backpack buckle with my teeth. The damn thing's got to open, it's just got to.

"McPhereson, stop!" Fredrique screeches, then clears his throat.

"What?" I spit out the unyielding metal, defeated. "It's stuck."

He takes off his beret, tossing it on the desk, and takes a deep breath. "Look, when I first took this job, it was a desperate move. My career was down the drain. I not only needed a way to fund my social life, I needed money to pay the bills. So Bradley called with the offer after Potter kicked the bucket and I said okay. But the moment I walked through the doors, I was a goner. And I knew it, I knew it. I'd look out at the class and the words 'Those who can't, teach' reverberated in my mind. I should be the one you're reading about, not the one reading to you. So everyone was my target. Some students, the ones with potential, maybe I was a little harder on than the rest." He shrugs. "Because I was once the star, the prize pupil. Seeing someone else with budding talent was a bit hard to swallow."

Could he be talking about me? He's not naming any names, for sure, but my first presentation found Fredrique at his most brutal, no doubt about it.

He glances at his watch. "Well, we can't change what's done, only move forward. And that's what I need to be doing if I want to make my acupuncture appointment."

I take the hint and gather my things in a daze, although my questions haven't really been answered. God, he's actually relating to me like a real person. My pulse is still racing. "You think I'll be alright?" I ask, voice full of hope, like Franco's when he asked to go to New York.

Fredrique looks into my eyes, unblinking. "Only you can answer that, McPhereson. The clues are in your designs, but the answer is right here." He pounds his velvet-covered chest with a slender fist. "It's right here."

— — —

"OKAY, HERE you go. Frank Sinatra tape, Yankees baseball card and a bagel. What do all these bring to mind?"

The booty spilling from Franco's arms elicits a smile from my stressed-out self. "Oh, Franco, we said we weren't bringing up the *N* word until after the show."

He really wants to go, I guess, buying all this shit. He is just the coolest. "I know, I know, but Tim and I hit the mall after the fertility clinic and I couldn't resist. He just dropped me off. Tim is so psyched about us moving, like he can't wait to visit."

I groan, looking back down at the list of models before me. As much as I want to think about Franco going with me, I cannot think about this now, I just can't. "Baby, I do appreciate it, really I do. But the agreement was that we wouldn't discuss it until after this hell week is over for me, okay? I have a million things left to do."

"A million?" he murmurs, wrapping his arms around my waist from behind. His lips press against my stiff neck. "I can think of a million things I'd like to do to you right now."

God, how many times did he ditch me for *Blow Me Blondes*, and the one time I'm too busy he wants to get fresh? But as his hands go lower, the tingling I'm feeling in all the right places is difficult to extinguish. Hard as it is, I must wriggle out of the untimely embrace. "Franco, no. As much as I'd love to, I can't."

"So I came over here for nothing? You don't even have five lousy minutes for your boyfriend and soon-to-be roomie?" he whines, plopping down on the dining room chair beside mine.

I cluck my tongue like a mother. "Sweetie, I'm happy you came to visit, but things are crazy for me right now. Five more days is not a lot when we're talking about my whole future here."

He nods slowly, guilt marring his features. "I know, I know. I just miss you being around."

I drop the clipboard with a clang and plant a kiss on his forehead. He really is sweet, I'm serious. "Believe me, so do I. Five days and I'm all yours again."

He squeezes my hand tight, hanging on and on. "Then we can make the plans."

My stomach stirs as I contemplate the magnitude of the plans to which he's referring. "The plans?" I repeat, scratching my head. "Yep, we can. But for right now, I've got a zillion other things to do. Let me take you home before Pat gets here. We've got so much to finish."

"Not anything I can help you guys with?" Franco asks hopefully, picking his teeth with the Yankees card.

"Nope." I grab my keys from the counter. "No offense, honey, but you'd really just be in the way."

"SAL CALLED. He wants me back, but I'm like forget it, you know? After the initial shock wore off, the breakup is actually more of a relief," Pat explains, unloading fish accessories from his bag onto the table. "The other guy is history, like Sal now sees the error of his ways. I was just like, 'Listen, you had your chance with me, get over it.' We are so done, it's not even funny. But really, it frees me up for the future. New York, here we come."

"Oh man, that's another thing I need to talk to you about," I say, not looking up from my clipboard. I don't want to tell him, honestly. I know he'll freak. Everyone is against me and Franco, especially Pat.

"What?" he asks, sounding scared. "Don't tell me you're bailing on me too?"

"No, you're not that lucky," I say, looking up. I'm telling you, he's going to go ballistic. Like he can't even get the guy's name right half the time. "Guess who wants to go with us?"

"Who?" he asks, totally knowing.

"Franco!"

Horrified look, then silence.

"Um, you know, he's really done a one-eighty since the X thing. I'm sure he's sincere." Memories flash like strobes—the baseball card, the sex initiation, the declarations of love.

"So now he wants to come to New York with you?" Pat exclaims, slugging my arm. He thinks I'll ditch him, it's all over his face. And that hand, running through his hair at lightning speed—he's scared, alright.

"Ouch. Yes, he does. It was practically like a marriage proposal or something, the way he said it," I say, trying to ignore

Pat's rolling eyes. "I'm pretty excited, but I just told Franco I can't think about it right now. Get me through this show and I can tackle anything."

I pick up the phone and dial the first number on the full model sign-up sheet. "Please let all these models be interesting looking—with five days, I can't afford to be choosy. If I was a real designer I would have had these people booked weeks ago. But then again if I was a real designer I would have a staff and not be slaving away setting up the music and getting hair accessories and sewing every piece stitch by stitch."

"Great change of subject, Ab. But yeah, I know what you're saying. I just met with my models yesterday. I lucked out with my aunt working at Jack Casablanco. The beginners' class she's letting me borrow is pretty cool. Although they were no Naomis, believe me."

I grin, then say into the phone, "Yes, hello, Joy please."

"Yes, hello, Joy-please-don't-be-a-dog," Pat whispers, sticking his tongue out at me. I lean over and slap him before asking her stats—height, weight, shoe size—and then making an appointment to check her out. I don't even care if she's a dog, just let her have a pulse and I'm happy. My last model call gets interrupted by a beep.

"Hold on, Pablo," I chirp, "call waiting. Hello?"

"Guess who? Your long-lost roommate!" Haven't seen her ass in forever, I swear. I get off the other line pronto. "Ohmigod, George, what is up? When are you coming back from your 'school holiday' at Mutha's? I miss the hell out of you." I'm talking so fast even I'm having trouble keeping up. Pat, used to my ramblings, rolls his eyes melodramatically.

"I know, the ten days I've been here feel like ten years. And can you believe she still hasn't suspected a thing with the boobs?" she whispers, I guess in case Mom's around.

"No way!" I gasp. It is pretty amazing, they're so jumbo and all. "How are you disguising them?"

"Little bra, big sweatshirt. I could be pregnant under here and no one would notice. I'm totally homesick for my bustiers and Hooters shirt."

Being homesick for a Hooters shirt is a frightening concept—

I really need to talk to her later about this one. "And they're homesick for you, George. Look, there's been some major Franco developments. You'll be back for the show Saturday, right?"

"Oooh, Franco developments? Can't wait. And as for your show, you know I wouldn't miss it!" She gives a dramatic pause. "And guess who I'm going with?"

I'm scared to ask. "Not someone you met at Hooters, let's pray."

"No, actually someone I met through you." Through me? Not Tim, I hope. "Chris!"

She did not just say "Chris." "Chris as in Pat's Chris?" Pat looks up with interest from the fish purse he's constructing.

"Yes. He called me this week here and we've been talking. He's nice."

"He is nice, but . . ." I'm taken aback. I mean, I used to go out with Chris, as we all know. Not that I liked him that way, really, but jeez. Pat mouths, "What? What?"

"Hold on, George." I put my hand over the phone. "George and your cousin are going to the show together."

"Like a date?" he asks incredulously.

"Like a date?" I repeat into the receiver.

"I don't know," she says, sounding really happy. "Maybe. You're not pissed, are you, Ab? I mean, I know you went out with him and I feel kind of weird about it. If you don't want me to go, I won't, you know that."

"Oh, please, George, you know I don't care. I'm totally happy for you. You both deserve the world." I guess this is kind of a lie. I do care a little, but I mean the part about them deserving the world. They both really do.

"So do you, Ab. And in five days, you'll have it by the balls," she says in cheerleader voice.

As I look down at the table at the mountain of things still left to do, her projection seems highly improbable. My eyes close in frustration, then I whisper into the receiver, "Let's hope so, George. Let's hope to God so."

Chapter 29

My apartment has become a sweatshop and believe me I'm getting paid way less than all of Kathie Lee Gifford's employees put together. I'm freaking out, I really am. Three days 'til the show and counting. I met with all the models yesterday, and I think I ended up with an okay mix. There were some stunning girls, absolutely stunning, and I was like, God, if I looked like that in high school my life would've been set. But as I said, the school is total "90210," like most of these girls get plastic surgery for their fifteenth birthdays or something. Some of the girls were just okay, but at this stage beggars can't be choosers, you know? And the boys weren't as flawless as some of the girls were, although since I really only have like six pieces for men I think I'm in alright shape. I was tempted to ask Franco to model because he has the absolute perfect look and walk and everything, but I think mixing business with pleasure at this point would not be wise. Plus I want him to be in the front row cheering me on, not backstage with a shirt pulled over his head when my most amazing dresses go down the runway. He has to be there to see every glorious inch of fabric and color and feathers and all of it. And if his ass doesn't bring me at least a dozen roses I'm going to be pissed.

The fittings today have been murder. Or maybe I should say nonfittings, because nothing fits. In a perfect world all the models I selected would have been the perfect size so I'd have to do little or no tailoring, but nothing at all seems to be going my way in that department. The skirts don't hang right. The jackets are too snug. One guy was practically busting out of his grape pants, and that means I basically have to sew a whole new pair, which I don't know how the hell I will have time to do. Some of the models were bitching, saying they looked fat or whatever. To top it off, it's hot as hell here and the air conditioner is on the fritz. Nothing like getting sweat stains all over my fall fashions. I'm a wreck, like I totally wish I had a Valium or something. Good thing I don't smoke, because if I did I'd be a chain-smoker by now.

My last fabric fitting is supposed to be here in five, this priceless girl named Linda, with dewy skin and legs that go for miles. Maybe she'll change my luck. She's the hottest girl by far, so I'm saving her for the best outfits. She'll be wearing my short swooshy skirt in mango with the plum feather jacket that is just absolutely weightless over the mango-and-plum-striped cotton knit top with the scoop neck. Then plum tights and mango boots and she's ready to face the world. I couldn't find any boots that were right so I had to handpaint some white go-gos I found at the Vintage. They're half a size too big for Linda but we'll stuff some Kleenex in the toes or something. Thank God I took out that extra student loan this term, because the collection is not coming cheap, believe me. I'm out like so much money I cannot even tell you. But luckily most of the clothes are in size 8, my size, so hopefully I'll get a fierce New York wardrobe out of the deal if I can undo all this tailoring that I have no time to do.

On my runway, the makeup will be glam—eye shadow, blush, eyebrows, lips, lips, lips—and the hair will be pulled up in big Barbie ponytails adorned with huge bows, or buns stuffed through lemon slices, or hair tucked under big Abbie-designed hats, like the daisy one I found Franco in. Or, correction: it will *hopefully* be that way. We have some volunteers doing the makeup and they could make everyone look like Tammy Faye, for all I know. With the way my luck is going today, I'm not banking on anything.

The doorbell rings and I hop over mounds of swatches and shoes and sewing machines to let Linda in. She looks even better than I remembered—jackpot—and I greet her with a harried grin. "Hey, supermodel, come on in!"

She gives me a high school hug and leaps into my apartment. "Hey!"

"Sorry for the heat. Are you ready for your fitting?" I ask, heading for the table where the clothes are piled.

"Sure. Jodi told me about hers." Jodi, I guess Linda's friend, was one of the bitchiest: *Do I have to wear this? It makes me look ugly. Damn, could it be any hotter in here?* I wanted to slap the wench, but my future depends on these girls and boys, no matter how much attitude they're giving me. So I kept my lip zipped.

"She said you poked her a lot, so could you be extra careful? I'm like terrified of needles," Linda confesses with a grimace.

I admit I "accidentally" poked Jodi a couple of times because she was being such a whiny prima donna. But as long as Linda is cool, she'll escape injury.

"I'll be careful," I say sweetly, handing her the plum-and-mango ensemble—shoes and tights and all—and directing her to the bathroom.

"You just have to put one leg of the tights and one boot on. And if anything doesn't work, just come out anyway and we'll adjust everything. Nothing has really been fitting, so it will be no surprise." As she disappears behind the bathroom door, I thank God this is finally the last fitting. Looking at the Polaroids I've taken, I can see there are some major problems. Major. And I don't know how the hell I'm going to solve them all by day after tomorrow. And I'm still waiting for the buttons for the tomato dress, which were supposed to be in like two weeks ago and hello are still not in yet. I don't know what the fuck I'm going to do about that.

Linda comes out in her fruity glory, looking pretty damn good, considering she's falling out of the skirt and busting out of the jacket. Earlier this would have sent me into hysterics but by now nothing shocks me. "So you're like a size six, right?" I ask, mouth full of pins.

"Six or four," she says, twisting around in front of the full-length mirror I've propped against the couch. "Even though the fit isn't so great, the outfit is really beautiful."

It is, too. The color combination works, I have to admit it. And the boots are perfection.

"Thanks, baby. But we do need a major overhaul here. Let out the jacket for the boobs, take in the skirt here and here." As I pinch and pin the fabric and feathers, we talk about what will go down on the runway. "Okay, this is outfit twenty-five, which is toward the finale. 'Copacabana' will be on. You'll walk out with twenty-six and twenty-seven, all in a row, side by side, and you're first, which puts you on the far right. As soon as twenty-seven turns to the audience, you go. Give a vacant gaze and walk like we practiced yesterday, hands hanging straight, don't look at anyone or anything, just straight ahead at nothing. Saunter to the end of the runway, deadpan, now hands on hips, turn completely, three-sixty, twirl the skirt, give a smile, back to deadpan, start back. The other girls will be behind you following suit. When you're halfway back—there'll be a small pink line on the runway—twirl again. Another three-sixty, chin up, and then back, coming backstage from the right because the left is where the next models are coming out, where you came out. Does any of this make sense? I realize it could be confusing until we're actually there for the run-through. Which is tomorrow from four to five, did I tell you?"

My words are coming a mile a minute—it's like my mouth is scrambling to narrate the video that's playing in my brain of the perfect show with the music and the lights and everything's to-die. Who knows if the reality will be as sweet. At this point I'm seriously doubting it. Linda does a run-through in the living room. Straight to the kitchen, gaze vacant, nothing, twirl, little smile, seductive, back, twirl again. On the way back, she trips over a sewing machine, sprawling to the floor with a thud.

"Oh shit! Are you okay?" I gasp, running to her side.

"My ankle! My ankle!" she cries, tears springing to her eyes. I lift her up and place her on my cluttered couch, removing the go-go and tights in a frenzy. I dart to the fridge for ice—please let the trays be full—thinking this is just fucking great. My best model probably has a broken ankle now thanks to me and my inability to keep my apartment clean. What next?

I come back with six cubes of ice wrapped in a wet paper towel. "Here you go, Linda. Ohmigod. I'm so sorry! Let's get these feathers off. How do you feel?"

She gives a half-smile as I extract her from the jacket. "Don't be sorry. My fault. But I think it's going to be okay. It's definitely not broken. Maybe it's twisted or something. But I hope it's not a serious sprain. I really want to do your show."

"And I want you to! This sucks. Let's just ice it for a minute and see if it feels any better." I try to flash a grin of encouragement, but inside, my heart is sinking. My best model. I can't even believe this. I should ask her a question or something, distract her brain from the pain.

"So do you do modeling here? You're really stunning."

"Thanks," she says, rubbing the makeshift ice pack on her ankle. "I've just done some catalog stuff here, local print work. I'm going to try New York this summer, go on some go-sees, hit some agencies with my book, see what happens." She looks up from her injury and flashes me this perfect supermodel grin, a smile full of all the hope and glitter I too feel when thinking about the shiny city. Even with a damaged body part, the girl has hope. Gotta admire that.

I snap a Polaroid, then another, of couch-ridden Linda for my scrapbook. I can look at it next semester, when I'll most definitely be back to school. I'm doomed. This was the beginning of the end, I'll think, stroking the photos' smudged surfaces, cursing the images that are slowly coming to focus before my eyes as I shake the pics from side to side.

"Did you say New York?" I ask, tuning into Linda's statement like two minutes later. Talk about delayed reaction—the girl probably thinks I'm a psycho. But the heat is making me delirious. "That's so weird! I'm heading there too this summer. With Pat, my best friend, whose show you'll also see Saturday. And my boyfriend, who actually also went to Highland Square. Franco Richards?" I say, turning my beloved's name into a question to find out if she knows him.

"No way! You mean Franklin? As in Franklin Richards the Third? Like who graduated about four years ago? Prom King Franklin?"

She knows him! My chest swells with pride. I am dating a prom king when the one at my alma mater didn't even know my name. I cannot even believe it. "Yep, the one and only."

"Oh man, that is so insane," she says, elevating her ankle. "My sister knew him pretty well. Chelsea DeRose? Wait 'til I tell her I'm modeling for Franklin's girlfriend, if in fact I get to. She's going to flip out."

"Small world! Your sister knew him? Like they were close?"

"Well, she was actually closer with his girlfriend at the time—

Zoe? But they all had this huge falling-out, apparently. I'm not sure what happened. But last I heard, Franklin was really big into clubbing. Is he still? I hear the club scene in New York is pretty intense."

The club scene. All the stories I've ever heard about New York clubs flood my brain: X parties, cute boys in cuter platform sneakers, Special K, *Bright Lights, Big City*, heroin, all of it. What if that's why Franco wants to go with me? So he can dance 'til dawn and shoot up and trip and try on all the new music and promoters and fashion and freedom like new pairs of shoes or something? Panic attack.

"Um, he's not so into it anymore," I say, hoping that is indeed the case. "He's the best. You'll see him at the show. He'll be there with bells on."

"Oh, I can't wait!" she says, rubbing a rescued cube from the ice pack all over her flushed forehead. "I really really can't."

"Me neither." I head over to the table, my head pounding to the beat of a jillion gyrating club kids. "How do you feel?"

"Um, okay I think." She sets the ice pack on the coffee table and gets up gingerly. "It doesn't hurt too bad. I think it's okay."

Thank you, God, thank you. I wipe my brow in relief. "That's great! Let me snap a few pics really quick." Perfect smile, not much weight on ankle, flash, flash and we're done. "Okay, all set. Only one more outfit. Do you feel up to it?"

"Yeah, really. I think it's okay. It doesn't hurt that much," she says, half limping toward the kitchen. "I'm good, really."

She doesn't look so good, with that limp and all. But I'll humor her. "Well, if you're sure you feel up to it. Next is a sparkly lime dress with this lemon coat and no tights. We'll skip the mules and finish up."

She pets the fake fur coat and smiles. "Wow, really cool. You're like a real designer!"

As I thank her, I can't help but wonder how much truth there really is to her super-sweet statement. I guess I'll find out soon enough.

"PAT, MY rehearsal is in two hours and I am so freaked out. I'm hyperventilating. I haven't slept in like three days," I cry, twirling the phone cord around my index finger until it's as red as my fire-engine nail polish. I'm on the floor surrounded by Polaroids and I just want to cry, to break down and bawl.

"Okay, baby, don't freak," he says, his voice sounding as jittery as mine. "Listen, I just finished. I'm not going to lie to you here, okay? It's hell. The Coliseum is sort of a wreck and the runway is still under construction. It's hard to hear anything over the buzz of the saws, we're talking splitting headache here. And Fredrique is being really erratic, like cheering one minute and hanging his head in his hands the next. But let's dwell on the bright side. The clothes are done, right? You've had the fittings. You've picked the music. You have the models. Do you want me to meet you over there? Maybe if I'm with you, you'll feel better."

I pick up a Polaroid—Linda on couch—and panic. "Pat, you have to meet me. I know you have a million things to do, but if you don't come I'm going to fall apart," I plead, winding the phone cord even tighter around my finger. "Let's look at your bright-side list. Are the clothes done, you ask? Why no, they're not. I'm only halfway done with all the tailoring and have to totally remake two pieces because the models pouring into them are all wrong. I've had the fittings, yes, but they were a nightmare. Like fucking endless. I've picked the music, yes, but I ended up mixing it myself and it sounds like shit. And the models, yep, I have them alrighty. But half of them are whiny and bitchy and think they look fat or whatever, and none, and I do mean not a one, of them fits into the clothes. To top it off, my best model sprained her ankle on my living room floor last night. After she hobbled out, I cried for two hours over my sewing machine and left you six messages, all of which you did not return. So the odds of all this coming together by tomorrow are slim to fucking none, okay? And if Fredrique yells at me today, I am just going to lose it. I cannot take it today, Pat. I simply cannot take it." The cord is wrapped so tightly around my finger by now I feel like it's going to fall off.

"Ab, you're having an anxiety attack, okay? Deep breath. Inhale, exhale, okay? It can't be that bad. It just can't," Pat insists as I unwind the tight white cord slowly, so slowly, and watch my tingling finger go from red to pink to white.

"Oh it can't?" I say in a dead voice. "Well, somebody please tell my collection that, because it thinks it can. It's falling apart at the fucking seams, Pat. I'm not lying."

"I'm coming over there right now," he says. "You're freaking my shit out, Ab. Almost sound like you're in shock or something, like someone off the 'Twilight Zone.' "

"Well, I feel more like Cindy Brady on that episode where she has stage fright on that quiz show and keeps staring at that hypnotic red light that says they're on the air. Like hypnotized or something. Get over here quick. Please."

"I'm there, baby. Don't slit your wrists or anything," Pat says, sounding like he's not totally kidding.

"I'll try," I groan, looking down at the blue veins and pale skin to which he's referring. Once a palm reader told me I have a very long life line but it's broken in two places, like I'll probably have two near-death experiences. I wouldn't be surprised if this was one of them, because I swear to God this collection is killing me.

Pat gets here in record time and soon my Karmann Ghia is packed to the gills with clothes and shoes and tapes and coats and hats and ribbons and tights and God knows what else. "It looks like a showroom exploded in this car," Pat says, parking his ass in the front seat. In lieu of answering him, I stick my show tape in the cassette player and start the engine.

"Here's the music. Four songs, fifteen minutes. My D.J. backed out and since my stereo sucks, it's definitely lacking. Like too much bass or something."

Pat runs his hands through his hair. "I'm sure it's fine. At least yours isn't fifteen straight minutes of the *Little Mermaid* soundtrack like mine. But what other fish songs exist?"

"Who knows," I answer, not caring about Pat's music or the glaring sun in my eyes or anything else besides my show. The Lemonheads are belting out their version of "Mrs. Robinson" as I get on the interstate. "When are your parents here?"

Pat rolls his eyes. "Tomorrow morning. I couldn't deal with having them here the night before the show. I'm already enough of a wreck. What about you?"

"Same thing, in the morning. I'm going to be up all fucking night as it is. I don't know how I'm going to pull this off. I really don't."

"Baby, you'll do it. If anyone can, it's you. And everyone's rehearsal is going like shit, I bet. If you have a bad rehearsal, it guarantees a good show. Isn't that how the saying goes?"

"Let's hope so," I mutter, pulling into the Coliseum parking lot. It's only like five minutes from my house, which is quite convenient. "Please let all my models show, please God. I'll go ballistic if they're not here, I swear I will."

Pat rubs my head. "Try not to freak, Ab. You don't even know if they're here yet and you're already preparing for the worst."

"Because that's how it's been so far. The worst." As we get out of the car, my stomach rumbles and tumbles as my mind twirls and swirls. Fredrique, Linda, the ankle, Parker, you're nothing, Franco, graduation, tomorrow, the reporters, my tape, the sewing, the two pieces, New York, my parents, cluttered apartment, failure. The sun beats down on me like a club. Heat, piercing, red red sun. I close my eyes for a moment then lean against my car and for a moment everything becomes white, so white. When I lift my lids, I'm staring at two sandals and ten red-tipped toes, all covered in vomit.

"Wow, THAT was weird, you getting sick like that. Are you sure you're okay? I mean, should I call somebody?" Pat asks, fanning me with an old newspaper he found on my back seat while I wipe off my feet with some Taco Bell napkins.

"No, I'm fine," I say, kind of like Linda told me yesterday after the fall. I hope I'm more convincing. "What time is it?"

"Fifteen 'til. Let's get you inside."

Pat parks me backstage and unloads the rest of my shit. I still feel a little woozy. I find a sink and splash some cold water on my face and feet. When everything is in, Pat leads me to the models. "I told them to all wait in this holding area, but I didn't tell them you were sick or anything. I just said I was your assistant," Pat hollers, trying to be heard over the loud sawing going on over on the runway. "You sure you're okay?"

My head's pounding but I give a feeble nod. I figure the day couldn't get much worse.

I approach the gaggle of models and, to my dismay, spy Fredrique hanging on the outskirts. "McPhereson," he says, pulling me aside, "bad news. There are some major runway problems. The guys just told me no more walking on it today if we want to walk on it tomorrow. So you can't have your actual run-through as planned. You'll just have to make do out here or backstage."

No run-through? How the hell am I supposed to stage a stunning show in twenty-seven hours when I'm allowed absolutely no dress rehearsal? I consider venting on Fredrique, but decide against it. I'm so freaked right now there's no telling what I'd say if you got me started. "Um, okay. So no run-through on the runway. What about the sound? Can they run that?"

"P.A.'s kind of faulty right now. Zambini just lost his tape, so I don't know that I'd risk it."

Did I just say the day couldn't get any worse? "Uh, so no sound either? What should I do?"

Fredrique pats me on the shoulder. "Designers face all sorts of pitfalls before a big show, McPhereson. It's part of the challenge."

Part of the challenge? I look at Pat in despair as Fredrique trots off, going who knows where. Say something, Abbie, anything.

"Okay, guys, roll call," I trill, taking a deep breath. There's no time to fall apart here. We run through the names. Two missing: Jodi, who told Linda to tell me that she couldn't make it but would come early tomorrow, and Joe, who didn't even call, send a message, nothing. Great. I toss Pat a quarter and send him on a search for a pay phone to figure out Joe's whereabouts, then go into director mode. "Pat's hung up all the outfits on the racks backstage—corresponding accessories are in the bags that are hanging with the clothes. They're numbered. Find your first outfit and get into it. There are no dressing rooms, as I explained, so just change anywhere. And watch for the pins. If you need me, holler, and Pat, when he gets back, or I will be over pronto. There's no runway or sound available, so I'll need everyone's cooperation please. We're gonna start this thing in five, so let's haul ass." I smile sweetly, directing the models to their outfits. Everyone is scrambling to get out of their clothes and into my fashions, and it seems every single one of them needs something at once.

"How does this shirt go?" "Will you help me into these boots?" "Ouch, this pin poked me!" "This zipper is stuck." "Um, will you button me?" "Will this be sewn by tomorrow?"—questions and requests bombard me like bullets, but I just keep breathing and try to persevere. Pat returns—Joe feels like hell, but promises to be here tomorrow in sickness or in health—and soon everything is somewhat under control.

I clap my hands for attention. "Alright, everybody. Since the runway is out of commission, we're going to have to use the aisles."

"And since the music's a no-go, I'll be providing musical accompaniment," Pat announces with a grin.

This is met by a groan from me. I've heard the boy sing, and it ain't pretty. But what's my alternative? "Okey-dokey, let's go." I herd everyone down to the red-carpeted aisle. "One through three, let's do it." I clap my hands and nudge Pat. "Go, music. 'Tutti Frutti.' "

As Pat's shaky version of "Tutti Frutti" fills the near-empty auditorium, my mind starts to fog. The forty-five minutes feel more like forty-five hours. Telling everyone how to look, walk, whirl, stand, smirk, slink and shake is exhausting, and when the last girl completes her final twirl I feel completely disoriented, like I've just run a marathon or something. Or maybe like I'm about to throw up for the second time today.

Problems: Most everyone tripped at one point. No one had the vacant gaze I was going for. Feathers were falling off. Linda was limping. Pat was totally off-key. Most girls kept running their fingers through their hair. Pins were popping out all over the place, meaning I'll have to repin later if I want to finish everything tonight. One of the guys had a big zit on his forehead I swear wasn't there yesterday. It was impossible to explain where I wanted the models to turn on the runway when we weren't even on the runway. And half the time we couldn't hear a thing anyway over the loud buzz of the power tools.

"Okay, everybody, if you have pins that fell out please come here and let me refit you. Otherwise, be here tomorrow by five.

Show's at seven. If you don't show, I will not graduate. I know this hasn't been a completely pleasant experience today, but I swear it will be better tomorrow." Or it better be if I want to have any hope of passing.

As I head backstage after the final refitting, I pass Fredrique, who gives me a nod. Not a smile or a pat on the arm, but a nod. What the hell does a nod mean? When I ask Pat, even he can't come up with an answer for that one.

The alarm that blares at 8:30 A.M. serves as the starting gun to the most important day of my life. On the first beep I'm incoherent, but by the second my stomach is completely in knots. The day of reckoning is finally here. I roll over and kiss Franco's shoulder, hugging him tight. Holding on to something somehow makes me feel less like I'm falling apart. I hit the off button and squeeze Franco as tight as I can, but he doesn't stir. At 8:33, I get up, rubbing my churning stomach like a Buddha.

Jane seems happy to see me, but I soon lose her attention to the can of dog food I just dumped into her bowl. I grab a Coke and then reach for the phone. An incoherent Pat mumbles "Hello" after the second ring.

"You up?" I ask, voice full of nerves.

"Of course. I haven't slept a wink. Where are you?"

"Franco's. I came over here about six this morning, once I finished the last piece. Just because I couldn't bear to be in my fashion-filled apartment one second longer. Oh God, I feel sick," I say, rummaging through Franco's cabinet for some Pepto. "Did you sleep long enough to have bad dreams like I did?"

"Uh-huh, like all my models strolled out totally naked and everyone was laughing at me, like cackling. Did yours go anything like that?"

"Sort of, only worse," I say, grimacing. "My models were covered in pudding and coming out to Michael Jackson tunes. What the hell does that mean?"

"Who knows, baby. But we're both going to be fine, I can feel it. So yesterday sucked. Okay. It's over. Everything is done now. The clothes are flawless. Our parents will be here soon and we're meeting with Fredrique at five and then the show is at seven.

You go on first, which has to be a good sign. He wants to hit them where it hurts."

"Or get me over with, as in, it has to get better from here. And you're going last, so what does that mean?"

"Not the best for last, I'm afraid. But it definitely means I have to sit through three hours of shows like a nervous wreck, while you're sitting there cool as a cucumber. Oh man, I really feel nauseous."

I swallow a tablespoon of Pepto. "Me too, but I just took some medicine. Do you have anything you could take?"

"Nope. And have you done your program yet of outfit order for the audience? Fredrique wants them first thing when we meet. And he said no graphics, total plain Jane."

"Programs? Programs?" I totally forgot Fredrique's request. And my Mac is on the fritz, of course, even though it's practically brand new. "Oh shit, I completely spaced on that. I guess I'll head over to the copy shop in a second to rent their Mac for an hour. It's open twenty-four hours, right? How many copies do we need?"

"Four hundred. Can you even believe there might be four hundred people there? I'm sick."

Four hundred faces turned my way. Eight hundred eyes on my fashions. Four hundred index fingers that could point my way in horror. Or, on the bright side, eight hundred palms that could clap in my honor—yeah, right.

"Ooh, I can't think about it. Like with everything that's gone wrong so far, I don't even want to speculate on what it will be like with four hundred people watching. Let's talk about something else. Um, what are you wearing?" I close my eyes, wishing the Pepto would take its effect on my roller-coaster stomach.

"Something basic, like black pants and white T. Maybe a cardigan. Don't want to compete with my fashions, you know."

"Yeah, that's smart. Maybe I'll go with something basic too." Preferably something that doesn't clash with the red roses that Franco better toss at my feet, no matter how much of a disaster the show is.

"Wear that black shift dress and lime cashmere cardigan. You look stunning in that."

How will the lime sweater go with the hunter green of the roses' leaves? I'll have to buy one on my way home to be sure. "I'll check that out. Okay, I'm going home. I have to pack up all my stuff again to bring to the Coliseum and then attempt to straighten up before Mom gets there. You know how she freaks when my house is a wreck. And tonight, not only do I have the show, but my family's meeting Franco for the first time. Aaah!"

"Oh man, can we say Red-Letter Day? Everything is going to be fine. Call me when you get home. I'm going to run for some Tums or something before I puke like you did yesterday."

I hang up and tiptoe in the bedroom to change, then kiss my man on the cheek. "Baby, I gotta go. Big day and all. I feel like hell, I really do."

Franco opens his eyes and smiles, giving me this totally concerned look. Like disoriented but worried, too. "Honey, you're going to knock 'em dead, no matter what happened yesterday. You've worked hard for this. And I'll come see you backstage, okay? For good luck."

"That's sweet. Okay, be there by six or I won't be able to see you. And I want you to meet my family too, remember."

"I'll be there, baby. Don't be freaked—everything is going to be just fine. You rule," he says, reaching up for a hug. As his arms wrap around my bod, I pray that Fredrique will agree.

"FOUR HUNDRED copies as requested," I say, handing over the stack of pages to Fredrique backstage at the Coliseum. "Do we really need four hundred?"

"That's a low estimate," he says, patting my arm. I must really look a mess to score a consoling pat on the arm from Fredrique. Pat confirms my fears when he strolls in a few minutes later.

"Ohmigod, you look so completely freaked out, like a ghost or something," he says, running a finger across my pallid cheek. "Get this girl some blush!"

"I know, right? I've thrown up three times today." Once before my parents arrived and twice after, I was wearing the Ty-D-Bol necklace. Not exactly accessory of choice on the most important day of my life.

"You too? I was puking my brains out just thirty minutes ago.

I think we're all regurgitating wrecks today, from the looks of it." I follow his gaze to the twelve others in the class, each face ashier than the one before it. Fredrique clears his throat to call for order.

"Okay, here we are. The day we've been planning for the entire semester has come at last," he declares, meeting each of our convict-in-electric-chair gazes with a determined smile. "I sat through your rehearsals yesterday, and I have to say that while some needed work, for the most part I am proud. There are a few of you I'm worried about, and I think you know who you are, but by and large I'd say we've pulled it off." As he shoots us a grin, I fire back a grimace. He thinks we failures know who we are? He's got to be talking about me, he's just got to. I was an idiot to actually think Fredrique was hinting around that I had talent the other day in his office. He totally wasn't talking about me. And even if he was, I'm sure yesterday's fiasco changed his mind, with my models tripping all over the damn place and feathers flying and me ralphing. Oh God, I am so fucked.

"One surprise. The graphic design department has created banners featuring each of your names to hang on the white backdrop when your collection is being shown. Just like the real designers in New York or Paris. I'll hand them out now, but give them back to Douglas here. He'll be hanging them before the appropriate show."

I stroke the white vinyl, rolled tight and tied with a ribbon like a diploma. This is real. The banner, my fashions hanging on the rack marked *Abbie McPhereson*, my models, Franco arriving in thirty minutes, *WWD* in the audience—all of it. And I'm not ready. It should be a dream but instead it's a nightmare. My eyes fill with tears as I unravel the banner. ABBIE MCPHERESON in bold black Times Roman, the *o* a lemon instead of an *o*. I guess a play on the fruit theme, but what a jinx. A lemon: universal euphemism for piece-of-shit cars or out-of-order appliances. Is that what my collection is now, an out-of-order piece of shit? My eyes are full as I look over at Pat.

"No backing out now, right?" he whispers, eyes also brimming with what must be tears of terror.

"Right," I murmur, as a tear splashes against my banner like an acid raindrop. "It's totally sink or swim."

NOTHING CAN save me now, I think as I stand before the lighted mirrors that have been set up especially for makeup application. Six o'clock. The backstage is becoming a zoo as models file in and assume their positions. Hair and makeup people—students donating their time out of the goodness of their hearts—are everywhere. Since all my models have their hair props and fake eyelashes as well as written instructions typed by yours truly at the copy shop today on how the hair and makeup should look, I guess it's out of my hands. I'll go around and approve everyone's look in about fifteen. But right now the only thing I want to inspect are my roses from Franco, which are for the moment nonexistent. He's not here yet. My parents will be here anytime, and I want to get the intro over with so I can devote full concentration to the matter at hand. What if he doesn't show? That would just be the topper, him not showing.

I want to find Pat to calm my nerves, but like I said, it's a madhouse backstage and he's nowhere to be found. Will Franco be able to find me in this mob of people? My fears dissipate as I see him strolling toward me a few minutes later, but then return as I notice his hands are roseless and that his stroll is more like a stumble.

"Hey, baby, how's my little Hat Gal, Hat Gal?" he calls, half falling on me, his whiskey breath stronger than pepper Mace. He's wearing an old flannel and jeans and his hair is a wreck, like he's slept on it for a year.

"Franco, what are you doing?" I whisper as I push him off, thinking I must be misperceiving this situation. He cannot be drunk. "Have you been drinking or something?"

"Yeah, I had a couple with Tim. Um, I think it was a couple. We smoked first, so everything's kind of hazy," he says, planting a sloppy kiss on my cheek. "But I'm celebrating, baby. Your big day. Our move. You know, us."

"Oh God, Franco," I whisper, not believing this. I look at our reflection in the mirror. Franco, bleary-eyed, fucked up, looking a wreck, trying to kiss my neck. Me, in cashmere and shift dress, perfect hair and makeup, on the biggest day of my life. Which is now being ruined by my so-called boyfriend, who didn't even bring me one goddamn rose, much less a dozen. Seeing us like this, reflected in the mirror, it's like I'm staring at every fucking relationship I've ever had. I'm struggling and scratching to get my shit together while boy gets fucked up to supposedly celebrate my victories.

"So, no flowers?" I ask in a sad voice, reaching out to smooth Franco's hair back into some sort of ponytail. He can barely stand and my heart is breaking, it is.

"Oh, man, I totally forgot. I'll get you some later tonight, okay baby?"

It's very not okay. Not this time. I glance up to meet Linda's gaze, who's looking over at me with sympathy. God, how pathetic I must seem. Here two days ago I was telling her that Franco would be here with bells on and how he is the best and that he's over the club scene, picturing him in the front row throwing roses at my feet even if I do in fact suck. And now I'm trying to fix his hair while he drools on my sweater, less than an hour before the most monumental event of my life. When I see her sympathetic gaze and little smile full of what can only be pity, I stare back at our reflection again and make the decision I should have made a long time ago.

"Look, Franco, since you obviously couldn't stay sober for the most important night of my life, why don't you just go? Get out of my life!" I say, voice trembling. My words are stronger than I am at the moment, and I know they're my only defense against this boy I have tried to rescue for so long. As much as I know I have to say goodbye, how many times I should have said it before to Franco and countless boys before him, my heart is breaking into a million slivers, like so many pieces of Unity confetti. A tear rolls down my cheek, the second one of the day. Both represent total terror, fear I won't be enough. But I have control over both situations. And it's time to take this one by the horns.

Without Franco, I'm not sure what will happen in New York. But with him, I know I'm screwed. He's proven that tonight, coming in wasted when I need his total support. And he's supposed to meet my parents, for Chrissakes.

"Ab? You don't know what you're saying, Ab. I love you, baby. I love you," he cries, clutching my shoulder, holding on and on and on like I've done to so many losers in the past. But I can't hold on to this one anymore, I just can't.

"Franco, you don't love me," I say, eyes closed, shaking my head side to side. "Or you wouldn't have come in here like this, not tonight."

He clutches my arm. "Baby, I was celebrating for you. You, baby. And we're going to New York. Together, just us. Look, I'm sorry. Tim and I got carried away. But it won't happen anymore, I promise. I love you, Abbie. I love you."

I know he thinks he does, that's what sucks. And how many times have I wanted him to love me, to say all the things he's saying now? But I know he only loves himself. And Jack Daniel's. And anything or anyone else that can make him forget. I tried to make him forget, too. That's why we never really talked much about his parents or his drinking or his drugs or any of it. I was hoping that my love would erase everything, fill all his voids. But that didn't work with Parker and it isn't working now. Nor will it ever.

"Baby, I just can't do this anymore. You come here wasted when I need you, what's going to happen in New York? We can't do this. We can't." My voice, like my heart, breaks.

"Ab, you don't know what you're saying," Franco says, voice getting more and more freaked out by the second as tears stream down his flushed cheeks. "I love you, Ab. I really love you."

It would be so much easier to do this if he would just be a dick to me, throw my keys in my face like Parker did that day I moved out. But Franco's done something equally awful by showing up wasted. And even if he isn't calling me a bitch like Parker did, he's disrespecting me just as much with his intoxication. No matter how many tears he cries or I-love-you's he spills, nothing's going to change that fact. "Please, baby, just go. My parents will be here any minute and I don't want them to see this, okay? Just go." Tears stream down my cheeks as Franco looks at me with desperation.

"Abbie, I love you. You're all I've got. Don't do this, please. I swear, it will never happen again. Never again. I swear." As he reaches out to me, his body shaking with small sobs. I think about how easy it would be to just fall into that embrace like I've done so many times before. How simple it would be to just take his word for it, believe something like this really will never ever happen again. Let him kiss my hurt away and simply forget the whole thing ever happened, just like that.

I close my eyes and reach out my hands. One swift shove—the hardest move I've ever made in my life—pushes him away. "Franco, if you really love me, please go. For me. Please."

He wipes his face with the back of his hand, trying to catch his breath. "Okay, I'll go. For you. But we're not over, okay? We're not."

I take a deep breath as hot tears barrel down my cheeks. "Look, we are. I do love you, but it's over. It has to be."

Franco doesn't say a word. No more protests, nothing. Just stands there for a second, looking at me. Like really looking. After maybe a minute, he leans over and gives me this sad little kiss on the forehead, his tears dripping on my nose like a faucet. And then he's gone.

As the sound of Franco's footsteps gets fainter, I stare into the mirror at the girl I see. Wrecked makeup, mascara down to her chin, heart splitting into a million pieces—sure. But in her eyes there's definitely a glimmer of something that wasn't there before: strength, pride, maybe even a little dignity.

Pat enters my mirror's view behind my cashmere-covered shoulder, looking completely worried. "What the hell happened? I just saw Franco crying and walking out the door and your parents are looking all over for you. Oh my God, your makeup. What's wrong? What did the bastard do?"

I sigh and white-knuckle the table before me. "He loved me, but it wasn't enough. Not anymore. It just wasn't."

Pat gives me a hug, saying nothing. I guess there's nothing to say. Behind his shoulder I see a clock: 6:15—oh God. I break the embrace in a panic.

"Shit, forty-five minutes. Get me a makeup person, quick. And tell Mom and Dad I can't see them, like I'm busy or something. With or without a broken heart, this show has to go on."

Pat kisses my forehead in the exact sad spot Franco just did. "I'm proud of you."

"I know, honey. I know."

As Pat goes to fetch me a makeup magician, I bend over a sink and splash my face with water. When I look up, face sopping, I meet Linda's gaze again. She saw the entire Franco episode, I'm sure of it. I give her a smile. And I am happy to say that there's not one ounce of pity in the one she flashes back.

"GIRLS, BOYS, we're almost on. Where's one through three? Jodi?" Seven o'clock on the dot. Everyone's here, and Pat's holding my hand. I meet Fredrique's gaze from the other side of the wings and give a nervous smile. I have to forget Franco, forget everything and just get through this. All the models showed, thank God, and we did manage a run-through. I bow my head in prayer, pleading for God's help. At this point, it looks like only a miracle will save the evening.

"Okay, go music, go music." The three models shuffle out as "Tutti Frutti" fills the dark auditorium. Lights up, ABBIE MCPHERESON banner in place, lemon *o*. It's happening, oh God, it's really happening. Jodi, Wes and Zanni go out and turn to the audience. Jodi, the bitchy one I poked, makes her way down the runway. The fuzzy leaf-necked brown banana dress, yellow tights, Chiquita-sticker-covered platforms, awesome, red lipstick, her hair in leaf-adorned ponytail. Vacant gaze, I love it. The twirl, then Wes, banana-covered white pants, no shirt, shaved head, yellow shoes, the pout, everything. Zanni, fuzzy leaf-necked orange dress, peach tights, Sunkist-sticker-covered platforms, bun adorned with orange rinds. She twirls, that smile, so on. Cameras are flashing like crazy, and it looks like a lot of people are scrawling in notebooks and on programs.

"Okay, four, five and six. Go, go." As Zanni's leaving the runway, I straighten Elizabeth's red fake-fur waitress cap. "Now." When they're all out, Elizabeth starts down the runway, deadpan, in white-with-huge-tomato-print Flo dress, red TOMATO name tag above her heart in honor of Arrow Mickey, red slippers. Hands on hips, red pencil behind ear, chewing gum. I swear I hear my mom holler with her high-pitched, dog-whistle squeal. Then

Doug, hair in Princess Leia buns, wearing watermelon-print white pants, shirtless, green shoes—just like Wes before him. Now Kimberly, same waitress dress, only this one covered with tangerines, TANGERINE name tag, orange pencil, orange slippers, orange hat, orange gum. Genius, absolute genius.

"Seven, eight, nine," I call, jumping up and down. "Wait." I turn up Linda's collar. "Tutti Frutti" blends into the Lemonheads' "Mrs. Robinson." I slap her five. "Go." Linda, hair in French twist, is first in lime glittery flapper dress, covered completely by lemon swing coat. As she twirls on her lemon mules—the ankle apparently fine now—she drops the coat to reveal the dress and drags the fake fur behind her like a poodle on a leash. Darcy, in raspberry dress and mules with coconut coat, and Lori, in blueberry dress and mules with apricot coat, follow suit, both wearing the identical blank look and sporting the same slinky posture. Just like I told them to do. Triplet temptresses, that's what they are.

"Okay—now," I say, shoving Betty, Freda and Billie out. "Go, girls!" They're in matching silk suits, very career—one boysenberry, one black cherry, one raisin. Long jackets, cinch waists, short skirts, totally corporate, matching tights, clunky pumps, hair in high ponytails with big satin Barbie bows. Twirling like carousels at the end of the runway, the quintessential working girls personified.

Pat leans over and whispers in my ear. "This is going awesome, you know." And no, I don't know as I straighten Joy's hat and signal her, Pablo and Kasey to make their debuts. I'm too freaked out to know anything at this point. Joy sashays down the runway wearing cherry silk-and-velvet slip dress and fetish heels, cherry-covered hat atop her head. Pablo follows in watermelon ruffled tuxedo shirt and watermelon-and-coconut seersucker pants with cranberry suede lace-ups. Kasey's in the same number as Joy, only her flavor is grape. I give her a wink as she struts off down the runway. I spot George and Chris in the front row, both glowing like Christmas trees.

The Cranberries' "Linger" blares, which signals that the show is half over already and no one's tripped yet, thank God. Time for Jodi, Wes and Zanni's second outfits. I blow them a kiss as they head out, looking scrumptious. Girls in shirtwaist dresses and grandpa sweaters in pineapple and persimmon with matching ballet slippers, hair in messy knots atop their heads; bald boy in kiwi linen pants, coconut T under cantaloupe corduroy jacket and loafers. Very "Leave It to Beaver" meets "Miami Vice."

I look over at Fredrique, who is singing along to the Cranberries tune and bobbing to the beat, eyes fixed on the runway. Does this mean he likes it? Instead of contemplating that one, I fake-punch Pat in the face as Elizabeth, Doug and Kimberly enter stage left. The girlies, hair in flouncy "I Dream of Jeannie" ponies, have donned tiny chiffon ballet dresses with tinier cashmere sweaters and short patent leather boots, in grapefruit and apple respectively, and Doug, in little-boy drawstring cowboy hat, is sporting a lemon satin jacket with cherry cowboy embroidery, raspberry cotton trousers and cherry snakeskin boots. As Kimberly does her last twirl, I hop up and down. It really seems to be going okay. Like I can't even believe it.

"The last leg, kiddos. Let's do it!" Barry Manilow's "Copacabana" fills the auditorium as my Charlie's Angels—a.k.a. Betty, Lori and Darcy—strut out in stretch nylon T's with nylon pants and gun belts filled with matching plastic guns, in pear, peach and plum. Feathered locks, silver sheriff badges and blackberry mailman shoes complete the tough-gal looks, and as Darcy makes her exit she squirts the front-row audience with her water weapon. And they love it, which means they might even love me.

"Okay, feather mamas, you're on!" Linda, Freda and Billie are next, all wearing outfits like Linda got injured in at my *casa*—feather jacket, striped shirt, short swoosh skirt, tights, handpainted go-go boots, hair up. Please Lord, don't let them fall. Linda's in the mango-and-plum combo—my fave, and she looks awesome—we're talking supermodel in the making here, Freda's in lemon and blueberry, and Billie's in strawberry and lime. The feather jackets are so weightless—think baby chicks—and the girls are slinging them over their shoulders as they make their first turn to show off the tiny shirts underneath. I take a deep breath and squeeze Pat's sweaty palm before he runs off to snap a pic of my last trio of models. The light at the end of the tunnel is shining brightly now, and I'm basking in its glow.

"Kasey's the last, kids. Get ready." Finale, finally. Joy, Pablo and Kasey all share a hug before hitting the runway. Joy looks amazing in long, poufy peach-with-lime-polka-dots taffeta skirt with peach short fake-fur hooded jacket over lime bra top. Truly breathtaking. Pablo is in pear cotton suit with apricot acetate-and-polyamide polo and bowling shoes, hair slicked back, the picture of hip. Kasey is a mirror of Joy in long, poufy cherry-with-watermelon-polka-dots taffeta skirt with cherry short fake-fur hooded jacket over watermelon bra top. As the last one disappears onto the stage, I hear a low voice in my ear. "You did it!"

I turn excitedly to give Pat a kiss. But it's not Pat by my side—it's Fredrique, of all people, leaning over to smack my cheek. As his collagen-enhanced lips press my skin, I think he's right, I *did* do it. He grabs my shoulders and looks into my eyes. "I knew you'd do it. I once had your talent. I did, but then got dumped by the fashion industry. So I was bitter. And when I recognized that talent in you, I was jealous. Because you were going to get to where I wanted to be. That's why I was so hard on you the whole time. But you did it anyway. You really did it."

Fredrique's confession, delivered at auctioneer speed, takes maybe seven seconds. But they're the most wonderful seven seconds of my life, I swear they are. Fredrique liked me all along! I will pass! I have talent! I'm not nothing! The realizations explode in my brain like fireworks on the Fourth of July.

The grainy monitor above Fredrique's head shows Kasey making her final twirl, skirt spinning like a record, as the audience bursts into applause. A jazzy instrumental fills the electrified air, signaling the end of my show and the beginning of my career.

It's over—I can't even believe it. Pat kisses my cheek and Fredrique breaks into applause as the models slowly file out on the runway one by one. Without thinking, I grab Fredriques and Pat's hands and dash out to take my bow. Pat has been there for me since day one. And so was Fredrique, I guess, in his own way, even though I didn't know it. It wouldn't be right to go out there without them.

I curtsy and give a wave to the audience, which is applauding wildly, and spy my mother in row one with tears running down her cheeks. George and Chris scream, "Go, Abbie!" Dad gives me a wink as he tosses a dozen red roses at my feet. Not from Franco, true, but somehow that doesn't seem to matter right now. Cameras flash, flash, flash and for a moment I'm blinded, eyes full of nothing.

As I drink in every last hoot and holler, Fredrique squeezes my hand and Linda gives me a hard hug. Then I'm floating backstage with everyone else. I throw one more wave to the audience as I pause underneath the ABBIE MCPHERESON banner, frozen. For this moment, this one glorious moment, I am quite possibly the happiest girl in the world.

"CHICKEN OR BEEF?"

I look up, startled, at the pert flight attendant looming before me. The same question Franco asked me on one of our first dates. "Definitely chicken," I answer, the exact words I said to him that night so many months ago. God, who knew that this was going to end in such psycho fashion? Whatever. All I can say is that it is totally his loss, just like it was Parker's and Arrow Mickey's and everyone else's.

As the flight attendant parks the dish I'm much too nervous to eat on my pull-down tray, I glance over for the millionth time at the three-week-old newspaper lying on the vacant seat to my right. *WWD*, page 9: "A Portrait of Young Designers on the Rise" screams the headline, next to a pic of none other than lovely Linda in mango feather jacket. *My* mango feather jacket. I pick it up and read the words I have long since memorized: "One of the surprises of our three-month search for ones to watch: Abbie McPhereson of Dallas Design Institute, whose fruit-inspired collection was full of the joy and color and whimsy you'd more expect from pros like Sui or Mizrahi. You can bet we haven't seen the last of this one. The name is Abbie McPhereson—and don't you forget it."

Damn straight. Especially now that I'm headed to New York, with a design assistant job beckoning like an expectant lover. Factor in Linda who, fueled by the *WWD* appearance, will be here next week to shack up with me in a SoHo two-bedroom, and Pat, who will be along to join us by the end of the month, when his costume gig starts, and you get a situation so perfect, it's almost surreal.

But just because something looks perfect doesn't necessarily mean it is. Case in point: Franco. God, even his name still breaks my heart. Letting go of him—of *us*—was the most grown-up thing I've ever had to do, especially when he was calling and begging me back every five minutes. But as tempted as I was to give in, the knowledge that I was way better off without him prevailed. It's not like I didn't love him—I did, with all of my heart. But sometimes love—even crazy, mad love like ours—just isn't enough.

What if things had worked out differently, if Franco hadn't shown up drunk at the show and had brought me dozens of long-stemmed roses and everything had worked out with us and he was holding my hand right now, on our way to our urban life together? I close my eyes and imagine the scenario: his fingers covering mine, the firm grip, the comforting squeeze. I feel a bit melancholy until I realize that if Franco was here, his hand would more likely be fondling a Jack-and-Coke instead of my polished digits. Reality check. It's time to quit thinking about the Parkers and the Francos of the world and just move on, into my new city and my new life.

I open my eyes to discover a cute boy spying me from the window seat.

"Hey, neighbor," he drawls, all flirtatious. "What's your name?"

"It's Abbie McPhereson," I say with a smile. And don't you forget it.

Printed in the United States
By Bookmasters